W9-BPL-104

THIS FALLEN PREY

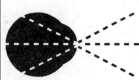
This Large Print Book carries the
Seal of Approval of N.A.V.H.

THIS FALLEN PREY

A ROCKTON NOVEL

KELLEY ARMSTRONG

WHEELER PUBLISHING
A part of Gale, a Cengage Company

Farmington Hills, Mich • San Francisco • New York • Waterville, Maine
Meriden, Conn • Mason, Ohio • Chicago

Copyright © 2018 by KLC Fricke, Inc.
Wheeler Publishing, a part of Gale, a Cengage Company.

ALL RIGHTS RESERVED
This is a work of fiction. All of the characters, organizations, and events portrayed in this novel are either products of the author's imagination or are used fictitiously.
Wheeler Publishing Large Print Hardcover.
The text of this Large Print edition is unabridged.
Other aspects of the book may vary from the original edition.
Set in 16 pt. Plantin.

LIBRARY OF CONGRESS CIP DATA ON FILE.
CATALOGUING IN PUBLICATION FOR THIS BOOK
IS AVAILABLE FROM THE LIBRARY OF CONGRESS

ISBN-13: 978-1-4328-5324-2hardcover)

Published in 2018 by arrangement with Macmillan Publishing Group, LLC/St. Martin's Press

Printed in the United States of America
1 2 3 4 5 6 7 22 21 20 19 18

For Jeff

ONE

The season may have officially started two months ago, but it isn't truly spring in Rockton until we bury our winter dead.

Dalton and Anders are digging the shallow grave. I'm wandering, trying to calm Storm. As a future tracking dog, she needs to know the smell of death. I've read books that say cadaver dogs can't do the job for long because every "success" leads to a dead body. I dismissed that as anthropomorphism until I showed Storm the corpses . . . and she promptly set about trying to wake the dead.

We're walking in ever-growing circles around the grave. Dalton's occasional "Casey?" warns me to stay close, while Storm's insistent tugs beg me to let her explore and forget what she's seen. The tugs of an eight-month-old Newfoundland are not insubstantial.

"Switch?" Anders walks over and holds

out a hand.

Storm isn't the only one who needs a break from this task. Every year, Dalton orders his deputy to stay behind. Every year Anders ignores him. As a former soldier, Anders might not need to see more death, but being a former soldier also means he refuses to grant himself that reprieve.

I give his hand a quick squeeze as I pass over the leash. "Remember, you gotta show her who's boss."

"Oh, she knows who's boss." The dog yanks, nearly toppling Anders. "And it's not me." He plants his feet. "Fortunately, I'm still a whole lot bigger. Go help Eric. We'll be fine."

I walk along a narrow caribou trail bounded by towering spruce. Green shoots have snuck up in patches of sunlight, and the air smells of a light shower, the rain already evaporating. I see no sign of Dalton. The forest here is too thick. Endless forest, the quiet broken by the scolding of a red squirrel as I pass.

I stay on the trail until I find Dalton standing beside one hole dug down to the permafrost. Three bodies lie beside it. Two are long dead, partly mummified from having been stashed in a cave by their killer. The third looks as if she could be sleeping.

Sharon was the oldest resident in Rockton until we found her dead of a heart attack this morning, prompting Dalton to declare the ground soft enough to bury our winter dead.

A shallow grave. Unmarked. As a homicide detective, I should be finding these, not creating them. But this is Rockton.

These three women came here in secrecy, fleeing threats from elsewhere. They came to the Yukon to be safe. And we failed them. One can argue it wasn't our fault. Yet we accept responsibility. To say "We did our best" is a slippery slope in Rockton.

We lay the corpses in the hole. There's no graveside service. I wasn't brought up in any religion, and our sheriff was raised right here, in this forest. I'm sure, if pressed, we could find a few lines of half-remembered poetry for the dead. But that isn't our way. We stand there, and we remember, and we regret.

Then we fill in the hole.

When we're done, Dalton rubs his face. He looks at his hands, as if thinking about what they just handled. I reach into my pocket and pass him a tiny bottle of hand sanitizer. He snorts at that and takes it, and when he's done, I lean against his side for a moment as he puts his arm around my

9

shoulders. Then we both straighten, job done, moment passed, time to get back to work.

"Will?" Dalton calls. There's exactly one heartbeat of silence, and Dalton's face tightens as he shouts, "Will?"

"Over here," Anders calls back. "Pup found herself a rabbit hole and —" A grunt of exertion. "And she really wants bunny for dinner."

We walk over to find him only lightly tugging on the leash, his big biceps barely twitching. I sigh and yank the lead with a "Hut!" Storm gives me a look, not unlike a sullen teen, and walks over to brush against Dalton.

Anders chuckles. "If Mommy gives you shit, suck up to Dad. Nice try, pup, but —"

He stops as we all hear the whine of a small plane engine.

Dalton shields his gaze to look up.

"Does that sound way too close to Rockton?" Anders says.

"Fuck," Dalton mutters.

"That'd be yes. Come on, pup. Time for a run."

We kick it into high gear. Dalton scans the sky as he tracks the sound. It's not a supply delivery — it's exceedingly rare for anyone other than Dalton to handle those, and he's scheduled to head out later today, releasing a few residents. But from the sound, that plane is heading straight to our airstrip.

The pilot shouldn't be able to *see* our airstrip. No more than he should be able to see our town. Structural and technological camouflage means that unless the plane skims Rockton, we should remain invisible.

I look up to see a small plane on a perfect trajectory with our landing strip.

Dalton curses again.

"Has anyone ever found the airstrip before?" I ask.

"Ten years ago. Guy was lost. Rookie pilot. I fixed his nav, gave him fuel, and pointed him to Dawson City. He was too shaken up to question. I just told him it was an airstrip for miners."

Having anyone stumble over Rockton even by land is rare, but we have a pocketful of cover stories. Today, Dalton decides "military training base" will work. We're all physically fit. Anders keeps his hair stubble-short, and Dalton recently reverted to his summer look — his hair buzzed, his beard down to a few days' growth. Suitable for a backwoods military camp.

Anders pushes his short sleeves onto his shoulders, US Army tattoo more prominently displayed. Dalton snaps his shades in place. I put on my ball cap, ponytail tugged through. And we have our guns in hand.

We arrive just as the propellers creak to a stop. The pilot's door opens. A woman gets out. When I see her, I slow, the guys doing the same. We've donned our best quickie military costuming; hers looks like the real thing. Beige cargo shorts. Olive tank top. Dark aviator shades. Boots. Dark ponytail. Thigh holster. Arms that make mine look scrawny.

She doesn't even glance our way, just rolls her shoulders and acts like she has no idea three armed strangers are bearing down on her. She knows, though. She waits until we're ten feet away. Then she turns and says, "Sheriff Dalton?"

Her gaze crosses all three of us. She rejects the woman. Rejects the black guy. Settles on the white one as she says "Sheriff?" again. I could bristle at that, but she's right in this case, and the certainty on her face tells me she's been given a physical description.

Without waiting for confirmation, she steps forward and extends her hand. "I have a delivery for you, sir."

Dalton takes her hand. While he's doing a good job of hiding his confusion, I see the tightness in his face. He might rule in Rockton, but he's only thirty-one, two months younger than me, and new situations throw him off balance.

"We weren't informed of any deliveries," I say.

She hands me an envelope from her pocket. "The details are in here, ma'am. I'm just the courier."

Dalton walks over to the plane. When a hand smacks against the glass, Storm and I both jump. Anders says, "Shit!" Dalton just peers inside. A man's face appears. A man wearing a gag.

Dalton turns to the pilot. "What the hell is this?"

"Your delivery, sir."

She opens the cargo door and disappears inside, with Dalton following. Anders and I wait. A moment later, Dalton comes out, pushing the man ahead of him. He's blond, younger than us, wearing a wrinkled linen shirt, trousers, and expensive loafers. He looks like he's been pulled off Bay Street midway through his stockbroker shift. He's gagged with his hands tied in front of him; a cable binds his legs so he can't do more than shuffle.

"I was told not to remove the cuffs," the woman says as she follows them out. "I was

13

also told to leave the gag on. I made the mistake of removing it. That lasted about sixty seconds. I have no idea what he's in for, but he's a nasty son of a bitch."

"In for?" I say.

"Yes, ma'am." She looks around. "There is a detention facility out here, isn't there? Some kind of ultra-maximum security?"

"Privileged information," Anders says. "Sorry, ma'am. You know how it is. Same in the air force, I'll wager."

The woman smiles. "It was. And it's no different in private security." She nods at his tat. "Cross-border job shopping?"

"Something like that. I appreciate you bringing the prisoner. We weren't expecting anyone new, so we're a bit surprised." Anders peeks into the cargo hold. "You wouldn't happen to have any beer in there, would you?"

She laughs.

"No, sir." She reaches in and pulls out a duffel. When she opens the zipper, it's full of coffee bags.

"Just this," she says.

"Even better," Anders says. "Thank you."

I look at the prisoner. He's just standing there, with Dalton behind him, monitoring his body language as Anders chats with the pilot.

14

"Thank you for bringing him," I say. "If you're flying back to Dawson City, skip the casino and check out the Downtown Hotel bar. Ask for the sour toe cocktail."

"There's an actual toe involved, isn't there?"

"It's the Yukon."

She grins. "I'll have to try that. Thank you, ma'am." She tips her hat and then motions to ask if she can pat Storm. I nod, and Storm sits as she sees the hand reach for her head.

"Well trained," she says.

"At her size, she needs to be. She's still a pup."

"Nice." She gives Storm a final pat. "I'll head on out. You folks have a good day. And remember, keep that gag on for as long as you can."

TWO

The bush plane has left, and we're standing by the hangar. I've opened the letter, and Dalton is reading it over my shoulder while Anders guards the prisoner. Storm lies at my feet, her wary gaze on the stranger.

As usual, Dalton reads faster than me, and I've barely finished the opening paragraph when he says, "Fuck, no. Fucking *hell,* no."

Anders leans over to see the letter — and the prisoner lunges.

Anders yanks him back, saying, "Yeah, it's not that easy, asshole," and the guy turns to see both Dalton and me with our weapons trained on him, Storm on her feet, growling.

"If you're waiting for us to get distracted and let you run, you'll be waiting a long time," Anders says.

"It wouldn't help anyway," I say. "You're hundreds of miles from the nearest community. Gagged. Bound. Your legs chained."

16

I turn to the guys. "Can we let him go? Please? Lay bets on how far he gets?"

"Nah," Anders says. "Lay bets on what kills him. I vote grizzly."

"Cougar," I say.

"Exposure," Dalton says.

I look at Dalton. "Boring."

"Fine, rabbits."

"But the rabbits haven't killed anyone."

"Yet."

The prisoner watches us, his eyes narrowing, offended that we find his predicament so entertaining.

"On the ground," Dalton says.

The guy lifts his bound hands and extends both middle fingers. My foot shoots out and snags his leg. He drops to his knees.

"Boss wants you on the ground, you get on the ground," I say. "Practice your yoga. Downward dog. All fours. Ass in the air."

When he doesn't move fast enough, Dalton says, "Do you really think this is the time to challenge us? I just read that letter."

The guy assumes an awkward downward-dog pose.

Dalton holds the letter out for me to finish. I don't need to — my gaze snags on a few key words, and I skim the rest to be sure I'm not misreading. Then I look at Dalton.

"Fuck, no," I say.

"Uh-huh."

We've left our prisoner with Anders and returned to Rockton. As we enter town, I imagine bringing him back. Imagine how we might explain Rockton, how we'd pass it off. Wild West theme town would be our best bet. Seriously. That's what it would look like to an outsider — a place where rich people pay serious cash to pretend they live in a rougher, heartier time. Wooden buildings, all in perfect condition, each adorned with very modern, oversize quad-paned windows. Dirt roads swept smooth, not a scrap of litter or whiff of horse dung. People milling about in modern dress, because we wouldn't want to take the fantasy *that* far. Living without electricity, cell service, and Wi-Fi is primitive enough, thank you very much.

We drop Storm off at the general store, where Petra will dog-sit. Then we head to Val's house, which seems like old times, going to her and demanding to speak to the council. For my first four months in Rockton, I never set foot in Val's house except on business. And I swear she never set foot outside it unless she had to.

Since then, Val has come to realize the

council set her up, that they wanted their local representative isolated. She's finally begun changing that, which means that when I say there was an unscheduled plane arrival, she doesn't hesitate to make the call. Phil answers right away, as if he's waiting.

"A serial killer?" Dalton says. "You sent us a goddamn serial killer."

"For six months," Phil says. "Not as a resident, but as your prisoner. You are free to impose any restrictions on him. We will not question your judgment. In fact, under the circumstances, we don't *want* Mr. Brady to enjoy his stay in Rockton. That is the point."

"The point?" I say.

"Yes, hello, Detective." There's relief in Phil's voice as he realizes I'm there. I am the reasonable one. Classic good cop, bad cop: the hotheaded, profane sheriff and the educated, professional detective. It's a useful fiction.

As Phil continues, his defensive edge fades. "Mr. Brady is in Rockton because he has refused other options."

"Like jail?" Dalton says. "Lethal injection? Because he's sure as hell earned those."

"Possibly, but Mr. Brady's father believes society is better served by saving the expense of a trial while removing him as a danger to

19

the public. He wants to keep Mr. Brady in what we would consider luxurious isolation, on an island, with caretakers and guards. Mr. Brady has refused. Which is why he is temporarily yours."

"So he'll come to see the appeal of a permanent Caribbean vacation," I say.

"Yes, and while we can argue that he deserves worse punishment, that isn't our concern."

"Your concern is how much you make from this arrangement," Dalton says.

"No, how much *you* make. For your town, Sheriff."

Phil proceeds to remind us how expensive it is to run Rockton, how the five-grand fee from residents hardly covers the expenses incurred during their two-to-five-year stays. How even the hundred grand they get from white-collar criminals barely keeps the town running.

Some white-collar criminals pay a lot more than a hundred grand, though, as do worse offenders. Rockton just never sees that money. The council keeps it. But with Oliver Brady . . .

"One million dollars," Phil says. "To be used at your discretion, Eric. And twenty percent of that is yours to keep personally as payment for the extra work."

Dalton glowers at the radio. "Fuck. You."

"Detective?" Phil says. "I trust you will speak to your . . . boss on this. Explain to him the benefits of a nest egg, should he ever decide to leave Rockton."

Explain it to my lover — that's what he means. Convince Dalton he should have money set aside in case he ever wants to leave Rockton with me. This is a threat, too. A reminder that they can kick him out.

I clear my throat. "I believe Sheriff Dalton sees that two hundred thousand as a bribe for endangering his town. While we could use extra money for Rockton, I think I can speak for both of us when I say we don't want it at the expense of endangering residents."

"People don't come here for feather pillows and fancy clothes," Dalton says. "They come for security. That cash isn't going to buy us a doctor, is it? Or radios that actually work?"

"We could certainly invest in better radios," Phil says. "Though I'm not sure that would be a wise use of the money."

The problem with the radio reception is interference. The same thing that keeps us safe and isolated also keeps us isolated from one another when we're in the forest.

Phil continues, "I'm sure if you asked the

21

residents, there are things they'd like to use the money for."

"Yeah," Dalton says. "Booze. And more booze. Oh, and a hot tub. That was their request last year. A fucking hot tub."

"We could actually do that, Sheriff," Phil says. "It wouldn't be a Jacuzzi-style with jets, but a deep communal tub with fire-heated water and —"

Dalton cuts him off with expletives. Many expletives.

"There are always things we could use," I say. "And if we went to the residents and asked, they might take this offer. That's because they trust us to protect them from someone like Oliver Brady. But we are not equipped for this, Phil. We have one jail cell. It's intended as a temporary punishment. It's not even big enough for a bed. We can't confine Brady to it for six *days*, let alone six months. If you wanted to send him here, you should have warned us and provided supplies to construct a proper containment facility."

"And maybe asked us if we wanted this deal," Dalton says. "But you didn't because you knew what we'd say. Which doesn't excuse not giving us *any* warning. You dropped off a serial killer and a bag of fucking coffee."

"Tell us what you need to construct a proper containment facility, and we will provide it," Phil says. "Until then, your holding cell will be adequate. Remember, the goal here is to convince Mr. Brady to accept his father's offer. Show him the alternative. Let him experience discomfort."

"You want us to waterboard him, too?" Dalton asks.

"If you like. I know you're being facetious, Sheriff, but the residents of Rockton are not subject to any governmental constraints or human rights obligations. Which you have used to your advantage before."

"Yeah, by making people sleep in a cell without a bed. By sentencing them to chopping duty without a trial. Not actual torture, and if you think that's what I'm here for —"

"You're not," I say. "The council knows that. What the council may not understand, Phil, is exactly what they're asking. Even with a proper facility, we won't be equipped for this. We don't have prison guards. You saw what happened this winter."

"But Nicole is fine now. She's staying by choice. That alone is a tribute to you both and everyone else in Rockton. You can handle this."

"They shouldn't have to."

That isn't me or Dalton speaking. It's Val, who has been silently listening.

"Eric and Casey shouldn't have to deal with this threat," she continues. "The people of Rockton shouldn't have to live under it. I don't know what this man has done . . ."

She looks at me warily, as if not sure she wants me filling in that blank.

"He's a thrill killer," I say. "He murders because he enjoys it. Tortures and kills. Five victims in Georgia. Two men. Two women. And one fourteen-year-old boy."

Val closes her eyes.

"Oliver Brady is a killer motivated by nothing more than sadism," I continue. "An unrelentingly opportunistic psychopath."

"We can't do this, Phil," Val says. "Please. We cannot subject the residents of Rockton to that."

"I'm sorry," Phil says, "but you're going to have to."

THREE

For the first three decades of my life, I didn't understand the concept of home. I had one growing up, and outwardly, it was perfect. My parents were very successful physicians, and my sister and I lived a life of privilege. We just weren't a close-knit family. That may be an understatement. Before I left for Rockton, I told my sister that it might be a few years before she heard from me again, and she acted as if I'd interrupted an important meeting to say I'd be out shopping for the day.

I don't know if my early life would have doomed me to an equally cold and comfortless adult one. Maybe I would have married and had children and formed a family there. But my future didn't proceed in a direction that allowed me to find that out.

When I was nineteen, my boyfriend and I were waylaid in an alley by thugs who took exception to him selling drugs on their turf.

I fought back enough to allow Blaine to grab a weapon so we could escape. Instead, he ran. I was beaten and left for dead, and he never even bothered calling 911.

I spent months in the hospital recuperating, post-coma. Then I went to confront Blaine. Shot him. Killed him. I didn't intend to, but if you take a gun to a fight, you need to be prepared for that conclusion, and at nineteen, I was not.

I spent the next twelve years waiting for the knock on the door. The one that would lead me down a path ending in a prison cell. I deserved that cell. I never pretended otherwise. Nor did I turn myself in.

Instead, I punished myself with a lifetime of self-imposed isolation, during which I threw myself into my job as a homicide detective, hoping to make amends that way. Create a home, though? A family? No. I gave up any hope of that life when I pulled the trigger.

Then I came to Rockton. I arrived in a place I did not want to be . . . and I woke up. Snapped awake after twelve years in what had been just another type of coma. I came here, and I found purpose and a home.

Yet my life in Rockton is an illusion. I know that. Our amazing little town exists inside a snow globe, and all the council has to do is give it a shake and that illusion of control shatters.

We do have options. We can refuse to accept Brady. And the council will send someone to escort Dalton to Dawson City. Ship him back "down south" — our term for anyplace that isn't here. Anyplace that Dalton doesn't belong.

You're on your own now, Sheriff. It might be hard to go anywhere when you don't legally exist. Might be hard to get a job when you've never spent a day in school. Might be hard to do anything when you don't have more than the allowance we paid. Oh, and don't expect to take your girlfriend with you — Detective Butler can't leave for another year. But go on. Enjoy your new life.

I'm sure Dalton's adoptive parents would help him. I could give him money — it's not like I've ever touched my seven-figure inheritance. The problem is that Dalton cannot imagine life anywhere else. Rockton is *his* purpose. *His* home.

We have a backup plan. If he's ever exiled, I will also leave, whether the council allows it or not. So will Anders. Others, too, loyal to Dalton and to what this town represents. We'll build a new Rockton, a true refuge.

Is that laughable idealism? Maybe, which

27

is why we don't just go ahead and do it. For now, we work within the system. And under these particular circumstances, walking out is not an option.

These particular circumstances.

Oliver Brady.

Twenty-seven years old. American. Harvard educated. His father runs a huge tech firm. I don't recognize the family name, but I'd presume "Brady" is as fake as "Butler" is for me. Also, his father is actually his stepfather.

What does that stepfather hope to accomplish with this scheme? I don't know. Maybe saving his wife from the pain of an incarcerated son. Or maybe saving his corporation from the scandal of a murderous one.

"Murderous" doesn't begin to describe Oliver Brady. I told Val there were five victims, but in cases like this, five is just how many bodies they've found.

During that interview with Phil, I made him give me details.

The police believe Oliver Brady took his first victim at the age of twenty. I'm sure there were other victims, animals at least. There are patterns for this sort of thing, and Oliver Brady did not burst from a

28

chrysalis at twenty, a fully formed psychopath.

Five victims over seven years. No connection between them or to himself. Just people he could grab and take to his hiding spots, where he spent weeks torturing them.

I'm not sure "torture" is the right word. That implies your tormenter wants something, and the only thing Brady wanted was whatever pleasure he derived from it. The detectives speculated that he never delivered what we might call a killing blow. He simply kept torturing his victims until they died.

This is the man the council wants us to guard for half a year. A man who likes to play games. A man who likes to inflict pain. A man who likes to cause death. A man who will not cool his heels for six months in a secure cabin. The first chance Brady gets, he'll show us how much he doesn't want to be here.

After we leave Val's, Dalton takes off to update Anders. I go in search of another person that needs to be told: the local brothel owner.

Yes, Isabel Radcliffe is more than the local brothel owner. I just like to call her that, a not-so-subtle dig at my least favorite of her positions. She owns the Roc, one of two

29

bars in town. The Roc doubles as a brothel, and she and I are still debating that. I say it sets up dangerous and insulting expectations of the majority of women who don't moonlight in her establishment. She says it allows women to explore and control their sexuality and provides safe access to sex in a town that's three-quarters male. I'd be more inclined to consider her argument if "brothel owner" were a volunteer position. I mentioned that once. She nearly laughed herself into a hernia.

I find Isabel upstairs at the Roc, walking out of one of the three bedrooms that serve as the brothel — for safety, paid sex must take place on the premises. She's wearing a kerchief over her silver-streaked dark hair, and it may be the first time I've seen her in jeans. Her only "makeup" is a smudge of dirt on one cheek. We can't find room for makeup and hair dye on supply runs, which is a relief, actually, when that becomes the standard. With Isabel, it doesn't matter. She still looks like she should be lounging in a cocktail dress, smoking a cigarette in a holder, with hot young guys fetching her drinks.

She's carrying an armload of wood, and I look into the room she's exiting and see a bed in pieces.

"Whoa," I say. "I hope you charged extra for that."

"I would skin a client alive if he did that." She hefts the wood. "Well, no, if he could do that, I'd want a demonstration. I'm repurposing the room, so I deconstructed the bed."

"By yourself?"

"Yes, Casey. By myself. With that thing . . . what do you call it? Knocks in nails and pulls them out again? Ah, yes, a hammer. Kenny was busy, and I didn't want to disturb him when he was getting ready to leave."

"You mean he was going to charge you double for a last-minute job, and you decided to do it yourself."

"Same thing. Make yourself useful and grab some wood."

I do, and as I follow her down the stairs, I say, "You said you're repurposing the room?"

"It will now be for private parties."

"Kinky."

She glances over her shoulder. "Not that kind. However, if you're *interested* in that kind, I can certainly arrange them. I'm sure we'd find no shortage of buyers. Though I also suspect our good sheriff would snatch all the invitations up."

"Nah, he'd just glower at anyone who tried to buy one. That'd make them change their minds. Fast."

"True."

"And, just for the record, I'm *not* interested in private sex parties."

She stacks the wood onto a pile. "As I said, it's not that kind of room. We very rarely have three clients requiring rooms simultaneously, which makes it an inefficient use of space. Instead, this one will host private parties. Drink and food provided, along with a dedicated server . . . who will offer nothing *more* than drink and food. You may feel perfectly comfortable holding your poker games up here."

"With people banging in the next room for ambience?"

"I'm installing soundproofing. Now, what was a plane doing landing on our strip?"

"You saw it?"

"I see everything."

Her network of paid informants makes sure of that. Isabel not only runs the Roc, but controls the town's alcohol, which makes her — after Dalton — the most powerful person in Rockton. She's also the longest resident after him. She's passed her five years but has made an arrangement with the council to stay on. I suspect that "arrangement" involves blackmailing them with information gathered by her network.

In a small northern town, I'm not sure which is more valuable: booze or secrets. Sex comes next. Isabel owns all three, while holding no official position in local government. Kind of like the Monopoly player who buys only Park Place and Boardwalk and then sits back to enjoy the profits while others scrabble to control the remainder of the board.

I hand Isabel the letter that came with Brady. As she reads it, her lips tighten almost imperceptibly. Then she folds it and runs a perfect fingernail along the crease.

"This is one time when I really wish you were given to practical jokes," she says.

"Sorry."

She shakes the letter. "This is inappropriate."

I choke on a laugh. "That's one way of putting it."

"No, it is the best way of putting it. Springing this on Eric is inappropriate. It is also inappropriate to ask the town to accept it."

"They're paying us. A million dollars for Rockton."

"It doesn't matter."

33

"Did you actually say money doesn't matter?"

She fixes me with a look and heads back upstairs for more wood.

"We don't need a million dollars," she says as I follow. "People didn't come here for luxury accommodations. They came for safety. This trades one for the other. Unacceptable."

"That's what Eric said. So they promised him twenty percent."

"Imbeciles. Did he tell them where to stick it?"

"Of course. Doesn't change anything, though. We are stuck with Mr. Brady for six months."

"And you want my advice on how to deal with it?"

"If you have advice, I'll listen, but I'm here for your expertise on Brady himself. Use your shrink skills and tell me what we're dealing with."

She picks up the headboard and motions for me to grab the other end. "I was a counseling psychologist. I had zero experience with homicidal maniacs. Fortunately, you have someone in town who is an expert."

"I know. But he's going to be a pain in the ass about it."

"And I'm not?"

"You're a whole different kind of pain in the ass."

"I'll take that as a compliment. He is your expert with Oliver Brady. You need me for another sort of advice: how and what to tell the general population. That is going to be the truly tricky part."

FOUR

I pace behind the butcher shop.

"The answer is no." Mathias's voice floats out the back door. "Whatever you are considering asking, the answer is no."

"Good. Thank you," I say. Or *Bien. Merci.* Mathias's English is perfect, but he prefers French, and I use it to humor him. Or placate him. Or charm him. Depends on the day, really.

"Wait," he calls after me. "That was too easy."

"You're imagining things," I call back as I keep walking.

A moment later, he's shed his butcher's apron and caught up. "This is a trick, isn't it? You wish my help. You know I will grumble. So you pace about, pretending you have not yet decided to ask me, and then you leave quickly when I refuse. My interest piqued, I will follow you of my own accord."

"You got me. So, now, knowing you've

been tricked, you should go back to your shop and not give me the satisfaction of victory."

"I could learn to hate you, Casey."

"Sure, you could. You could even find someone else to speak French to you. We're mostly Canadians here, so almost everyone knows rudimentary French. It's a little rusty, but I'm sure they —"

"Death by a thousand cuts would be less painful. As will whatever fresh torture you've dreamed up for me. I presume we have a rash of phantom chest pains in the wake of Sharon's demise, and you want me to assure them they are not about to die. William would be better suited to the task. He will tell the truth."

Mathias may be the town butcher, but he was a psychiatrist, which means he has a medical degree. He's just never practiced — the medical part, at least.

"No phantom chest pains." I glance around. Even if we are speaking rapid-fire French, I want to be sure no one is nearby. "We had a delivery today."

"I heard the plane."

"They dropped off a new resident."

"And he is ill?"

"In a manner of speaking."

I pass over the letter that accompanied

Brady. As Mathias skims it, his eyes begin to glitter. By the time he finishes, he's practically beaming.

"I think I love you," he says.

"Fickle man."

"We all are. So, what does Casey Butler wish me to do? Assessment? Or assassination?"

"I haven't decided yet."

After talking to Mathias, I walk to the hangar. Inside, Kenny and Paul stand on either side of Brady, watching him so intensely I suspect they literally haven't taken their eyes off him.

"Hey," I say to Kenny. "You didn't need to be here. Your ride out of Rockton might be delayed, but you are officially retired from duty."

"Hell, no," he says. "As long as I'm here, I'm working. Especially something like this."

"We appreciate that, but for now, you can both head back to town. I've got this."

Paul looks over my shoulder. "Where's the boss?"

"Busy."

Paul opens his mouth to question, but Kenny shoulders him out, saying, "See you back in town."

They leave, with Paul casting regular

glances my way. I wait until their boots tromp down the well-used path. Then I walk to Brady. His hands are still bound, feet chained.

I lower myself in front of him. He's watching me carefully. Analyzing the situation and struggling to hide his confusion.

I don't cut the most intimidating figure. I'm barely five foot two. A hundred and ten pounds. I just turned thirty-two, but the last time I was in the US, I got carded in a bar. My mother was Filipino and Chinese, and physically I take after her more than my Scottish father. In other words, absolutely nothing about me screams threat.

When I reach out, Brady draws back. Then he steels himself, shame flooding his eyes, as if he's been caught flinching from a Pomeranian.

I tug down his gag.

"I didn't do it," he says.

I shove the gag back up, and his shame turns to outrage. He doesn't move, though. Not one muscle. Still considering. Still analyzing. Still confused.

"Never been in prison, have you, Oliver?" I say.

He doesn't respond.

"If you'd like, you can blink once for yes, twice for no, but nodding and shaking will

39

be easier. In this case, it's a rhetorical question. Guys like you don't go to jail. That's why you're here instead. But having probably never even spent the night in a drunk tank, you need some advice. Telling the guard you didn't do it is pointless. He doesn't care, and even if he did, he can't help you. No one here is your judge or jury. We're all just guards. Now, let's try this again."

Gag down.

"My goddamn stepfather —"

Gag up.

"Your escort was right," I say. "Best to leave that on."

His eyes blaze hate. Hate and powerlessness from a guy who has never known a moment of either in his life.

"Do you have any idea where you are?" I ask.

He doesn't respond.

"Nowhere," I say. "No place that exists. No place that falls under any law or jurisdiction. If I shoot you, the sheriff's just going to say, *Oh, hell, another body to bury.* We buried three this morning. Our winter dead. And sure, it's easy enough to reopen the mass grave and toss your ass in, but I wouldn't do that. None of those people deserves to share their final resting spot with thrill-killing trash."

His mouth works behind the gag. He so desperately wants to tell me he didn't do it. I don't look forward to six months of hearing how this is all a big mistake. Could be worse, I suppose. Could be six months of him regaling us with the details of his crimes.

"My job here is to protect people," I say. "And you threaten my ability to do that. Yet killing you seems problematic. I'll have to give it more thought. I haven't worked out all the factors."

"In other words, don't give us an excuse," Dalton says as he strolls in.

"I wasn't going to say that."

"It's the truth."

"Far too Clint Eastwood for me."

"Which is why I'm the one who said it." He stops in front of Brady. "Did you take off the gag?"

"Twice. I got 'I didn't do it' and cursing about his stepfather." I turn to Brady. "Get up. We're taking you to town."

A press conference in Rockton is a strange thing. First, we don't have a press, which may make the entire endeavor seem rather pointless. Instead, it only makes it all the more critical. Without official media, the

41

only way to disseminate information is word of mouth, and as anyone who's ever played telephone can imagine, that's a dangerous game when you're dealing with a matter of public safety.

In a Rockton press conference, I am the physical manifestation of the printed page. I climb onto the front porch of the police station, give the news, and take questions. Dalton stands off to the side, arms crossed, his expression warning that those questions better not be stupid.

Brady is safely ensconced in the station cell. We brought him in through the back door. So no one has seen him yet as I stand on that porch and tell them that the council has asked us to take custody of a dangerous criminal. I get that much out, and then I wait, knowing exactly what will come.

"How dangerous?" someone asks.

The first time I spoke to a community group, my sergeant told me not to give details. They don't need to know, he said brusquely, and I bristled at the implication that a frightened community didn't deserve to know the exact nature of the predator in their midst. Which wasn't what he meant at all. It wasn't patronizing; it was protective.

I must know what Brady has done to fully understand what I am dealing with. That's the nightmare I must welcome into my head so that I can do my job. No one else needs that.

Even Dalton, who'd insisted on listening earlier, now shifts behind me, porch boards creaking, that subtle movement screaming his discomfort at the memory. Whatever Dalton has seen, whatever tough-guy face he puts on, I know his overwhelming thought on Brady's crimes.

I don't understand.

I cannot fathom how one person could do that to another.

I can't either, but I must stretch my imagination there as much as possible.

For the town, I provide the roundabout blather of the bureaucrat, words that seem like an on-point answer.

He's dangerous.

Murderously dangerous.

While I understand that you may wish to know more, you must also understand that he comes to Rockton as a prisoner, to await a decision on his fate, which means we are not at liberty to discuss his exact crimes, for reasons of security.

Words, words, more words, spun out until I see nods of understanding. Or, at least, of acceptance.

I continue talking, imparting data now.

He will be here six months. He will be confined for the duration. He is being held in the station until we can construct a special building to house him.

"How long will that take?" someone asks.

"We're assessing the feasibility of constructing a new one versus retrofitting an existing one," I say. "We're aware that the holding cell is far from ideal. That's why we want to move quickly on an alternative."

"Can't we just free up a house? Guard the exits?"

"No," says a voice from the crowd. Everyone follows it to Nicole. When they see who has spoken, a murmur runs through the assembled. They remember what happened to her.

"We understand that whatever this man has done, he is due his basic human rights," I say.

I feel that creak of the boards, Dalton recalling what Brady did and not convinced he concurs. I would agree. As far as I'm concerned, Brady can *get* comfortable in that cell. But that isn't an option, because the people of Rockton would not allow it without hearing the extent of his crimes.

I already see the crowd pulse in discomfort. I could tell them what he has done. *Do not let yourselves be concerned on his behalf.*

Just tell them.

Take the outrage and the anger and the impotence that Dalton feels. Multiply it by two hundred. An entire town, furious that the council has done this, furious that we have "allowed" it.

If we tell them his crimes, any civil rights we've accorded Oliver Brady will be held against us. Mob mentality will rise. Against him. Against us.

I love my town, but I do not trust them in this. So I remain silent.

FIVE

I'm in the station. It's a small building, with one main room and a door leading to the cell area. I've got that door open.

Brady is pretending to sleep. When I turn my back, moving about the station, I know he peers out to assess. I'm here alone, and again, he doesn't know what to make of that. But he is pleased. He gives that away in the curve of his lips. He's growing confident that this will be easier than he dared hope, that the alpha dog foolishly leaves the weakest in the pack alone with him time and again.

Kenny comes in while I'm settling behind the desk.

"No, Eric is not here," I say as he looks about.

He glances at Brady, slouched on the floor, knees up, eyes closed. Kenny lowers his voice and moves closer to me. "I know you can look after yourself, Casey, but maybe . . . You know."

I arch my brows.

"Look, I don't *want* to know what this guy did. If you say he's violent, that's enough for me. But whatever it is, I'm sure it involves women. Maybe leaving you here isn't . . ."

"Because I'm a woman?"

"No, just . . ." He makes this awkward motion, waving at me, top to bottom.

He's trying to come up with a respectful way to say that I'm attractive. When I arrived, Kenny was one of those guys who wouldn't see a problem with telling a co-worker that a pair of jeans really showed off her "assets." He wasn't a jerk — he honestly didn't realize that was inappropriate. But as soon as someone points it out, he trips over himself to correct the behavior. Sometimes to rather comic effect.

"He's not that kind of killer," I say.

Kenny frowns, like he can't imagine any other kind. I could also tell him that *those* predators don't always target women they find attractive. At some point, though, that starts to sound like lecturing. So I just say, "He's an equal-opportunity killer, so watch yourself."

"Sure, sure. But then, maybe no one should be alone with him."

"Mmm, I'm not worried." Through the open doorway, I see Brady's lips twitch. "I am sorry it screwed up your departure, though. I know you were looking forward to getting out today."

Kenny shrugs and sits on the edge of the desk, positioning himself between me and Brady. "It's not like I have plans. I'm going to bum around, visit a few places before I decide where to settle. Which reminds me. . . . I know Eric got Storm because you like Newfoundland dogs. How about Newfoundland itself? You been there?"

I shake my head.

"You know much about it?" he asks.

"I had a detective partner who came from there. He said he spent his life waiting to leave . . . and now can't wait to retire and move back. City life wasn't what he expected, and he missed the open spaces, small towns, slower pace, friendlier people."

"That's what I'm looking for, I think. A place like here but . . ."

"With Wi-Fi? Microwave ovens? Real indoor plumbing?"

He chuckles. "All the twenty-first-century amenities, which are the only things I missed from down south. I might even build my own house. Never imagined that before I came here. I barely knew how to hold a hammer."

"Join the team."

"Yeah, but at least you had the muscles to lift one. I want to keep doing carpentry. Become that local guy people call if they need a new bed or cupboards."

He settles on the desk, gaze going distant. "Maybe I'll meet someone, have a kid or two. Never did that. I always figured I would — it just seemed natural, you know. Then it didn't happen. I'll try harder this time. Put myself out there. Find someone who might not mind settling down with a guy like me."

Jen walks into the station, saying, "You want my advice, Kenny? Skip Tinder and go straight to mail-order brides."

"Personal experience, huh?" he says. "Or is that the real reason you stay in Rockton? There are so many guys, even you can get sex. You can get them to pay for it, too. Not much but . . ."

She scowls at him.

I shake my head. "You walked into that, Jen."

She walks around the desk, where she can put her back to Kenny, and then shoots her thumb toward the cell. "I want to talk about him."

"Casey doesn't need —" Kenny begins.

"It's fine," I say. "We should refill the

49

wood, though. We're going to need to run the fireplace all night."

Kenny hesitates, as if considering whether he can pretend not to get the hint. Then he says he'll grab some logs and be back soon.

Once he's gone, Jen looks around. "Where's the fur beast?"

"With Eric."

"So you're here doing paperwork alone while lover boy walks the pooch . . . and we have an allegedly dangerous killer in town?"

"When is the last time you saw us walking the dog during work hours?" I say.

Her jaw sets, like that of a petulant child countered with the indignity of a reasonable response.

"Eric is working," I say. "Storm is with him because she's a work dog."

"Then shouldn't she be here, guarding you?"

"Nah, if this guy escapes, I'll throw you into the line of fire."

Her snort awards me a point for the comeback. I'm trying to work with Jen, no matter how many people tell me it's a waste of time. I must be that idiot who keeps trying to pet the stray cat, knowing I'm just going to end up with bloody scratches. One could see this as a sign of deep compassion and the belief in inherent human goodness.

It's not. As Dalton says, I'm just stubborn. Jen is an obstacle I will overcome. Which is not to say I'm winning the battle. We have reached an uneasy truce, though. I champion her continued role in the town militia, and she doesn't address me as "Hey, bitch." At least not in public.

Jen walks to the cell. She's spent her share of time in there, more than anyone else in Rockton. I first saw her at the Roc, Isabel having come by the station for help breaking up a bar brawl. There'd been no brawl. Just Jen, looking like a middle-aged schoolteacher enjoying a glass of wine with her significant other. Then Isabel tried to kick her out — for freelancing on brothel property — and that's when the brawl began.

I later learned that Jen really had been a schoolteacher. She still looks it to me — late thirties, average appearance, nicely groomed. When she walks to that cell, Brady cracks open one eye. He can't help it. He heard her talk — insulting Kenny, snarking at me — and he's looked, expecting to see a rough and bitter woman. Instead, she looks like the schoolteacher she'd once been, and his eye opens a little wider, just to be sure.

"How many?" she says.

I don't need to ask what she means.

"Five," I say.

"And you buy that?"

"I'm sure there's more. There always are."

"That's not —"

"You mean do I think he really did it. I don't give a shit. That's not my job, and after what we've been through, I'm not taking the chance."

"So the council — which I know you don't trust — tells you this preppy-assed brat has murdered five people, and you're just going to believe them?"

Brady's eyelids flicker, and I'm tempted to grab her by the arm and haul her onto the back porch. But it's too late, so I say, "And I'll repeat — I don't give a shit. If he was a citizen of this town, I'd care. He's not. And if I did decide he was innocent, you'd be first in line howling that I was putting your life in danger."

She looks at Brady again. "This just doesn't seem right."

"Well, considering I'd never expect you to agree with any choice I made, I'm not too worried."

Except I am. Jen is my Greek chorus — the voice that will never let me enjoy a moment of hubris. Every choice I make, she questions. So this should not surprise me. Should not concern me. But I expected her to walk in here and tell us we're *under*react-

ing, being too lax. When she instead says
the opposite, I begin to worry.

Six

I'm lying on our living room floor, fire blazing over my head. Dalton sleeps beside me. Storm whines, and I snap out of my thoughts and give a soft whistle that brings her bounding out of the kitchen. When she was a puppy, we'd barricade her in there whenever Dalton and I needed private time. Now we only need to kiss, and she'll give a jowl-quivering sigh and lumber off to the kitchen and wait for that whistle.

When she bounds in, I signal for her to take the exuberance down a few notches. She creeps over and sniffs Dalton's head, making sure he's asleep. I give her a pat, and she settles in on my other side, pushing as far onto the bearskin rug as she can manage.

As I rub behind her ears, I pick up on her anxiety. She knows something is bothering us, our stress vibrating through the air even now, as Dalton sleeps.

I don't think he has taken an easy breath since Brady arrived. So I may have intentionally worn him out tonight. But I'm wide awake, tangled in my thoughts.

I give Storm one last pat, head into the kitchen, and pull tequila from the cupboard. One shot downed. Then a second. I'm standing there, clutching the counter edge, when I hear a gasp from the living room.

"Casey?"

I jog in, and Dalton's scrambling up, eyes open but unseeing.

"I'm right here," I say, but he still doesn't seem to notice. He's on his feet now, looking from side to side.

"Casey?" Louder now.

I hurry beside him and put my hand on his arm. "I'm right here."

He turns, exhales hard. His arms go around me, and he's only half awake, as I lower us back to the floor. His head hits the rug, and he pulls me in, clutched like a security blanket, his heart rate slowing as he drops back into sleep.

An hour passes.

I'm still entwined with him, my head on his chest as I listen to the beat of his heart. That usually lulls me back to sleep after my nightmares. Tonight it doesn't. It can't.

I would get up and read a book, but if I

leave, he'll wake, and he needs his sleep. So I lie there, listening to the dog's snores. Then Dalton's breathing hitches. His heart thumps, and he bolts up, gasping again.

"I've made a mistake," he says.

I don't answer. I just wait.

He says it again. Not "I fucked up," but "I made a mistake." His voice is soft, a little boyish, a little breathless. He's awake but with one toe in that twilight place.

I adjust so I'm sitting with him as he squeezes his eyes shut.

"With Brady," he says. "We need to do something else."

"Like what?"

He runs his hands through his hair. "I don't know. That's the problem."

Which is exactly what I've been lying here thinking. He says, "This isn't the way to handle it, but I don't know what is," and that articulates my thoughts as perfectly as if he's pried them from my brain.

"Fuck," he says, and I have to smile, hearing him come back to himself. He looks at me. "We're screwed, aren't we?"

"Pretty much."

Silence. When he speaks again, his voice is low. "I keep wanting to ask what we could do differently, but if you had an idea, you'd give it."

"I would."

Dalton's eyes shut. A sliver of moonlight bisects his face, half light, half dark. It's a lie. There's no darkness there.

Light doesn't mean carefree or easy or saintly, though. It's not even light so much as . . .

If the absence of light is dark, what is the absence of dark? To say "light" isn't quite correct. Even "good" doesn't work.

"If I knew for certain he was guilty . . ." He lets the rest trail off.

If I knew for certain he was guilty, I could kill him. To protect the town. To protect you. To eliminate any chance that he hurts someone here.

That's what he means, and maybe it should prove that he *does* have darkness. But this is sacrifice. It's a man saying he would take another life and suffer the guilt of that rather than let anyone else be hurt.

Dalton's lack of darkness, though, means he can never take that step as long as there's a chance that Brady is innocent.

We both know innocence is a possibility, but I wasn't lying when I told Jen it didn't matter. We cannot prove Brady's innocence or guilt. We cannot even investigate his crimes. He didn't kill here. We can't go there. Which reduces our options for deal-

57

ing with Oliver Brady to two.

Keep him.

Kill him.

We can devise the most secure prison, staffed with our most reliable and loyal guards, while knowing we cannot truly guarantee safety.

Or I can conclude that we can't care whether he's innocent or guilty, but I must treat him like a potential patient zero and — without equipment to test for the virus — decide he must die.

"No," Dalton says, and I haven't spoken a word, but his eyes bore into mine with a look I know well.

Drilling into my thoughts. In the beginning, that look meant he was trying to figure me out. Now he doesn't need to. He knows.

"If you make that choice, Casey, you need to tell me first."

Which means I can't make it. I'd never allow Dalton to be complicit in Brady's death. Nor can I do it behind his back, for the purely selfish reason that it would be a betrayal our relationship would not survive. I'm not sure I could survive it either. I've had my second chance at a good life. I won't get a third.

He continues, "If it comes to that, it has to be both of us deciding." He settles back onto the rug. "I think we can handle him. Build a cabin like the icehouse. Thick walls. No windows. One exit. Only you, me, or Will carries the key. That door never opens without one of us there. Brady gets a daily walk. We'll do it when no one else is in the forest. At least one of us will accompany him, along with two militia. That's the only time he comes out. We'll gag him if we have to, so he doesn't talk to anyone, doesn't pull his innocence shit." He looks at me. "Does that work?"

It's the course of action we've already come up with. He's just repeating it, like worry beads, running plans through his mind, trying to refine it and seeing no way to do so.

"It works," I say.

And I pray I'm right.

Day three of hosting Oliver Brady in our holding cell. We're constructing his lodgings as fast as we can. The new building will serve as a food storage locker once Brady is gone. We have to think of that — construction like this cannot go to waste. That also keeps us looking toward the time when he *will* be gone.

I remember reading old stories of barn-raising parties, a building erected in a day.

It's a lovely thought, but this is being built to hold something more dangerous than hay. We must have our best people on it. Which would be so much more heartening if we had actual architects or even former construction workers. We have Kenny . . . who builds beautiful furniture.

Dalton is the project foreman. Since he was old enough to swing a hammer, he's built homes meant to withstand Yukon winters. Solid. Sturdy. Airtight. He got up at four this morning to start work, after returning home at midnight.

It's ten in the morning now, and I'm waiting for Mathias so we can get Brady's side of the story. Part of me would rather not; I fear it will ignite doubt I cannot afford. But that gag can't stay on forever, and we must know what others will hear once it's off.

Brady is pretending to sleep. That's what he does for most of the day. He must figure the law of averages says that at some point we'll forget he's awake and say something useful.

When the door opens, I say, "I hope you brought plenty of anesthetic," in French. I'm kidding, while testing whether Brady knows French. He's American, but he's also a private-school kid.

Brady doesn't react. Nor do I get a rejoin-

60

der from Mathias . . . because the man walking through the door is Brian, who runs the bakery. He has a Tupperware box in hand and slows, saying, "Did you just ask if I brought a nest egg?"

I snort a laugh at that and shake my head.

"Yes, I failed French," Brian says as he comes in. "You must be expecting Mathias."

"I am."

He lifts the box. "I brought cookies, since I know you're stuck here with . . ." His gaze slides to Brady, and I tense.

The cookies are an excuse. With almost anyone else, I would have foreseen that, but Brian has been to our house for poker. We've been to his for dinner. I talk to him almost every morning as I pick up my snack. He's my best source of town gossip, but it's the harmless variety, local news rather than rumor and innuendo. He has never once asked me for information on a case.

But now he's here to see Brady. To assess the situation. And when his gaze falls on the prisoner, his lips tighten in disapproval.

"A gag?" he says. "Is that really necessary?"

I want to snap that if it wasn't, I wouldn't do it.

"Yes," I say. "For now, it is. We've replaced

the original with something softer, and Will's watching for chafing. Given what this man is accused of, I'm okay with him suffering a bit of temporary discomfort. The gag will come off soon."

Brian eyes Brady. "What does he try to say when it comes off?"

"What would you say?" asks Mathias as he walks in. "If you were in this man's position, what would you say?"

"I-I don't know."

Mathias throws open his arms. "Look at where he is. Who he is with. He came to stay among strangers, accompanied only by a piece of paper accusing him of crimes. What is he going to say? That it is all a terrible mistake. That he did nothing."

"Then why not just let him say that?"

"Because it grows tiresome. For twenty years, I studied men like this. It is banally predicable. It begins with 'I am innocent' and escalates to 'You are a nasty human being for not believing me' and continues to 'Let me go, or I will slaughter you and everyone you have ever loved.' Tiresome. It is bad enough Casey has to sit here all day babysitting him. Does she need to endure that as well?"

"No, but . . ." Brian sneaks another look at Brady.

"The gag will come off," Mathias says, "once he realizes he wastes his breath with protestations of innocence and threats of terrible vengeance. Now go." Mathias waggles his fingers.

Once Brian leaves, Mathias makes a very indecent proposition to me *en français.* Then he watches for a reaction from Brady. There is none, confirming that if he does speak the language, it's probably limited to being able to order champagne in a Monte Carlo casino.

"Are you ready to interview him?" Mathias asks, still in French.

I make a noise in my throat. I'm unsettled by Brian's visit, seeing a friend and supporter question our decisions.

People want their monsters to look monstrous. At the very least, they want them shifty-eyed, thin-lipped, and menacing — a walking mug shot. But reality is that a killer can be a petite Asian-Canadian woman, well educated and well spoken. Or a killer can be a handsome all-American boy, a little soft around the edges, a young man you expect to see on the debate team and rowing team, but nothing overly rough.

When you look at Oliver Brady, you see wealth and privilege, but you don't really begrudge him that, because he seems innocuous enough, the type who'll attend a fund-raiser for the Young Republicans on Friday with friends and a Greenpeace meeting on Saturday with a girl.

Mathias opens the cell door. I'm standing guard, my gun ready.

"Step out," I say to Brady.

I don't tell him to put his hands where I can see them. It's not as if he's hiding a shiv in his pocket. He puts them up anyway and takes exactly one step beyond the cell door. Then he stops. Waits.

I motion to the door leading from the cell to the main room.

"In there, please."

There's the slightest narrowing of his eyes as he assesses my *please.*

He walks into the next room and sits on the chair I've set out. He puts his hands behind his back. I ignore that. I'm not binding him.

When I circle around, Brady's head swivels to follow. I've holstered my weapon, but his gaze dips to it, just for a split second, as if he can't help himself.

"Detective Butler is going to remove your gag," Mathias says. "If you wish to scream for help, please don't restrain yourself on my account. It will give her the excuse to replace the gag, and me the excuse to get on with my day."

Brady grunts. I read derision in that. He looks at Mathias, hears his diction, and smells weakness. Mathias is twice his age. A slender build. Graying hair and beard. An air of the bored aristocrat, the French accent on precisely articulated English adding to that sense of the bourgeois. Brady comes from wealth, but it's new-world money, won by frontier ingenuity. In Mathias, he sees old-world rot and weakness. An old man, too, compared to him.

Brady's grunt dismisses Mathias, and the older man's eyes glint.

"Remove the gag, please, Detective. Let us begin."

Seven

I take off Brady's gag. He reaches up and rubs at his mouth, wincing as his fingertips massage a tender spot.

Mathias turns away as he pulls over a seat. It's a deliberate move. He could have placed the chair sooner, but he puts his back to Brady.

Brady's gaze flicks to me. He expects to see my hand resting on my gun. When it isn't, he looks back at Mathias, now tugging the chair over, his attention elsewhere. He sees that, and he frowns, as if to say, *I don't understand.*

Good.

Mathias sits. I back up to perch on the edge of my desk. Brady looks from me to the older man. As he does, his sweep covers the back and front doors.

His nostrils flare, as if he quite literally smells a trap, as if Dalton and Anders are poised outside those doors, praying he makes a run for it.

"Detective Butler says you have been very eager to tell your story, Oliver," Mathias says. "Now is your chance."

Silence. When it reaches ten seconds, I open my mouth, but a subtle look from Mathias stops me. Five more seconds pass. Then:

"Is there any point?" Brady says. "You don't want to hear it. You've all made that perfectly clear by the fact you've kept me gagged for seventy-two hours. I try to say a word when it's removed at mealtime and *she*" — a glower my way — "threatens me with starvation."

"*She* is Casey Butler. *She* is a detective who has been placed in a very frustrating position, forced to babysit you when she has other work to be done."

"And I'm supposed to, what, apologize for the inconvenience of my captivity?"

"No, you are supposed to recognize that Detective Butler has done nothing to deserve the inconvenience of your care. And recognize that she attempted to relieve the indignity and discomfort of that gag, and you called her . . ." Mathias purses his lips. "I will not repeat it. It is rude. Uncalled-for in any circumstances, but particularly these."

"I was pissed off. I vented." He glances my way. "I apologize." His gaze swings back to Mathias. "But you aren't interested in what I have to say. Neither of you is. You're treating me like a child throwing a tantrum. Let me get it out of my system, and maybe I'll shut up. Gregory Wallace has convinced you all that I'm guilty, and the only thing that surprises me about that is how easy it was."

Brady pauses. "No, I shouldn't be surprised. I've seen it my whole life. Got a problem? Drown it in money, and you'll drown all doubts. Don't look a gift horse in the mouth and so on. How much is Greg paying you?"

"Hot tubs," I say. "He's paying us in hot tubs and big-screen TVs. Oh, and diamond necklaces, to wear to the next town picnic."

Brady's eyes narrow.

I wave at the police station. "Look around. We don't have electric lights or gas furnaces, and that's not for lack of money. We have what we need. You're here because of what you did. Not because we're being paid to take you."

"No, I'm here because of what I know."

"Which is?"

"Does it matter?"

"Your plan is ill-advised," Mathias murmurs.

Brady turns to him. "And what is my plan? You obviously know, so how about letting me in on it. Maybe it'll be something I can use, which is a damn sight better than *my* plan — the naive one where I thought you people might be smart enough to question the lame-ass story my stepfather gave you."

"It does not seem 'lame-ass' to me," Mathias says. "Uninspired and unoriginal, and yes, that is the colloquial definition of lame, but I believe the word you meant was 'dumb-ass,' implying anyone who believes the story is not very bright, rather than that the crimes themselves suggest a lack of intelligence on the part of the criminal."

"What?"

"Is my accent impeding your comprehension? Or are you simply proving my point?"

"I'm not going to sit here and be insulted —"

"Yes, you will. We are not forcing you to speak. I spent my career interviewing psychopaths, sociopaths, and garden-variety sadists, and I always told them that they were free to cut the session short at any time. Do you know how many did?" Mathias holds up his thumb and forefinger in a zero.

"But please, feel free to show some original-ity in this, if you could not in your crimes."

Brady seethes, and it is like watching a weasel in a cage, being poked with a cattle prod. All it has to do is retreat to the other side. Instead, it snarls and twists and snaps at the prod. That may feel like grit and cour-age to the weasel, but to an outsider, it looks like submission. Mathias holds the power; Brady is trapped.

"Ignore him," I say to Brady, and he starts at the sound of my voice, as if he's forgot-ten there's someone else in the room.

"He's baiting you," I say. "He gets little amusement up here, and you're his enter-tainment for the day."

Brady's lips tighten. He wants to smirk and lean back in his chair and say he isn't falling for the good cop, bad cop game. But my expression doesn't look like the good cop's.

Seconds tick by. Then he makes up his mind and twists to face me.

"I can't fight a bold-faced lie," he says. "I don't even know where to start."

"Try."

"How? We're not in San Jose right now. We're thousands of miles from it. So how exactly do I prove I wasn't the shooter?"

Mathias clears his throat, and I know my

poker face has failed. Mathias's throat-clearing pulls Brady's attention away, and I recover.

"Try," I say. "Tell me what proof they had against you. What they were using to charge you."

Brady laughs. There's a jagged bitterness to it. The weasel has realized that attacking the prod does no good, but it can't help itself. It has no other recourse. Keep doing the same thing and hope for a different result, knowing how futile that is.

"Greg said I was being charged? Of course he did. It's not like you can call up the district attorney and ask. Not like you'd expect an honest answer if you did. *We can neither confirm nor deny* — that'd be the sound bite, and you'd take it to mean yes, they have a warrant out for my arrest, when the truth is" — he meets my gaze — "it's like me telling this old man that you think he's hot. You know it's bullshit. I know it's bullshit. But he'd love to believe it, and there's nothing you can say to defend yourself."

"Actually, no," Mathias says. "I find the thought rather alarming. I would have to disabuse Casey of it immediately, and inform her that, as lovely as she is, I really do prefer women who were born before I graduated university."

"Whatever," Brady says. "My point is that I wasn't even on the investigators' radar. Why would I be? What's my motive? Did Greg even bother to mention that? 'Cause I'd love to hear it."

"Haven't you asked *him*?" Mathias says. "Or are you testing us? Seeing if your stepfather's story changes, depending on the handler? That would be odd, given that we could simply compare notes, as they say."

"Do you think any of my 'handlers' were talking to me?" He shakes his head. "Everybody's looking for the shooter, so it was an easy story to tell. Greg just had to move fast, before they caught the real guy. Get me up into Alaska, some off-the-grid place where no one can check the news."

"But someone *did* tell you what your stepfather said."

"No, I overheard two guards talking about it. Couple of jarheads, must have thought gagging me also took away my ability to hear. When they fed me, I tried to reason with them. They gave me this." He pushes aside his hair to show a scabbed gash. "The gag stayed on for the next eight hours. No food. No water. That's what a guy who shot six kids deserves. Which is why Gregory used that story. The whole damn country

72

wants that bastard to burn in hell."

"What's your stepfather's motive, then?" I ask. "You said you know something."

He eyes me. Sizes me up. Finds me lacking and eases back into his chair as he says, "That's my leverage, and I'm not giving it up until it'll get me somewhere. For now, let's go with the obvious motive. The one that's partly true. Money."

"From what I understand, it's his company. Your mother married into it."

"No, it was my father's company. My biological father. Gregory Wallace was his employee. After my dad died, Greg took his wife and his company. But my dad made sure no one would get their hands on my inheritance. On my twenty-eighth birthday, I get a trust fund of fifteen million. Do you know how old I am now?"

"Twenty-seven."

"Yep. Last year, I heard something that made me suspect there wasn't fifteen mil in that fund anymore. I tried investigating. Greg blocked me. Gave me some song and dance about the stock markets and poor investments my father made. He promised there will be plenty of money but . . ."

"Not fifteen million."

"Far from it, I bet. That's part of the reason I'm here. I'm not a stand-up guy.

I'm a bit of an asshole. But I'm not a sociopath. That would be the guy who sent me here."

EIGHT

When I walk into the Roc with Mathias, Isabel is already pouring a shot of her top-shelf tequila. She holds it out for me.

"It isn't noon yet," I say.

"It is somewhere."

"And I'm on duty."

"True." She downs the shot herself. "I have a feeling I'm going to need that."

She pulls over a bottle of single malt and pours a shot for Mathias. He arches his brows. She points to the side.

"Glasses over there. Ice, too, if you insist on ruining good Scotch."

"I do not ruin it. I chill it. Two shakes around the glass and out it goes."

"Waste of good ice, then, which isn't cheap this time of year."

"Put it on my tab, and come winter I shall replace the cube with an entire block."

Isabel grants him a chuckle for that. She even gets him a glass, though she draws the line at adding the ice. Mathias still smiles, pleased with his victory, and then admires her rear view as she crosses the bar to start the coffeemaker.

"Eyes off my ass, Mathias," Isabel says. "I'll put that on your tab, too, and it's more than you can afford."

"Oh, nothing is more than I can afford, *chérie.* And I do not need to pay. You would be offended if I were not looking. I am simply bowing to your iron will."

She rolls her eyes.

The door opens. Dalton walks in and says, "Coffee ready?," as if this is his biggest concern, but his gaze slides my way, asking how it went with Mathias and Brady. I make a face. He grimaces and eyes the beer display but doesn't ask for one. The door opens again, and Val joins us.

"Gang's all here," Isabel says. "Before we begin, would you like a drink, Val?"

"Yes. Tea, please. Strong."

Isabel's lips twitch. From anyone else, that might have been a joke. Not Val. Strong tea *is* her equivalent of my tequila shot.

First, I tell them Brady's story about the shooter in San Jose.

"Bullshit," Dalton says. "Bullshit to make you do exactly what you're doing."

"Wonder if I've been misled."

"Right. He pretends he's been accused of an entirely different crime, and you start wondering if there are multiple stories going around, which makes it seem like we're being played."

That's the answer I like. I'm not sure it's the right one, though. I walk them through the rest of the interview.

When I finish, Isabel looks at Mathias. "Well, that was a mistake."

His brows shoot up.

"You just antagonized a man who viciously murders people for no provocation."

"Then perhaps, having given him provocation, I have removed myself from danger."

"You just can't help yourself, can you, Mathias? You are incapable of learning the lesson life has tried to teach you: don't piss off the psychos."

"I am stubborn."

"Stubbornly suicidal."

From that exchange, I presume Isabel knows why Mathias is here. One of those "psychos" accused Mathias of brainwashing him into emasculating himself and then managed to escape and come after Mathias, leaving dead bodies in his wake. Which should sound as if the innocent psychiatrist was targeted by a delusional psychopath spouting obvious nonsense. Yeah, I'm pretty sure that isn't actually how it worked. Not with Mathias.

Dalton cuts in. "I'll side with Mathias on this. Rattling Brady's cage might not be the worst thing. Get him worked up enough to snap, prove he's not Mr. Innocent. We just need to make sure his cage is locked tight. And if he does lash out?" Dalton shrugs. "He's got a target now."

"Thank you, Sheriff," Mathias says. "While I would think my approach is somewhat more nuanced than 'rattling his cage' —"

Dalton snorts and rolls his eyes at me, but Mathias continues, "— yes, that is part of my approach."

"Never learned the idiom about honey and vinegar, did you?" Isabel says.

"It doesn't work for me. Now, if *you* were to offer Mr. Brady honey, I suspect that would be an entirely different thing. He doesn't want mine."

"Should we do that?" Val says. "Should we allow Isabel to handle this instead? Or perhaps not *instead,* but in conjunction *with* Dr. Atelier. The honey and the vinegar."

"I can consult if you truly see the need," Isabel says. "But if you're hoping for me to charm and disarm, I suspect I'm twenty years too old for that. Brady seems like a classic narcissist, which implies he'll have no use for older women — they would not satisfy his self-image. He would only expect to charm *me.* To disarm *me.*"

"Then he would prove himself a very poor judge of character," Mathias says. "Which I believe he is not, as evidenced by the fact that he has not attempted to charm Casey. He knows better. The same would go for you."

"But what about someone he felt he could charm?" Val says.

"That's actually a good idea." I make a face as I hear myself. "Sorry. I didn't mean it like that. But we could provide contact with someone we trust. Someone Brady will find an easy dupe. He needs an ally. He needs someone championing his cause and seeding doubt. Maybe even someone he thinks he can con into helping him escape. A woman who will, at least to him, seem ripe for his charm. Lonely. Uncertain. Over-looked."

Mathias turns to Val. "I do hope you're volunteering."

I glare at him.

"What?" he says. "Have you not just described Valerie?" At a harder glare, he deigns to add, "In the sense that Valerie can *appear* to be all of that."

"No," I say.

"He's right," Val says. "I *wasn't* volunteering but . . ." She looks from me to Isabel, as if searching for an answer there. Then she squares her thin shoulders. "I *am* perfect for the job. We can even tell him I'm the town leader. That will make him feel as if he warrants special treatment. And he'll know I have power here, which makes me even more useful to him."

"Yeah, no," Dalton says.

"You think I can't handle it, Sheriff?"

He meets her gaze. "No, I think it's dangerous."

"And you think I can't handle *that*."

"No, Val. I think nobody should be put in that position. Don't pull this bullshit."

I know what he means. When Val first arrived in Rockton, she'd wanted to join a patrol. Dalton argued against it. She took offense — clearly he was discriminating against her because she was a woman. The council had backed Val . . . and she'd been attacked on that trip. Kidnapped by hostiles and almost certainly sexually assaulted, though she vehemently denies it. The truth is that Dalton has never let anyone — even Anders — into the forest so soon after arriving. But even now, Val hears only "*You* can't handle this," because she's been hearing variations on that all her life.

"Casey?" she says.

"No," Isabel says. "Don't do that, Val."

"Isabel's right," I say. "You're asking me to intercede with my *boss,* Val. This is a law enforcement issue. He's the sheriff."

I can feel Dalton studying me. Trying to figure out what my answer *would* be.

"You can still voice an opinion," Val says, and Isabel makes a noise, low in her throat, a warning that Val ignores.

"You think we should try it," Dalton says.

"I . . . I would rather not put Val in that situation," I say.

"In ideal circumstances," he says. "But under these ones, you think it's worth a shot."

I want to say no. Support him. He *is* my boss, and I never want to undermine his authority. That opens up a situation where residents will act like Phil, coming to me as the calm and reasonable one who can intercede with Dalton. Worse, they'll come to me as his lover, in hopes that I can use leverage.

So I want to just say Dalton's right. But he knows that isn't my answer, and he'll take more offense at a lie.

"I don't like the idea," I say carefully. "But if Val is willing —"

"I am." She straightens and meets Dalton's gaze. "I can do this. Whatever you think of me, Eric, I believe I am more, and I'd like the opportunity to prove it."

He mutters, "Fuck." It's like when Nicole asked to join the militia after her ordeal. I wanted to say no. Tell her to take more time. Not to push it. But I understood that need to push. Val is trying to step up. She's trying to be a valuable member of the community. Unless we are vehemently against her doing this, it's difficult to deny her that opportunity.

"Fine," Dalton says. "You have a week. If it doesn't go anywhere, I'm pulling you out."

Val wants to start right away. As hard as she fought for this task, once the meeting breaks up, I can tell she's having second thoughts. Yet when I offer her the chance to change her mind, that only solidifies it. She wants to meet him now. Before she loses her nerve.

Val and I walk into the station, talking town business. I give her some files. As she's preparing to leave, I ask her to send Kenny in to relieve me for lunch. She goes . . . and returns to say he's been called off and she'll stay instead. I hem and haw, but she insists.

I tell her I'll be back in thirty minutes. I actually do leave — I go for coffee at the bakery — but I've warned Kenny to keep an ear on that door.

When I return, it's with Dalton, and it hasn't been nearly thirty minutes. She knows to expect that, and when we walk in, she acts surprised, scurrying from the cell room.

"Sheriff," she says.

"Everything okay?" Dalton slows, his gaze moving from Brady to Val.

She stammers a response, and she overdoes it, but Brady doesn't seem to notice and comes to her rescue with, "We were just talking about my meals. I need more protein. And I'd like hand weights. Twenty-pounders."

"If you don't get the weights, you won't need the protein," Dalton drawls, but when Brady's lips tighten, he says, "We'll arrange trips to the gym later. We're not giving you dumbbells, though. We call those weapons."

"Oh, I think that's overstating the matter," Val says.

"Then you think wrong," Dalton says. "Now, if you'll excuse us . . ."

Val bristles. Dalton turns his back on her. Brady follows the exchange and allows himself the smallest of smiles.

NINE

It's now day five, and we need to get Brady out of that cell. Time for his first walk.

Anders, Dalton, and I lead Brady into the forest through the station back door. I've removed his gag, and he's trudging along, gaze down, docile and quiet. We make it three steps before he spots a woman by the forest's edge and raises his bound hands.

"Help me," he says. "Please. This is a mistake. They're going to —"

"Yeah," Nicole says. "You definitely want to keep that gag on."

She walks to Brady. "Oh, I'm sorry. Did I look like a gullible passerby? There aren't any of those here. You know what is here? People who'll take one look at scum like you and —"

He snaps forward to crack heads with her, but Nicole pulls back and their foreheads barely graze. Then she plows her fist into

Brady's stomach, and he staggers, gasping in pain.

"Like I said," she says. "Don't bother."

She continues past him. Moving out of his field of vision so he doesn't see her flushed face and quickened breathing. I resisted bringing her on this walk. She's militia, which means she's trained for it, but she became militia after her ordeal. I understand her need to get past that, toughen up and move forward. I also know the dangers of doing it too fast, and that quickened breathing tells me that as badass as the encounter looked, she's quaking inside.

While Dalton replaces Brady's gag, I look over and Nicole mouths, *Please.* I know she means please let her come. I nod.

We've barely taken three steps when Dalton hears something, and we see a trio of residents, who just happen to have decided to stroll along the town border. Brady turns their way, his head bowed, bound hands lowered. He makes no move to get their attention, but he does, of course. He looks as pathetic as he had for Nicole.

Please help me.

They've made a mistake. You see that, don't you?

He says something against the gag, and I don't even think it's words. It's not meant to be. He's just drawing their attention to his situation.

This is the dilemma we face. Remove the gag, and Brady can plead his case. Leave it on, and the very gag pleads it for him.

Look at me.

Look what they're doing to me.

"You done gawking?" Dalton says to the trio. "Come over and take a closer look. See if Nicki has a bruise yet, from where he head-butted her."

Of course, there isn't a mark, but that's enough to make them decide to head back into town.

We set out. As we walk, Anders glances at me, as if feeling the urge to make small talk. I'm not sure that's wise, though. It feels too easy to let something slip, something that might suggest Brady isn't in Alaska.

Except that's not all he knows. He has seen faces. Heard names, even if they're fake. We are making an enemy here, one who does not seem like a stupid man. One who is not going to forget us.

I'm only beginning to realize the full extent of the danger the council has put us in.

We're a couple of kilometers into the forest when I turn to Brady and say, "Enough exercise?," and he looks around, as if he's considering, but it's more than that. He's processing his surroundings, and when he shakes his head, I know it's not that he wants more exercise — he wants to see more.

"We can go back and come out again," Nicole says.

"Nah," Dalton says. "We'll walk as far as he wants. He's enjoying the scenery. Plenty of it out here."

Endless scenery, that's what he means. Endless trails that go nowhere Brady will want to go. They lead to mountains and caves for us to explore. Lakes and streams for fish and fowl. Hunting blinds. Overnight campsites. Berry patches. Yes, one of those paths might hook up with a trail used by miners or trappers, which could ultimately get you to the nearest village. But Brady would still need to *survive* the trek with no weapons or skills.

As we continue, Nicole asks if anyone has seen our resident man-eating cougar recently. It's a heavy-handed attempt to tell Brady what he'd face out here, but Dalton goes along with it, mostly for conversation. The silence is starting to smell of fear, as if we're too shaken by Brady to talk around him.

They're discussing the big cat when I see

a figure around the next bend. My left arm flies up, stopping Brady. My right goes for my gun.

"It's just me," Jacob calls as he breaks into a jog. "I was about ready to give up on you guys. I thought we said noon . . ."

Jacob slows as he rounds the bend and sees us. His gaze travels over Brady, and I'm waiting for a *What the fuck?* Except he won't say those exact words. Dalton's younger brother does not share his propensity for profanity.

Instead, he just says to Dalton, "You forgot about me, huh?"

Now we get the "Fuck," from Dalton, and, "Yeah, sorry."

We're close to the spot where Dalton and his brother trade, and I'm guessing that's what they had scheduled for today.

I wave at Brady. "We had a situation."

"I see that. I heard Eric and Nicki talking, and I thought maybe she'd come along to help him carry supplies."

"Or to visit," Nicole says. "I hope I'd be more than a pack mule in that scenario."

"Course," Jacob says, his cheeks flushing over his beard, which I do not fail to notice has been trimmed short. His hair is tied back neatly, and he's dressed in the new jeans and new tee he'd requested at their

88

last trade. Which isn't to say that Jacob *normally* looks like he's just crawled from a cave after a winter's hibernation. But he does live out here, without access to showers and department stores.

This extra effort was in hopes Nicole would accompany Dalton, as she often does, part of the slow dance between her and Jacob. They've been circling each other, not unlike a couple of fifteen-year-olds, trying to figure out if the other is interested before making any embarrassing moves.

"Eric did forget," Nicole says. "Otherwise, I'd have expected an invitation. But, yes, as you can see . . ." She nods at the man beside me. "We have a situation."

Jacob nods.

"You're not even going ask *why* we're walking a bound and gagged man through the forest, are you?"

Jacob shrugs. "Figure he pissed Eric off."

Nicole laughs at that.

Jacob looks at his brother. "You want me to store the game?"

"Nah, we'll take it off your hands."

We walk around the bend to the spot where Jacob left his trade goods — a brace of rabbits, one of ducks, and one of pheasants.

"Good hunting," Dalton says.

" 'Tis the season, as Dad used to say."

Dalton nods, expressionless, as he always is when his brother mentions their parents. When Dalton was nine, the former sheriff of Rockton "rescued" him from the forest. And by "rescued," I mean kidnapped. So Dalton went from one loving set of parents to another. And the first set never came after him, while the second never realized that what they'd done was wrong. It's an impossible situation to reconcile, and Dalton refuses to even discuss it.

After Jacob mentions their dad, Dalton just bends to examine the game and discuss the price. If there's any haggling involved, it's Dalton trying to get Jacob to take more. Another impossible situation — Dalton wants to help his brother, and Jacob sees that help as charity.

Dalton has tried to get Jacob to come to Rockton. Jacob refuses. I wonder sometimes how much of that is choice and how much is fear that he won't fit in, that he will be seen as a freak. Dalton already feels that about himself. But if I presume Jacob chooses the forest out of fear, then am I any different from the women who presumed Dalton stayed in Rockton out of fear he wouldn't fit in down south?

Those women meant well, but in their

90

way, they were no different from Dalton's adoptive parents. The Daltons found a boy living in the forest and decided no one could voluntarily want that life, so they rescued him. When Dalton and I look at Jacob's life and wish for better, we fall into that same trap of thinking what we have is clearly superior.

When Dalton and Jacob finally agree on a price for the game, Jacob says, "You can get me your stuff next week. If the weather holds, I want to head north for a few days. Got a spot up there that's all-I-can-haul hunting."

"Or all-two-can-haul," Nicole says. "Someone agreed to take me on a hunting trip once the weather improved."

When Jacob doesn't answer, Nicole quickly says, "Oh, I'm kidding. Maybe another trip."

Jacob shoves his hands into his jacket pockets. "No, this might be a good time. I could use the help. Let me check a few things. If it'll work, I'll leave a message in two days."

One might think it'd be easier for Jacob to just pop into Rockton, but very few residents know he exists, and while I'm uncomfortable adding Brady to that list, there's nothing to be done about it now.

Dalton says he'll check for the note. As they talk, Anders subtly directs my attention to our left, where I see another figure in the forest. My hand goes to my gun again, but slower this time. With Jacob, I could clearly see a human shape on the path. This is a big shape in a tree about fifty feet away. The only creature that size you'd find treed up here is the one we were just talking about. The cougar.

Anders's gaze shifts to Dalton, asking if we should tell him. I shake my head and take a step off the path, trying to see past a tree that partially blocks my view.

For the most dangerous creature in these woods, humans win hands down. But after that, the runner-up is a matter of debate. Grizzly or cougar? Pick your poison. One is seven hundred pounds of brute force. You'll see it coming. Question is whether you can stop it. The other? About my size. Much easier to kill. The problem is getting that chance — before it silently drops onto your back and snaps your neck.

Yet in this particular situation, a grizzly would worry me more. If this is a cougar, we see it, and that's really all we need. The question is whether it's the big cat we're looking for. She was the only one around — we're north of their usual territory — but we've seen signs that her cubs may have stayed. If it's the mother, I don't want to miss the chance to kill her. She's a man-eater, which makes her an indisputable threat. But her offspring?

Here is the question we face, not unlike our dilemma with Brady. If we see one of the younger cougars, do we exterminate it, just in case? That isn't our way. But if we let it live, and it kills someone, we have to take responsibility for that death . . . and *then* deal with a proven threat.

I edge around the tree. The figure is still too hard to make out, between the distance and blooming tree buds. All I can say for sure is that it's the right size for a cougar or a human, and it's lying on a branch watching us, which fits for either, too.

I glance at Anders. He gives a helpless shrug. We don't have binoculars — we were so distracted by Brady that we didn't grab our hiking pack. I survey that shape on the tree, and I know we can't walk away without seeing what it is. But we'll need to send at least two of us in for a closer look, and that leaves only two with Brady. No, wait, there's also Jacob. That'll work. Jacob and Dalton can go —

The figure moves and sunlight glints off —

"Down!" Anders shouts. "Everyone down!"

TEN

Anders's hand hits me square between the shoulder blades. Even as I fall, I look up to see Dalton spinning toward me. That's his first reaction. Not to drop, damn him, but to make sure Jacob and I are. Both of us *are* dropping, and I'm shouting "Eric, get down!" but he's already doing that. Then he sees that one person hasn't moved.

Brady.

Our sudden movement threw him into defensive mode, his hands rising as if to ward us off.

"Oliver, get — !" I shout.

Dalton lunges at Brady just as I see the distant muzzle flare. I shout "No!" and I'm scrambling up as Dalton knocks Brady out of the way. Then blood. I see blood.

Anders grabs my leg, but I yank away and lurch, bent over, toward Dalton as I shout, "In the woods! Roll into the woods!" Anders echoes it with his trained-soldier bark, and

Brady, Nicole, and Jacob crawl off the path.

Dalton doesn't move.

He's on the ground. And there's blood. That's all I register. Dalton is on the ground, and there is blood.

Even when I see him rising, I think I'm imagining it. My brain has already seized on the worst possible scenario and refuses to let go.

"Down!" Anders says. "Both of you! Now!"

I'm close enough to grab Dalton, and then Anders is there, and we both get him off the path as Dalton says, "I'm fine, I'm fine."

There are no more shots. When Jacob tries to rise, though, Anders says, "Stay down! It's a sniper."

Jacob stares at him, uncomprehending.

"There's a shooter in the trees," I say. "Get off the path. We have Eric."

"I'm fine, Jacob," Dalton calls. "He winged me. That's all."

Which is a slight exaggeration. Dalton has been shot in the upper arm. A small-caliber bullet passed through what I hope is just muscle. It should be, but blood streams from the entry and exit holes, and I'm still fighting the panic that insists that it's more serious.

When I prod Dalton into thicker brush,

96

he doesn't argue. I get my belt and shirt off and fashion a padded tourniquet around his arm.

"It's fine," he says. "We need to —"

"I know."

Anders motions. I peek around a bush and see what he's trying to show me — that the sniper's perch is empty.

"Go on," Dalton says. "You and Will."

I hesitate. I'd rather have Anders stay to properly assess him, but Dalton's stable and our shooter is on the move. He squeezes my fingers with his good hand and says, "Be careful."

"I'm not the one leaping in to save serial killers."

"Yeah, didn't think that one through. He'd better appreciate it."

I shake my head. Oliver Brady will consider rescue no less than his due. While Dalton can say he didn't think it through, I'm not sure that would have mattered. Brady is under his protection. Dalton isn't going to stand by and watch him die.

Anders and I slip from bush to tree to whatever will hide our approach. Every few moments, we stop to listen. There's nothing to hear, just the usual noise of the forest.

When we're about halfway to the tree, I pop up enough to scan our surroundings.

Anders does the same. A shake of his head says he sees nothing either. When I frown, he jerks his chin, asking what's bugging me. The calm suggests our shooter has retreated, but I'd have expected to *hear* that — in the thump of a foot on hard ground, the crackle of undergrowth, the cry of a startled bird.

Our sniper hasn't beat a hasty retreat, crashing through the forest. Has he retreated at all? I whisper that possibility to Anders, and he nods, his gaze shifting to where we left the others. As much as we want to go back and warn them, Dalton will keep them safely hidden until we say the coast is clear.

We continue on, step by careful step. Listen. Step. Look. Step. *Feel.* Yes, that last one seems strange, especially if I admit I'm trying to catch a sense of someone nearby. Out here, I've learned not to be too quick to dismiss the raised hairs on my neck, the sense that I am not alone.

Dalton is the most pragmatic person I know, but he'd also be the first to tell me to pay attention to my sixth sense. He puts it into a context his brain understands — humans are both predator and prey out here, and so logically we might have something that is not quite premonition, but rather an awareness of another presence. Maybe it's vibrations underfoot or a scent in the air or a sound too soft to be identified.

I detect none of that.

We reach the tree and circle it, guarding each other while scanning the forest.

"Gone," Anders whispers.

I process the scene, but there's nothing to find. Not even a fiber trapped in the bark where he climbed. I shimmy onto that limb and find nothing. Then, as I'm climbing down, I catch the glint of metal in the undergrowth.

"Will . . ." I say carefully.

He's been circling the tree, searching. Now he halts, one foot still raised.

"Stay right where you are," I say.

"Can I put my foot down?"

"Very carefully."

He does that as I say, "There's something metallic on the ground to your left."

"Bear trap?"

"Not unless they come in long, barrel-shaped form."

"Shit. There's a gun pointed right at me, isn't there?"

"Yep."

"Of course there is." He curses some more. "Okay, if it's a trap, you're looking for a trigger. Presumably it would be tripped from the direction the gun is aimed. It could be a pressure plate under the soil."

"I don't see any soil disturbance around you."

"Good start."

I crawl out on the tree branch over him to conduct a full visual sweep. I don't see a trip wire, and I tell him that, adding, "But don't take my word for it."

"Oh, I'm not. Sorry. Can you climb out over the gun?"

"Yes, but I can already tell that won't help. It's nestled in the vegetation. I'm going to check it out. Just hold on."

I retreat down the tree. Then I circle wide. When I'm on the far side of the gun, I walk toward it, checking before putting each foot down. Finally, I reach the spot. I crouch. Then I swear.

"That doesn't sound good," Anders says.

"No, it's — Just hold on."

I swore because I know this gun. I'm temporarily putting that on the "not important" shelf, along with the ramifications of having a sniper in our forest.

I hunker down. Then I lie on my belly, getting a straight-on view of the gun.

"And . . ." Anders says.

"I don't see any sign of a trigger device. It looks as if the shooter just left it behind."

"That's actually kinda disappointing."

"At the count of three, I'll knock the barrel aside, and you'll dive for cover. We'll tell everyone else it was rigged, and you narrowly escaped death. Plus, of course, I saved your life, and you owe me forever."

"Yeah, no. But you *can* move the barrel aside. Carefully please."

I lean over the gun and take another good look, running my fingers along the perimeter for a trip wire. The trigger is clear, and the gun seems fine. I ease the barrel away from Anders.

"Thank you."

I start to rise, and he says, in a low voice, "Stop."

A low growl sounds behind me. I look over my shoulder to see a muzzle and eyes peering from a clump of weeds.

ELEVEN

"Is that a . . . ?" Anders begins.

He doesn't finish, but I know what he was going to say. It looks like a wolf — the size, the build, the ears, the muzzle shape, and the white and gray fur. But there are brown spots in that gray, and its face is freckled.

"Wolf-dog," I murmur.

"Shit," Anders says.

It's the dog part that worries me. I hear wolves almost every night, but I've only spotted them deep in the forest, as they catch wind of us and disappear like ghosts. Dogs are another matter. They're feral, descended from those either released or escaped from Rockton, back in a time when pets were allowed. Those canines don't always slip away like wolves. Even a few generations removed, they retain their fearlessness around humans.

I aim my gun. I don't want to. But this is Dalton's rule. If a feral dog makes an aggressive move, we must shoot to kill.

I can't tell with this one. It's watching me just as carefully as I'm watching it.

"Got your gun ready?" I ask Anders.

"I do."

"Count of three. Three, two, one —"

I lunge at the wolf-dog and let out a snarl. I'm hoping it'll run. It doesn't. Nor does it attack. It just hunkers down and snarls back, fur bristling. Anders curses some more, and I agree. We like our decisions cut-and-dry, and the universe isn't complying these days, not even with a damn dog.

"Protocol is to shoot," Anders says. "If it doesn't *back* down, we *put* it down."

I notice he doesn't actually shoot. He's waiting for me to say yes, that's what we have to do. When I say, "Wait," he exhales in relief.

I hunker to crouch.

"Good idea," Anders says. "Submissive pose. See if it attacks."

Which isn't what I'm doing at all. I'm taking a closer look at something I've spotted.

"She's nursing," I say. "Her cubs must be nearby."

"Right. Okay. So we leave her."

"As long as she doesn't attack, yes. I'm going to pick up the rifle, and we'll back off slowly."

The wolf-dog stands her ground, allowing me to get the gun and start backing up. Then she follows, stiff-legged.

"Making sure we leave?" Anders says.

"I hope so."

When we've made it about halfway to the others, I call, "Eric?"

"Here."

"Our shooter is gone. He left his gun. But we've got a wolf-dog backing us off. It's a nursing mother."

"Fuck."

I don't ask if he wants us to shoot. If he does, he'll say so. Instead, he calls, "Jacob?"

There's a murmur of voices. Jacob appears. He ducks to peer under a branch and gets a look at the canine.

"That's Freckles," he says. "She's not usually a problem. It's the cubs making her defensive."

I don't comment on him "naming" the wolf-dog. That's not what he's done. It's just a way to identify her, the same way people name ponds and hills and other landmarks.

Jacob tells us to keep backing away. When the canine continues to follow, he lunges and growls, and she freezes. There's a five-second stare-down. Then the wolf-dog snorts and stays where she is, letting us retreat.

"You need to be more intimidating, Case," Anders says.

"Nah," Jacob says. "You just need to learn the stare . . . and know which animals you can use it on. Do that to a boar grizzly, and you're dead where you stand. She was just making sure you got away from her litter."

We return to the others. Anders and I go straight to Dalton. That's when our sheriff sees the rifle.

"Fuck, no," he say.

"Fuck, yes," Anders says. "Now give me that arm."

"We need to —"

"Arm. Now."

Dalton lifts his arm for Anders to examine. Residents joke about Dalton being the alpha dog in Rockton. He is, and no one disputes that. But people aren't animals, and the idea of one person being in charge, at all times, in all situations, is bullshit. This winter, when Dalton contracted the flu in Dawson City, Anders happily turned to me and said, "You're up." *You play sheriff for a few days.* He didn't want the job. Yet all he has to do is adopt this tone, and Dalton shuts up and listens.

As Anders examines him, Dalton shoots

glances my way. He's trying not to look at the rifle. Trying not to tip off Brady, who's watching us intently. He's also trying to hide the worry in his eyes.

"Does it matter?" I say. "Threat-wise? Six of one, half dozen of the other."

Brady's brows furrow. Dalton nods. He understands my verbal shorthand. This gun is from Rockton. That suggests our shooter is also from Rockton. On the surface, that's alarming, but what's the alternative? An external sniper would mean someone sent to kill Brady. Someone who came from Brady's world.

The two situations are equally dangerous.

Most pressing right now is Dalton's arm. Jacob and I are both hovering as Anders works. I see Brady watching, and I want to pull back, tug Jacob with me, but that's pointless. One glance at Jacob, and Brady can tell he's Dalton's brother. And if Brady hasn't figured out that Dalton and I are lovers, he's going to soon.

Dalton's injury isn't as serious as I feared, but it's still a bullet wound. It will be temporarily debilitating. Or so it will seem to a guy who agreed to stay in bed with the flu only when we warned he could infect others. It's his left arm, which is a problem.

When I say, "Good thing you're right-handed," there isn't even a moment of confusion. Instead, Dalton exhales, and says, "Yeah," and Anders agrees. Jacob looks up but covers his surprise fast. Having our prisoner realize that our sheriff has lost the full use of his dominant arm is the last thing we need. It really is.

In town, Dalton strides straight for Val's place. I catch his good arm. My gaze shoots to the station. He hesitates but nods, and we follow Anders and Nicole with Brady. When they head inside, though, we veer off to the supply shed.

The shed isn't part of the station — our building is too small to have the militia tramping in and out all day. Inside the supply building is a secure gun locker, which I examine for signs of tampering. There are none.

We have two sets of keys for this locker. Dalton carries one. Anders has the other. The militia use handguns on patrol, and they typically just pass their weapon on to whoever takes over their shift. Otherwise, they need Anders to open the locker. He never just hands over his key. Neither does Dalton.

Dalton reaches into his pocket with his left hand — force of habit — and then winces. With that wince comes a growl of frustration.

"As tempting as it is to play the tough guy," I say, "please remember that every time you do that, you pull at the wound, and it's going to take that much longer to heal. I'm going to suggest — strongly suggest — that you let me put your arm in a sling, if only to remind you to keep it still."

"Fuck."

"Yes, but it'll heal faster."

He nods. Then he switches his key to his right hand. When he fumbles to get it into the hole, I resist the urge to do it for him. The key goes in, and the cabinet opens, and sure enough, one of our rifles is missing.

I read the log. "It hasn't been checked out since last weekend, when we took the rifles for hunting."

"It was here yesterday, when I had to grab a gun for Kenny. So how the hell — ?"

"Someone picked the lock," Anders says as he walks in. "That's the only explanation."

"Agreed," I say. "But it's not a standard lock. Whoever did this has some serious skills."

"So we go to the council and demand . . ." Dalton begins, and then trails off, grumbling under his breath.

"Yeah," Anders says. "You can demand to know if we have any thieves in town, but they aren't going to tell us."

"Do you know, for a fact, that there are only two keys?" I ask. "I'm guessing you didn't install that locker yourself."

Dalton shakes his head.

"So there could be a third key floating around . . . or the council has always had one."

Anders looks at me. "You think the council brought in a sniper?"

"I'm afraid to even start considering the possibilities. We'll need to report the attempt, but I'm going to suggest we don't mention finding the gun or realizing it's missing. If the council is responsible, their sniper could have brought his own weapon. Using ours suggests they wanted to frame us. By admitting it was ours, we set ourselves up to take responsibility if they succeed next time."

Twelve

"I don't understand," Phil says after I explain what's happened.

"Someone tried to shoot Oliver Brady," I say.

"Yes, I understand that's what you're telling me, Detective, but I'm not sure I follow your reasoning. You presume Mr. Brady was the target."

"If Eric hadn't pushed him down, he'd have been —"

"And what proof do you have of that?" Phil cuts in, his voice edged with impatience. "I'm sorry to interrupt, Detective, but I am concerned that you are leaping to conclusions here. There is no way of telling that the bullet would have hit Mr. Brady. Even if there was, that doesn't prove he was a target. It may have been simply a random shot fired by a settler."

"The shooter was in a tree. That's a targeted attack."

"Perhaps because you were trespassing on territory the shooter considers his."

"So it was a complete coincidence that we were walking the prisoner in the forest when someone fired a shot from a tree — which has *never* happened before — and that bullet just *happened* to seem aimed at our prisoner. Presuming it was a random attack —"

"— is like seeing a grizzly barreling in your direction," Dalton says, "and standing your ground because there's a chance he's not actually charging at *you*."

"A colorful analogy, Sheriff," Phil says. "But I take your point. Obviously extra steps will be required to secure the prisoner."

"Like what?" Dalton says. "Keeping him locked up six months with no exercise?"

"I do not have an issue with that. Nor does his stepfather."

"Our residents will. They already think he's being mistreated."

"I'm sure you can handle that, Sheriff."

"I can. What I can't handle is the loss of respect they'll have for me — and Casey and Will — for a situation that is not our fault. We don't want Brady here."

"And did you take steps to rectify that?"

"Excuse me?" I say.

111

"Yeah," Dalton says. "We put one of our guys in that tree to shoot him. Stupid me forgot *we* planted the sniper and nearly got my ass killed trying to save the target. Whoops."

"What I mean, Sheriff, is that you might have let your dissatisfaction with the situation be known, and one of your citizens decided to relieve you of the responsibility. Are all your guns accounted for?"

"They're all in the locker," I say. Which is technically true.

"Then I don't know what to tell you, besides my suspicion that this was one of your forest people, and regardless of whether Mr. Brady was the target, you should reconsider walking him outside of town boundaries."

"On another subject," I say, "do you know anything about a shooting in San Jose?"

Silence. "A shooting . . ."

"In San Jose."

"There are many shootings in America these days, Detective. To the point, sadly, where they begin to blur."

"This was in a school playground, and the shooter is still at large."

"That does sound familiar. But I fail to see what . . . Are you suggesting that has something to do with *this* shooting?"

"Brady mentioned it."

"All right . . ." A long pause. "I'm still not seeing the connection. I seem to recall a sniper was involved in the playground incident, but I'm at a loss to even guess what the connection might be."

"I thought it was odd that he brought it up."

"Ah. What you're saying is that it's odd that he mentioned a sniper shooting . . . and then seems to be the target of one. You're wondering if Mr. Brady himself had something to do with the attempt this afternoon."

"Sure." That wasn't where I was going at all — I just wanted to verify that there *had* been a shooting in San Jose and see how Phil reacted to Brady mentioning it.

Phil continues, "You're asking whether Mr. Brady knew where he was going. Or if he might have been followed there by a confederate."

"Yes."

"There was no indication of a partner in his crimes. However, Mr. Brady has the money to hire someone to do what you are suggesting — appear to shoot at him, in hopes of bolstering his claims of innocence. He is proclaiming that innocence, I presume."

"To anyone who'll listen, which is why we're keeping the gag on."

"A wise idea."

"Yeah," Dalton says. "It really helps those who think we're mistreating him."

There's a pause, and Phil manages to sound borderline sympathetic when he says, "I can see that would be a problem. It will need to be dealt with very carefully."

Dalton snorts.

Phil continues, "Back to the issue, while I will agree that Mr. Brady could hire someone to do this, I don't see how he would carry it out. We were exceedingly careful with transport, funneling him through multiple handlers, none of whom knew the situation or the destination or had any experience with Rockton."

"*None* knew the situation?" I say.

"That is correct. They were told only that they were transporting a dangerous prisoner. We advised leaving the gag on, and we said they could not trust any story he told if it came off. The warning wasn't really necessary. For those we hired, this would go without saying."

"The woman who brought him here was ex-military," I say.

"Most were."

"Any with sniper training?"

He pauses. "I have no idea, but I will look into that, particularly with the woman who delivered him. That would be the only scenario I see working here — that he communicated with her and she agreed to help. She knew where he was being held. And she *is* a mercenary. Excellent deductive reasoning."

Or, maybe, just an excuse he can utilize. *Why, yes, Detective, it turns out she was trained in distance shooting, and we cannot track her current whereabouts. Good job, Casey. Gold star. Case solved. Move on.*

"What about the stepfather?" I say. "Does Gregory Wallace know where Oliver is being held?"

"Not specifically. And I can't imagine why he'd pay us to keep the young man safe . . . and then hire an assassin to kill him. That's hardly cost-effective."

Actually, it would be very cost-effective. If Oliver Brady is innocent, that will be proven when someone else is accused of the same crimes. Even if that never happens, his mother might begin questioning. It's far more convenient for Brady to be dead. *I'm so sorry, darling — I tried to keep him safe for you, and I couldn't.*

If Brady is guilty, there's still a reason to assassinate him. How long will Wallace want to pay to keep his murderous stepson safe? Whatever the scenario here, killing Oliver Brady is both efficient and cost-effective. The only reason Wallace wouldn't have done that right away is his wife. Better for her to think Wallace tried to save her boy, no matter what crimes he's committed.

I talk to Phil for a while longer, but there's nothing more to get. Before we sign off, he says, "Sheriff?"

"Yeah."

"I know we've put you in a bad position."

"The word you want," Dalton drawls, "is 'untenable.' "

There's a long pause, and then an almost reluctant "I'm not sure that's the proper term," as if he's loath to correct his uneducated sheriff, when the poor guy is trying to expand his vocabulary.

"Yeah," Dalton says. "It is. Untenable. A position or argument we cannot defend. We have a killer who has done seriously fucked-up things, yet I cannot explain that to people or they'll revolt. But if I don't tell them, they'll think we're mistreating a common criminal. Or that he didn't commit a crime at all. Maybe we're afraid they'll discover the truth if we take off that gag. An untenable situation."

Another long pause. Then, "You'll work it

116

out, Sheriff. I just need you to understand, particularly in light of this shooting, how important Mr. Brady is to Rockton. The cost of hiding the town against modern technology is skyrocketing. We need to take advantage of opportunities like Oliver Brady."

"Bullshit." Dalton's voice is low, nearly too low to hear, and there's a note in it that has the hairs on my neck rising.

"I beg your pardon?"

"That's bullshit, and you know it. You want to cover skyrocketing costs? Look at reducing your profit margin."

Phil's voice cools. "I don't like your implication, Sheriff. Anytime you would like to see our fiscal reports, I will have a copy sent to Dawson City for you."

Which wouldn't do any good. It's not the official income that counts. It's the hidden profits, from those who buy their way in under a false story.

"Oliver Brady is your responsibility, Sheriff," Phil says. "You only have to keep him safe for six months. I'm certain you can do that. If you can't, we'll need to find someone who can."

THIRTEEN

It's almost ten at night, and there's still enough daylight for me to squeeze in an hour of training with Storm. She's graduated beyond obedience lessons. We covered those as soon as she was old enough. We've passed manners training, too, which is particularly critical given her size. Greeting people by jumping on them ceased to be adorable about twenty pounds ago. By the time she's full-grown, even leaning in for attention could topple people. Roughhousing is for playtime and only with a select few people. For the rest, she must comport herself with queenly dignity.

Tonight's lesson is also critical for her breed: distraction and dominance training. She'll weigh more than me in a few months, which means I will physically be unable to restrain her. I'm putting her through her basic paces — sit, stay, come — while Dalton sits on the porch and tosses her favorite ball in the air.

"Storm . . ." I say when she looks his way.

Her ears perk, but her gaze doesn't move. "Eyes on me."

Her head shifts, just enough so she can see me out of the corner of her eye.

"Uh-uh. *Eyes* on *me.* Both of them."

Her gaze shoots to me. Back to Dalton. He chuckles.

"Storm."

She sighs, a deep one, her jowls quivering. Then she looks my way and keeps her attention there.

Dalton fake-fumbles the ball. As it thumps to the ground, her head whips toward him.

"Storm," I say. "Eyes on me."

Another sigh, as she looks my way with a glower, like a teen saying, *Happy now?*

"Stand."

She does.

"Sit."

She grumbles at that, having clearly hoped the stand meant she was about to be released.

"Down."

She flounces to the ground. Dalton pitches the ball. It springs past us, and her muscles bunch.

"Stay."

She hesitates, muscles still tense. Then she

gives in and tears her gaze from the ball.

"Are you ready?" I say.

She whimpers, body quivering. But she doesn't rise. Doesn't look at Dalton. Keeps her gaze on me.

"Wait . . . wait . . . and . . . *go.*"

She leaps up and tears toward Dalton . . . and I see that sling on his arm.

"Shit!" I say. "I mean, no, wait —"

He falls on his ass before she can get to him. As she pounces, I'm running over with, "Storm, no —"

"It's fine," he says. "We've got this."

He sits on the ground and rubs her with his good hand as she dances on his lap. Then he raises his arm for me to toss him the ball. I do, and I retreat to the deck to watch them play fetch. Except Dalton has never actually known a dog, so his version of fetch is, well, unique. He throws the ball, and they *both* run after it, which usually results in a football tackle. That's more his style, getting in there and working off energy, and Storm loves it, so I wouldn't argue . . . if he didn't have his arm in a sling.

When I try to intercede again, though, he waves me off, and he *is* being careful, so I settle on the deck. I watch him shrug off his day and become the guy he can be only in the relative privacy of our backyard. The guy who slides on the grass and tackles a dog and gets a faceful of fur and comes up sputtering and laughing and crowing in victory, too, as he waves a slobbery ball over his head.

I think of Phil's thinly veiled threat to exile Dalton, as if he's committed some terrible crime. That "crime" is devoting his life to this town, risking his life today to protect a man who did not deserve protecting. Dalton might stride through Rockton like he owns the place, but it owns him, too, and it owes him better than this.

I never want to lose the guy I see tonight, playing with a dog. This problem isn't mine to fix, and it's patronizing to try, but sometimes I peer down Dalton's life path, to a future where he becomes the front he shows others — harsh, tough — and then continues along that road until he reaches bitter resignation, no longer even bothering to fight back, because he knows it won't do any good.

I fear for a future where Dalton is no longer Rockton's protector, its best advocate, its biggest cheerleader. A future where he's just a guy doing a job, putting in his time here because he has no place else to go, hating the town and himself for that.

I want to tell myself I'm overreacting. I

see him playing with Storm, and I want to say, *See, even amid all this, he's fine.* But I know Oliver Brady will not be an anomaly. Phil hinted at that today. If Brady survives his stay here, there will be others. If he doesn't? I don't know what happens then, but I fear that outcome would be even worse. For Dalton. For Rockton. For all of us.

FOURTEEN

That afternoon, I run fingerprints from the gun locker, which is a far cry from the way I used to do it down south. I'm a technology-era baby. From my earliest experiences in a police department — when I told my parents I was volunteering at the Y — I saw fingerprints run on computers. I remember my disappointment at that. It seemed so dull compared to what I'd read in old crime novels. I also remember, when I became a detective, looking back and rolling my eyes at my younger self, unable to imagine the work involved in manually processing fingerprints.

Now I can.

It might be possible to process them by computer. Dalton has a laptop for when he goes down south on business. It will run here if I charge it from the generator. I could buy a scanner and input the townspeople's fingerprints into a database and then find a program to compare them to crime scene prints. But honestly, with a small and constricted population, that's more work than manually processing.

So, in this, as in many other aspects of my job, I have become that Victorian-era detective. I have my fingerprint powder and my index cards of exemplars. And I love it. Sure, there's some misplaced nostalgia there. The public is better served by modern crime-solving methods. Yet I'm not sure that applies in Rockton, and I *feel* more like a detective when I dust prints from the gun cabinet, see whorls and ridges, and say "That one's mine, and that's Will's, and Eric's, and Kenny's . . ." without needing to consult my cards.

I've lifted all the prints and brought them home. I'm stretched out on my stomach on the bearskin rug. Storm has her head on my legs. She snuffled the cards once, withdrawing at an "Uh-uh" from me, though not before leaving a string of drool.

While I eliminated most prints at the site, I still lifted them to pore over here. Yet I'm not seeing any other than the ones I'd expect.

"The problem," I say to Storm, "is overlapping prints. A computer is so much better at analyzing those." I lift a card. "All I see is a mess of whorls. It's like a reverse jigsaw. A very imperfect science. I hate imperfect."

"Does she ever answer you?"

Dalton's voice drifts in as the front door clicks shut.

I wait until he appears and say, "She's not supposed to. She's my Watson."

He lowers himself beside me. "I thought I was your Watson."

"Watson is the guy Holmes talks *at*. A sounding board to hear his theories and tell him he's brilliant. You can do that last part if you like."

"Better stick with the dog." He reaches for the card I'd been examining. "Is it even possible to separate these?"

"With computers, there are algorithms. Even those are still works in progress. I can separate out the ones at the edges, but not once I get into the middle. I'm not sure this isn't just busywork anyway. I've got enough smeared prints to suggest whoever took the gun used gloves. The stock is totally wiped down."

"Which supports the theory that we're dealing with a pro."

"No, just a non-idiot. The fact fingerprinting works in any of our cases shocks the hell out of me. It's not like it's difficult to find gloves around here."

He stretches his legs. "Think there's any chance Phil's right? That this could be the woman who flew Brady in?"

"On paper, she looks good. Trained soldier. Mercenary. She admits she removed his gag. If he got the chance, he'd have offered her money. No doubt about that."

"Because he knows she's a mercenary."

"Right. But *how* mercenary? Adjective versus noun. Just because she uses her army skills to make a living doesn't mean they're for sale to the highest bidder."

"Yeah." He scratches Storm behind the ears. "And there's no chance she snuck into town without being noticed."

"Young, female, attractive . . . yep, they'd notice."

"Female's enough for this town."

I chuckle. "True. If the sniper *was* the pilot, why steal our gun? She'd have access to her own."

"But framing us would still help. Set us chasing our tails looking for a shooter internally."

"This is why you aren't Watson. You come up with good ideas."

Dalton rises. "Pretty sure Watson *had* some good ideas. Coffee?"

"Yet another good one." I watch him start

the fire to heat water. "Does Tyrone have military experience?"

"Ty Cypher?"

I sit up, crossing my legs. "Sorry. Mental jump there. Thinking about the pilot made me wonder who in town has military experience. That's just Will and Sam, right?"

"Kenny was in Air Cadets."

"Which is a youth group. I don't think they train snipers. At least not in Canada. And Sam served in the navy."

"That's the one with water."

"It is."

"Any snipers?"

"The Canadian Navy has one destroyer, which is on its last legs. Lots of tugboats, though."

"Uh-huh."

"I think Sam was in peacekeeping."

"So . . . snipers?"

"That's one way to keep peace. But no. Not usually. I don't think a military connection is the answer. Marksmanship doesn't need that, though. Not by a long shot, pardon the pun. I'd like a list of our best shooters."

"That'd be Will."

I shake my head. "Good thing he was on the scene then. Otherwise, he'd be our key suspect, which is just awkward."

"After him? The best shooter is you."

"Even more awkward. Let me guess, you come after me?"

He taps his sling. "I am definitely out of the running. So that's top three. Next is the militia."

"Our boys like their target practice."

"As do Jen and Nicki."

"True enough. Are any of them good enough to make that shot, though?"

"Depends on what 'that shot' is," he says. "I hate giving Phil credit, but there's no way to say for sure that the bullet would have hit Brady."

"Are you thinking maybe he *wasn't* the target?"

"Who the fuck knows at this point? It seemed aimed at him. No one else was standing there until I got in the way. But would it have killed him if I didn't inter-fere?" Dalton throws up his hand.

"If it didn't kill him, would that have been intentional — trying to spook us rather than assassinate Brady? Or would it have missed because our shooter *isn't* a crack shot? We could just be looking at a decent shooter with an overinflated sense of his — or her — skills. So . . . Ty?"

Tyrone Cypher was sheriff of Rockton before Dalton's father. When the demotion to deputy rankled too much, he'd gone to live in the forest.

"Are you looking at Ty for this?" The wrinkle in Dalton's nose tells me what he thinks of that. He doesn't say it, though, just keeps making coffee in our French press.

"I'm looking at everyone for this. He was a professional assassin, though."

Dalton snorts. "Hit man. There's a difference."

Which is true. "Assassin" conjures up an image that is *not* Tyrone Cypher.

"What's his firearm prowess?" I ask.

"On a scale of one to ten? Negative three."

I give him a look.

"I'm serious," Dalton says. "The guy prides himself on not using guns. You know that."

"So when he says he worked with his hands . . ."

"If Ty says it, it's true. He's serious about *that,* too. I've never actually caught the guy in a lie. Which, like you said, might not mean he never lies — just that he saves the falsehoods for the big stuff."

"Has he ever *said* he can't shoot? His comments about the military make Will think he served."

"Tyrone doesn't volunteer information.

129

He's never said he can't shoot — he just chooses not to. The problem is motive."

I rub my fingers together and then I realize the gesture means nothing in Dalton's world.

"Money," I say. "Ty killed for money before, and he doesn't seem to have any moral qualms about doing it again."

Dalton shakes his head. "I see where you're going, but Tyrone doesn't give a shit about money. Now, if they offered him a barrel of coffee creamer, maybe. But even then, it'd mean working for the council, and you know how he feels about that."

"So you trust Ty."

He makes a face as he passes me a filled mug. "I wouldn't say trust . . ."

"We've been trading with him since last winter."

"The man works for coffee and powdered creamer. Can't beat the price. But trust him? He's . . . What's the scientific term? Loony tunes."

I have to laugh at that. "True. He has his own special brand of crazy. But you trust him enough to trade with him, send him on scouting missions, and let him into Rockton."

"As long as he's escorted."

"Only because you don't want to freak

out the locals."

"Yeah, okay, sure. I trust . . ." He stops. "Fuck. I just stepped into it, didn't I?" He sighs. "Where is this leading?"

"I'd like you to deputize Ty for a few days. I need information I can only get from the internet, and the only person who can fly out of here is you. It's a lousy time for you to leave, but I think the need outweighs the danger. I'd like you to take an overnight trip to Dawson City, with a list of what I need researched. I'll stay here and Ty can help guard Brady."

Dalton snorts. "Because he'll scare the ever-loving shit out of Brady?"

"Possibly." I smile. "Ty won't buy Brady's stories. He might even be able to give us some insight into how likely it is that he committed these murders. Mathias knows one side of killers. Tyrone knows another."

"It'll take a day or two to find Ty. By then, Brady's permanent residence will be done so I won't mind leaving. What do you want online?"

"Everything you can get on these crimes he supposedly committed. Including whether they actually exist."

"Actually exist?" He looks at me, his mental wheels turning fast. "Fuck."

"Yep. I need information on the San Jose

131

shootings, information on the Georgia murders, plus anything that can help us figure out whether Oliver Brady is responsible for either."

FIFTEEN

It's the next afternoon. Val has conveyed Dalton's message to the council. They're "considering" letting him go to Dawson.

I'm the sole officer on duty right now. Dalton and Nicole have gone into the woods to get Jacob's message and look for Cypher. An hour ago, someone from the logging party came running back to say there's been an accident. Nothing serious, but a hatchet injury always requires immediate attention, so Anders has left with his first-aid kit.

I'm on Brady duty, all of our militia having been repurposed into construction workers. That's fine — Brady's cell is secure, and it's not as if he's going to ever talk me into letting him out for a walk. Still, Petra has come over to keep me company, and we're on the rear deck.

I haven't accidentally left Brady unattended. I'm testing him. He knows Dalton

133

and Anders are gone. He knows the militia are doing construction. And now his sole guard has just wandered outside to chat with her friend. I want to see what he'll do. So far, the answer is "Nothing."

Petra has her sketchbook out. She was a comic-book artist down south, and up here, she draws art as a sideline — people buy it to decorate their homes.

"Looks like someone's hungry." Petra nods at a raven, who keeps circling to the deck railing and then pulling up before landing. "That's yours, isn't it?"

"It's not really —"

"Yeah, yeah," she says. "Wild animals are not pets. I once made the mistake of asking Eric if I could adopt a bear cub. I was kidding. I still got the lecture. Since he's not within earshot, though, this is your raven, right? The one you've trained."

"It is." I take a piece of muffin from my pocket. "It won't come close to Storm, so you'll need to hold her."

"Have you thought of training them?"

The raven swoops past, but it knows better than to snatch the muffin chunk from my hand.

Petra puts her sketchbook aside. "I grew up rural. We had chickens, and we had dogs that we didn't want devouring the chickens.

You can train them both. Teach Storm not to go after the raven, and teach the raven that the dog is safe."

Petra explains how to start, and then she puts her hand on Storm's collar, while I set the muffin on the railing.

The raven lands at the far end and begins inching along, while croaking at me, telling me to move it farther from the dog.

I start to pocket the muffin chunk. The raven lets out a loud squawk.

"Oh, it doesn't like that," Petra says with a laugh.

I put the muffin down again, and the raven waddle-walks as fast as it dares —

The station front door slams, and the raven flies off. Storm growls. Petra glances through the rear door and pats Storm.

"Good baby," she says. "Excellent instincts."

The back door slaps open, and Jen barrels out.

"What the hell?" Jen says. "You're leaving him unguarded now?"

"We're on the back porch," Petra says. "And he's locked in a cell. We aren't concerned."

"I see that. I guess maybe he's not such a dangerous criminal, huh?"

"Jen?" I say. "Don't."

"Why? Because you're busy chatting with your buddy and playing with your dog? Are you even trying to find out whether this guy is guilty?"

I don't answer that. I remember a time when I'd check out online articles for crimes I was investigating. I'd read the comments section, in hopes of getting a lead or a fresh angle. Instead all I got were complaints. The cops are lazy. The cops are incompetent. The cops are corrupt. Why can't they just run DNA? Why can't they arrest the guy everyone knows did it? I'd log in under a fake name and try to explain, but those commenters didn't want explanations. The same goes for Jen.

Before I can speak, I see a paper in Jen's hand.

"What's that?" I ask.

"A petition."

"Oh, for God's sake." Petra reaches to snatch it.

Jen yanks it back with, "Hey!"

I put my hand out. Jen holds the paper up but doesn't pass it over.

"I have fifty names," she says. "Residents who demand a public inquiry into the department's handling of this situation."

"An inquiry?" Petra says. "Do you even know what that is? Or is it just something you heard on TV?"

"Tell me exactly what you want," I say. My voice is calm, but my heart's hammering.

Fifty names. One-quarter of the population doesn't trust our handling of this.

No, only a quarter agreed to sign Jen's petition. How many others disagree and fear saying so?

"Give me the list —" I say.

I'm stepping toward her, but she swats at my outstretched arm. Storm lunges at her. That's all she does. It's a feint, with a warning growl, nothing more, but Jen kicks Storm. Her foot slams square into the dog's chest.

If asked what I would do in this situation, I would say that I'd go after Jen. I'd be unable to help myself. But the thought does not cross my mind. Instead, I throw myself between them, stopping Jen, and then all my attention is on Storm. She's only staggered back, with a yelp that is more confusion than pain, but I'm on my knees, cradling her.

Then I hear a snarl and a thump and a gasp, and I turn to see Jen pinned against the wall. And the person pinning her is Petra. She has Jen against the wall, shirt bunched in her fists. The look on Petra's face is exactly the one I would have expected on my own. Blind rage.

"You do not ever touch that dog," Petra says between clenched teeth. "You do not ever touch Casey."

"I-It was a mistake," Jen stammers. "I'm sorry, Casey. Is she okay? Should I get someone?"

I ignore Jen as I check Storm. She's breathing fine. My finger prods make her flinch but not whimper. She's rubbing against my legs, looking for comfort, and that upsets me more than the kick itself. My dog has known nothing but kindness from humans. People here fawn over her, sneak her treats, pet her, offer to take her for runs. As the only pet in town, she's a pampered princess. Now someone has hurt her. She keeps sneaking glances at Jen.

"Just go," I say without looking up.

"Is she — ?"

"You *kicked* her. Whether she's physically hurt or not, she isn't okay."

"I'm sorry. I really am. When I was a kid, a dog attacked . . . I'm sorry. I just reacted."

I pat Storm and get to my feet.

"I was trying to accept your petition," I say, my voice cold. "You brought it. I was taking it. We all know there's a problem. We know people aren't happy. And we're trying

138

like hell to figure out what to do about it."

"I was afraid —"

"That I'd burn the petition before Eric saw it? Tell me, Jen, what have I *ever* done to make you think I'd do *anything* except present it to him?"

"I —"

"Use your goddamn brain for once. I know you have one. Fifty people can swear they signed your petition, so how the hell could I make it disappear?"

I shake my head. "Just go, okay? Take the petition or leave it. I don't give a damn. Just —"

A crash sounds inside the station.

Sixteen

I race for the door, and I don't even have it open before I hear voices. I throw open the door to see a half dozen people bearing down on Brady's cell.

"What the hell?" I say.

The guy in the lead — a new resident named Roy — points at me. "You, stay back."

"What the *fuck*?" I barrel in. "You do not ever tell me to do anything. Get the hell out of here. All of you."

Everyone except Roy stops. They don't leave, though. They just stop. He keeps going, barging into the cell room.

"Talk to me," Brady says, gripping the bars. "Please just talk to me."

I march past the mob. "Roy? You have ten seconds to get out of there or you are under arrest."

"Yeah?"

He steps up to me. He's at least six-two

and probably two hundred and fifty pounds. It's not muscle, but he's still more than twice my size.

"Try that again, girlie," he says.

I reach for my gun. Then I stop. I see myself pulling it. I see myself pointing it. I see him laughing. And then I see Blaine, hear *him* laugh. A drop of sweat trickles down my hairline. I leave my gun holstered.

"Yeah, I didn't think so," he says. "Get out of my way."

I cannot get angry. Cannot get defensive. Cannot show this asshole what a mistake he's making, because if I do, I know how this ends up. With a bullet through his chest.

At a noise behind me, I glance to see Petra. Her eyes still blaze with that fire from earlier, and I put up a hand to stop her.

"Go get the boys, please," I say. "We seem to have a situation."

She stands her ground. I meet her gaze. She nods, abruptly, and then shoulders past the others.

"Yeah," Roy says. "Run and get 'the boys.' Their girlie needs some help."

"What do you want?" I say.

It's Brady who responds first. "These people see what you're doing to me, the injustice, and they aren't going to stand for it."

"Yeah, he's right," Roy says. "We see the injustice here. The injustice of being forced to live with a killer."

"No one said he —" I begin.

"I haven't killed anyone," Brady cuts in. "I didn't shoot those people. I'm being framed."

"See?" Roy says, his voice rising for the others. "Told you it was murder. *Multiple* murders, like I said. That's the only reason they'd build him his own private jail. He's a fucking psychopath."

"What? Wait," Brady says. "No. I didn't —"

"We want a trial," Roy says. "Now."

"How?" I say. "He didn't commit any crimes here."

"See?" Brady says. "I haven't done any —"

"Shut. Up." I glower at him. "These men aren't here to set you free, you idiot."

"Hell, yeah. We'll set him free," Roy says. "Swinging from the end of a rope."

"Are you fucking nuts?" It's Jen, shoving her way through.

"What the hell?" Brady says. "Did he say —"

"It's called a lynch mob," I say. "But if you want them to let you out and give you a trial, just let me know."

I turn to Roy. "Get the hell out of my station."

"*Your* station?" He snorts. "You're the sheriff's playmate, little girl. Now hand over those keys and let us clean up his mess."

"I'm going to count to three. When I finish, if you're still here, you'll be sharing the cell with this guy, and I really don't think you want that."

He laughs. Then he lunges. I duck, grab him by the arm, and throw him down. He hits the floor with a thud. I'm on him in a blink, pinning his arm behind his back.

"Holy *shit,*" Brady says.

"I'm making the same offer to everyone else," I call. "Three seconds to get out. Which doesn't mean I won't remember all your faces."

Two leave as Roy rants and writhes beneath me. A guy named Cecil sidles into the cell room.

"Just let him go, Casey," he says. "We don't need to get Eric involved."

Jen laughs, "Seriously? Hell, yeah, Casey, just let that asshole walk away. No harm, no foul." She moves up to Cecil. "You cowardly piece of shit."

"Cecil, get out of here," I say. "You —"

I notice the knife at the last second. I'm distracted, pinning Roy's arm, his other one free to pull a penknife from his pocket. I see his arm move. I see the knife flash. But I'm too late to stop it, and it rams into my jacket. It gets caught there, and only the tip sinks into my side, but my reaction gives him the leverage he needs to throw me off. Before I can recover, he plows his fist into my jaw.

I fly backward. Jen lets out a squawk of alarm. Outside, Storm is going crazy barking. I barely hear her, just like I barely notice the remaining mob surge forward. I see only that knife coming at me again.

I am on the floor, pain throbbing through me, looking up at Roy, and I don't see him — I see four thugs in an alley. It's like I'm back there, and it's happening again, only this time I know what's coming. This time, I will not go down under a hail of blows and kicks. This time, it's *one* guy, and I am prepared, and he is going to pay.

Roy slashes at me. I catch his arm, and I wrench. He drops the knife. I kick it away, and then I throw him down. He falls and I'm on him, my fists and boots slamming into him.

A hand lands on my shoulder. I wheel, fist flying up. I see Jen's face. See her eyes widen. I manage to divert my blow, but then Cecil has me by the collar, dragging me off

Roy, saying, "Hey, that's *enough.*"

"Fucking hell it is," Jen says.

She goes at him, and I see Roy crawling for the knife. I lunge and land on it, and he slams his fist into the side of my head.

I grab the knife from under me and flip over, brandishing it, and he lunges at me with a snarl . . . just as Kenny and Sam race in. They manage to haul him back.

I'm getting to my feet when I see Brady out of the corner of my eye. He's grinning. When he catches my glance, he shoots me a thumbs-up.

"That was fucking awesome," he says. "I gotta say, I've been complaining about the entertainment here, and you guys delivered. Hey, big guy, that 'little girl' kicked your ass, huh?"

"Shut the fuck up," I say as I rise. "Kenny? Secure —" Blood trickles into my mouth. I wipe it away. "Secure Roy. And —" I hear the slap of the front door. "Hey! No one leaves —"

The thunder of running boots cuts me short. Dalton barrels through with, "What the hell is going . . ." He sees me, staggering, blood dripping.

His eyes go wide. Then he pulls himself up short and wheels on the remaining mob. "You heard Casey. None of you fucking

145

moves. Anyone who does will spend the rest of the *year* on shit duty."

"We —" one begins.

"You witnessed an officer being assaulted, and you stood and fucking watched it happen. I don't want to hear a word from any of you. Sit on the floor. Shut your mouths. And pray that when it comes time to pass sentence, I'm not *half* as pissed off as I am right now. Sam? Get out there and watch them."

As soon as Sam leaves the cell room, Dalton kicks the door shut with, "Better if I don't see their fucking faces right now."

He strides to me.

"I'm fine," I say. Which is a lie. I'm seeing double, my nose is streaming blood, and my lip is split. But I'm upright, and that's the important thing. I'd seen the look in Roy's eyes when he came at me with that knife, and I know I got off easy.

Dalton takes my chin in his hand, and he's checking my injuries when I catch his eye and shake my head. His lips tighten. He knows what I mean. It's what stopped him on his way in — made him tend to the mob before me. The job comes first, as long as I'm standing.

"Where's Will?" he asks Jen.

I answer, "Hatchet mishap with the lum-

146

ber party. Nothing serious."

He grunts and tells Jen to get the backup first-aid kit from the clinic. She takes off. Then he strides into the next room, without a word to anyone there, and returns with a wet cloth. He hands it to me, and I press it against my lip as he walks to Roy.

"What the fuck happened here?" Dalton asks.

Roy blinks, as if surprised he's asking him first.

Before Roy can answer, Brady says, "These rednecks formed themselves a lynch mob, Sheriff. Took advantage of you and the deputy being gone and tried to storm the station. Your detective stopped him. He pulled a knife on her. Knocked her around. But she took him down. Too bad she wasn't carrying her sidearm."

"She's got her fucking sidearm," Dalton says, his gaze on Roy. "She knew she didn't need to use it on a useless piece of shit like you."

"I wanted to try him," Roy says. "A trial. Not a lynch —"

"You said you were going to string me up," Brady says. "We call that a lynching where I come from."

"Can you add anything to contradict what I just heard?" Dalton asks Roy.

"She went off on me. Started beating the shit out of me."

"*After* you stabbed and punched her." Brady glances at Dalton. "The stabbing was unprovoked. She took him down after that. There was a commotion, and he got free and started hitting her. That's when she went off on him." He smiles. "It was awesome."

No, it wasn't. I lost control. I don't say that now. I've been a cop long enough to know this is a situation I discuss with my superior officer . . . alone.

"Feel free to correct him," Dalton says to Roy.

"You're listening to a murdering — ?"

"Feel free to *correct* him."

Roy glowers.

"Yeah, that's what I thought." Dalton returns to the main room and comes back with a handcuff strap. He tosses it to Kenny. "Let him chill in the icehouse until I feel like talking to him. Better grab him a parka, too. It'll be a while."

SEVENTEEN

Dalton deals with the mob. None of them may have thrown a punch, but in Rockton, witnessing a crime and doing nothing about it is a punishable offense. This law of Dalton's wouldn't fly down south, but up here, with such a small police force, we can reasonably expect better.

I've let Storm in, and I'm consoling her while Dalton chews out the mob. When Jen comes in with the first-aid container, I point to the back porch. She hesitates, but I march her out.

"Here's —" she begins, holding out the kit.

I thrust the discarded petition at her. "You set this up. You knew Eric and Will were both gone. You chose that moment to hit me with this."

"Yes, I did. I wanted to talk to you alone because you're the only person who actually listens to me."

"You took advantage of that to distract me while the others —"

"What? My petition was for a public inquiry, not a trial. Sure as hell not a lynch mob."

"Bullshit. You kicked Storm, knowing that was a guaranteed distraction —"

"No." Guilt flits over her face as looks at the dog. "I'm genuinely sorry about that. If Eric wants to come up with a punishment for animal abuse, I'll take it. I kicked her, and that was uncalled-for. My past experience with dogs isn't an excuse. I reacted badly." She eases back and eyes me. "I think you know something about that, considering those scars on your arms and the way you went after Roy."

"That —"

"In your case, it was justifiable anger. Mine was not."

She's being reasonable, and I'm not sure how to handle that. I feel as if I'm being set up, and I'd prefer the old Jen, someone to snap back at me, someone I can rightly vent my rage on.

"You guys need to do something about Roy." Before I can snarl a response, she lifts her hands. "Yeah, I know, you don't need me giving you more work right now, but he's a nutjob."

"We've had a few run-ins with him already. He has issues with authority."

She snorts a laugh. "That's putting it mildly. What you just saw didn't come out of nowhere. I can tell you stories . . . and he's only been here a month."

"If you can tell stories, you should. As part of the militia."

"I did not have anything to do with what happened in there," she says, ignoring my comment. "You aren't going to find any of those names on my petition. I knew you were alone here, and Roy knew you were alone here. Two totally separate incidents."

I open the first-aid kit.

"People don't like what's happening with this Brady guy," she says.

"Really?" I scrunch my nose. "Personally, I can't see it, but that may be because I'm seeing two of everything right now, after getting clocked by a guy who . . . Wait, *he's* upset about Brady, isn't he?"

"I'm just —"

"You're pointing out the obvious, as usual." I yank out a bandage and lift my shirt. "You have your petition because you think we're overreacting. Roy tried to lynch Brady because he thinks we're *under*reacting."

"You need to clean that wound first." She

picks up my discarded wet cloth from the railing.

Dalton peeks out the door.

"She's fine," Jen says.

Dalton ignores her and says to me, "I'm still dealing with these idiots, but if you need anything . . ."

I manage a smile for him. "I can stitch myself, remember?"

"Yeah, but don't. You need me, shout. Otherwise, I can help in five minutes."

He retreats inside.

I turn to Jen. "I know how you feel. You've made that abundantly clear. I'm fucking up, as usual. Now just go."

"I just think it's a dangerous situation. Especially after this. Whatever Brady did, does it really deserve this treatment?"

I stare at her. Then I march inside.

Dalton stops lecturing the coconspirators and arches his brows. I wave for him to continue. Then I unlock a drawer and remove the letter that came with Brady. I walk outside and hand it to Jen.

After she's read it, I give her the details.

When I finish, she's pale. Then she says, "Maybe Roy has the right idea."

"Really? That's your takeaway from this?" I throw up my hands. "I try to share information with you, so you understand why

152

we're keeping him locked up, and you do a total one-eighty. Now we're wrong for not lynching him."

"I never said lynching."

"We are doing our best here," I say. "We need people to trust us. Like I trusted you with that letter. If I find out that anyone else knows those details? I know where it came from."

"I don't like this," she says as I walk away.

"No one does," I say, and take Storm inside to help Dalton.

The council has decided not to let Dalton go to Dawson. After what happened today, the situation is "too precarious." I can bitch about that, but they aren't wrong.

We're on Dalton's balcony, which is our bedroom in good weather . . . and sometimes in bad. I've been here nine months, and the allure of falling asleep to the howl of wolves and the perfume of pine hasn't worn off. We have a mattress out here, and we're lying on it, with Storm at our feet as we talk.

Roy is still in the icehouse. We gave him winter gear and a sleeping bag. He'll be fine. One of the militia guys is in there with him, just in case he decides to sabotage the ice. I wouldn't put it past him. Jen's right that he's been trouble. What happened today, though, was worse than I expected. Far worse.

"He's going back," Dalton says. "As soon as we figure out the shit with Brady, Roy is going home."

"Is that . . . a good idea? They made Diana stay because she posed a security threat."

"Nah, they made Diana stay because they're assholes. They've kicked people out before. They have blackmail to make sure they keep their mouth shut about us. We'll work it out. He's not staying, though. He could have killed you. His so-called backstory says nothing about violence, meaning his file is bullshit."

I don't pursue this. After Dalton finished dealing with the mob, he'd gone to the icehouse, and then Roy got to see how Dalton really felt about him attacking me. It wasn't physical. Dalton isn't going to rough up a bound man. But he managed to scare the shit out of Roy without lifting a finger. So while Dalton's calm now, I'd like to back-burner the issue of Roy.

We discuss the mob. Dalton's furious about that, too, especially since they waited until I was alone at the station. That is unacceptable. They've each been sentenced to six months of chopping and sanitation duty, the worst punishment I've seen Dalton inflict since I arrived. This was an uprising. A revolt. We cannot afford that in our little powder keg of a town.

The petition doesn't help. The fact that we have residents complaining that we're erring too far on *both* sides means we're, well, screwed. We can't inch in either direction without pissing someone off.

"Stay the course," I say. "That's my advice, if you want it."

"Course I do."

"Then we continue on as planned. Ignore those who argue that Brady deserves more freedoms. The bigger threat is Roy's gang. If that continues, we clamp down."

"Martial law." Dalton shakes his head. "I saw it done when I was growing up, and I was kinda proud of the fact that I've never had to resort to that. Thought that meant I was a better sheriff. Bullshit. It just means I got lucky."

"Rockton has never dealt with anything like Brady before. Right now, I think we're just in the unsettled phase. People are on edge. Once his cabin is built, they'll settle." I stretch out on top of him. "We'll be okay."

His arms go around my waist. "We will be."

Which is true. We'll be okay, as both a couple and as individuals. We'll weather this, however it plays out. The problem is everyone else. Everyone we are responsible for.

EIGHTEEN

"That is *not* perfect," Anders is saying early the next morning. "Casey cut the board backward."

"I was just —" Kenny says.

"Being supportive. Encouraging." Anders puts the board in place, and the angle is indeed the wrong way. "Well, at least it's straight. A for effort, Case."

I take back the board, with my middle finger raised.

As I carry it to the sawhorse, Anders says, "Casey *hates* the effort award. She wants the honest A-plus overachiever award."

"Ignore him," I say. "But yes, Kenny, you can tell me I did it wrong. I'll survive. And I'll do it right the next time."

"Overachiever," Anders calls.

Kenny comes over and helps me line up the cut. I don't tell him I can handle it. He means well. While I've chopped wood, even that was a new experience for me six months ago. When I was growing up, we never had so much as a saw in our garage. My parents would say sharp tools were unsafe, but part of it was also the mentality that such tasks were meant for people who lacked a surgeon's IQ.

Brady's new quarters are almost done, and we're spending every spare minute building.

I hand the fixed board to Kenny.

"Now it'll be a half inch too short," Anders says. "It'll leave a gap, and Brady will get his fingers through and pry it open and escape."

"It's for the bathroom interior wall."

"He'll still escape through it. Just watch. All because you cut an angle backward."

"Didn't we have to take down half a wall because someone put the damn door on the wrong side?"

"You said the door went on the west wall, and you know I'm directionally challenged."

"The sun was setting. It doesn't set in the *east.*"

Jen walks by with a bucket of nails. "You two keep bickering like that, the sheriff's gonna get jealous. Sounds like someone has a crush."

"Only if you're twelve," Anders says. "Grown-ups bicker 'cause it's fun."

"The word you want is 'annoying,' " she says.

"You only say that because you feel left out. Hey, Jen, can I have a few of those screws?"

"They're nails."

"I know, but yesterday I asked you for screws, and you brought me nails."

She shakes her head.

"That's an opening," he says. "You're supposed to make a sarcastic retort."

"The only ones I can think of are puns on screwing and nailing, and every woman in Rockton knows not to mention those words around you, Deputy, or you'll think it's an invitation."

"Ouch."

"Good one, though," I say. "A little below the belt, but it's an A for effort."

Kenny snorts at that, and he starts to say something when I hear "Will? Will!" and Paul races around the neighboring building, pulling up short when he sees us. "Will *and* Casey. Perfect. I need you both at the station. There's something wrong with the prisoner."

Anders takes off ahead, Storm follows at my side.

"You didn't leave him alone, right?" I ask as Paul runs a pace behind.

Silence. Then, "He was sick, and I had to get Will, and there was no one else —"

"Is his door locked?"

"The station door?"

"*Cell.* Did you open his cell?"

"I don't have the key. Eric took it. He got called across town. As he was leaving, the prisoner said he had to take a shit, and Eric said to hold it or use the bucket. He wasn't leaving the key."

I send up a silent thanks to Dalton.

I yell ahead to Anders, "Careful! I think it's a trap," and he raises a hand, as if to say he's already figured that out. The medical emergency is a hackneyed escape ploy. The fact that it happened while Dalton was out? And after Brady tried to get him to leave the key? Yeah, this screams setup, and not a very clever one at that.

I race into the station to find Anders outside the cell. Inside, Brady is on all fours, vomiting. Vomiting hard, as if he's going to puke up his stomach lining. His back arches like something out of a horror movie, his body convulsing before he spews more of his stomach contents onto the floor.

Paul looks at me. "Should I go find Eric for the key?"

I take mine from my pocket. Then I proceed with measured steps toward the cell. Paul stares at me, and I see that once again, we are trapped in this dilemma, where caution seems callous.

Anders looks at me, his mouth set in a tight line. He knows this can be faked. Stick your finger down your throat to start the vomiting and then act out the rest.

"Guys?" Paul says.

"Lock the back door," I say, and then I do that with the front. As Anders holds open the back door, he says, "Out," to Paul . . . who hasn't moved.

"But he —"

"— could be just hoping we throw open the cell door and let him make a run for it."

"You think he's faking?" Paul says.

I say, "I think every second you debate whether to do as I said, you delay us helping him if he's *not.*"

Anders shuts and locks the rear door as he says, "Stay here then. And don't expect me to forget that you disobeyed an order."

We don't hear Paul's protest. I'm at the cell door with my key in one hand, gun in the other. Storm stands beside me. I hand Anders the key, and he unlocks the door. Brady is still doubled over, dry-heaving now, panting hard and letting out whimpers of pain between breaths. The stink of vomit fills the room.

161

Anders opens the door and steps over a puddle. His gaze goes to something behind Brady. He motions to me that he's going to bend over the heaving man to retrieve it. I stand poised while he crouches. What he lifts is Brady's breakfast tray. He backs out of the cell to set it on the floor. Then he starts in again.

Anders makes it one step. Brady lurches. I shout "Will!" but Anders is already on him, pinning him to the floor, a slap as Brady's body hits the vomit pool. Brady's arms fly out to the sides, as if in surrender.

"Dog," he rasps. "The dog."

He points in my direction, and I'm not sure if I'm mishearing, but he just keeps pointing. Then he starts heaving again, his body jerking and convulsing under Anders.

"Lock the door," Anders says.

I hesitate — I'm loath to lock Anders in there with Brady — but it's only a split second. Then I lock it and train my gun on Brady as Anders rises off him.

Brady stays facedown, racked with dry heaves.

"I need you to put your hands behind your back," Anders says.

At first, Brady just moans. Anders repeats the command, and Brady complies. Anders snaps on a wrist strap. He looks from me to

162

the puddles to the food tray. It's mostly empty, the water and coffee drained. If Brady just finished his meal — including two drinks — that could account for the quantity of vomit. That tray, though, also suggests he might *not* be faking.

"Here?" Anders says, and I know he's asking whether we should attempt to care for Brady in the cell.

If it is poison, we need him at the clinic. He can't even lie flat in the cell, and it's such a mess that it'll impede our efforts.

"He's secured," I say.

"Can you walk?" Anders asks Brady.

The younger man puts one foot out and begins to rise. It's slow, unsteady, but even if he forced the vomiting, he will be weak.

Anders helps him to his feet. Then, "Paul?"

"Yes, sir." Paul hurries over from where he's been watching in silence. "I can help you carry him."

"Not you. Get Kenny."

Paul flushes. He knows Anders is saying: *I don't trust you.* He bobs his head and runs out the front door. I relock it behind him. Then I move to the cell and unlock that. Anders has Brady up, supporting him. I open the door and move in to help, but

163

Anders says, "I've got it. Just stand point, please."

I step back and keep the gun ready as they walk out of the cell. A key scrapes in the front door lock. Then it stops.

"Casey? Will?"

I call for Dalton to come in, and he finishes unlocking the door. He steps through, sees Brady, and curses. Then he hurries over to help.

If there is an advantage to having parents who raised me to be a doctor, it is that I don't need to consult our medical texts to recognize the signs of poisoning. I assess Brady as Dalton and Anders carry him to the clinic.

He has a fever. He's struggling to breathe. His heart is racing.

Oliver Brady has been poisoned.

At the clinic, we pump his stomach. It's only our second time using the procedure. In Brady's case, after all that vomit, there really isn't much to pump, but it's all we know.

Brady is thankfully unconscious by this point. I say thankfully, because we would not have earned his confidence if he'd been awake, hearing Dalton reading aloud from a chapter on emergency poisoning treatment as Anders and I worked.

And he really wouldn't want to hear us concur that pumping his stomach is the extent of what we can do. After the pumping, we put him on an IV to replace fluids. Then we wait.

It's two hours before he wakes. I'm collapsed in a bedside chair. Anders sits on the floor beside me. Dalton has gone back to the station to secure the scene.

Brady wakes, and the first thing he says is, "Dog."

I remember him saying that in the cell, and again I think I must be mishearing.

"Doug?" I say. We do have a resident named Doug . . . who also works as a chef.

He shakes his head and rasps, "Dog. Your dog food."

Anders rises. "You think someone served you dog food?"

More head shaking, Brady's face screwing up in frustration. "Your dog. The food. Poison. Did she eat — ?" He coughs and winces as the cough sets his raw throat aflame. "Did your dog eat the food? Tried — tried to warn —"

"You were trying to warn us that your food was poisoned," I say. "Before my dog ate the rest."

He nods, eyelids fluttering as if even keeping them open is too much effort.

"Is she okay?" he manages.

"She doesn't eat anything without permission. The sheriff got your tray out of there. We'll be analyzing it for poison."

He gives a harsh laugh, wincing again. "Pretty sure it'll come back positive."

NINETEEN

I've lied to Brady. I have no way to analyze his food. Down south, we'd just ship the sample off to the lab. Up here . . .

Before I requisitioned a Breathalyzer and urine-testing kits, Dalton used the old-fashioned methods — walk in a straight line, recite the alphabet backward, let me see your eyes . . . I need something more scientific. To be honest, though, I've never used the formal tests and gotten a result *different* from his assessment. It just stops people from protesting their innocence when I have hard evidence.

Our poison-testing method is not unlike Dalton's sobriety testing. Someone finds berries or mushrooms in the forest, brings them back to town, and he says, "Yeah, don't eat that." Food spoilage is a bigger poisoning risk, but Rockton has very stringent food-handling rules, and the problems occur only when someone says, "I'm sure that meat I left out of the icebox is fine."

The one person who might have been able to help us here is Sharon — the woman we just buried. Not only was she a gardener — familiar with poisonous plants — but for Sharon that was more than theoretical knowledge. She was one of the residents the council snuck in, a wealthy woman who'd poisoned her husband and his pregnant mistress. Even in that case, though, we could hardly have gone to her and said, "Hey, you wouldn't know anything about poisons, would you? Random question."

We don't have any chemists either. The two residents with that sort of experience are both dead, which has at least temporarily fixed Rockton's drug problem.

So I'm not sure what to do, beyond saying, yes, Brady was poisoned, and it seems unlikely that it *wasn't* in his food. As for what it could have been, I'm stumped. We don't use pesticides in our greenhouse. We certainly aren't spraying our yards to control "weeds." Nor do we use poison for vermin. That's just too dangerous.

I'll need to dig up all the chemicals we *do* have. I'm hoping to narrow the field by figuring out suspects and what sources of poison they have access to. The obvious place to start is by tracing the path Brady's breakfast took.

Dalton was the last person to handle it. He took the tray from the delivery person and gave it to Brady while Paul stood guard and the delivery person waited. So two people were watching the whole time, meaning I can eliminate Dalton, should anyone else suspect him.

Who delivered the food? That'd be Kenny.

Then I need to consider those who prepared the food. There's Brian, who made the muffin and poured the coffee. Before that comes the person who brought the tray — with scrambled eggs and sausage — from the kitchen. Then the person who made the eggs and cooked the sausage, as well as everyone else who was in the kitchen at the time.

Finally, the chain goes back to the guy who made the sausage. Mathias.

"I did not poison the sausage," Mathias says when I walk into the butcher shop.

"Yes, I know."

That stops him, bloody knife in hand. He wipes it on a cloth, slowly, as if awaiting a punch line.

"You delivered that batch of sausage yesterday," I say. "There was no way of knowing which links would go to Brady, and you wouldn't poison innocent people."

"Thank you." He sets the knife aside and removes his apron. "I did not shoot at Mr. Brady either. I was expecting to see you after that."

"It was the wrong kind of murder."

He chuckles, pleased. When Brady first arrived, Mathias had asked if I wanted him to assess or assassinate the prisoner. If I'd pursued that, he'd have claimed he was joking. He wasn't. I have no doubt that Mathias has killed murderers. He has a modus operandi, though. Poetic justice. What Brady is accused of requires a more fitting punishment than a shot in the head.

"Also," Mathias says, "you are not convinced he is a killer."

"Are you?"

"No. But I am rarely convinced until they confess. Even that is never a guarantee. In Mr. Brady's case, though, I require more interviews to make an educated guess. Which would still not be enough to warrant capital punishment. One must be absolutely certain. Hypothetically speaking."

"I should have you speak to Roy and his crew about that."

Mathias sniffs. "Roy is a cretin. I would like to interview *him.*"

"That can be arranged. We'd appreciate

it, actually."

"So if you did not come to question me . . ."

"Even if there's no way you poisoned the sausage, I must be seen coming in here to question you. Otherwise it'll seem as if I'm excusing you because we're acquainted."

" 'Acquainted'?" His brows rise. "That is an odd word to use, and I will presume you choose it because you have temporarily forgotten the French word for *friend.* Otherwise, I would be insulted."

"If I said we were friends, you'd make some comment about *that.* Now, I do need to get back to the business of finding who poisoned the prisoner. If you have more of that batch of sausage, I'll take some for analysis."

"You mean you'll eat it."

"That's the best way to test it. Also, I missed lunch."

He walks into the back, leaving the door open. "So it *was* poison."

I list the symptoms.

"Interesting," he says as he returns with a package of sausage. "Did Mr. Brady say anything?"

"Sure." I make retching noises.

He shakes his head.

"At the time, he only mentioned Storm.

When we removed his food tray, he was worried she'd eat what was left and get sick."

His lips purse in thought. "Or worried she would eat it and *not* get sick, proving the food was not the source of the poison."

"If so, he could just say it must have been in his water or coffee. That was also the first thing he said when he woke. He was concerned that she'd eaten his food."

"Interesting," he says again.

I eye him. "In what way?"

"Just . . . interesting. I would like to speak to him later."

"I don't think he'll be in the mood for your brand of conversation."

"We will discuss dogs."

"Uh-huh . . ."

"He apparently has a fondness for them. It would be a topic of conversation — other than himself — that he might respond to."

I have a suspect for the poisoning. I'm just trying not to fixate on him, because, well, he couldn't have done it, considering he was locked in the icehouse at the time. Roy is the most obvious possibility. Less than twenty-four hours ago he wanted to try Brady, a sham trial that I'm sure would have resulted in a guilty verdict and a death

172

sentence.

Obviously Roy didn't do it. But he didn't act alone yesterday. When I track the path that Brady's food took, I'm looking for one of those names, somewhere along the line. When there are none, I start to investigate the whereabouts of those five residents who'd been with him.

I've found a possible lead. Cecil was supposed to work at the main food depot this morning. He would have prepared Brady's breakfast . . . if Dalton hadn't yanked him onto chopping duty. It would be easy, though, for Cecil to pop into the food depot and wander around a bit, poison Brady's tray . . .

I'm heading to the depot when Val hurries up alongside me.

"It seems I've been trailing one stop behind you," she says. "I wanted to ask if I can sit with the prisoner."

"Hmm?" I catch a glimpse of Diana up ahead, coming out of the bakery.

"Take a turn playing nursemaid," Val says. "I think Diana's up next. Looks like she's got a coffee to keep her awake."

"Right." I'm distracted, and it takes effort to follow what Val's saying. "So you want to take her shift?"

"Oliver was awake when I went by earlier.

Nicole refused to talk to him, so I think he's getting bored. If I go in when he's feeling lonely and groggy, it will help establish me as an ally." She gives a look, like a five-year-old whispering plans to eavesdrop on her parents' party. "I've managed to establish a rapport that I feel will be useful."

"Uh-huh."

I could tell her that I'm no longer convinced we need this. But that look really is childlike, her eyes glittering. Val wants to be helpful, and the idea of playing spy with Brady makes her feel both happy and useful.

"Sure," I say. Then I call, "Diana?" When she stops, I say to Val, "Tell her you're taking her shift. I'll swing by in a couple of hours to see if he's ready to go back to his cell. If not, Diana can take over then."

TWENTY

No one at the food depot saw Cecil there that morning. It's still possible he was — he'd have access. It's also possible there were more than five people following Roy's madness. I'm going to need a complete list of everyone who could have come in contact with Brady's food.

First, I want some idea of what kind of poison could have been used, in hopes of linking the two — who had access to both the food and the poison. Dalton's helping me compile a list of potential toxins. We're walking around Rockton checking labels on everything he can think of. We're in the brewery at the Roc, where Isabel is explaining that not only is this the most secure location in town, but the only poison there is methanol.

"He'd have spit it out," she says. "He's not going to think we just brewed a batch of cheap coffee."

"We *don't* brew cheap coffee," Dalton says. "He'd know that by now."

Which is true. Supply issues in Rockton are a matter of transport and storage rather than cost. Our milk might be powdered, along with most of our eggs, but when it comes to dry goods, we can get the good stuff. Which is one reason why the money Brady brings us won't impact our basic lifestyle.

"Are we sure he *was* poisoned?" Isabel continues. "I treated enough bulimic patients to know how easy it is to make yourself sick."

"He had symptoms other than vomiting. They were consistent with poison."

She's not the first person to mention this possibility. Each time someone suggests that Brady faked it, I feel a nudge at the back of my mind, the one that says *You're missing something.*

"Could it be environmental?" Isabel says. "God knows, there's enough in our forest that can kill you."

"We do have water hemlock and false hellebore," I say. "Which vie for the title of most poisonous plant in North America."

Isabel sighs. "Of course they do."

"Hey, at least it's not Australia. Everything's poisonous there."

"I would rather face a kangaroo than a grizzly. Or a cougar. Or a wolf. Or a wolverine. Or a feral dog, feral pig . . ."

"There are no feral pigs in the Yukon."

"Just the ones Rockton released. Like the dogs, the cats, the hostiles . . . Because our forest really needed *more* threats."

"Water hemlock's rare," Dalton says. "Only seen it twice this far north. False hellebore is the problem. Which is why I don't tell folks that real hellebore is edible. Can't take the chance. The symptoms fit, though."

"But it'd be tough to get and mix into his food or drink," I say. "That's why we're looking in town for poisons —"

There's a shout from outside. Then what sounds like . . .

"Is that the bell?" I say.

We installed a bell this winter. Another of my suggestions, after a fire burned down the lumber shed. Dalton resisted — there hadn't been a problem alerting people for the fire, and I think he didn't like the intimation that he needed a bell to make residents listen. A bell wouldn't have saved the lumber shed, so I didn't get one . . . until after Nicole was taken and rousting searchers five minutes faster might have helped.

"If that's another goddamn prank . . ."

Dalton says as he strides from the brewery.

Shortly after we installed the bell someone rang it in the middle of the night. Drunk, obviously. Rang it and ran . . . leaving boot prints in the snow, which I matched to a perpetrator, whom Dalton then sentenced to go to each and every person in town and say, "I'm the fucking idiot who rang the fucking bell at two in the fucking morning. I'm sorry."

No one has touched the bell since.

As Dalton jogs out, I hear "Eric? Eric!" from several directions.

Jen races around the corner and sees us. "Finally. The lumber shed is on fire."

Dalton stops so abruptly that I bash into him. I know exactly what he's thinking. That the lumber shed cannot possibly be on fire nine months after we rebuilt it. Jen must be making a very bad joke. And yet one sniff of the air brings the smell of wood fire.

He shouts for everyone to "get to the goddamn fire," infuriated that they went looking for him rather than tackling the actual problem.

As we run, Jen explains that Anders is already at the shed, with as many people as he could gather. He sent her to find Dalton and me.

People join us as we run. They hear the

178

bell and smell smoke and see us running, and they fall into our wake. This is Dalton's success as a leader. People don't smell that smoke and retreat. They join the fight.

As we run, Dalton barks questions. How did the fire start? *When* did it start? Who saw it first? How bad is the damage?

Jen doesn't know. She wasn't first on the scene. Dalton keeps questioning; I retreat into my head, into my own questions.

There is no chance that the lumber shed accidentally caught ablaze. We are a town made of wood surrounded by a forest of the same. Whatever dangers lurk in the wilderness, none approaches that of fire.

On the drive up from Whitehorse, one of the most memorable sights I saw was the markers by the roadside, memorials to past blazes. Each was labeled with a year, and I hadn't really understood the power of fire until I saw those signs and the forest they marked. Vast swaths of wasteland left by flames that had blazed before I was born. Dalton would point out the signs of rejuvenation in that seeming wasteland. He'd even say that fire served a purpose in the forest: rebirth. He saw hope and new life; I saw death and destruction.

The precautions we take against fire border on insane. Smoking is prohibited.

Only a select few can use kerosene at night. Candles are restricted to certain areas, like the Lion and the Roc, where the staff can ensure they're put out at night's end. Fireplaces are inspected weekly. Bonfires are permitted only in the town square, only on designated days, and only with supervision and sand buckets. The list goes on. Before the lumber shed, the last fire had been years ago, when lightning struck a building.

This is arson, as it was before. That fire had been set to cover a crime. This time . . .

There is only one explanation.

"Eric," I call as I jog up to him.

He looks over as if startled, having been too busy to notice that I'd fallen behind.

"I need to . . ." I trail off. "To check something." Which is not an excuse at all, and any other time, he'd call me on it, but he's focused on that burning shed.

"I'll be right back." I turn to Jen. "Make sure he watches his arm."

A nod from her, and she will, if only because she's one of the few who'll tell him off. Whether he listens is a whole other matter, but the risk of him injuring his arm is minor compared to what I fear.

I'm running as fast as my bad leg will allow. I tear down the narrow passage between

180

two buildings, and I fly out onto the street just as another figure heads the opposite way.

"Kenny?" I call.

He looks over but doesn't stop. "There's a fire."

"I know, but you're posted at the clinic."

"Val's there." He keeps running. "Brady's secure. She said I can go help . . ."

The rest is muffled as he runs into the passage between buildings.

"No!" I shout. "Get back to your post!"

He's gone. I slow, torn between running after him and —

A bang comes to my right. From the direction of the clinic. My brain screams gunshot, but as I spin, I see it's just a door slamming shut as Diana runs from her apartment.

She sees me. "Casey?"

Come with me. That's what I want to say. *I need you. Come with me.*

I can't, though. Both because I don't trust her, and because I can't put her in danger.

"I need someone at the clinic," I say. "Get . . ." I trail off. Get who?

"Mathias," I say. "Get Mathias for me."

She nods, no question, presuming it's a medical emergency. Also, she's happy to avoid going near the fire. I don't blame her

181

for that — she nearly died in the last one.

I run for the clinic. I know what this is. A diversion. Everyone in town is dealing with that fire. No one is paying attention to Oliver Brady.

Even Kenny is gone, because Val wants to prove herself. As soon as Kenny asked Val what she wanted him to do, she would tell him to go help with the fire. Brady's hands were secured. He was weak from the vomiting. He was no threat.

The possibility that he was *under* threat? I could not trust her to realize Brady had faced two assassination attempts, and Kenny wasn't only there to make sure Brady didn't escape.

As soon as I dash into the clinic, there's a crash in the examination room. I already have my gun out. Now I put my back to the wall. The door is beside me. I watch the knob. When it turns, I aim, take a deep breath —

The door opens, and Val appears, stumbling through. A hand on her arm propels her forward. She sees me. "Case —"

She's yanked back before she can finish. The door slams shut.

"Lay down your weapon, Detective," a voice says. "Or I slit Valerie's throat."

TWENTY-ONE

When I hear that voice, my gut clenches.

"Put your weapon on the floor. Open the door. Kick the gun through. Then follow with your hands up. Otherwise, I'll kill her. You don't want to call my bluff."

I glance at the exterior door. Hoping for what? Divine intervention? Even if Diana finds Mathias, he's not going to get me out of this. There are exactly two solutions.

I do as I'm told.

Or Val dies.

And here is the terrible truth: I should stand my ground.

It is the coldly correct answer to this dilemma. The only way out of the clinic is the door behind me. When a suspect escaped through the back last winter, Dalton ordered that exit boarded up. I thought he was overreacting. Now I am glad of it. There's one way out. I'm blocking it. If I do not respond to the threat, it ends here.

I should let it end here.

I cannot let it end here.

I put Val in that room. I need to get her out of it and stalling won't help because there is no magical third solution.

"I want to trade," I say. "Val and I will switch spots. You can take me hostage."

"I don't want you, Detective. Val here will do as I say. Won't you, Val?"

"Casey?" Val's voice quavers. "Just do what he wants. Please."

I set my gun in front of the door. "My weapon is down."

"Good. When I open the door, you'll kick it through." A pause. "Step back first. I want to see you across the room. Then on my signal, you'll walk forward and kick it through. If I see you charging the door or doing anything other than giving me your weapon, Val dies."

I back up across the room, within the sight line from the door. It creaks opens just enough for me to boot the gun inside. The waiting figure makes no motion to bend and retrieve the gun. That would give me an opening for attack.

"Walk my way," he says.

I reach the door, pull back my good leg, and . . . kick the door with everything I've got.

It flies wide open, and Brady falls back.

"Knock him down!" I shout to Val as I go for my gun.

Val flies at Brady. She swings, and her fist connects with his jaw, and her eyes widen as if in surprise at actually making contact. But it's not enough. Not nearly enough.

Brady barely staggers, recovers fast and lunges at me, and I see a knife raised and twist out of the way just as it comes down. But that twist lands me out of reach of the gun. He scrambles for it. I kick. My foot strikes his jaw.

"Val!" I shout. "The gun."

She runs and snatches it up. Brady comes at me again. My fist plows into his jaw, in the same spot my foot had. He falls back snarling, but it's only a moment and then he's charging me with the knife.

I dodge his slash and dive over the hospital bed. There, on the floor, are the remnants of his wrist restraints. He cut them free with the knife. Where did he get — ?

He circles around the bed, advancing as I retreat.

"Val?" I say. "Can you shoot?"

Her eyes round, as if I'm asking her to turn backward cartwheels. Shit. That means the gun is useless — Brady knows she won't fire it.

At least it isn't in *his* hand.

Brady keeps coming. I grab the rolling medical tray and fling it. The clatter startles him. I leap over the bed to get the gun from Val and —

She's backed across the room, and now she's by the door, weapon raised.

"If you can't shoot that," I say, "then run. Just take it and run. Get Eric."

"Val?" Brady says. "If you leave, I'll kill your detective."

"I can handle this," I say. "Just —"

He flies at me. I stand my ground, and he doesn't expect that and stops short. I slam my hand into his arm. The knife goes flying. He hits me, and I can't avoid that. The powerful blow slams into the side of my head. I stagger. Fall to one knee.

The knife. Damn it. Get the knife.

I see it. I lunge as he walks over, confident he's put me down. I slam my hand into the back of his knee. It buckles. I dive and hit the floor, shoving the knife along with me. I pick it up and —

I recognize the knife.

It's a pocket one. That's not unusual here. If you want one, you can buy it. The only reason I don't have mine is that I took it out on the jobsite to pry open a can.

"Here, Case, let me get that for you." A

186

pocketknife appears.

"Got my own," I say. "But thanks."

I see the hand that grips the knife in my memory. I want to tell myself I'm wrong, but I have seen this knife too many times. I know who owns it.

Kenny.

I have Kenny's knife in my hand, as I'm backing into the wall. Brady keeps coming at me. I'm ready for him, ready to —

A muzzle flash from across the room. I swear I feel the bullet whiz past my head.

Val gasps in alarm. "Casey!"

"I'm fine."

"Oliver?" she says. "Stop or I'll —"

"Shoot?" he says. "Please do. With that aim, you're going to hit your own detective."

"Val?" I say. "The door is to your left. It's open. I want you to step left and back out. I've got this."

"If you leave, I'll kill Casey," Brady says.

"I'm the one holding the knife," I say.

"Doesn't matter. We both know how quickly that can change. I'm fighting for my life here. I will get that knife. I will stop you. I might kill you, but I don't want to. I just want to walk out of here."

"Do you really think I'd let a serial killer —"

"Serial killer?" He chokes on the words. "Is that what Greg told you? Figures. He didn't even keep his story consistent. Had to adapt it for the audience. A salesman to the core."

"You threatened to kill Val. You're threatening to kill me. And you're still proclaiming your innocence?"

"Because I *am* innocent. I'm fighting for my life. My actual life. I was shot at two days ago, nearly lynched yesterday, poisoned this morning —"

"Your accomplice gave you the poison."

That's the possibility that I failed to see. The niggling question in my head. I kept coming back to the possibility he'd faked it when I knew that couldn't be true. Yet faking it wasn't the only way he could be complicit.

"You're saying I knowingly put myself through that hell?" he says.

"It got you what you wanted, didn't it? And like you say, you're a desperate man."

"An innocent man, desperate to escape a death sentence. I will kill you if I have to. I don't want to. Just let me —"

He lunges, hoping I'm distracted. I feint to the side and slash. The knife slices his arm. He lets out a hiss and slams his fist into my gut. I double over, and he grabs my arm, trying to get the knife, but I grip it.

Val runs at us. She kicks at Brady, but he twists out of the way. He bodychecks her, and she goes flying. The gun fires.

I see the muzzle flare, and I dive, but Brady still has my arm. He yanks it and the knife falls. I manage to smack it away. That's all I can do — get the knife where we both can't reach it. But that move costs me a split second and in that second, Brady is on my back. He has my ponytail wrapped around his hand, wrenching my head. Then he stretches toward the knife.

"No!" It's a woman's voice, but not Val's. I manage to turn just enough to see Mathias and Diana behind Val.

Diana tries to get past, but Mathias pulls her back and shakes his head, and she turns on him with "We need —" but he silences her. Mathias is hoping Brady *will* go for that knife. It's just far enough out of reach that he'll need to shift his weight to stretch for it, and that will give me what I need to throw him off.

Brady reaches, but as soon as he sees how far it is, he stops.

"Give me the gun please, Valerie," Mathias says, his voice as calm as if he's asking her to pass the salt. "I can shoot him. You cannot."

Val steps toward him, gun outstretched. Before she reaches Mathias, Brady says, "If you take that gun from her, old man, I'll break this bitch's neck."

Val stops.

"That is misguided," Mathias says. "That *bitch* was the one keeping you alive. The one who was injured trying to save you from a lynch mob. The one attempting to determine whether or not you were guilty of your crimes. I suppose now she has her answer."

"I'm *not* guilty. I —" He stops, unfortunately, as if realizing he's about to go into a rant that could distract him. He settles for, "Damn you. Damn you all."

"Valerie?" Mathias says. "The gun please."

"Give it to me," Brady says.

Mathias chuckles. "Speaking of misguided . . ."

"I just want to get out of here," Brady says. "Either I take Casey as my prisoner, or I take the gun. Your choice."

"Take Casey," Mathias says. "Please. That will go *so* much better for you."

Brady scowls at Mathias. "Shut up, old man. I know it's a fucking strain for you, but shut the hell up." He looks at Val. "I don't want to take your detective. I know she fights to win. She will not come quietly, and I'll have to kill her. I do not want to do that. I just want to leave. Put the gun down and push it into the middle of the floor. To get to it, I'll have to let her go."

Val looks at me.

"No," I say.

Mathias echoes it. Diana says nothing, as she looks anxiously from me to Brady.

"Just give the gun a push," Brady says to Val. "If I get it, I'll walk away. If anyone else goes for it, we'll be right back here again, and I won't get out of this goddamn town without killing someone. Let me leave. Please just let me leave."

Val takes a deep breath. I can see her steeling herself. Then she exhales and pushes the gun into the middle of the room.

"Count of three," he says. "I'll let Casey go. No one moves."

He counts down. At two, he lunges for the gun. I can tell I have no chance of getting it, so I dive for the knife instead and come out in a roll. I leap to my feet, holding the knife. Brady is already across the room with the gun.

"Yeah," he says. "Don't even bother, Detective. Now, Val? I need you to come over here."

"No," I say. "She did what you asked, Oliver. You have the gun. We'll escort you to the edge of the forest. Then you're on your own."

Except he's not on his own. Never has been. Someone in this town betrayed us, and the knife in my hand tells me who that is, but I don't want to believe it.

Forget that for now. Focus on this.

Brady shakes his head. "I don't trust you."

"Then you are a fool," Mathias says. "Casey stopped that cretin from lynching you. Eric took a bullet for you. William pumped the poison from your stomach. These are not your enemies."

"Right now, they are. They won't let me walk away. They only want me to think I'm home free, so they can come after me the moment I turn my back. I need a guarantee. Val will come with me. If no one follows, I'll leave her at the spot where the sheriff got shot. If I hear anyone in pursuit, I'll have to shoot Val. Otherwise, she's yours. I just need a head start."

"And you expect us to believe that?" I say. "You told us that all you wanted was the gun. You lied."

"All I want *is* the gun. I'm borrowing her. You'll get her back. Now come over here with me, Val."

"Don't," I say. "We can't trust him."

"I'm going to count down now. Walk

toward me, or I shoot."

I discreetly motion for Val to stay where she is. The moment he begins counting, I'll charge. I'm far enough to the side that it'll take him a moment to realize it. I will charge, and Mathias will get Diana and Val out and shut that door. That's all we need. I can handle Brady.

"Three."

I charge. Brady fires. I dive and the bullet hits the wall behind me. When I roll up, Val is walking toward Brady.

"Val, no," I say.

"I have to," she says. "I can do this. I'll be fine."

The gun swings in my direction.

"Val made her choice," Brady says. "The smart choice. If no one comes after me, I'll leave her at the spot where Greg's assassin shot your boyfriend. Give me one hour. She'll be fine."

Val reaches Brady. He has her turn around and raises the gun between her shoulder blades.

"Everyone step outside," Brady says. "Do not test me. If you do, you'll see exactly how desperate I am. Please. Just let me go."

Mathias and Diana retreat. I back out of the building, one slow step at a time.

TWENTY-TWO

As I back through that door, I'm torn between wanting to see someone out there . . . and praying no one is. Dalton, yes. Anders, yes. Even some of the militia could be trusted to keep a level head and help me end this. Sam, Nicole, Jen, Kenny . . .

Kenny.

I squelch the reminder.

There is no one outside. Not everyone will be helping with the fire. We aren't a town of saints or heroes. Given what we actually are — criminals and victims — it is a testament to Rockton that so many put aside fear and self-interest to help. Those who have not, though, certainly aren't going to come out now, as Brady steps onto the street with a gun at Val's back.

"If you're truly innocent —" I begin.

"Trust the system?" Brady gives a harsh laugh. "There is no system here. There's just my stepfather and a mountain of money. That old man there tells me to remember that you guys saved my life. That's a lie. You saved an asset. If I die, you lose your share of Mount Fortune."

"And what would we do with it?" I wave at the town. "We have nothing to spend it on."

"Sure you do," he says. "You can spend it on the only thing that matters. Freedom. You're trapped in this hellhole, same as me. For money, I presume. Like guys who work on oil rigs. No one does that for fun."

I keep arguing, but I keep moving backward, too, because I know my arguments are pointless. A rich kid like him looks around and sees the wilderness equivalent of a ghetto. No one would choose to live here.

In talking, I'm only hoping that my raised voice brings Dalton or Anders running. It does not. I hear shouts over at the lumber shed, and I know they're still fighting the fire.

The fire that Brady's accomplice set.

I want to seize that as proof it isn't Kenny. He'd been outside the clinic door when it started. But it's easy to delay a fire. Start it small enough, and it could take an hour or more to be spotted. He's our carpenter.

He's in charge of the lumber shed. In charge of the firewood stocks.

"Val?" I say.

She looks at me. Her eyes are fixed wide, and I know she's praying for me to save her. I cannot. Unless something startles Brady, I can't get the jump on him, and even if he is startled, it's just as likely he'll squeeze the trigger accidentally. I must let him take her and hope he is telling the truth. That he will free her.

I tell her that. Reassure her. *Do as he says. We'll be there within the hour. Don't leave that spot.* I'm not sure she hears any of it.

Then I ask what I must ask, as cruel as it seems to speak of anything except her immediate situation.

"Did you tell Kenny he could leave earlier?"

"W-what?" she says.

I repeat the question.

"*Tell* Kenny he could leave?" she says. "Why?"

"He was guarding the door."

"No, I —"

Brady prods her in the back. "Enough talking. I know you're hoping someone will hear us, Detective, but you also know that's not a good idea. Just let me leave. An hour from now, you'll have Val back."

■ ■ ■ ■

I ask Mathias and Diana to go home. Diana
hesitates, but Mathias says, "Casey fears we
will raise the alarm, however unintention-
ally. Valerie may not be our town's most
popular resident, but if people hear she has
been taken hostage, and we are not running
to her rescue . . . ?"

"Someone will decide to play hero," Diana says. "And he'll shoot Val." She looks at
me. "You did your best, Case. Brady will let
Val go — he knows if he doesn't, you'll
chase him to the end of this damn forest.
You can hunt for him as soon as she's safe.
And it's not like he's going to get very far.
Not alive, anyway. You made the right
choice."

"All completely true," Mathias says. "But
at this moment, Casey does not need re-
assurances. She needs to inform Eric. And
we need to get into our homes and stay
there until she requires us."

"Thank you," I say.

I take off at a jog, my expression neutral,
so no one sees me running in a panic.

When I reach the shed, the fire is almost
out. I can't see much damage from here.
Just spirals of smoke that people with

blankets are desperately trying to squelch. That smoke is a beacon for anyone who sees it, as dangerous as the fire itself.

Dalton is giving orders to wet more blankets and put them over smoldering wood.

"Save what we can," he says. "The shed's fine, but that's a shitload of wood at risk."

I look around for Anders. He's treating a burn. I walk up as he's saying it's not serious, just keep it dry.

"Will?"

He sees me. "Good. I was about to go look for you. Eric asked me to send someone ten minutes ago, and I kinda ignored him. We needed all hands. But I was getting worried."

"I'm fine. Just had to take care of something." I motion for him to follow me and walk out of earshot. "I need you to keep an eye on Kenny."

He starts to turn, but I say, "Don't look. He's supervising people carrying out wood. I need you to watch him while I talk to Eric. Do not let him out of your sight. If he even needs to go to the bathroom, make some excuse why he can't. I need about fifteen minutes."

"He isn't the one who poisoned Brady, is he?"

I pause. "I'll explain when I can. Just

198

watch him, please."

"I will."

Dalton has spotted me, and he heads over with a quiet "Everything okay?" and a look that says he knows it's not.

"If you're done here, Storm's acting a bit off. I don't think she'd go into Brady's food, but I'm worried. Just come, and tell me I'm being paranoid."

Storm is in the station. We left her there what seemed like a lifetime ago. She whines as soon as she catches our footsteps.

We go inside, and I drop to a crouch to pet her and reassure her.

"She's fine, isn't she?" Dalton says.

I nod. Then I straighten. "The fire was a diversion."

"What?" He winces before the word is even out. "Someone tried to kill Brady. Shit. Tell me he's okay."

"It wasn't that kind of a diversion. I thought so, too — that's why I went to check —"

"No." He spins to the door. "Fuck, no. Do not tell me —"

I grab his arm. "Yes, I'm telling you he's gone, and that there's a reason why I didn't come running to get a search party. Just listen. Please."

He nods, and I explain.

TWENTY-THREE

You did the right thing.

That's what Diana told me. That is, I know, what I will hear from Anders, from Nicole, from everyone else who believes in me and wants to offer support.

That is not what I get from Dalton.

Fucking impossible situation.

That's what he says, and it's what I need to hear. Acknowledgment that there was no right choice here. There were only choices.

He doesn't tell me he'd have done the same. That goes without saying. Because what is the alternative? That I raised the alarm and hoped someone took Brady down before he could shoot Val?

Fucking impossible situation.

I put Val in that situation, so I could have done nothing that would end in her death. Even though what I *have* done might still kill her.

I don't trust Brady to let her go. Like Diana, Dalton argues that Brady has no reason to kill her and no reason to take her with him. But he says that because, to him, this is logical.

To Dalton, if Brady has no reason to kill Val, then he won't. He understands that we may be dealing with a man who kills for pleasure, but he cannot comprehend the implications because they don't exist in his world. Even with the hostiles, he presumes they attack us for a reason.

When I correct him, though, he says, "Yeah, but will he endanger his life for the enjoyment of taking hers? I like sex, but I gotta warn you — if our house catches on fire midway through? I'm leaving. Taking you with me, but leaving. If Brady kills Val, we're going to be all over his ass. Far as I'm concerned, if he gives us Val back, I'll do a rudimentary search — that's it. I'm not risking lives to recover him. But if she dies . . ."

"You'll hunt him down."

"*We* will."

Back at the shed, Dalton tells people to carry on. Then he asks a few to help him tackle "security shit — 'cause it doesn't stop even for a fucking fire." He takes Anders, Nicole, Sam, and Kenny. Paul feels the sting of being passed over. Paul is core militia, and Nicole is not yet, but Dalton's commitment to women in the militia means show-ing that they won't be tokens, left off the front lines when situations get serious.

Anders runs Storm over to Petra's. Our first stop is the station, where Dalton asks Nicole and Sam to wait outside. We take Kenny in.

Dalton closes the door behind us.

"I'm going to ask you to step into the cell," Dalton says.

"Sure," Kenny says. "You need me to check something?"

"No, I'm going to lock you inside until I get back."

Kenny lets out a strained laugh. "Is it something I said?"

"When you showed up here three years ago, I thought you were useless. Couldn't hold a saw. Sure as hell couldn't fire a gun. Nothing I could do with you except make sure you didn't get your damn ass killed before you could go home. Then you de-cided to apprentice in carpentry, and I thought, huh, maybe . . . Still, when you asked to join the militia, I thought, fuck no. Another desk jockey fancies himself a law-man. Gonna shoot yourself if I give you a gun. But you proved you could handle it. You became Will's right-hand man. You still drive me fucking crazy sometimes, but I came to respect you. And that respect is why I'm not throwing you in the cell. I'm asking you to walk in yourself."

"I don't under —"

"The only thing to understand right now is that I gave you an order. Either you do it or this gets uglier than I want."

Kenny walks into the cell. Dalton closes the door.

"Oliver Brady is gone," I say.

"What?" Kenny says. "Someone killed —"

"He escaped."

Kenny's mouth works. Then he stops. "Because I left him unguarded. Shit. I'm sorry, Eric. He was secured and the fire —"

"He got himself unsecured," I say. "With this." I hold out Kenny's knife.

Kenny pats his pockets. "No. *No.* He must have — I know this looks bad but —"

"You told me Val let you leave. She says she didn't. After you told me that, I called you back. You kept going."

"I didn't hear — Wait. Val says she didn't tell me to leave? I heard the bell, and then I smelled smoke, and I told her and she was freaking out over the fire, and maybe she didn't understand what I was asking. You know how she gets. Bring her here. Let me talk to her."

"Brady took her."

204

"Wh-what?"

Dalton says, "He took Val hostage. You're staying in that cell, and we'll talk when we get back. Just hope we have Val with us to straighten this out."

Before we go, Dalton changes his mind about bringing Anders. That would leave Rockton exposed. The fire was a distraction, and Dalton failed to see that, so now he's madly spinning out all the possibilities we might be missing. One is that Brady expects we'll do exactly this — gather our law enforcement and troop into the forest, leaving the town with a guard or two on fire cleanup. He could take more hostages, steal an ATV, even try to steal the plane.

I explain the situation to Anders, Sam, and Nicole as we walk. Then Anders runs back to town, where he'll have the remains of the militia guard the vehicles and patrol the town while citizens handle the fire fall-out.

We move at a brisk walk. Val will be alone in the forest, which she has not set foot in since she was attacked here shortly after she arrived. Now she's about to be abandoned in these woods after being marched in at gunpoint. I cannot imagine what that will be like. Nicole can. She's moving faster than any of us, and Dalton has to call her back, saying, "If Brady thinks we didn't give him an hour, that gives him an excuse."

An excuse to kill Val.

We're approaching the final curve when Dalton's gait catches. A split-second hesitation as his chin lifts and his nostrils flare, finding some scent in the breeze.

"Eric?" I say as I come up beside him.

His nostrils flare again. His gaze fixes on the path, and when Sam whispers, "What's the plan?," Dalton doesn't seem to hear him.

"You two stay here," I whisper to Sam and Nicole.

I slant a look at Dalton, giving him the chance to contradict the order. He just keeps moving, his gaze fixed on that corner.

"Guns out," I whisper to the other two. "Watch the forest. Do *not* fire."

I jog to catch up with Dalton. He's rounding that final curve to the place where we should find Val —

The breeze hits, bringing with it the unmistakable coppery smell of blood.

I cover Dalton. He doesn't have his gun out. His arm isn't good enough for that. Instead, he reaches his right hand into his pocket for his knife.

I have my gun ready as we continue around the curve . . .

206

There's something on the path. Dalton stops short, but he doesn't look at the object. He's scanning the forest. I give the object one quick glance, and then pull my gaze away after I'm sure it's not a person.

As I survey the forest, though, I recall the image. A bloodied heap. Something brown.

What was Val wearing?

It's too small to be her body. Too small to be her *entire* body.

I don't pursue that thought.

I know why Dalton is ignoring the heap — he can't be distracted from a potential trap. But the unknown pounds at my head, my mouth going dry, and all I can think about is Val agreeing to be our spy with Brady.

And me letting her, despite Dalton's reservations.

So I look. I suck in breath. Dalton tenses, shoulder blades snapping together under his T-shirt.

"It's not Val," I say quickly.

His gaze drops then. And he lets out a quiet oath.

It is a dog.

No, it's a puppy.

On the path lies what looks like a shepherd puppy, with brown speckles on its muzzle. As soon as I see those, I remember the wolf-dog, the nursing mother.

The cub is dead.

Slaughtered and left on the path.

I pull my gaze from the cub and wrap both hands around my gun. Dalton steps over the tiny corpse.

I lift my foot to follow. Then I stop. Eyes on my surroundings, I crouch and lay my fingertips against the side of the cub's neck.

Still warm.

I hurry to catch up with Dalton, continuing around the curve and —

He stops and lets out a string of curses under his breath.

There is another heap on the path.

We don't stop for a better look. I see bloods and entrails, and my stomach churns. I've seen plenty of dead animals up here, often in worse shape, half devoured and rotting, but this is not a predator's kill. These cubs have been planted — a trap that Dalton and I are expected to fall for because we have a dog of our own. So we will see these poor dead cubs and stop, and then —

A whimper sounds in the bushes, and Dalton lets out another curse, this one softer, almost an exhalation.

Fuck, no . . .

What will be worse than seeing dead wolf-

dog cubs in the path?
   Seeing one that is not yet dead.

TWENTY-FOUR

We take a step. Then the sound comes again, that deep-throated whine, from the brush beside the path.

Dalton glances back at me. It's the briefest of glances, no more than a flicker of eye contact.

We should keep going. We're suckers if we don't, playing right into the trap Brady has set. A third cub has been left alive, horribly injured, as the cruelest of taunts. Punishment for the fact that we are not monsters.

Can you walk by this dying dog? You know you should. It's a wild thing, a feral beast. But I saw how you left the wolf-dog alone. I heard you say that she must have pups nearby. Heard the relief in your voices when she didn't attack, an excuse to let her live.

Suckers.

I'll leave Val by that spot where the sheriff got shot. You know the one. Just go there, and you'll find her.

The cub whines again.

"Fuck."

"Val?" I call. Then louder. "Valerie?"

She doesn't respond, and I know she won't. She isn't here. It would make no sense to kill these cubs and leave her with them, where she can warn us of a trap.

Brady is out there, in the forest, with my gun.

He's watching us. Figuring out how to put us both down before we can fire back. And this is the way to do it. Get us to lower our guard as we go after the wounded cub, because we will do that, of course we will.

Suckers.

I remember reading folklore that said one way to escape a vampire was to throw rice on the path, and it will be compelled to stop and pick up every grain before continuing on. I remember shaking my head at the absolute ridiculousness of it. But that is what Brady has done. He has thrown rice in our path, knowing we must stop to gather it up.

"Sam?" I shout. "Nicki?"

"Here!" Nicole calls back.

"Stay where you are, and stay alert. Brady's set a trap. There's no sign of Val. We're fine. Just hold there while we look for her."

"Got it!"

I cover Dalton as he takes another step. Then he bends to grab a stick with his bad hand, his knife still clenched in the good one. He pokes the stick around the brush where the noises come from. He jabs the cub by accident, and it lets out a startled yelp. Then it growls, and when he withdraws the stick, a pair of tiny jaws come with it, clamped on the wood before they fall away.

"Well, that's a good sign," he murmurs.

Confident he's not about to step into a literal trap, Dalton walks to the undergrowth, bends, and pushes fronds aside. Inside is a cub. I catch one glimpse of it before I remember what I'm supposed to be doing.

Don't be any more of a sucker than you need to, Casey.

I stay back and let Dalton handle it. The cub whines and whimpers and then —

"Fuck!"

I look over sharply. He's pulling back his hand, puncture wounds below his thumb welling with blood.

"It attacked you?"

"Nah, just snapped at me. It's caught in something."

"How badly is it injured?"

"I see blood where it's caught, but otherwise nothing. Looks like a snare wire. I'm probably going to get nipped again, so ignore the cursing."

"Got it."

I survey the forest. I know this is a trap. It must be. But there's no sign of anyone. Dalton works on the cub, swearing as he's nipped. Then there's a sound from the forest.

"Eric . . ."

"I hear it."

He backs away from the cub, who begins whining and yelping in earnest. However much freeing it hurt the cub, it's even more worried about being abandoned again, and it's making enough noise that I can't hear what's happening in the forest.

Dalton retreats to me, knife still in his hand. "Sound came from that way."

"Could you tell what it was?"

"Footsteps maybe? Hard to say."

The brush crackles, loud enough for us to catch it between the cub's cries. I see it, too, a wave of movement, branches pushed aside, something big crashing toward the path . . .

I aim my gun.

There's another movement. A dark shape *below* where I'm aiming.

The mother wolf-dog staggers onto the path. Her gray fur is matted with blood, and she moves with a stiff-legged gait, breath coming so hard I can hear it.

Dalton says, "Fuck, no," and that seems odd. Yes, it's a tragedy that the wolf-dog has also been mortally wounded, drawn back by the cries of her cub, but there's a note of fear in his voice that I do not understand until I see what hangs from her jaws.

Saliva.

Bloody, foaming saliva.

"Rabies?" I whisper.

"I hope not, but presume yes. We're going to have to take her down. You got a bead on her?"

I nod.

"Okay, take the —"

The wolf-dog charges. One second, she's shambling along, seeming a heartbeat from keeling over. The next she is in flight, jaws snapping, bloody froth flying.

I fire.

The bullet hits her. And she doesn't care.

I fire again, and Dalton stays right there, beside me, and I want to shout at him to *move.* Get out of the way. Dive for cover. Run!

But he just waits as I fire more rounds, and by then she's so close I can see the proverbial whites of her eyes as they roll.

"Eric!" I shout as I fire one last time.

He pushes me to the side. It's not a shove, just a push, and I'm scrambling out of the way, and he's just moving aside and . . .

The wolf-dog falls. Midflight, she collapses, this weird movement, almost like she's dancing as she folds in on herself. Then she drops, and when she hits the ground, those wild eyes are frozen open in death, a bullet hole between them.

"Nice shot," he says.

"Next time, can you *not* stay in the path of a charging wild animal?"

"I knew you'd get her."

"Just humor me, okay?" I walk over to see I *did* get her — with every bullet. Two to the chest, both of which would have been fatal, but she'd been too far gone to care.

"Got another one here where the blood's drying."

It's the spot I'd seen on her flank, matted with blood. Dalton pokes at it.

"Bullet's . . ." he says.

He uses his knife to cut it out. I've stood in on countless autopsies without flinching, but I swear Dalton makes me look positively squeamish. There is a question to be answered here, and he digs that bullet free without a moment's hesitation.

He holds the bullet up, his fingers red with blood.

"Nine-mil?" he asks.

"Yes."

One of the perks of being on the Rockton police force is that we get to choose our own sidearms. Mine's a Sig Sauer P226. Dalton is a revolver guy — the product of growing up here and using older guns. He carries a .357 Smith & Wesson. Anders prefers a gun that might actually stand a chance of taking down a grizzly: a Ruger Alaskan .454, which requires more wrist strength than I currently possess.

The bullet Dalton found fits my weapon . . . the one Brady took.

"Yes," I say. "It is possible we've misread the scenario. Brady shot this dog, which appears to have rabies or some other infection that drove it mad. It might have killed its own cubs. That one" — I nod toward the third — "could have gotten tangled in a settler's snare. Then Brady comes along, finds the mad dog and shoots. Even if it was a trap, it only seems to have been designed to slow us down, because he's missed the chance to attack."

"Or he was setting a trap. He killed the cubs, and the mother unexpectedly returned and attacked. He shoots her and takes off."

"Possible. Right now, though, we have two problems, leading in polar opposite directions. Finding Val and getting that cub back to town."

He frowns at me.

"No," I say. "As much as I love dogs, I'm not equating that cub's life with Val's. But this is about *yours.*"

His frown deepens.

I wave at the wolf-dog. "If she had rabies, there's a chance her cub is also infected. The cub that bit you. We need to quarantine it."

"Yeah." No curse for this one. He hasn't considered this possibility, but now that I raise it, he doesn't freak out. *Huh, you're right. I could have a terrible and deadly disease.*

"Casey?"

I jump at Nicole's voice. I'd forgotten we've had two militia around the corner. The only reason they haven't come running is that they know how much shit Paul is in for disobeying an order. So they stayed put, our voices assuring them we aren't lying in agony, shot on the ground.

I tell them to approach, and I warn about the cubs, but when they appear, both are obviously rattled.

I'm standing point while Dalton continues freeing the cub. Nicole sees what he's doing and jogs over with, "Here, let me —"

"No," I say. "The mother may have been rabid. Eric's already been bit."

"Rabid?"

I struggle to keep scanning the forest. Dalton may not be freaked out about the possibility, but I sure as hell am. I feel him glance at me.

"It's unlikely," he says, his voice softer than usual. "Highly unlikely. There's never been a confirmed case in the Yukon. But, yeah, I've seen reports of it. We'll quarantine the cub. First sign of trouble, I'll get my ass south."

I don't answer, just keep looking for trouble, hoping that if it exists, it's out there, not here in the form of a small and terrified cub.

"Casey?"

"Hmm?"

"There's *never* been an incidence. Not one. The mother could have had a seizure. Could have been poisoned."

"I vote poisoning," Nicole says. "If that bastard did this, poison is your answer."

Dalton continues, "Even if, by some very slight chance, it was rabies, I'm not seeing any sign that this little guy was bit by his mother. His leg's messed up from the wire, so yeah, we have to consider the possibility that wound hides a bite. But what are the chances that she's got rabies — in a territory that doesn't have it — and she bit him . . . on the leg that he then got caught in a snare?"

"One in a million," Nicole says.

"We'll still take this guy back to Rockton to be sure."

He hefts the cub as he stands and holds it out. The wolf-dog lies over his hands, as if too exhausted to squirm.

"Male," he says. "Probably more wolf than dog. Which means it's not a pet. But, yeah, we gotta take it back. Sam, give me your jacket. You and Nicki will run him to town. Casey and I need to search for Val."

Dalton puts the cub inside Sam's jacket and pulls up the sides. "Carry it this way, like a bundle. Keep it tightly closed, and he won't escape. He can breathe — don't let him try to tell you otherwise. He stays in there until you're back at Rockton. Then take him to Casey's house. The door's unlocked. Put the whole jacket inside the door like this" — he demonstrates — "and then give it a push, and get that door closed before he escapes. Leave him be. His leg's bad, but it'll hold until we come back."

Sam takes the bundled cub.

"Nicole?" Dalton says. "While he's doing that, tell Will to announce what's happened.

Minimal details. Arrange search parties. Let's get them out before dark."

TWENTY-FIVE

We search for Val. Call for Val. There's no sign that either of them was here except for that bullet in the wolf-dog, and even that's hardly ballistic proof. It just means someone shot her with a 9 mm.

I don't know what's going on here. I can speculate, but the whole thing is just fucked-up. There's no other term for it. Too many puzzle pieces could fit the hole, and yet none are exactly right.

Did Brady set all this up? That's the answer I both like and hate. My gut likes it for the lack of coincidence. My head hates it for the complexity of the plan.

Also, do I like it a little too much because it proves Brady is a monster, which makes this easier? If it wasn't for Val, having Brady escape might be the best possible solution — let him die out here, no longer a threat to Rockton. But if he is indeed innocent . . . ? Then he is like any other resident, and we failed him. He ran because we failed. He took Val because we failed. We put his back to the wall, and he lashed out.

Do not test me. If you do, you'll see exactly how desperate I am.

Please. Just let me go.

Val is the priority here. But she's nowhere to be found.

We return to the dead wolf-dog, and I examine the site. I find traces of footprints, but the ground is hard enough that they're only smudges, too faint to even tell if they're ours. Hell, even a perfect print of Brady's sneakers could be from our first time here.

When we're finished, I check Dalton's hand. The puncture wounds are red and inflamed.

" 'Cause it's a bite," he says. "Trust me, I've had them. Gotta get it cleaned and then bandaged so it stays clean."

I nod.

"I'm okay, Casey."

I nod again. He puts his fingers under my chin and tilts my face up and bends to kiss me. It's a very sweet kiss, and when it breaks, I say, "You do realize that's an invitation for us to be attacked."

"I'm setting a trap."

I smile at that, and he kisses me again and then feigns stretching a kink from his neck.

"You gotta get taller," he says.

"I'll work on that."

I smile again, because I know he's trying to coax one from me.

He rests his forearms on my shoulders. "This sucks."

I do laugh at that. He's right, though. It might not be the most erudite description of the situation, but it's completely apt. There is nothing we can do about this. Maybe not even anything we could have done to prevent this. It just sucks.

"I should have gone looking for you during the fire," he says. "Should have realized something was up. Fuck, I should have realized *what* was up — obviously someone set that fire for a reason. We might have stopped him."

"Or gotten Val killed. Gotten me killed. Forced Brady into a panic and sent him over the edge. In hindsight I should have told you what I was doing. But I was playing a hunch, and my hunch was that someone was using the fire as a distraction to *kill* Brady. While I wasn't going to sit back and let that happen, it wouldn't be the biggest tragedy in the world. Even if he's innocent. That's a shitty thing to say, but he was a threat either way."

"Impossible situation."

I nod.

He looks out at the forest. "Still plenty of daylight left. You okay with walking another hour or so? Gives us a chance to get farther in while heading for a destination."

"Jacob's camp?"

He nods.

"You're worried?"

"Nah. Brady's not going after anyone out here. I still want to warn Jacob, though. I also want to let him know what's going on, get him to talk to Brent, maybe Ty, set them looking for Val."

"Good idea."

Jacob's camp is empty. That's no cause for alarm. He's packed it up, which means he headed off on his hunting trip. I feared that after he didn't leave the note yesterday. I know Nicole will be hurt, and I hate seeing that.

On our way back to town, we take a different route to widen the search. There's still no trace of Brady or Val. Tomorrow we'll visit Brent and swing by the cabin that Cypher used for the winter, see if he's still lurking about. Brent's easy to find, though, and he's a former bounty hunter, which makes him as good a tracker as Jacob.

Back in Rockton, the first thing I do is

treat Dalton's hand. He's right that it just looks like a bite, but that won't keep me from worrying.

Anders has explained the situation to the residents. Oliver Brady used the fire as a distraction to escape. He took Val hostage, with a promise to leave her at a set location in an hour. If we hadn't agreed, he'd have killed her on the spot. Val was not at the promised location. We are currently searching for them.

He doesn't mention that we suspect the fire was deliberately set. That implies an accomplice, and people might jump to the conclusion it's the guy we locked up. We won't do that to Kenny. After Roy's bullshit, we don't trust people not to take justice into their own hands.

We passed a search party as we were coming in. Dalton told them to keep at it for another two hours and then switch off with a fresh group. We have the advantage of daylight at this time of year, and we can keep hunting until nearly midnight.

Next stop is the wolf-dog cub. When we enter my house, Dalton blocks the exit, expecting the cub to charge for freedom. He doesn't . . . because he's hiding behind the sofa.

I pull him out. I'm dressed in long sleeves

and gloves, but he doesn't try to bite. Just shakes and whines. I've brought sedative, and he yelps at the needle, but a few minutes later, he's limp in my arms.

I work on his injured front leg. It's not as bad as I feared. It's just messy, flesh ripped as he'd struggled against the snare wire.

I bandage the wound. Then Dalton covers the cloth in a goop we use with Storm, when she insists on licking a cut or sting.

Once I'm done, I lean back on my haunches. He looks more like a lion cub than a wolf or a dog, with thick tawny fur, gray and dark brown striping, and an even thicker mane around his head. He has the same freckles as his mother, though.

"Do you think the father was a dog?" I ask.

"Probably not. Take away the coloring and those freckles, and he's wolf."

"Which is a problem."

"Either way, it's a problem. I'd rather face a wolf, but dogs have the genes for domestication. Wolves don't." He looks down at the cub and sighs.

"We'll keep him until we know he isn't rabid," I say. "Then we can . . . do whatever."

He slants me a look. "Do you really think either of us is going to be able to 'do whatever' after we've nursed him back to health?"

I don't answer.

"Yeah." He heaves to his feet. "We'll wait and see. But if anyone comes looking to adopt a puppy, the answer is fuck no. This isn't a pet. We can't turn him out into the woods at this age, though. Can't raise him and then release him after he's lived with humans. That's just as cruel. Dangerous, too." He runs a hand through his hair and sighs again.

"We'll figure it out," I say. "You and I both understand this isn't a pet wolf. But it's not a rabid dog either." I pause and look down at the sleeping cub. "Or so we hope."

"He's not. Just gotta wait to be sure and then we'll . . . figure shit out."

Figure shit out.

That's what we're doing, on so many levels, over the next twelve hours. There's still enough light for us to get to Brent's that evening, but Dalton doesn't want to leave town. We'll go at first light.

Dalton joins the last evening search. That's where he's best right now, as our top tracker.

He takes Storm. We're hoping to make a search-and-rescue dog out of her. That's what the breed is used for, though more commonly water-based, given their webbed feet and double coats. But her sense of smell is excellent, so that's our plan. She's only eight months old, just entering doggie adolescence, with the attention span to match. This is the one area of her training where I've discovered I can't push. I've introduced her to the concept of tracking, and we work on it weekly, but it's mostly play at this point — I give her the scent of someone in town, and if she can find her target, she gets a treat. If the trail's too convoluted, though, she loses interest.

Still Dalton takes her, along with Brady's and Val's dirty clothing. Storm has spent enough time around Brady that we hope that helps — she's definitely better at finding residents she knows. She knows Val less well — big dogs make Val nervous — but Storm only takes a quick sniff at Val's blouse, as if to say, "Okay, I know who you want." Which is promising.

They leave, and I stay behind to "figure shit out."

Some of that is investigating, some is talking to people, and some is just staring into space and thinking, and then jotting those thoughts into my notebook.

Brady had an accomplice in town. That is

a fact. There is absolutely no way someone coincidentally set fire to that shed when Brady was out of the cell. His accomplice put poison in his food, enough to make him violently ill. That gets Brady out of the cell and into the clinic, which was exactly the scenario I expected the moment I saw him throwing up. *Not this old chestnut — prisoner fakes illness to get to a less secure environment.* Except he hadn't been faking. He'd gone the extra step and let himself be poisoned.

From there, I'd supplied Brady with a hostage. A nurse at his bedside. Then his accomplice sets the fire and Brady grabs Val as insurance to get him out of town.

Next Brady knows the wolf-dog is near that spot. He poisons her — and kills her poor cubs — to slow us down. It also gives him an "excuse" for Val not being there, in case we catch up with him. He couldn't exactly leave her with a frothing canine, right?

And the sniper? It could very well have been his accomplice, hoping to convince us Brady was in danger. Or hoping to scatter us so he could rescue him.

As a hypothesis, this solidifies Brady's guilt. He is a monster. A killer.

But it's only a hypothesis. The assassin

might have come from his stepfather. That would give Brady reason to panic. Then Brady enlisted a local mercenary of his own, with promises of a rich reward.

Was Kenny that local mercenary? He *is* just about to leave, and he'll need money. Still, when I consider him as a suspect, I feel sick. I won't interview Kenny until both Dalton and Anders are back. The point is that Brady has a confederate in Rockton, and it doesn't matter right now if it's Kenny or . . .

There's another possibility. One person that I know suspects Brady is innocent. The one who delivered that petition. Also the one who came running to notify us of the fire. Jen.

Too much to think about. It's a puzzle of configuration, and each piece in it has two sides — guilt or innocence — and the meaning changes depending on which side I place up. If Brady is innocent, then x. If he is a monster, then y. Two ways of looking at everything, leading to two ways of investigating.

Stop. Focus.

Take it apart. Look at the trees, not the forest. That's what my first detective partner taught me. There are times when, yes, it's good to step back and see the whole. But there are also times in police work when you must focus on the minutiae. On the trees. On one puzzle piece. Figure out where that fits and that'll help you find where another goes. Get a few of those done and then step back, or you'll go crazy with possibilities, each configuration sending the investigation spiraling in a new direction.

Focus.

Start with the fire.

The problem with determining the cause of a fire? The evidence has gone up in smoke. Which is why there are trained experts for this — experts who are *not* police detectives. But I am every investigator in Rockton, and this is one of the many areas I've been researching. I've always been a believer in lifelong learning. I took every course my department would send me on. Learned every new technique. Subscribed to every journal. Attended every local conference on my own dime, even as my colleagues rolled their eyes and said, "We hire experts for that, Casey." True. I did not need to know anything about forensic anthropology, because I wouldn't ever be the person analyzing buried remains. But I wanted to know. And now I *am* that person. Jack-of-all-trades, feeling truly master of none.

Arson investigation.

I evaluate the scene. Document it. Process the evidence.

This time, the building has been saved. There's damage, but it can be repaired. And it doesn't take much investigating to know it's arson. The smell of kerosene gives it away, as it did the last time.

It is an arson easily set by anyone with any knowledge of wood and access to kerosene. Which really doesn't narrow it down in Rockton.

Dalton comes back ahead of the others. A dripping black rug trails behind him with a look that is unconvincingly contrite.

"Got too close to the lake, didn't you?" I call as I walk toward them.

Dalton only sighs.

"We need to take her there more often," I say, "so the siren's call of water is a little more resistible."

"I'm not sure it ever will be. Been thinking of buying one of those pools."

"The plastic kiddie ones? She's a little big for that." I gingerly pat her wet head, and she slumps happily.

"I mean the ones you set up," he says. "The bigger pools."

"Then we'll have to keep the humans out of it."

"If they want to swim in dog fur, they can go ahead. Just make a rule: you use it; you clean it."

He walks over. I take his hand to examine it, but he wraps his fingers around mine, holding tight. His expression is calm, as if he's just returned from a walk in the woods, but his tight grip tells me the rest.

"Not a trace," he says. "Storm did well. She found the trail out of town and followed it along the path. They turned off before the spot with the wolf-dog."

"Turned off or doubled back?"

"That's the problem. The trail left the path, and Storm followed it awhile, but the undergrowth thickened and hit a whole warren of rabbit holes. She went nuts and lost the trail. I couldn't get her to focus. So I took her backwards, in hopes she'd pick it up again."

"And?"

"And I don't know. She kept finding the same end point. I moved higher up the path in case he rejoined it, and then we were too close to the dead dogs."

He looks down at her. "She smelled those, and she was upset. Really upset. She got away from me and kept nosing the first cub and . . ."

He exhales. "It wasn't good. I got her out

of there. Which means I can't answer the question. All I know is they left the path at one point and neither of us could figure out where they'd gone from there."

TWENTY-SIX

It's time to notify the council. Except we can't. Without Val, we don't know how.

We have a radio receiver. We understand the basics of how to use it, and Anders knows specifics. But we don't have a frequency. That's top secret, need to know only, and no one other than Val, apparently, needed to know.

We move the radio to our house and wait for Phil to call in. That's all we can do.

We're up at four. I play double nursemaid, first tending to Dalton's arm and his hand. The former is healing well; the latter shows no sign of infection. Then, while he cooks breakfast, I go to see the cub.

Storm comes with me. I'm not about to let her into the house — I'm still worried about rabies — but she smells him from outside and seems to think it's another dead wolf-dog. Her whines escalate to howls. So I lift the cub up to the front window . . .

and then she goes nuts because there's another canine in town and I'm keeping him from her.

I try to calm her by cracking open the front door just enough for her to snuffle him. The poor cub sees this massive black nose and he freaks. I shut the door and Storm starts howling again. The cub stops quaking in mortal terror . . . and begins howling back.

It's an interesting way to start my morning. I don't think my neighbors agree.

The cub is otherwise fine. I'd left a bed and food and water. I have to clean up piddle and poop, but I'm not taking him out for a walk until that leg is better. I moved all my blankets and cushions and rugs upstairs, so the damage is minimal. I tend to his leg, replace the food and water, and then I return home for my own breakfast.

At dawn, we're off to visit Brent. It's a long hike to the mountain where Brent has his cave. Before we leave, we remind Storm of Brady and Val's scents, and every time the path branches off, we have her sniff. She finds nothing. As we draw near the mountain, though, she starts getting excited. Which *would* be exciting . . . if we weren't on the path Brent uses daily. Storm is very fond of Brent, who always has dried bones for her.

When we reach the cave entrance, she plunks down with a sigh. She still fits, but she won't for much longer. Once we get through, we shove a rock into the opening, the last thing we need is her wedging in and getting stuck. She sighs again and then sticks her head into the remaining opening to watch us mournfully.

Or that's what she usually does. This time, when she sticks her head through, her nostrils flare, and she sniffs wildly as she whines.

"Storm, no," I say. "Brent will come out. He'll bring your bone."

She keeps whining, but I've told her to stay and she obeys.

We're going down the first passage when my light catches something on the wall. Dalton is ahead of me, and as I stop for a closer look, he glances back.

I have the penlight between my teeth so I can crawl. Now I take it out and shine it on the wall to see . . .

A handprint.

A red handprint.

"Eric . . ."

"He's been hunting," Dalton says. "Must

have butchered up top. That's what Storm smells."

He says that, but he still moves faster, and I remember Storm whining on the path, getting excited, presumably she smelled Brent.

And if it *wasn't* Brent? What if, instead, she picked up the very scents we asked her to find?

As we crawl, I tell myself I'm overreacting. Brady doesn't know anything about Brent. He has no reason to come for him. No idea where to find him. The chances that Brady would just happen to take shelter in the same cave where Brent lives? Infinitesimal. The opening isn't even visible from down the mountainside.

We reach the cavern that Brent calls home. There's blood on the floor, large drops, some smeared. A shelf has been pulled down, contents spilled, another bloody handprint on the wall.

"Brent?" Dalton's voice echoing through the cavern. "Brent!"

I'm following the blood. More smears here, like drag marks. They lead to the smaller cavern Brent uses for storage. I pull back the hide curtain. And there is Brent, lying on the floor, curled in fetal position, blood soaking his shirt, one hand pressed against it. His eyes are closed.

I bend to clear the low ceiling. Then I crouch beside him. My fingers go to his neck, and he stirs.

Dalton's figure fills the entrance.

"He's alive," I say.

Barely. Brent's eyelids flutter, but he can't open them. His face is almost as white as his hair. He isn't breathing hard enough for me to even see his chest rise. Then there's the blood. A pool of it under him, his shirt soaked with it.

We get him out of that small cavern. That wakes him, crying in pain. Dalton wets a cloth as I gingerly peel up Brent's shirt. I take the cloth and clean as carefully as I can. Brent whimpers, his eyes still shut, and Dalton tries to rouse him.

There's a bullet hole through Brent's stomach.

"Diagnosis dead?" a papery voice whispers.

I turn. His eyes are barely open, but he's trying to smile.

"I know the diagnosis," he says. "Dead from the moment the bullet hit. Body just hasn't realized it yet."

He's right. If he'd been steps from a hospital when he'd been shot, he might have survived. Even that is unlikely. And now . . .

Tears well. I blink them back hard.

"Casey?" Brent says. "I already know."

"I can try —"

He reaches for my hand and squeezes it. "Let's not waste my time. Not much left."

"You want a drink?" Dalton asks.

Brent manages a hoarse laugh. "I would *love* a drink."

Dalton takes a bottle from the backpack we brought. A gift for Brent, in return for his bounty hunting services.

Brent cranes his neck up. "Is that . . . ?"

"Scotch. I'm told it's the good stuff. Bought it a while back, in case you ever had anything better to trade than skinny-assed bucks. Never did. But I guess you can have it now."

Brent laughs, knowing full well that Dalton would have bought this on his last trip, after Brent and I argued over the merits of Scotch versus tequila.

Dalton pours him a glass full.

"Trying to get me drunk?" Brent says.

"Yeah, hoping those conspiracy theories of yours might make more sense if you're loaded." He hands him the glass. "Got any theories on who did that to you?"

"It's the bastard you were keeping in that town of yours. Kid told me you think he's some kinda killer. Insisted he's not." Brent looks down at his gut. "Seems he lied."

"Okay," I say. "Just rest and —"

"I'm not resting, Casey. I'm helping you catch my killer. And drinking. Heavily. If it starts spilling out my guts? Don't tell me."

He takes a deep drink. "I was down the mountain, shooting grouse at twilight. Kid got the jump on me, the fuck —" He stops. Apologizes to me for swearing, as always. "He got me dead to rights. I was picking up my game, had put my gun down. He wanted to know where to find Jacob."

"Jacob?" Dalton tenses.

"Relax, Eric. You think I told him?" Brent slurps more Scotch. "Said he wanted to hire Jacob. As a guide. Get him out of here. I said I could do it. He said no, had to be Jacob. That's when I knew something was up."

"He didn't *just* want a guide," I say.

"Right. So I confronted him, and he told me that story about being a prisoner in your town, falsely accused. Says he needs Jacob as a guide and as insurance, but he won't hurt him. Offers to pay me to take him to Jacob. I say no. He threatens to shoot me in the shoulder. I go for the gun. We fight. I get gutshot instead. Maybe that was an accident, but the bas — the jerk put his fist on my gut and pushed down. Made me howl, I'm ashamed to say. But I got the gun

241

away from him. Fired a shot. He took off. I hauled ass back here. Lost the damn gun on the way, pardon my French. But I made it. Holed up with my rifle, in case he came back."

"He didn't?"

"Nah, ran and kept running. Little pri — prat."

"Was there anyone with him? Any sign of a hostage?"

Brent shakes his head. "He was alone. Never mentioned anyone else. It was all about him. How everyone done him wrong." Brent coughs and then gasps in pain with the movement. "Damn country song, he was. You don't need to worry about Jacob, though. I don't even know where he's camping right now. Left his last spot a couple of days back."

"So he's gone duck hunting," Dalton says.

"Not yet. Came by to say he was holding off — he was tracking a bull caribou and wanted to get that first. And he was trying to decide if he should ask that girl from your town to go duck hunting. Came to me for advice." Brent gives a weak laugh. "Like I'd be any help. I faked it, though. Told him yes, he should do it."

"So he's mobile right now?"

Brent nods. "Until he gets that caribou."

I help him lift the glass to his lips. His hand is trembling. He takes two big gulps. When he speaks again, his words are slurring, exhaustion and alcohol mixed.

"Eric?"

"Right here, Brent."

"You gotta bury me in my jersey, okay?"

"The Maple Leafs one?"

Brent raises his middle finger. Then he drinks more Scotch with my help. "You know how I want to go, right?"

"I do."

"Up in one of those platforms. Like the Indians used to do it."

"I know. I'll do it just like you wanted."

Brent's eyelids flutter. Then they open. "Almost forgot. Eric? You gotta get something for me."

His words are slurring badly now, and it takes a while for Dalton to interpret his directions and bring what he wants. It's two carved wooden figurines.

"Give it to me," Brent says. "You'll do it wrong."

He takes the figures and arranges them on his palm. It's a woman in a ponytail, kneeling in front of a rolling ball of fur.

"That a bear cub?" Dalton says.

Brent raises his middle finger again.

"It's me and Storm," I say. "When she was

a puppy."

"First time you brought her here. I remember you two playing in the grass. Been a long time since I heard a girl laugh like that. I wanted to capture it. She's not so little anymore."

"Yeah, Casey, gotta watch what you're eating."

We both raise our fingers for that. Then Brent hands me the figures. Up close I see the detail, the hours spent carving them. I thank him, and we talk for a little more. He's flagging, and I tell him we'll build that platform and put him in his beloved Canadiens hockey jersey. And I say we'll get Brady for him.

"I'm sure you will," he says, "but I'm not too worried about that. I'm just glad you came. Not a bad way to go. Good Scotch. Pretty girl."

I squeeze his hand and bend to kiss his weathered cheek as his eyes close.

"Eric?" he whispers, voice barely audible.

Dalton bends by Brent's head.

"I figured it out," Brent says. "The secret behind that town of yours. This is what it's for, isn't it? Harboring the worst criminals. The ones the government wants to make disappear. Save folks the expense of a trial and hide them up here, let their sorry asses rot." His eyes half open. "I'm right, aren't I?"

"Took you long enough."

Brent smiles and his eyes close again. A few more breaths, and then he goes still.

TWENTY-SEVEN

I make Brent comfortable. I know exactly how ridiculous this is, but I do it anyway, arranging his body on his sleeping mat and pulling up a blanket, as if tucking him in for the night. Dalton doesn't say a word.

Then I stand and march to the exit. "I'm going to find Brady. I'm going to find him and put a bullet through his gut and leave him out there. Let him drag his ass to shelter so he doesn't get eaten by a pack of damn wolves. I will *watch* him drag his ass, and I will pray that the wolves come. Wolves or a wolverine or ravens. I hope it's ravens. I hope they find him, gut-shot, and they rip out his . . ."

I don't go further. Dalton knows what I mean, and he doesn't need to hear the details.

I stoop for the passageway, and Dalton grips my arm.

"Casey . . ."

"I'm going to find him."

"You will. But Brady's not waiting outside this cave."

I wheel on him. "You think I don't know that?"

"It's been twelve hours."

"I need to process the scene."

"Twelve hours."

The crime scene isn't going anywhere. That's what he means. He glances back at Brent's body.

"No," I say. "We're not doing that right now. We need tools."

"He has everything."

"Later. He's fine. He'll be . . ."

Fine. He'll be fine.

Brent is not fine. Brent is dead, and I don't want to lay him to rest because it feels like acknowledgment. Feels like acceptance. Feels, too, like I'm stalling when I need to be acting.

"We need to —" I stop myself.

Find Jacob. Warn Jacob. That's what I want to say, and that's where I must draw the line. I can't remind Dalton his brother is in danger, as if he doesn't know that, as if he's not holding himself back from running out to find him.

It has been twelve hours. Another hour won't matter. Not for finding Jacob. Not for examining the crime scene.

For Brent, though . . .

"We made a promise," Dalton says, his voice low.

"I . . . I . . ."

I look over at Brent's body. And I burst into tears, and Dalton's arms go around me, holding me tight as I sob against him.

We lay Brent's body to rest, the way he wanted it, on an open platform, with him wearing his Canadiens jersey, a reminder of the season he'd played for the team, fifty years ago.

Afterward, I examine the crime scene. That's what Dalton insists on for the next step. Jacob can wait — the crime scene could be disturbed.

Storm easily tracks Brent back to where he'd been shot. Blood and trampled grasses mark the exact spot, as do the grouse Brent shot. There's a bow and arrows there, and I remember he was new to bow shooting, having finally agreed to let Jacob teach him.

Too old for this, he'd said, *learning new tricks at my age. But it saves on ammo.*

Dalton said he could bring more ammunition with his trades, but Brent had blustered that he needed the other items more. Which was a lie. He *wanted* to learn something new. Wanted to challenge himself.

Dalton takes the grouse. When we first met, I'd have been horrified by that. Stealing from the dead? Now I know better. It is a sign of respect. Brent killed these birds, and his efforts should not go to waste. Nor should the lives of those birds. We'll eat them, and we'll remember where they came from.

Dalton takes the bows and arrows, too.

"Jacob made these," he says. "I'll give them back when we catch up to him."

Not *when* we find him. Certainly not *if*. There's very little chance Jacob is in any danger, and it really is just a matter of catching up to him. I know that. Dalton knows that. *Feeling* it, though, is another matter.

Brent said he got my gun away from Brady, and he's right. It's there, hidden in the grass.

I see nothing at the crime scene to contradict Brent's version of events. Not that he'd deliberately mislead us, but maybe he misunderstood. Maybe I'll find something that proves the gunshot *wasn't* an accidental discharge.

"What would prove that?" Dalton says when I admit what I'm hunting for.

"I have no idea. But I want it."

He wisely says nothing and just lets me keep scouring.

"Brady is still culpable," I say. "He held Brent at gunpoint. Whatever happens after that, it's still murder, even if it's second-degree."

"It is."

"And he ground his *fist* in the injury. I don't care how desperate he was to find Jacob. That's sadistic."

"It is."

I crouch and stare at the bloodied ground.

"You want proof he's exactly what his stepfather says," Dalton says. "Proof Brady is more than what he claims — a desperate man driven to desperate measures."

"Yes."

I want justification for my rage. I do want to see Brady gutshot for this. Gutshot and left in the forest. And that scares me. It's the sort of thing Mathias would do, and I tiptoe around the truth of what Mathias is, alternately repelled and . . . Not attracted. Definitely not. But there's part of me that thinks of what he does and nods in satisfaction. I could not do it, but it doesn't horrify me nearly as much as it should.

"I should have come out last night," Dalton says.

I look up at him, as I stay crouched.

"I decided not to come see him last night. I waited until morning."

I rise and walk to him. "Doesn't matter. This happened at twilight. We wouldn't have made it here before Brent got shot."

Dalton says nothing, and I know that will weigh on him. Like my poor choices with Val weigh on me. We haven't discussed that yet. It's not time. Not time for this either, as he pats Storm and then peers into the forest.

"Should see if she can find Brady's trail."

She can't. The blood seems too much for her. It's upsetting or confusing, and she grows increasingly anxious until I release her from the task.

Next we try to "catch up" with Jacob, while continuing to search for Brady and Val. We put up the markers, telling Jacob we need to speak to him. There's no way to warn him otherwise. Despite Dalton's best efforts, Jacob is functionally illiterate. Their parents taught them the language of the forest, the one they needed to know. I get the sense that Dalton had learned how to read and write before he came to Rockton, but presumably he sought that teaching from his parents and Jacob had not.

We head to the cabin Tyrone Cypher has been using as a base. There's no sign of him.

We leave a note, though I'm not sure that will do any good either. Cypher can read; he just might choose not to.

Back in Rockton, there's been no word from the council. Petra and Diana have been taking turns with the radio. We aren't even sure how often they make contact with Val. Maybe, with us being pissed off over our unwanted prisoner, they'll just wait until we call and hope we don't.

The search for Brady and Val didn't stop while we were off with Brent. We join that, and by the time we return home, it's after nine at night. Dalton and I are exhausted. We have one more task, though. Kenny has been in the cell over twenty-four hours, as Dalton lets him stew. We need to talk to him, as much as we're both dreading it.

Kenny was the first true Rockton resident I'd met. My first taste of what to expect in this town. I'd spent time with Dalton, in my admission interviews and then over twelve hours of travel together, yet I had no idea what to make of him. There was so much about Dalton that reminded me of the worst kind of cops — swaggering through life, a bully with a badge. He seemed to fit that slot . . . and then he'd do something to pop him out of it. That was uncomfortable.

I'd met Anders, briefly, and he seemed more my kind of colleague, competent and personable. But after maybe five minutes in Rockton, they'd both had to rush off to an emergency, and I'd made my way to town alone.

Go in the back door of the station. Stay there. Anyone comes into the office? Tell him to come back when we return.

Those were Dalton's orders, which seemed a little disconcerting, as if the locals were wolves who might pick me off while the alpha was away.

It was Kenny who came into the station. As I discovered later, a bunch of the militia guys had drawn straws to see who got to introduce himself to the "new girl" first. That's what I'd been to them. Not their new superior officer. Not the new detective. A new woman in town. An addition to Rockton's meager dating pool.

Kenny had exactly two minutes with me before Isabel showed up and shooed him off. I remember her asking if I could guess what he'd done in his former life. Given the size of his biceps and the perfume of sawdust, I'd guessed carpenter or construction worker. High school math teacher, she said.

When he arrived eighteen months ago, he'd never have worked up the courage to talk to you. People come here, and it's a clean slate. A chance to be whoever they want for a while.

What Kenny wanted to be was one of the cool kids. For a guy like him, cool meant tough. Except he lacked that edge and wasn't terribly invested in finding it. So he settled for hitting the gym and joining the militia. He became the guy he wanted to be. And now he'd been about to leave his new life. Had he panicked at that? Worried he'd end up back in a job he'd hate because his new skills wouldn't pay the bills? Had he been an easy target for Oliver Brady? I desperately want to say no. But the evidence must be acknowledged.

When we walk in to question Kenny, the first thing he says isn't *I didn't do it* or *Guys, come on, you know me.*

"I know how bad this looks."

"Good," Dalton says.

We pull up chairs outside the cell. Kenny has one inside. We've granted him that, in recognition that he's had to wait a very long time for this interview.

"Your knife was found with the prisoner," I begin.

He starts to speak, but Dalton says, "Be quiet and listen."

"Brady used that knife to cut his bindings," I continue. "He used it to take Val

254

captive. You were his guard at the time —
and you were in charge of the guarding
schedule."

"I —"

A look from Dalton silences him again.

"You assigned yourself to that time slot.
You abandoned your post. The prisoner was
left unguarded, with a weapon, while a fire
brought everyone else running. A fire set in
the lumber shed, which you know very well.
It was a delayed-start fire, giving you time
to go on guard duty."

"I —"

"You brought Brady his breakfast. You offered to bring it. We realize now that it was
poisoned — not to kill him, but to get him
out of that cell. So Brady is in the clinic
with his wrists tied and under guard. Fire
breaks out. Everyone runs . . . including his
guard. He is left with a knife and the perfect
hostage."

He slouches in his seat. "Shit. I'm not
even sure where to start."

"Well, that depends," Dalton says. "If
you'd like, you can start with explaining why
you were the one bringing that food tray."

"I took it from someone. She was in a
hurry and complaining about her workload,
and I wanted to be nice." He lowers his
voice to a mutter. "Even if she'd never do

the same in return."

"Jen," I say.

"I'd rather not name names —"

"You have to," Dalton says. "But in this case, you don't need to. That description says it all."

"So you volunteered to take the tray," I say. "Then you volunteered for guard duty at the clinic."

He shakes his head. "I was scheduled for guard duty with Brady here at the station. Will asked me to make up a twenty-four-hour schedule, with me and Sam alternating four-hour shifts. Will picked us two for it."

He pauses and then hurries to add, "Which made sense. Paul's in the doghouse right now, and Will wanted his best two guys. His two most experienced. That'd be me and Sam."

"And the knife?" I say.

"After I offered to help you open that can, someone asked to borrow it, and I said sure, just leave it on the sawhorse when you're done. When I went back to get it, it wasn't there."

"Who borrowed it?"

"I'm not even sure. I was cutting wood, and someone asked behind me. I never turned around. I barely heard him over the saw."

"Tell me about leaving your post."

"I heard the bell. I went outside, and someone said it was a fire. I ran back in. Brady was sound asleep. Val was doing one of her algebra puzzles. I'd talked to her earlier about it, said I remembered giving those to my students. She assured me this one was much more advanced."

An eye roll and a slight smile. "You know Val. Anyway, when I came in, she was absorbed in that. I said there was a fire at the shed, and I should go, and she said, 'Yes, yes.' Those were her exact words. 'Yes, yes.' She never even looked up. I double-checked Brady's restraints, and told Val I'd send someone to take my place. But then I saw you coming, Casey, so I thought it was covered."

Kenny shakes his head. "I made a mistake. A big one. But my mistake was leaving my post. *Not* helping Brady escape. I'd never do that."

TWENTY-EIGHT

We place Kenny under Dalton's version of work release. He'll do the lumber-shed repairs during the day and spend his nights in Brady's new residence, as we give his cell to Roy instead. As for our suspicions with Kenny, we will say nothing to the council. As far as they'll know, we are punishing him for letting Brady escape on his watch.

Kenny will be leaving as soon as this is over, and we will let him go, even if that means he's going to collect a reward down south for helping Brady. Otherwise, if the council knows, we cannot trust he'll survive the trip south, and whatever mistake he's made, it doesn't deserve the death penalty.

We spend the next day combing the forest for Val and Jacob. Dalton's trying not to freak out about that. There is no sign that anything has happened to his brother, and this *is* how Jacob lives. He moves with game and the seasons and whatever whim strikes him.

Jacob's life, though, means Dalton can't pick up a phone and call to warn him about Brady. Jacob comes and goes, and that stresses his brother out at the best of times. The fact we can't find him means absolutely nothing. It's just driving Dalton crazy.

We take an ATV out the next morning. We have three of them — two smaller ones that can take a passenger on the back and a side-by-side that only travels on the widest trails.

I've been trying to talk Dalton into dirt bikes for getting deeper into the forest. In fact, when the council told us we'd get a windfall from Brady, that's what Dalton said to me, trying to find an upside — *we'll get a couple of those bikes you've been talking about.* Which apparently isn't happening now.

We're riding one of the smaller ATVs. I'm on the back. We'll switch at some point — Dalton knows there's no way I'm taking the bitch seat for the whole trip.

Storm runs along behind us. We aren't going that fast, and we don't really have a destination in mind. We're just covering ground and making a lot of noise doing it, in hopes that if Jacob is around, he'll pop out. Or that Val will come stumbling from the forest, having been abandoned by Brady three days ago.

We're zipping along a straightaway. I have my visor open as I scan the forest. Dalton's turning to say something just as a massive shaggy shape tromps onto the path.

"Bear!" I yell.

Dalton hits the brake. The figure in front of us shouts, "Bear? Do I look like a fucking bear?"

The man is over six feet tall. Massive shoulders. Grizzled shaggy hair and beard. Dressed in a brown jacket that he's pieced together from skins and fur.

"A fucking bear, no," I say as I hop off the ATV. "A standing one? Absolutely."

"Ha!" Cypher jabs a finger my way and says to Dalton, "See, boy? That is what we call a sense of humor."

"You get our note?" Dalton says.

"Good to see you, too," Cypher says as he bends to pet the dog. "I'm fine, thank you for asking. Weather's been clear. Hunting's good."

"We have a problem."

Cypher plunks his ass down right on the path and then pulls a kerchief full of jerky from his jacket. One piece goes to Storm. He holds out another for me.

"I said —" Dalton begins.

"That you have a problem. I was hoping you'd say something new and original. You want to know how to solve your endless problems? Take your girl here and leave that piece-of-shit town. I did not get your note. I haven't been to the cabin in days. I heard the ATV and thought I'd say hi. Beginning to regret that."

"Brent's dead," Dalton says.

Cypher stops. He looks at me, as if checking whether he's heard wrong.

"He was shot by a prisoner who escaped from Rockton," I say. "Gutshot. We found him the next morning. He lived long enough to confirm who killed him."

"Fuck." A moment's pause. Then, *"Fuck."* Another pause, this one followed by a knitting of his brows as he looks up. "Did you say *prisoner?*"

When we finish explaining, he says, "You let the fucking council —"

"We didn't *let* them do anything," I cut in. "You know how it works."

"Yeah, which is why I got the hell outta Dodge. You couldn't stop them from dropping off that guy, but you didn't need to accept the delivery."

"Yeah," Dalton says. "Coulda just left him there, a few hundred feet from town. A guy who tortures people to death for fun. What could possibly go wrong?"

"Okay, fine. You had to take him — onto the back of your ATV there, and then head to the swamp and dump his ass. I'd give him three days. If swamp fever doesn't kill him, the mosquitoes will."

When we don't answer, he looks from me to Dalton. "Fuck, no. Do not tell me this guy said he was innocent. No, scratch that. Of course he told you that. The *fuck no* is *fuck no, tell me you didn't consider the possibility.* Well, I guess you know better now."

"Because he ran?" Dalton says. "Yeah, if I was brought up here, held prisoner for crimes I didn't commit, I'd just plop my ass down — like you on this damn path — and sit it out."

"My ass is on the damn path because I'm tired. So is your puppy. I'm resting for her."

"We entertained doubts about his guilt," I say. "Those doubts had no impact on our treatment of him."

"Except that they kept you from dumping him in the swamp. Or taking him behind the hangar and putting a bullet through his skull. That's why you're in this situation, kids. You don't have what it takes to run that town properly."

"No, we don't have what it takes to *be*

run out of that town," I say. "If we killed Brady, the council would have put Eric on the next plane out."

"Not if you did it right. Hire an expert. I'd have taken him out cheap. You could even blame me if you wanted — we took that kid for a walk, and Ty Cypher came roaring out of the forest. You know what he's like. Fucking certifiable. Dragged the poor kid off, and a hail of bullets couldn't stop him."

"What we *should* have done doesn't matter," I say. "The point is that he's out there, and he took Val, and he killed Brent, and I don't care if that wasn't what he had in mind, if I see him, there *will* be a hail of bullets. Our priority right now is twofold. Find Val and warn Jacob."

"Well, I can't help you with the first. If I'd seen a lady out here, I'd have noticed. I'd have come to her rescue right quick, hoping she'd have been grateful."

"Uh-huh."

"Don't give me that look, girlie. I mean I'd have hoped for a reward of the material variety. I'm not a perv."

"Didn't you tell me that you came to Rockton because you slept with a mark instead of killing her? And you slept with

263

her because she was grateful for your warning?"

"Which means I have learned my lesson about gratitude. It is safer in tangible form. However, I can help you with Jakey. Saw him yesterday morning, carving up a bull caribou over by Elk Ridge. He let me have the heart. I am very fond of hearts. Builds strength."

"You ate a raw caribou heart?"

"Fuck no. I cooked it." A grunt as he hefts himself to his feet and hands Dalton the last piece of jerky. "I'll take you to the site. You gotta leave the wheels, though. I'm too old to run behind it with the dog."

"You need more caribou hearts," I say.

"Evidently."

TWENTY-NINE

Dalton is calmer now. Cypher has seen Jacob, and he's doing exactly what Brent said, which explains why he left his last camp and why he hasn't been easy to find. Elk Ridge is north, and we haven't searched in that direction. Brady will head south to find civilization. Actually, the nearest village is west, but he doesn't know that. South makes sense. North does not.

We hide the ATV. It wouldn't have done us any good anyway. The fastest trail to Elk Ridge isn't more than a footpath, soon cutting through sheer rock. As we walk, Storm has a blast, tramping through the mountain streams.

"I want a dog," Cypher muses as she whips past, water droplets flying.

"Well, we do find ourselves in possession of a very young wolf-dog cub," I say. "His mother seemed like she might have been rabid, and the cub bit Dalton, so we're holding him under quarantine."

He glances at Dalton. "Doesn't look like he's quarantined."

I roll my eyes. "The cub."

"It's not rabies anyway. Never seen that in all my years up here." He walks a few more steps. "Wolf-dog you say? How much of each, you figure?"

"More wolf than dog. Just your style."

He gives me a hard look. "Do I strike you as an idiot? Only a fool thinks he can domesticate a wolf. You should give him to your boyfriend there. Seems *his* style. Raised by wolves, weren't you, boy?"

Dalton ignores him.

"If there's a decent amount of dog in the pup, you might be okay," Cypher says. "Too much work for me, but at least dogs are domestic animals. Wolves aren't. Can't be."

"They probably *can* be," Dalton says. "The root genus is the same. The question is time frame. It takes generations."

"You letting him read again, kitten?"

Dalton continues, "There was an interesting study using silver foxes in Siberia. They keep breeding them with human contact. After forty generations, they had domesticated foxes. That's *forty* generations. Going in reverse, with dog DNA already in the cub, it should be easier. You still have the

266

wolf to contend with, though. The question would be mostly one of dominance. Not domestication so much as establishing a leadership position."

"I like you better when you act stupid, boy."

"I like you better when you don't."

"Who says I'm acting? You keep your wolf-dog. Getting too old for that dominance shit. Had that already with a dog like yours. Bull mastiff. Took it in partial trade on a job. I liked the dog. Didn't like the way its master was treating it — the guy figured he'd beat the dog into submission. So I persuaded him to part with the beast."

"Uh-huh."

"It was a civil conversation. I asked nicely. The guy laughed, said the dog was a fucking purebred, too rich for my blood. So I asked again, said he could take five hundred off my pay. He agreed. Well, he nodded. Had some trouble talking dangling two feet off the floor with my arm crushing his wind-pipe."

"You're very persuasive."

"You have no idea, kitten." He looks at Dalton. "I want a dog. You got this fancy purebred for your girl. I don't need anything that nice, but I don't want some mangy mutt either. If I find this Brady guy and take

267

him off your hands, I get a dog, okay?"

"If you find *Val,* you get a dog," Dalton says. "After Brent, the other bastard can die out here. If he hasn't already."

Cypher keeps us entertained on the walk. Or I'm entertained. When it comes to Tyrone Cypher, I can never tell how Dalton feels. If asked, he grumbles and rolls his eyes and grumbles some more. I believe he sees Cypher the same way one might view the grizzly the big man resembles — potentially dangerous, potentially useful, trustworthy enough if you know how to approach him but, really, you should probably avoid it if you can.

I like Cypher, but I respect Dalton's wariness. Cypher is the only person here who knew Dalton when he was brought to Rockton. When we first met, Cypher mocked Dalton by calling him "jungle boy" and making his "raised by wolves" jabs. Having gotten to know the man better, I think he was teasing. But those jabs cut deep. Dalton might not be that boy anymore — and he was never the half-wild savage Cypher claims — but he feels like he was, like he still is in some ways, and that's the sharpest needle you can dig into someone, piercing straight into their best-hidden insecurities.

268

There's more to it, too. I've never met Gene Dalton — the former sheriff — but I used to presume Dalton inherited his personae from him. The profanity. The swagger. The creative punishments. The hard-assed sheriff routine that is fifty percent genuine and fifty percent bullshit. Then I met Cypher, and I realized it wasn't Gene Dalton the boy from the woods had admired and emulated.

That boy wouldn't have necessarily admired the man I've since realized Gene is — quiet, thoughtful, fair and reasoned. No, if that boy was going to look up to someone, it'd be Cypher, larger than life, everyone scurrying from his path, a man both feared and respected.

The problem is that Dalton didn't stay a boy. He grew into a man who sees Cypher's shortcomings. Who realizes Cypher was more feared than respected and that maybe he enjoyed meting out his creative punishments a little too much.

But the die had been cast. Dalton still subconsciously emulates his first role model.

We're nearing Jacob's camp.

"He should be here," Cypher says. "When I talked to him yesterday, he said he wanted to finish butchering the caribou. If he's gone, he won't be far.

"Jake!" Cypher booms. "Yo, Jakey!"

There's a sound from up ahead, and through the trees I make out the side of a hide tent. Another sound comes, a grunt, and Dalton's arm shoots up to stop me.

Cypher swears under his breath. Storm catches a smell in the air, and her fur rises as I grab for her collar. Dalton pulls back a branch.

"And *that,* kitten, is a bear," Cypher whispers.

It is indeed, and it's right there, next to Jacob's tent, ripping through a pack on the ground. It's not a grizzly, which is some relief. It's a big black, though. A boar in his prime, maybe three hundred pounds. When he stands to sniff the air, he stretches to my height.

I cast a quick look around the camp. There's no sign of Jacob, and I exhale. While black bears aren't nearly as dangerous as browns, they can kill if provoked. Jacob knows better than to provoke one. Cypher on the other hand . . .

"You got a clear shot at it, kitten?" he asks.

"Only if it attacks," I say.

"If you've got a clear shot, take it."

"No," Dalton says. "She won't. We can't skin it here, so we're not taking it down unless we have to."

"Fuck, don't tell me you're one of those. Doesn't like killing things unless they need killing."

"Weird, I know," I say.

"Life's a whole lot less dangerous if you just take out everything in your path. Kill or be killed. It's the way of the jungle."

"We're not in the jungle," Dalton says. "This is boreal forest."

"Stop reading, okay? Just stop." Cypher sighs. "Fine, so how you want to do this, nature boy? Ask the bear if we may approach?"

"We're going to spook it. Casey can cover —"

Storm growls.

"I think your pup wants in on the fun," Cypher says.

Storm growls louder. She's straining at my grip, every hair on her body raised, head lowered. The bear rears up again and looks our way.

"Fuck," Cypher says. "Can we shoot it now?"

"Well, that depends," Dalton says. "Unless you've actually learned to aim a gun, you'd have to hold the dog while Casey shoots. And pray that Casey's nine-mil will take the bear down in one shot from this distance."

"You've got a three-fifty-seven."

"I'm left-handed."

Cypher glances at the sling on Dalton's left arm. "Can't just be right-handed like normal people. Fucking inconvenient, you are."

"Eric?" I say. "As fun as this debate is, I'm going to back Storm up before that bear decides to charge. Ty, take my gun. Eric, if you need to shoot, even with your right, you'll probably do better than him."

"Guns are unsporting," Cypher says. "I fight with my hands."

"You do that then, and I'll keep my gun."

"I'd rather you kept it anyway," Dalton says.

I start backing Storm up. It's a tug-of-war, but she allows me to inch her away. Dalton lopes off to the side, making just enough noise to pull the bear's attention.

I continue backing off until we've lost sight of them, and that's when Storm finally settles. She grumbles and grunts, not unlike a bear herself, her shaggy head turning from side to side as she sniffs the air. I manage to get her lying down and park my butt on top of her.

I hear a "Hie! Hie!" from the camp. That's Dalton. Cypher uses more colorful language to convince the bear it's time to go. Both crash through the undergrowth, making as much noise as they can. When a shot fires, I tense and Storm whines, but it's a warning shot, followed by crashes heading the other way and accompanied by the grunts of a fleeing bear.

"Casey?" Dalton calls.

"Right here!"

"He's taking off. We're going to check out the camp. Are you okay where you are?"

"I am."

"Then stay there with Storm in case the bear circles back."

"Got it."

I listen to the forest, gun in hand, but all I can hear is the rustle and murmured talk of the men at Jacob's campsite.

And then Storm leaps up. Leaps up, toppling me off her, and by the time I realize what's happened, she's a black blur disappearing into the forest.

I race after her. It happens so fast that I presume she's heading for the campsite, and I'm not too concerned about that. Then I realize we're heading in the opposite direction.

I should have shouted. If I'd even just yelled for Storm, Dalton would have heard it. I do now. I call for her, and I call for him, but I'm still running, stumbling through thick undergrowth, and I can tell my voice isn't loud enough to carry back to Dalton. But I cannot stop because in that moment, I am absolutely certain that if I do not catch Storm, I've lost her. She's running, and I see her, and as long as I can do that, I still *have* her.

I stop shouting for Dalton and call to her instead. *Storm. Get back here. Stop. Come. Wait.*

It's too many commands. I know that. I'm panicking and shouting whatever comes to mind, and she is not stopping. Goddamn it, she is not stopping. I should have her on a leash. She isn't ready for this, not well enough trained, and my hubris has failed her.

The ground opens up as we veer toward the mountain base. I can see her easily now, bounding over the rock. She's chasing something. I catch a glimpse of brown fur. Tawny. A deer? It leaps over rock, and as it jumps onto one, I see . . .

I see that it's not a deer.

THIRTY

When I realize what Storm is chasing, I scream at her. "Stop! Storm! Stop now!"

She just keeps bounding after a massive tawny brown cat.

A mountain lion.

"Stop!" *Please, please, please, baby, stop.*

She does not stop. Does not seem to hear me. She scrambles over the rocks, letting out a happy bark as she closes in on her quarry.

Quarry? No. Storm has no sense of other animals as prey. We have not taught her that.

We *should* have taught her that.

We didn't get her as a hunting dog, and we don't want her chasing down animals. She's had exposure to many — foxes, deer, rabbits. But they aren't prey. They're chase toys. They run, and she pursues until they take cover, and she loses the game. She's never caught anything bigger than a mouse that she once surprised, and then she just tossed it about until we got it away from her.

In failing to teach her, I have been, in my way, like my parents, failing to prepare me for life's dangers. Because what she is chasing right now is not a chase toy. It will not take cover. It is a predator, and when it turns on her, she will not flee. She will not attack. She'll think the game has taken an exciting new twist — not a chase toy, but a playmate. An animal her own size who is turning around to say, "Tag, you're it," like her human playmates do.

I'm screaming at her, and I know she can't hear me. There's a sharp wind coming off the mountain, blowing my shouts away. I'm not even sure she'd hear me without that. Her ears are filled with the pound of her oversized paws and the heave of her panting breaths and the thump of her adrenaline-charged heartbeat.

I have my gun out. I've had it ready since I realized what Storm is chasing. But I can't get a shot. She's too close to the big cat.

The cat is drawing her into its territory, its comfort zone. Cougars are death from above. The silent plunge from a tree or a rocky overhang. A deadweight thump on your back. Powerful jaws clamping around your neck. Spinal cord severed, you're dead before you hit the ground.

This cougar is luring Storm in. It will make one incredible leap onto a rock — a leap that requires feline hindquarters — and will leave the canine scrambling at the base. Then it will pounce. And that will be my chance. I'll see it spring onto that rock where Storm cannot follow, and when the big cat turns around, I will shoot. I will empty my goddamn gun if I have to.

We're scrambling up the mountainside. The cougar looks back a couple of times, obviously shocked that such a massive canine is keeping up. Storm is big, but she's young and agile, not yet the lumbering Newfoundland she'll become.

The cat veers suddenly. I see where it's going — the perfect overhang. But it has miscalculated. That rock is at least twenty feet above the path. The cougar can't possibly make the leap. Yet it intends to try. Still running, it hunkers low, gaze fixed on that spot. It slows, and Storm is gaining and oh, shit, no. Storm is gaining, and the cat will realize it can't make that jump. Storm will leap and —

The cougar jumps. I see it crouch, see its hind muscles bunch, see it spring, and as terrified as I am for Storm, I cannot help but mentally freeze-frame the sight, awed by the beauty and perfection of that huge cat in flight.

It lands squarely on the ledge. The shock of that freezes me again. Then the cat disappears, turning around, and I jolt from my surprise to remember my shot.

I raise the gun and look down the sights. The moment the cat appears, I will fire.

At the base of the overhang, Storm barks, jumping and twisting, as if she can reach it.

The cat's ears appear first. Tawny black-rimmed ears. Then the top of its head, dark line down the middle, perpendicular dark slash over each eye. When the pink nose emerges, I start to squeeze the trigger. A chest shot would be better, but any shot at all should spook it, and if it runs the other way instead of pouncing, Storm will be safe, stuck below —

Storm gives one last bark . . . and tears off. I glance away from the gun just in time to see her racing along the rock. Looking for another way up.

Damn it. This is one time when I really wish I had a dumber dog.

"Storm!" I call. She has to hear me now. The cougar does. Its gaze swings my way, and I'm close enough to see those amber irises. Close enough to make eye contact and feel a stab of regret and a hope that my bullet will miss, and the big cat will be frightened off —

Another bark. The sound of paws scrabbling on rocky ground. The sound of paws finding purchase, finding a path, pounding up the mountainside . . .

Shit!

The cougar's head disappears. I fire anyway. Fire and hope the sound will send it running. But I only take that one shot, and then *I'm* running, tearing in the direction Storm went. I can see her, black against the gray rock, making her way up the mountainside, determined to win this game of catch-me.

"Storm!" I call as I run.

She hears me then. Looks back and gives a happy bark. *Mom's playing, too, this is awesome!*

"Storm, come —"

I stop myself. Focus. Breathe. I'm cold with panic. Literally icy with it, cold sweat dripping down my face as I shiver, each breath scorching my lungs, my heart pounding so hard my vision clouds. This is terror. Like seeing that sniper in the tree, Dalton lunging, Dalton falling — but that was a mere second of panic, the thin space between seeing him fall and seeing him alive and breathing. This seems to go on forever.

When I saw what Storm was chasing, I knew she could die. I realized death was a very real possibility and maybe even a probability, and it was all my fault. She trusted me, and I should have known better, and who the fuck — who the *fuck* — was I to think I could protect anything. I have never in my life been able to do that. I've spent years barely able to keep myself moving forward.

Don't rely on me. Just don't. I will do what I can, *everything* I can, but please do not rely on me. Do not give me that responsibility. I will fail.

I am about to fail.

Stop. Focus. I have one last chance. Storm can hear me, and any moment now, that cougar will appear and leap from a rock I can't even see down here.

"Storm? *Stop.*"

I don't shout it. I say it. Loud. Firm. Angry even. Let her know I'm angry. That is the key here. She doesn't understand fear. She doesn't understand shrieking panic. That is not the language I have taught her.

"Storm. Stop."

She skids to a halt and glances over her shoulder and in her eyes, I see confusion. Hurt and confusion.

"Storm. Stay. Storm? Bad girl."

Her ears droop at that, muzzle dipping. She knows she has misbehaved. Knows she has run from me. I must use that.

"Storm? Come."

I'm still walking, as I extend my hand, reaching for her, my gaze on the rocks above. She's almost to me when I see a flash of tawny fur. That's all I see — a blur, as the cougar leaps and shit, oh, shit, no, the big cat is in flight, dropping toward Storm, who is making her way slowly to me, her head and tail down.

I fire. Shot after shot, I fire as the cougar is in flight. The big cat jerks, bullets ripping through its underside in a burst of blood. But it is still falling. Still on trajectory to hit Storm.

"Storm!" I yell, and that only confuses her, and she slows, her head lifting.

The cougar lands square on Storm's back, and I'm flying forward. A voice in my head shouts for me to stop, just stop. It's Dalton's voice, not mine. Mine is silent, accepting, and I'm sailing at the cougar, gun dropped, hands out as if I can physically wrench the big cat off Storm.

The dog bucks, her eyes rolling in terror. The cougar's jaws open. I hit it, both hands slamming into its side. One massive fang slices into Storm's shoulder. Slices in and

281

rips as the big cat falls. I'm on it then, and a memory flashes, Cypher telling me he wanted me to teach him aikido so he could take down the man-eating cougar out here. I remember rolling my eyes at that. He was joking. Had to be joking. No one would attempt anything so stupid.

I'm falling, my hands wrapped in brown fur. Fur slick with blood, blood pumping from multiple shots in the cougar's white underbelly. We go down, and I'm atop the big cat, and all I can think is *What the hell are you going to do? Wrestle it to death?* I grab for my knife. I'm still pulling it out as we roll, and I rear up, knife raised.

The cougar stays on the ground.

I'm poised there, adrenaline pounding. The big cat lies on its side, flanks heaving, blood pumping from the bullet wounds. The cat's mouth opens, and it is breathing hard. Its eye rolls to look at me, and in it, I see a look I know well, from Storm when she is injured.

I don't understand.

I hurt, and I don't understand.

Storm moves up beside me. Blood seeps from her shoulder, but she's walking fine. She sniffs the cat's injured belly and whines. Then she lowers herself at my side and lays her big muzzle on my foot as she watches the cat.

I tentatively reach out and place my hand on the cougar's shoulder. That amber eye meets mine, but the cat just keeps breathing hard, gasping for air.

Dying.

When I shot Blaine, I saw him die. It took only a moment, but I had to watch it — the outrage, the anger, the disbelief. While he had not deserved what I did, he was not blameless. The punishment simply did not fit the magnitude of his crimes.

This cougar *is* blameless. It ran from a predator. It tried to stop a threat. It did what it needed to survive. And I shot it. Emptied my gun into it.

It's a young cougar. I see that now. A male, the size of Storm, which means it isn't more than a couple of years old. One of the man-eater's cubs. A beautiful creature, covered in blood, dying and confused.

Storm whimpers, and I know I have to tend to her, but I can't leave the cat to die alone. Maybe that's overly sentimental, but I feel I owe it something.

No, I *know* what I owe it. The question is whether I can do it. I don't want to. I have to. It is gutshot, like Brent, and if I walk away, it will lie here for hours, slowly dying.

I steady my knife. Then with my left hand, I rub the fur behind its ears. I half expect it to snarl, to tense, but that eye closes and the big cat relaxes under my fingers. I grip the knife firmly in my right hand, find its jugular, and slice, as quickly as I can. The cat's eye flies open, but it doesn't lift its head. With the pain from its stomach, it barely notices the cut. I keep rubbing its head, and that eye closes, and after a moment the cougar goes still.

THIRTY-ONE

I take only a second to regroup. Then I'm checking Storm's shoulder. There's a gash where the cougar's fang pierced and then sliced, and that, too, is my fault — I'd hit the cat as the fang caught.

Of course, if I *hadn't* hit, all four canines would have ripped out the back of Storm's neck. But I'm good at taking blame. Two seconds faster, and I could have saved her from any injury at all.

I have a rudimentary first-aid kit on my equipment belt. When I was a constable, I hated the equipment belt. Gun, baton, radio, cuffs, flashlight . . . The damn thing weighed fifteen pounds, and I consider myself in good shape — need to be in my profession — but I was still half the size of my partners, and my belt was just as heavy as theirs. I would long for the day when I could trade my belt for a shield. It came quickly — my education fast-tracked me to detective — but I still remember the damn belt. Now I must wear one again, and I'm fine with that. I've actually added items to what Dalton considers essential for venturing into the wilderness. The mini first-aid kit is one of my extras. God knows, we need it often enough.

I clean and suture Storm's shoulder. She is remarkably good about that. Part of it is that she's been stitched before, more because her owners are anxious new parents than because her wounds actually required stitches. I suspect her stillness is also because she knows she's in trouble. And part is, I fear, shock. Shock that this beast hurt her. Shock that her attacker now lies warm and motionless and bloody on the ground.

I don't understand.

I hurt, and I don't understand.

I rub her ears and pet her and talk to her. She nudges the cougar a few times, as if seeing whether it will rise. Nudges. Sniffs. Lies down with her head on its foreleg and sighs.

I'll come back for the cougar's hide. While that sounds callous, it is the opposite. I don't want this hide. I want to say it's ruined and leave it here. But only the belly is shot, and this is what Dalton has taught me, that if we must put down a wild animal and there is any use to be made of its remains, then we must do that. Leaving it to rot is a last resort when, as with the mother wolf-dog, there is nothing to be taken.

I heave to my feet, and maybe I'm in a bit of shock myself, because it's only then that I think, *Oh, shit. Dalton.*

In everything that has happened, I've forgotten how it started. That Dalton and Cypher were checking Jacob's campsite while Storm bolted, and Dalton never realized I'd taken off. He's certainly realized it by now.

I need to get back to him.

I look around, and . . .

Which way is back?

Down the mountainside. I know that much. But from there . . . ?

I ran after Storm, focused only on her, paying no attention to my surroundings.

Shit.

No, I'm fine. There's a damn mountain here, a massive landmark. I know Jacob's encampment was near the base. It's just a matter of orienting myself.

I tell Storm to stay. She doesn't appreciate that, but when I insist, she wisely decides she has disobeyed me enough for one day, and she plunks down with only a grumble.

I climb up to where the cougar had leapt from. I walk to the edge and look out to see forest. Endless miles of forest.

"Eric!" I shout. My voice echoes over the woods below.

I scan for any sign of Jacob's campsite. Of Dalton. Of Cypher. Of anything that doesn't belong in this forest.

I see trees.

Lots and lots of trees.

Forget landmarks, then. I know I am on the proper side of the mountain. We approached from the south, to the southeast side of Hawk Peak — so called because it resembles a hawk's head, with a jutting rock for a beak.

The problem? From where I stand, I can't tell if I'm *on* Hawk Peak. I'm too close to see the rock formation.

If this is Hawk, then I should be able to see a smaller unnamed peak to the east and . . .

I do see rock to the east. Is it the smaller peak . . . or just rock? Damn it. I'm just too close to judge.

I know my way home. That is the main thing. The problem is that Dalton won't go home until he's found me.

I see a stream below. Possibly a small river. I didn't cross one, but I do recall running through marshy land. There's mud on my boots, so that seems to be the generally correct direction.

I unwind a strip of bright yellow cloth from my belt. Last winter I got lost in the woods during a snowstorm, and I'd been grateful for a particularly ugly scarf Anders gave me. So Dalton now insists everyone carry a strip of bright fabric. I fasten it to this rocky ledge to mark the spot where I've left the cougar. I also attach a note for Dalton.

We're fine. I'm going to try to find the campsite again. If you aren't there, I'm heading for the ATV. I know where I am. I won't wander.

Except, of course, I have already wandered, and by saying I know where I am, I mean only the rough geographic area. Rockton encompasses about fifteen acres. It seems a huge and exposed parcel of land, but it is tiny in this massive forest. It isn't as if I can just keep heading in a compass direction and not miss it.

I won't worry about that. I have my gun and extra ammo. I have energy bars. There's plenty of fresh water. It's good weather. Storm and I will be fine. This is the mantra

I repeat to myself as I make my way back to my dog.

She's where I left her. I give her a strip of dried meat and a pat, and we set out. I watch her movement. Going downhill isn't easy with her shoulder. She takes it slow, growling now and then, as if frustrated by the impediment. I know exactly how she feels — I do the same, as old injuries in my leg protest the steep downward climb.

As we near the base, I know this isn't the spot we went up — it's too steep. I'm looking for an easier route down when Storm goes on full alert. She starts to whine, her tail wagging.

"Eric?" I ask her.

Her whole body quivers as she dances from paw to paw, her nose raised to catch a scent.

I say "Eric?" again, to be sure. She whines louder, giving me this look as if to say, *Well, obviously. What are we waiting for?*

"Slow," I say. She bounds forward. I call, "Slow!," and she gives me a reproachful glance as she takes it down to a walk.

We make our way down the steep incline. I hope it's Dalton she smells. Names are something she's learned only from general usage. If I say "Where's Eric?" she'll look for him. And one of Dalton's favorite games

290

is to hear me coming up the steps and hold the door closed, saying to Storm "Is that Casey? No, I don't think that's Casey. Are you sure it's Casey?" while the poor puppy goes nuts. I've said one of these days, she's just going to get fed up and bite him, and I won't blame her. If she doesn't, I will — especially if he's holding the door shut when it's thirty below.

I test Storm, saying "Is that Eric?" as we walk, but that only makes her pick up speed, leaving me stumbling over rocky ground to keep up. I quit that before I lose her again. Another thing to add to my duty belt — nylon rope for a temporary lead. I search for something else to use, but I'm not wearing a regular belt, and I have gauze pads, not strips. So, I just keep calling "Slow!" when she bounds ahead, and then I get those looks, like she's humoring Granny with the bad hip.

We're definitely not going the same way we came in. I try not to worry about that. I still have my landmarks, and Storm is on a scent that is almost certainly Dalton's. When I hear something in the trees ahead, I call, "Eric? Tyrone?," and the long muzzle of a caribou rises from a grassy patch. The caribou sees us. Storm sees it.

"Stop!" I say.

Wrong move. The sudden shout sends the doe running, crashing through the trees. I dive for Storm, and I land on her, my hands gripping her collar. But she hasn't moved. She's quaking, watching that fleeing caribou as if fighting the urge to turn tail and run, the memory of the cougar still fresh.

I pet her and tell her it's fine, and I'm fretting about that, whether one bad encounter will now have her terrified of every creature in the forest. But as the caribou bounds off, Storm's shaking turns to another kind of quivering, the kind that says she wants to give chase, and it's a good thing I have both hands on her collar and my deadweight holding her back. The surge of fear has passed, and now all she sees is yet another fleeing play toy.

I sigh, shake my head, and say, "Stay, stay," and then I'm the one fighting an urge. A horrible urge to touch her shoulder, that raw line of stitches, a quick jolt of pain to remind her why she cannot chase things in the forest.

I feel sick even thinking it. Here I was worrying that this bad experience will traumatize her . . . and then I'm struggling against the urge to *reinforce* that?

I finger a tiny scar on my jawbone. Compared to all the other scars on my body, this one is invisible, but for so much of my life, it was "the scar." A permanent reminder that I had disobeyed my parents, and this was the price I'd paid — that my face would never be "perfect" again.

I got the scar rollerblading. I wasn't allowed to rollerblade, of course — looking back, I'm surprised my parents let me own a bicycle. But I'd been at a friend's place and borrowed her blades, despite knowing I was not allowed. I'd fallen and this scar, maybe a half inch long, was the result. After that, whenever I complained about not being allowed to do something, my mother would take out her compact mirror and hold it up for me, and I knew what that meant. *Remember the scar.*

In my head, a barely noticeable blemish became hideously disfiguring. A guy I dated a few times in high school touched it once, when we were sitting on the curb, and he told me it was cute, kinda cool and badass. I dumped him after that, convinced he'd been mocking me. As a child, though, when my mother showed me that mirror, I never felt angry at the reminder. It meant she loved me. It was the only way I knew my parents did. They might not hug or kiss me or call me endearments, but they cared about my safety. Now, as an adult, I'm not sure that was love at all, and yet, when I feel that urge to touch Storm's wound as she watches the fleeing caribou, *that* is what goes through my head. I will touch it and remind her of the danger because I want her to be safe. That is love.

I swallow hard and squeeze my eyes shut. That's not me. That will never be me. But even knowing I'd never do it, the urge still hurts. And on the heels of that comes the reminder that maybe it's a good thing my attack meant I can probably never have kids. I have no experience of how to be a proper parent, and so perhaps it's a decision that *should* be taken out of my hands.

I shake off the thought. Clearly not appropriate — much less helpful — at this moment.

Storm twists and licks my face, whining softly.

"Sorry," I murmur, giving her a pat. "Let's get on with it. Take me to Eric. That's who you smelled, right? Eric?"

Her tail thumps, and I nod, relieved that it wasn't the caribou.

I carefully release her, ready to lunge and grab her back, but she stays at my side for a few steps before venturing into the lead again. As she walks, she lifts her muzzle to catch the breeze, snuffling it, and I call

"Eric!" each time to reinforce that's who we're looking for. There's no sign or sound of him, though, and I'm getting nervous. Nothing here is familiar, and there's no way to be sure he *is* what Storm's tracking. We just seem to be wandering deeper into the forest.

When a distant sound catches my ear, I home in on it, thinking, *Eric.* It's not the sound of people, though. It's water. The rushing water of the river I'd seen from the ledge.

Good, I'm on target. We'll go another couple of hundred steps, and if Storm doesn't track down Dalton, we'll swing east and try to find our way back to Jacob's camp.

Storm gives a happy bark and looks at me, tail wagging.

"You smell Eric?" I say.

She whines and dances.

I smile. "Okay then."

She takes off like a shot. I jog after her. The ground is more open here, and I can easily track her as she runs. I don't see anything ahead, but she very clearly does, tearing along, veering to the left, me jogging behind, my footfalls punctuating the burble and crash of water over rapids —

Water.

River.

To the left.

That's what Storm is running to. Not Dalton, but the one thing she can resist even less than fleeing prey: the siren's call of water.

I shout, calling her back, but she keeps running. I don't know if she literally can't hear me, being too far away, or if she figuratively can't hear, the call of that water too great.

Damn it, we need to work on this. Buy a whistle and train her to come to it.

We also need to seriously consider that pool. It might help with her water fixation. I can't blame Storm — Newfoundlands are water dogs. She'll even try getting into the shower with us if we don't close the door.

I'm chasing her at full speed, but I'm not worried. We'll be delayed for a few minutes while she splashes and plays. Then I'll continue on with a very wet but happy dog.

I hear the crash of the water over rocks, and I realize I know where I am. We came this way a couple of months ago with Anders, just as the spring thaw was setting in. He saw this river, rock-filled and fast-running, and said it'd be perfect for white-water kayaking. Dalton said sure, if he could —

My steps falter as I remember the rest . . . standing on the edge of rock and looking down at the river as Dalton said, "Yeah, if we can airlift you down there."

Down into the canyon river, fifty feet below.

THIRTY-TWO

"Storm!" I shout. "Stop!"

She doesn't slow. I yell louder. She keeps going.

I need a whistle. I need a leash. I need to do more goddamn training with her.

All of which is a fine idea, and perfectly useless at this moment.

We reach the rocks, and she's leaping over them, heading for that gorge.

"Storm! Stop!"

I shout it at the top of my lungs.

Less than a meter from the edge, she stops. Then she looks back at me . . . and begins edging forward, like a child testing the boundaries.

"No!"

Another step. A look back at me. *But, Mom, I really want to go this way.*

"No!"

I'm moving at a jog now across rocks slick with moss. Storm has taken one more careful step toward the edge. Her nose is working like mad, picking up the scent of the water below.

"No."

Please, no. Please.

She whines. Then she takes another step, and she's almost to the edge.

"Storm, no!"

Goddamn you, no. Damn you, and damn me for the idiot who didn't bring a lead.

She's stopped mere inches from the edge.

As she whines, I hunker down and say, "Come."

Whine.

"Come. Now!"

She looks toward the edge.

"Storm, come!"

I hear a noise. At first I think it's the water below. It must be. It cannot be what it sounds like.

Storm is growling. At me.

She growls again, jowls quivering.

My dog is growling at me.

I know it can happen. I've read enough manuals to understand that a growl is communication, and not necessarily threat. What it communicates is a clear no. A test of dominance. Yet it feels like a threat. Like I have failed, and she's questioning my authority. Telling me she's not a little puppy anymore.

"Storm," I say as firmly as I can.

Don't show fear. Don't show hurt.

She lowers herself to the rock in submission, as if I misheard the growl.

"Storm. Come here."

Still lying down, she begins belly-crawling toward the edge.

"Goddamn it!"

I don't mean to curse, but my words ring through the canyon. She whines. Then she continues slinking toward the edge.

My heart thumps. There are only a couple of feet between us, and I want to lunge and grab her by the collar and haul her back from the edge. Yet if she resists at all, we'll go over.

I keep moving, as slowly as I can, trying to figure out how to get her back without turning this into a deadly tug-of-war.

Please, Storm. Please come back. Just a little. I can grab you if you come a few inches my way.

She puts her muzzle over the edge, and I have to clamp my mouth shut to keep from screaming at her, from startling her into falling. She lies there, looking down. Then she glances back at me. From me to the river below. Her nose works. She whines.

"I know it's water," I say as I get down

onto all fours. "I know it looks wonderful. If we keep going down the ridge, there's a basin. You can swim there. I promise."

I'm talking to myself. I know that. But I hope my voice calms her, even casts some kind of spell luring her from that edge.

Again, though, she looks from me to the river. Sniffs. Whines.

I form a plan. It's dangerous, but there's no way I'm taking a chance she'll go over the edge. I creep along on all fours. When I reach Storm, I rub her flank. My hand travels up her side, still petting, aiming for her collar. I carefully hook my fingers around it.

I won't pull Storm until I'm farther from the edge, with a better footing. Before I inch backward, I glance down into the gorge. I'm getting a look at what we face, so I will be prepared should we go over. And the moment I look down, I know I do not want to go over. Glacial ice coming off the mountain has been wearing away rock for centuries, and the walls go straight down. Below, there isn't even a safe amount of water to drop into. It's a shallow mountain river, more of a stream, filled with rapids and —

There is something in the water. An unnatural shape, unnaturally colored. Long and slender. Black on the bottom. Purple and yellow on top. It's the purple and yellow that I focus on. It's a pattern of some sort, and it jogs a memory of me thinking:

I haven't seen that shirt before. It's pretty. Far more colorful than usual. Did she bring it with her, tuck it at the back of her closet, an unwanted reminder of a time when she hoped for a brighter future in Rockton?

This is Val's shirt.

It is the blouse I last saw her wearing.

I tell myself she's lost it, that maybe she removed it to wash in the stream and it floated away and that's all this is. *All* this is.

That's a lie. An obvious, blatant, ridiculous lie.

I see that blouse trapped on the rocks. I see the black below it — the dress trousers she always wore. I see one shoe. One bare foot, pale against the dark water. I see her arms, her hands, equally pale. I see the brown and gray of her short hair.

I am looking at Val.

At her body.

Battered against the rocks below.

Storm whines. I glance over, and she has her muzzle on the edge, her dark eyes fixed on Val. That is why we're here. Not because she smelled water and wanted to go for a swim. She has located her target. We set her on a scent, and she has tracked it to its source.

I reach to pet her and whisper, "I'm sorry."

She nudges me, and then looks at Val again.

Well, there she is, Mom. Go get her.

I can't, of course. Not from here. I'm not even sure I can get to her from below. It's a narrow gorge, and she's trapped on the rocks.

Sure, Val, go ahead and play spy.

It's okay, Val. Just go with Oliver. You'll be fine. We'll get you back.

My fault.

My responsibility.

There is no surge of grief. No tears. I move slowly, looking around for a way to get down, my body numb, the crash of the rapids muted. Storm's muzzle against my hand feels as if she's nudging me through a thick glove.

I nod, and I murmur something to her. I'm not even sure what it is. All I know is that I need to get Val out of the water for a proper burial.

Like Brent.

How would you like to be buried, Val? Before you go, just answer me that. In case I fuck up and get you killed, how should you be laid to rest? Any final words you'd like said?

Tears do prickle then, but they feel like self-pity, and I swipe them away with the back of my hand.

I will get her out of the water. I see jutting rock down there, with sparse vegetation, a bit of windblown soil and a place for me to lay her body, safely out of the water. We'll come for her later. Just get her out before the current dislodges her body and whisks it away.

I survey the cliff. It's impossible to climb down right here — it really is an edge, with a straight drop below. But if I travel farther down, I see a route with a bit of a slope.

I head to it. Storm follows. I reach the spot and tell her to lie down and then, firmly, to stay. She does, head on her paws.

I crouch at the edge. From here, the route looks steeper than it did farther up. But I can do this. Just a bit of rock climbing. I see the first stone to put my feet on. It's a half meter down. Easy. Just back up to the edge and lower my feet over.

I do that. I'm holding on to a sturdy sapling with one hand, the other grabbing the rock edge. The rock should be right . . .

It's not right there. I'm past my waist, and I don't feel anything underfoot. I glance down. I'm about six inches short, that rock farther than it seemed. I take a deep breath and lower myself until my toes —

My foot touches down and keeps going. I grab my handholds as tight as I can and find my footing before I carefully look. I see my boot and the rock beneath it. A sloping rock. Okay, that's not what I expected but —

No.

I hear Dalton's voice in my head.

Hell and fuck, no, Butler. Get your ass back up here now.

I look over my shoulder and see Val's body.

You feel guilty? Fine. You're going to risk your own life to get her out of there? Not fine. Stupid. Unbelievably stupid, and you know it. You aren't saving her. She's dead. She doesn't give a damn if you bury her body or not. Get your ass up here, come find me, and we'll see if there's a way to do this safely.

He's right, of course. This is unbelievably stupid.

The second time I met Dalton, he called me a train wreck, hell-bent on my own destruction. I corrected him — that implied I was a *runaway* train, not a wreck. I didn't argue with the principle, though. After killing Blaine, I never contemplated suicide. I never tried to die; I just didn't try to live, either. Didn't try to stay alive or enjoy that life while I had it. I felt as if I'd surrendered my future when I stole Blaine's from him.

305

Now, seeing Val's body below, I feel as if I have pulled that trigger again. If anything, this is worse, because I didn't act out of hate and rage and pain. It was negligence. Carelessness. But when I think that, I hear Dalton's voice again, telling me not to be stupid. Yeah, he understands the impulse — fuck, yes, he understands it — but we *aren't* shepherds with our herd of not-terribly-bright sheep. Mistakes were made. Mistakes will always be made. But I didn't throw Val to this wolf. I tried everything I could to keep Brady from taking her into that forest.

I still accept responsibility for Val's death. Yet I have to take responsibility for my life, too, for not doing something stupid because I feel guilty. That leaves Rockton without a detective and Dalton without a partner. I have made compacts here, implicit ones, with the town, with Dalton, even with Storm, and those say that I won't do something monumentally risky and stupid, or I will hurt them, and they do not deserve that.

I dig my fingers into the soil, and I test the sapling I'm holding. It's sturdy enough. I brace and then pull myself —

My hand slides on the sapling. It's only a small slip, but my other hand digs in for traction and doesn't find it and . . . And I'm not sure what happens next, it's so fast.

306

Maybe when the one hand loses traction, the other loosens just enough to slide off the sapling. All I know is that I slip. I *really* slip, both hands hitting the ravine side with a thump, fingers digging in, dirt flying up, hands sliding, feet scrabbling for that rock just below. One foot finds it. The other does not. And the one that does slides off, and I fall.

I fall.

Except it's not a clean drop. It's a scrabble, hands and feet feeling dirt and rock and grabbing wildly, my brain trapped between *I'm falling!* and *No, you're just sliding, relax.*

The latter is false hope, though. It's that part of my brain that feels earth under my hands and says I must be fine. I'm not fine. I'm falling, sliding too fast to do more than notice rock under my hands and then it's gone, and I try to stay calm, to say yes, just slide down to the bottom, just keep —

I hit a rock. A huge one. My hands manage to grab something and my feet try, but they're dangling, nothing beneath them, kicking wildly, and *why can't I feel anything beneath them?*

I've stopped. Both hands clutch rock — a shelf with just enough accumulated dirt for my fingers to dig in and find purchase. There. I'm fine.

No, you're not. Where are your legs?

I'm fine.

Look down.

I don't want to. I know what's happened, and I've decided to pretend I don't.

See, I stopped falling. No problem. I've totally got this.

I look down. And I see exactly what I feared. I am holding on to a ledge. Dangling from a rock thirty feet over the water. No, over a thin stream and more rock.

The wind is howling, and I think, *That's just want I need.* But the air is still, and I realize I'm hearing Storm.

Newfoundlands have an odd howl, one that makes them sound like a cross between a dinosaur and Chewbacca. It's a mournful, haunting sound that has scared the crap out of every Rockton resident. It's been known to wake me with a start when she begins howling with the wolves.

"I'm okay!" I call up to her. "Storm? I'm fine."

Even if she understood me, she'd call bullshit, and rightly so. I am not fine. I'm dangling by my fingertips over a rocky gorge.

I flex my arms, as if I might be able to vault back onto that ledge. My fingertips slide, and my heart stops, and I freeze, completely freeze. My left hand finds a rocky nub on the ledge. I grip that and dig in the fingers of my right hand until they touch rock below the dirt.

Then I breathe. Just breathe.

I glance over my shoulder. Even that movement is enough for my brain to scream for me to stop, don't take the chance, stay still. But I do look, as much as I can without loosening my grip.

It's a drop. There is no denying that, no chance I could just slide down. I will fall. At best, I will break both legs, and even as I think that, I know that is extreme optimism. Death or paralysis are the real options here.

I'm going to die.

If I don't die, if I'm only paralyzed, I won't be able to stay in Rockton, and when I think that, it feels the same as death. I want to tell myself I'm being overdramatic, but I know I'm not. Leaving this place would be death for me, returning to that state of suspended animation. I don't think I could ever return to that. I've had better. So much better. If I can't stay here . . .

I squeeze my eyes shut.

Breathe. Just breathe.

My arms are starting to ache. One triceps quivers. I strained it last week in the weight room with Anders, twisting mid-extension as he made a joke. Now it's quivering when it should be fine.

It is fine. It will be fine.

Breathe.

I don't breathe. I can't. That quivering triceps becomes a voice, whispering that even holding on is foolish. I can't hold on forever, and there's no other way to go but down.

The triceps is quaking now, and my right hand slips. I grip tighter. The rock edge digs into my forearms. Blood drips down my arm.

I look left and then right. Maybe that's the way to go. Perpendicular. Get to a safer spot and then slide. I can see one possibility, maybe ten feet to my left. Between here and there, though, the rock is smooth, and I'm not sure I could find hand grips.

Well, you're going to have to try, aren't you?

My left hand has a good hold on this rocky nub. I release my right a little and begin inching it left. It's slow going. Millimeter by millimeter it seems, excruciatingly slow as my dog howls above.

I'm almost there. Get my right hand wrapped around that nub and then —

My right hits rock. Solid, slick rock. My fingers slide. I try to dig in, but there's nothing to grasp, and my nails scrape rock and

there's a jolt, excruciating pain shooting
through my left arm and . . .

THIRTY-THREE

I'm dangling by one arm. My left hand still clutches that jutting rock, but that's the only thing keeping me on the rock face, and the pain, holy shit, the pain.

I grit my teeth and focus on the fact that I'm still holding on. Not how *barely* I'm holding, or how much that jolt hurt. I'm still okay.

Well, relatively speaking.

I make a noise at that. It's supposed to be a chuckle, but it sounds like a whimper.

Still hanging on. Still alive.

I need to find purchase. Whether it's my right hand or right foot or left foot . . . Just find purchase somewhere. Being slightly lower means I have fresh places to check.

Optimism. Awesome.

I start with my right hand. Reach up and . . .

All I can do from this angle is scratch the edge of that rock ledge, and my nails are already torn. I reach down instead. There's a rock there, a nub that I can at least grip to brace myself and take some of the pressure off my left arm. I do that, and then I try with my legs, but of course, that would be too much to hope for.

I'm still hanging off a ledge, my dangling legs nowhere near the cliffside.

I'm okay. I'm okay. I'm okay.

Two fingers on my right hand twitch. I'm holding them in an awkward position trying to keep some semblance of a grip, and they have had enough. Two fingers twitch. Then a third joins in.

No, no —

My right hand slips. That jolt again, my left shoulder screaming as my right hand clamps tighter and —

"Casey? Casey!"

I am hearing that, right? Not hallucinating?

Fresh pain stabs through my arm.

"Casey!"

The voice comes from right above me, and I peer up to see Dalton on his hands and knees, looking over the side, his face stark white. He pulls back, and I want to scream, *No, don't leave me.*

I remember my nightmares after finding Nicole in the cave, nightmares where I'm in

313

the hole and everyone leaves me, and Dalton stays the longest but eventually he, too, gives up on me.

I'm hallucinating. He's not really here. It's the pain and the shock and that memory finding a fresh variation to torture me with.

Even Storm has gone silent above.

Pebbles fall, pelting my face. "Are you crazy, boy?" a voice bellows. "Get your ass back . . ."

The words trail off, and I see a foot over the edge. A boot. Dalton's boot. Vanishing as Cypher hauls him up.

"You want to *knock* her down into that gorge?"

Dalton reappears, looking over the edge. "Casey? Can you hear me?"

"Course she can," Cypher says. "The whole damn mountain can. Now stop panicking and get back from that edge. Your girl is fine."

Dalton snarls something at him. Cypher's bearded face appears over the edge.

"Hey, kitten," he says. "How are you doing?"

He gets a string of obscenities from Dalton for that, but I say, "I've been better," and Cypher laughs.

"Okay," he says. "I'm going to ask you to try something for me. Take your right hand

and bring it up on the *other* side of your left. You need to reach maybe four inches to the left of it."

I do that, and I find a crevice in the rock, one I can dig my fingers into. It's an even better grip than I have with my left, and I ease a little of my weight that way.

"Don't get too comfortable, kitten. I'm going to make you switch hands. Which will be tricky, but a whole lot easier to maintain. Okay?"

"Okay."

He guides me through it, and a few minutes later, I'm still hanging, but in a far more secure position.

"I'm going down —" Dalton begins.

"No, Eric, you aren't," Cypher says. "I'm not rescuing both of you today. How about you help me figure out how Casey can rescue herself?"

"I'd rather —"

"I know you would. But if you try, I'll throw you down there with that poor drowned woman and save the trouble of having to rescue you."

As he says "poor drowned woman," I turn to see Val's body, directly below. Her one arm is stretched over her head, the current catching it in a macabre wave.

"Yeah, she's still there," Cypher says. "Still

dead. Like she was when you apparently decided you had to go after her."

"I wanted to retrieve her body."

"Why? She doesn't give a damn." He shakes his head, grizzled hair hanging. "You almost kill yourself for a dead woman. Your boy here tries to turn this into a double suicide mission. And people say I'm crazy."

"Casey?" Dalton calls. "Don't move just yet, but I'm going to have you keep shifting left. Once you get past that overhang, you'll be able to get footholds."

"Oh," Cypher says. "You're back with us, are you?"

"Have to, or you'll *talk* Casey to death." Dalton leans out. "You're going to be fine, but if at any point you feel yourself slipping, or if a hold doesn't seem as safe, I want you to stop. No heroics. I *can* get down there. Got it?"

"Yes, sir."

Dalton guides me. Whenever he hesitates, Cypher points out possibilities, and they debate them quickly, before coming to a consensus. I move about five feet left and then I'm clinging to the cliffside, hands and feet secure.

"Up or down?" I ask.

"You can make it up," Cypher says.

"I'd rather you went down," Dalton says.

"Please."

When I pause, he says, "It's a crawl with no serious obstacles. It's safer."

I start down. Once I'm securely heading that way, Dalton heads along the cliffside to find a more gradual decline. He'll join me, and we'll see if we can get back to Val. Cypher grumbles about that, but we outvote him.

I make it down. It is not an easy trip. Nor painless or even remotely graceful, as I slide down the last ten feet on my ass, try to put on the brakes, and land in the icy stream.

"It's not a waterslide, kitten," Cypher booms down the gorge.

I wave at him as I get to my feet. Dalton is already down, picking his way along the stream. I wave to him, too, as I start toward Val. She's still bobbing, her shirt hooked on a rock. I can't get very close. She's on the other side, and the stream is a good ten feet across and moving fast with spring runoff. One wrong foot placement, and I'll hurtle downstream.

"Wait," Dalton calls.

"I am."

I sit on a rock. He's discarded his sling, not surprisingly. He's almost there when his foot slips, and I leap up, my hand swinging out. He grabs it, but only gives it a squeeze and says, "You okay?"

"I am."

He nods, and I feel his assessing gaze, stopping on every gash and rising bruise, his lips tightening.

I hug him. Throw my arms around his neck and squeeze, and that's meant to reassure him, but as soon as I feel him against me, my knees wobble and every muscle unclenches, and if he didn't hug me back tight, I'd have been on the ground.

"You're okay?" he says again as he releases me.

"I'm fine, Eric. But Val . . ."

"Yeah, I know. Bastard." He looks over at Val's body. "I don't see the point, Casey. I really don't."

"With people like Oliver Brady, I don't think there needs to be a point. He killed her because he could."

He nods, as if he understands, but I know he doesn't. He can't.

"Let's just take her . . ."

I'm about to say "home." Rockton is *our* home; it wasn't hers. I'm not sure it ever could have been.

"Is there some other place to . . ." I'm being foolish when I need to be practical, so I don't finish voicing the thought.

"We'll figure something out."

He looks over at her. "All right. Trick will be getting her free without losing her. I'm going to grab her leg closest to this side." He starts untying his boots. "It looks about a foot deep. I'll wade. Safer than rock jumping."

"There's a clear path just above that rock. Stick to it or even in water that shallow, you can get your foot caught, and the current will take you down."

"I know. If it feels too strong, I'll drop."

He means that he'll fall on his ass and crawl. That's the way to do it. Twelve inches of water *does* seem like a simple wade, but between the current and the slippery rocks below, it's treacherous. He takes it slow, placing one foot down and making sure it's secure before lifting the other. Twice he just stops and waits until he has his balance.

Seeing Val's body this close up leaves little doubt she's been dead and in the water since not long after she disappeared. Her thin face has bloated, and her slender body strains against her clothing. That amount of water retention suggests he killed her on the first day. I can't see *how* — there's no obvious sign of injury — but I will once I can examine her body.

Dalton is close enough to reach Val's leg. Then he looks about, assessing.

"If you're considering whether you should drop," I say, "the answer is yes."

He lowers himself. A quick gasp as the icy glacial runoff soaks him. He's on his knees, stable now and less than a foot from Val.

Dalton reaches for her trouser leg. Her corpse rocks, as if even his body mass disrupts the rush of water. He lets out a curse and grabs for her, but that movement unsnagged her blouse and her body shoots off downstream.

I take a running leap along the rocky path, but Dalton shouts "No!" and he's right. The water is moving fast, and Val's body is hurtling faster than I can run along this uneven shore.

"She'll come to rest farther down," he says. "It lets out into a small lake. We'll get her there."

We're up on the cliffside with Cypher and Storm. Dalton has explained that he saw my yellow flag, and they'd been by it when Storm started howling. Which means I suspect she really *had* initially scented Dalton and only diverted when she smelled Val — the target I'd set her on. Doing as she'd been told, while her master freaked out, mistaking her for a feckless puppy.

When we reach them, Cypher has something for me. The young cougar.

"You went back for that?" I say.

"Fuck no. I was busy watching you two fools, in case you needed grown-up help. We found him" — he hefts the carcass — "up by your flag. When your pup started yowling, I grabbed the cat and . . ." He swings the cougar over his shoulders to demonstrate.

"And ran down the mountain with a hundred-pound cougar on your back?"

"Wasn't going to leave him for scavengers. That's some fine shooting. I'm guessing by the placement of those bullet holes the cat was midleap when you put them in him."

I nod. "They didn't kill him, though."

"Disabled him. That's all that matters. And you knew what to do next. Put the kitty out of his misery. See, now *that's* what I need."

"Someone to put *you* down?" Dalton says.

Cypher rolls his eyes. "I mean a girl like Casey to keep me company. Smart and pretty, a good conversationalist, knows how to take care of herself. If I found one who could cook and clean, too, I'd be set." He looks at me. "What do you figure my odds are?"

"Excellent," I say. "If you're twenty-five, gorgeous, have a Ph.D., and can bench-

321

press triple your body weight."

"Two outta four ain't bad."

"Never knew you had a Ph.D.," Dalton says.

"And the boy makes a proper comeback. The next step? Make one that's actually funny."

THIRTY-FOUR

Shortly after that, Cypher leaves us. He'll drop off the cougar at his camp, where he insists on preparing the skin for me. We continue on to retrieve Val's body, but we can't find it. She's out of sight by the time we reach the top of the cliffside, and we follow the stream along until we reach the lake where Dalton is certain her body will stop. We don't see her there. At some point, her clothing must have caught again and submerged her body.

I'm not sure what we'll do about this. I want to find her, obviously. But someone else is missing, too, someone who is almost certainly still alive: Jacob.

Dalton tells me his brother's campsite seems to have been abandoned before the black bear found it. It's a hunting camp — a basic tent, sleeping furs, and the backpack we saw the bear rummaging through. The only thing missing? Jacob. That could suggest he was just out hunting . . . if he hadn't left his gun. And the food bag he'd hoisted into a tree was full.

"That makes no sense," I say as we walk. "If Brady found Jacob at his camp, he'd take the gun and food."

"Then he must not have found him at camp. Jacob could have been out scouting."

"Without his rifle?"

Dalton shrugs. "Getting water then."

"And you're sure it was Jacob's site?"

"One hundred percent. His gun. His pack."

I want to say that I don't think Jacob could be captured so easily. Or that Brady would have forced him back to take his supply stash. But, yes, Brady could have surprised Jacob, and he might not have realized Jacob would have food nearby.

"We'll stop at Rockton," he says. "Get Will and a couple of others and head out to look for Val."

Which seems to be the right move. But it's not. This winter, when we had a fatality in town, Anders had said, "I can't fix dead." It wasn't just a gibe, though. It was hard truth.

We can't fix dead.

Val is dead. Brady killed her. We know those two things; so autopsying her body will only tell us how he did it. Brady won't ever see the inside of a courtroom, though, especially for anything he does up here.

I do want to put Val's body to rest, but how much of that is about me and not her? She's gone, and I blame myself, and I want to do something for her, and the only thing I can do is retrieve her remains. Would she care?

No. The only thing she'd care about is justice. If we think Brady might have taken Jacob, that's all the more reason to focus on him.

We retrieve the ATV and return to Rockton. With everything that has happened, it feels as if it should be nightfall by now. Instead, it's two in the afternoon, and we're still able to grab a late counter-service lunch.

Dalton takes Anders, Jen, and another militia member and heads back on the ATVs to search for Val.

I stay behind. One of us should, and Dalton wants me to tend to my various scrapes and bruises and pulled muscles. When I don't argue, he gives me a look, as if to ask what I'm up to, but I tell him I don't want to slow them down, and someone *does* need to be here in case Brady circles back.

Plus, I have to tend to the wolf cub, change his dressings and look for signs of rabies. I think it's the last excuse that convinces him. I'm still worried about Dalton's bite, so that makes sense.

I put Storm in the house. I hate locking her in but the alternative is a recap of pup versus cub.

When I open the door to my old house, I hear the scrabble of claws as the cub races behind my couch. This time, I can lure him out with meat scraps. I haven't proven dangerous so far, and that monster isn't howling and scratching at the door.

I replace his dressings and check for signs of rabies. I see none, and by this point, I'm starting to agree he isn't infected.

As I change his dressing, I resist the urge to scratch behind his ears or cuddle him. That is oddly difficult, more than it would be with a human patient. We're already crossing a line by feeding him — associating humans with food. Yet we aren't sure what else to do, besides declare him rabies-free and dump him into the forest to fend for himself. Abandon him to die. That's what we'd be doing, and neither of us suggests that.

When the door opens, I grab for the cub.

I'm accustomed to Storm as a puppy, where an open door meant freedom. Instead the wolf cub dives back behind the sofa.

Mathias walks in. Before I can give him shit for not knocking, he says in French, "I want the wolf-dog."

"Uh, yeah . . . no. He's not a —"

"Pet. I realize that. No one else will." He purses his lips. "Except Dalton. And of course, you, but you already have Storm, therefore giving you guardianship of another animal would be unfair."

"No one is taking this cub. The whole 'not a pet' issue."

"Which is why I am requesting guardianship." He crouches to peer at the cub. "Australian shepherd."

"Hmm?"

"The dog blood is Australian shepherd. I am familiar with the breed — my family owned several. It's a working dog, like all shepherds. I believe that will help counteract the wolf blood and the combination of the two will produce an excellent guard dog. Possibly even an acceptable hunting dog, given the wolf instincts."

When I say nothing, he looks over. "What is the alternative? It cannot be returned to the wild at this age. It cannot be released once it is grown. It cannot be given to anyone in town who will, despite all protestations, expect a dog like Storm. I have scraps to feed it. I have the time to train it. I am bored. It will be a project for me."

"I'm not sure an animal should be a cure for boredom, Mathias."

"Then consider it a favor. To you. Otherwise you will be placed in an impossible situation. You'll never euthanize an animal you have rescued and cared for. So you will be forced to add it to your household, which introduces a dilemma. It cannot sleep by your bed like Storm, or roam freely as she does. Yet if Storm bonds with the cub as a pack mate, you must treat them the same, which means either restricting her or being dangerously lax with him."

I hunker back on my haunches. "Did you hear about Val?"

"All right. You are not outright refusing me, which means you are changing the subject so you may consider my request. Also you are reminding me that this might not be the time to make such a request. Yes, I heard she is dead. I also know you will feel responsible. If you wish to discuss that, I would remind you that Isabel is the therapist."

"I'm not looking for therapy. Or absolution. You were there. You know what hap-

328

pened. I chose to let Brady take Val because that seemed the best chance for her survival."

"True."

I carry the wolf cub's bowl into the kitchen for fresh water. "The question I want to ask you is *why*. Why would Brady kill her? Yes, we suspect he's a serial killer, but his MO suggests he likes torture and captivity. Would a quick kill serve the same purpose?"

"No," he says as I return with the water. "But the urge to kill is . . . People often use the analogy of hunger or thirst. I prefer sex. Most of us enjoy it, and it satisfies a need, yet we can survive without it. For a murderer who likes to torture his victims, a quick death is akin to shower masturbation with someone banging on the door telling you to hurry up. It won't scratch the itch, but it does the job in a pinch."

I set the bowl down along with more meat scraps. When the cub comes out from behind the couch, Mathias crouches and takes a piece, holding it out.

I make a noise in my throat, and he says, "That is an excellent Momma Wolf impression, Casey."

"You know what I mean."

"Oh, but I do. The same thing Momma Wolf would. Watch myself because you have not yet decided whether I pose a threat to your little one." He feeds the cub. "Are we certain Brady murdered Val?"

"He murdered Brent."

"Which is not the same thing. And yet it is to you, isn't it? If he murdered your friend Brent, then you are not wasting time wondering if he is also responsible for Val. You will determine that when you have the body, but for now, it does not matter."

"Should it?"

"I suppose not."

I want to snap, *Then why bring it up?* I don't. He's only nudging doubts I don't want nudged. Brent is dead. There is no question that Brady shot him. But the question of *intent* is murkier. The gun went off during a fight. I want to say that doesn't matter. Death as a result of an armed robbery is still homicide. Brady also failed to do anything to help Brent after he'd been shot. He ground his *fist* into the injury. Therefore, he must be the monster his stepfather claims he is.

Yet I keep hearing him in the clinic, telling me not to test him, not to underestimate his desperation.

Desperate enough to take a hostage. Desperate enough to threaten to kill me. Desperate enough to waylay Brent in hopes of finding Jacob.

And Val?

When I realized she'd been in the water for a while, I jumped to the conclusion that this proved Brady killed her. Of course it doesn't. In fact, if I'm being brutally honest, the location of her corpse suggests he might not be the culprit. While it's possible that Brady led her up the mountainside and then killed her, I don't see the point of that. My theory was that her body had been dragged upstream by a large predator.

Yet is it not equally likely that Val herself fled in the wrong direction? That she escaped Brady, or he let her go, and she ran toward the nearest landmark? Climbed the mountain hoping for a good vantage point and then slipped into the gorge?

I don't want to think that. I need the simple answer for now — that Brady murdered her and therefore, if I see him, I am free to shoot.

He killed Brent. He killed Val. He is a killer. The end.

THIRTY-FIVE

Dalton returns at dinner hour. They didn't find Val. The stream is too narrow and shallow to miss her body, but there are several pools along the way. We have no equipment for diving, and the glacial water is still too cold for sustained searching. So they return, tired, frustrated, and empty-handed.

Dalton finds me in our house. I'm taking a shower with Storm — kind of — having trained her to lie with her head inside the partially open door so she can enjoy the spray without actually getting in with me.

Afterward, I'm dressing while packing a bag. He's too preoccupied to notice the latter.

"I've decided you're right," he says as he lounges on the bed, watching me scurry about in my bra and panties.

"Am I?"

"About Jacob, that is. There are other reasons he might abandon camp temporarily. Bears for one. And I didn't see his bow. He might have been out with that, got led off by good hunting."

"Uh-huh." I tuck one of his shirts into the bag.

"Even if Brady did get the jump on him, that doesn't mean he *kept* him. Jacob isn't some kid wandering the forest. He knows how to take care of himself."

"He does." I grab toothbrushes and paste from the bathroom. Then I start pulling on my jeans and shirt.

"But if it wasn't easy — or safe — to escape, Jacob would do the smart thing and give Brady what he wants. Lead him in the general direction of the nearest community. It'd take a fucking week to walk there. But that's a week for Jacob to escape."

"True." I heft the bag. "Needs marshmallows."

"Marshmallows?"

"For the bonfire," I say as I head downstairs.

I'm on the first level by the time he calls down, "What bonfire?"

"The one we'll have when we stop to camp. We should get going, though, while we still have light. You grab the marshmallows and bring Storm. I'll meet you at the stables."

■ ■ ■ ■

Dalton doesn't argue with my plan, which is that we're going hunting for Jacob — immediately. All the self-talk in the world won't keep us from worrying. At least searching eases the tension, making us feel as if we are accomplishing something productive.

First, we check the marked tree and find the flag to tell Jacob we want to talk. Next we travel to a spot he sometimes uses for a temporary camp. There's no sign he's been there. He has a more permanent site where he hides his gear, but Dalton has no idea where it is.

He grumbles about that tonight, like he always does. Usually, that's just hurt feelings, and I tease that it's like when the brothers were little and Dalton had hiding spots to escape Jacob. Now Dalton knows what that feels like. It's a good analogy, too. Jacob avoids questions about his main camp because he doesn't particularly want his brother there. Part of it might be privacy, but I think more is fear of being judged.

Dalton is physically incapable of keeping his opinions to himself, particularly when those opinions relate to how others are living their lives. We occasionally need that blunt honesty and hard push toward what we secretly know is the right path. But there's a limit to how much honesty — and pushing — anyone wants, and Dalton struggles to find that line. I think Jacob imagines his brother seeing his permanent camp and finding all the faults with it, all the reasons he should make Rockton his base camp. Better to just firmly draw that line for Dalton. *I love you, brother, but this is my space, and thou shalt not pass.*

Now, though, not knowing where to find that permanent camp gives Dalton a real reason to complain.

We return to the abandoned camp to search it better. We confirm that, yes, Jacob's bow is missing. While he has the rifle, that's mostly for protection. It's the bow he keeps strung across his back in case he spots dinner.

We set Storm to work here. I pull a sweater from inside the tent and let her sniff, and she does a little dance of joy. On the long list of people she adores, Jacob is near the top, and she's been racing about camp already, sniffing and looking for him. Now realizing that *he* is her target makes her far happier than when we gave her Val and Brady.

The moment I let her sniff Jacob's sweater, she's off like a flash. Fortunately, I learned my lesson with the cougar. She's on a lead now, and Dalton is holding it — she can't take him butt-surfing, no matter how hard she pulls. She snuffles around the campsite for about three seconds and then zooms into the forest. She doesn't go far. Apparently, she's found the path Jacob uses for his latrine, which means it's well traveled . . . and goes nowhere useful.

When she comes back, she takes it slower, unraveling scent trails. She follows the one we came in on and then pauses, as if considering. We've been working on teaching her to "age" scents — parse older ones from new.

She circumvents the camp again. Then she takes off on a trail leading into the forest. She commits to this one, which makes things tricky when it goes through trees too dense for the horses. I go back for them, climb onto Cricket and take Blaze's reins. Dalton's gelding isn't thrilled with that plan, but he follows and we circle around while whistles from Dalton keep us going in the right direction.

We spend an hour like that. I ride and lead Blaze while trying not to stray too far from Dalton's signals. Twice Jacob's path joins a trail, which makes it easier, until he cuts through the bush again.

Dalton finds no sign of trouble. No indication of an ambush or a fight. But eventually we hit a rocky patch, and Storm loses the scent. She tries valiantly to find it again, grumbling her frustration when she can't. We have some idea of the general direction Jacob was headed, though, so we continue that way, both on horseback now, while Storm runs alongside, her nose regularly lifting to test the air.

"Satellite phones," Dalton says after a while.

"I know."

I've been advocating sat phones. I remember when I first moved here, I thought that's what Val used. When it turned out to be some kind of high-tech dedicated radio receiver, I presumed that was because nothing else would work. But Dalton and I did some research when we were down south, and we discovered there was no reason sat phones *shouldn't* work. We just don't have them, because they'd allow us to call out, which is against Rockton rules. Also, even calls between phones in such an isolated region could trigger unwanted interest.

We have discussed getting them anyway, for emergencies, and now is the perfect example of when a satellite phone could be a lifesaver.

"We'd need to know whether they could be detected," I say. "And figure out how to get an account without a credit card and ID. They aren't like cell phones. You can't grab a prepaid."

"Yeah."

"It might be possible to buy one on the black market. Yes, I'm talking about that as if I have a clue how to get *anything* on the black market. But I might be able to figure out . . ."

I trail off as Storm stops. She's sniffing the air. Then the fur on her back rises, and she reverses toward me . . . which means toward Cricket, making my horse do a little two-step before snorting and nose-smacking the dog.

I pull Cricket to a halt and swing my leg over, but Dalton says, "Hold," and I wait. Storm growls. I resist the urge to comfort her. If she senses trouble, I *want* her warning us.

Storm is sitting right against Cricket's foreleg. The mare exhales, as if in exasperation, and nudges the dog, but there's no nip behind it, and when Cricket lifts her head, she catches a scent, too.

"Step out."

Dalton's voice startles me. The animals, too, Storm glancing back sharply, Cricket two-stepping again. Only Blaze stays where he is, rock-steady as always.

"We're armed," Dalton says as he takes out his gun. "I know you're there, just to the left of the path. Come out, or we'll set the dog on you."

THIRTY-SIX

Silence answers. I haven't heard whatever Dalton and the animals must.

Then he says, "Storm? Get ready . . . ," and there's a rustle in the undergrowth ahead.

A boy steps onto the path. He can't be more than twelve. I see him, and the first thing I think of is Dalton — that this boy is already older than he would have been when the former sheriff took him from the forest.

The boy looks so young. It's easy to think of twelve as the cusp of adolescence, but it is still childhood, even out here, and that's what I see: a boy with a knife clenched in one hand, struggling to look defiant as he breathes fast.

Dalton looks at the boy, and his jaw hardens. Then he aims his glower into the forest.

"That's a fucking coward's move, and you oughta be ashamed of yourselves, pushing a kid out here. Did I mention we have guns? And a dog?"

The boy's gaze goes to Storm. He tilts his head, and I have to smile, remembering how Jacob mistook her for a bear cub.

"Storm?" I say. "Stand."

She does, and her tail wags. The boy isn't the threat she smelled, proving Dalton is right about there being others.

"If you're planning an ambush," he calls, "you do realize that the person I'm going to shoot at is the one I see, which happens to be a *child.*"

"I'm not a child," the boy says, straightening. He pushes back his hood . . . and I realize he's not a boy either. It's a girl, maybe fourteen.

"And I'm alone," she says. "I came hunting and —"

"Yeah, yeah. There are three other people over there, who obviously think my night vision sucks."

"Sucks what?" the girl says.

I chuckle at that, and she looks over at me. "You're a girl," she says.

"Woman," Dalton says. "And a police detective. Armed with a gun. Now sit your ass down."

"You can't tell me —"

"I just did." He points the gun.

341

The girl sits so fast she almost falls.

I say, "Storm, guard." Which is a meaningless command, but I pair it with a hand gesture that means she can approach the girl to say hello. The girl shrinks back as the big canine draws near. Storm sits in front of her and waits to be petted. Patiently waits, knowing this is clearly coming.

"Three people," Dalton calls. "I want to see you all on this path by the count of ten. Your girl seems a little nervous, and if she runs, I can't be held responsible for what our dog will do."

Storm plunks down with a sigh, her muzzle resting beside the girl's homemade boot, as if resigned to wait for her petting.

"Just don't move," I say to the girl. "You'll be fine."

Dalton begins his countdown. By the time he finishes, a man and a woman have emerged from the trees. Both are on the far side of fifty.

"It's only us," the woman says. "You have miscounted."

"And you have mistaken me for an idiot incapable of counting." He raises his voice. "I see you coming around beside me. Do *you* see the gun pointed at your fucking head?"

Silence. Then a dark figure appears from

the shadows, heading for Blaze.

"Yeah, no," Dalton says. "If you're planning to spook my horse, thinking he'll unseat me?" Dalton lowers the gun a foot over Blaze's head and fires. Cricket does her two-step and whinnies, but Blaze only twitches his ear, as if a fly buzzed past.

"Now get up there with the others," Dalton says.

A young man steps out. He has a brace of rabbits over his shoulder.

"Good hunting?" I say.

He only stares. Keeps staring, his gaze traveling over me a little too slowly.

"Answer her, and keep your fucking eyes on her face," Dalton says. "She asked you a polite question, as a reminder of how civilized people behave when they come across one another, each out minding their own business in the forest."

"You his girl?" the young man asks.

"She's . . ." Dalton hesitates, and I know he wants to say "my detective" because that is the respectful way to introduce me. But it might imply I'm single, and from the looks this kid is giving me, we'd best not go there.

"I'm his wife," I say, and Dalton's gaze cuts my way, but he only grunts and says, "Yeah. My wife *and* my detective."

"What's a detect —" the girl begins, but

the older woman cuts her off with a look.

"I was a police officer down south," I say. "Law enforcement."

"Down there and up here," Dalton says.

"Here being Rockton," the older man says. "I know you. You're Steve's boy. Jacob's brother."

"And you're from the First Settlement."

The man nods.

"We're looking for Jacob," Dalton says. "You seen him?"

The older man and woman nod. The younger man's gaze alternates between me and Blaze, the look in his eyes suggesting we are of equal value, both chattels he covets. When he glances at Dalton, I see the dissatisfaction of a child looking on an older one, wondering what he's done to deserve all the good toys.

The girl is busy staring at Storm, and while Dalton talks to the woman and older man, I murmur, "Storm? Up."

The dog rises, and the girl falls back. No one else notices, and I tell her not to worry, the dog is safe unless I give her a command.

I lean over Cricket's neck and murmur, "Do you want to pet her?"

The girl frowns, as if "pet" is as foreign a word as "detective."

I say, "Storm?," and she bounds over to

me. I bend as far as I can and scratch behind her ears.

"This is petting," I say. "She likes this, as you can tell."

The girl rises and approaches carefully.

"Put out your hand," I say. "That gives her a chance to sniff you, and it warns that you're going to touch her."

The girl lays down her bow first. It's a beautiful one etched with wolves. Then she lets Storm sniff her fingers and lays a tentative hand on the dog's broad head. As she strokes Storm's head, she says, "It's soft."

I smile, and as Dalton continues talking with the older settlers, I show the girl where to pet Storm, and I point out her black tongue and webbed feet. She runs her hands over the dog, fingers in her thick fur, and smiles when Storm licks her arm. She asks questions, too, like whether Storm hunts and if she ever runs off. I tell her about the cougar, and her eyes round at that. I may give Storm a little more credit for "rousting" the cat than she deserves, but it makes for a better story.

By the time Dalton is done, the girl is throwing sticks for Storm, fascinated by the dog fetching them back.

"Harper?" the woman says. "It's time to go."

The girl pats Storm again and gives her the stick.

The younger man says to Dalton, "If you're looking to camp, there's a good spot just west of here. Follow the path and take the first left. You'll see the clearing."

"Sounds good," Dalton says. "Thank you."

I straighten on Cricket. "Jacob isn't the only one we're looking for out here. There's a man. Young, maybe your age." I describe Brady. "He's dangerous. He doesn't look it, but he is."

The young man curls his lip, and even on the faces of the other two adults, I see contempt. Sneering at me for warning them.

"We will be fine," the older man says. "No one out here is a threat to those of the First Settlement."

I want to say no, he doesn't understand. *Do not underestimate the danger. Please.* But I can tell that would be interpreted as weakness. If I fear Brady, that means I am simply not as strong as they are.

Dalton says, "If you see him, the same reward applies. We want him alive, but in his case, we're more concerned with catching him than keeping him healthy."

"Understood," the older man says. Then

346

he calls to the girl, still lingering by Storm, and they return to the forest.

THIRTY-SEVEN

We head off in the direction where the young man suggested we camp. We won't be stopping there. Dalton veers off on another path and cuts back to our initial route. We continue along for another couple of kilometers before we make camp, well off the trail, in a spot sheltered by rock on two sides.

We brought a small tent — a simple pop-up — and we tie the horses right outside it. The clearing is large enough that nothing will get the jump on them, and they are capable of looking after themselves. Storm will sleep inside, on our legs, which makes the tent a bit crowded, but I can't rest if she's outside alone.

Once the tent is ready, Dalton rigs up a simple intruder alert system. Rockton has never had problems with the First Settlement. Its elders are from the town, and while they may have chosen to leave, they respect what Rockton stands for. The problem, as I know Dalton fears, is that those who settled the community are getting old. The girl — Harper — is likely third generation. The farther removed the settlers get from the originals, the easier it will be to look on our town and covet its relative riches.

It's not just Rockton's horses and women they'll want — the differences in our standard of living are clear right down to our store-bought boots and fresh-scrubbed faces. Once the hold of the first generation relaxes, Rockton can expect raids. We both fear that day, and we know it's coming fast.

I start a fire while Dalton sets up the alert system. I'm still a fire-building novice — it really is a skill — but I manage to have one going by the time he finishes. Then we settle in, sitting on a blanket, his arm around my back. From his pocket, he pulls a flask.

"Tequila?" I ask.

"Of course."

He passes it to me for the first slug. There's not much in the flask. I max out at two shots — always. He'll go to two, if we're alone, but tonight he won't, not with settlers in the woods. So he just takes a long sip and hands it back.

"I've got vacation time coming up," he says.

"Do you?"

"Yeah, apropos of nothing except the fact that it's been a shitty day, and I'm trying to think of something good."

"Vacation time is always good."

I feel him shrug, and he says, "Guess so."

"You go to visit your parents, right?"

"Normally." Five seconds of silence. "Think it's okay if I skip that?"

"I think a guy who works his ass off is entitled to do what he wants with his vacation time. They'll want to see you at some point, but not all your breaks need to be family visits."

"Yeah." He pauses. "You like Vancouver?"

"Sure, and if you want me to suggest some places you can visit, I know it well enough."

He glances over. "I'm not going on vacation without you."

"Uh, I don't qualify —"

"Already worked it out. Before all this shit started. I get a week. I agreed to cut it to five days if you can come. I sure as hell wouldn't go to the city by myself." He shudders.

"Too many people?"

"People. Concrete. Noise. When I go to interview newcomers, if it's in a city, sure,

350

I'll go sightseeing. Museums. Galleries. Libraries. Theater. But . . ." He makes a face. "I feel like people look at me and wonder if I took a wrong turn. Like everyone can tell I'm a country mouse in the city. I know that's bullshit. They're too busy to even notice me."

He pauses. "Which isn't how this conversation is supposed to go at all. I think I'd like the city a lot more if you were there, and I'm sure you'd like a civilization break. The way city people take a camping break."

"Am I allowed to suggest alternate vacation plans?"

"Sure."

"Down south, we have what's called staycations, which means you don't travel far from home. That's what I'd like. A five-day hike or horseback trip up here. Would that be okay?"

He looks over. "Is that what you want? Or what you think I do? Because it sounds like backpedaling to me."

He means "backpedaling" to the old Casey. The one who frustrated him because she never *wanted* anything. No likes. No dislikes. Every choice weighed according to practicality and the needs of others.

I scoop up the marshmallow bag and put one on a stick I've set beside us. When it's in the fire, I say, "If it's just five days of camping, then I might prefer a trip to Vancouver. But if it's five days of scouting for a potential site for a new Rockton, then that's what I want. Not a place to start building right away, but a place we know we *can* build at. A spot maybe a day's ride away that we can visit over the seasons and see how it seems, for water, game, other inhabitants, and so on."

"That would work."

"Then it's a date?"

"It is."

I pop the roasted marshmallow in my mouth. As I'm moving back, he pulls me into a kiss. Then he licks his lips and says, "Tastes like marshmallow."

"Shall I roast you one?"

"Hmmm." One brow lifts, his eyes glinting. "Tell you what. You roast one. Wherever you put it, I'll take it off."

"Oh?" I take another marshmallow from the fire, blow it out, and tear off one crisp corner. Then I put my finger in and pull out a dollop of gooey marshmallow. "So if I put this someplace . . ."

"On *you*."

I laugh. "Okay. Well, let's see."

I lick the marshmallow off my finger. Then I have him hold my stick while I slip out of my shirt. My jeans follow in a striptease. Bra. Then panties. Then I'm kneeling beside him, naked, his breath coming fast. I reach out for the marshmallow, take another fingerful, and lower it down. Then I slowly draw it up, over my belly, past my breasts, careful not to let it drip.

"Anywhere?" I say.

"Uh-huh."

"Hmmm, how about . . ." I streak it across my chin. "There?"

He laughs and his arms go around me as he does indeed lick it off, while toppling us onto the blanket behind.

THIRTY-EIGHT

We're sleeping soundly when a scream cuts through the night. Dalton scrambles up with, "Casey!" as his hands wildly pat the blankets. I've rolled just far enough away that he's panicking, and before I can say anything, the scream comes again.

"Casey!"

"Here," I say. "I'm right here."

I fumble in the darkness and find him as he turns on the flashlight. He's looking around, eyes still wide, as if getting his bearings. Storm is on his legs, whining.

"Is that a cougar?" I ask.

A moment's pause. Then he nods. "Could be."

The night has gone silent again. I replay the sound. I know what a cougar's scream sounds like only from anecdotal evidence.

"Have you ever heard one?" I ask.

"Once." Another pause. "I'm not sure that was it."

"Vixen then?"

I *have* heard those screams — female foxes at mating time — and they're chilling, but not quite what I just caught, and Dalton agrees.

"Do you think it's a trap?" I ask.

"Maybe."

A woman's scream to bring us rushing out. Riding to her rescue, worried and still sleepy. Ripe for theft.

"We shouldn't ignore it," I say. "Even if it's a trap, that means those settlers are looking for us. Better to confront them, while we're prepared."

"Yeah," he says, and I can tell he's relieved. Neither of us wants to be the chump who falls for a trap, but we can't ignore it, either.

We dress and then step out carefully, in case the "trap" was just to have us race — weapon-free — from our tent.

The horses are uneasy, Cricket stamping her feet, Blaze casting troubled looks in the direction of the screams. I glance at Storm. She's gazing about, on alert but calm enough that I know no one is nearby.

We gather our valuables — that's another potential trap: lure us away and then raid our camp. We leave only the tent and sleeping blankets behind. Then we set out, leading the horses.

There's been no other noise, and we take it slow. Dalton goes first. He'll have a better idea of where that scream came from. We follow the path to a spot that has Dalton pausing and looking about. He bends to check something at ground level. A grunt of satisfaction before he leads Blaze off the path, following a trail only he can see.

We've only gone about twenty paces before Cricket whinnies. She flattens her ears, her nostrils flaring, eyes rolling. Blaze snorts and shifts uneasily. Storm gives a long-drawn-out whine, her gaze fixed on the forest ahead.

Dalton motions for me to tie Cricket to a tree. He leaves Blaze untethered. His horse has been known to wait half a day by a stream. Cricket is too young and temperamental for that.

After I've tethered my mare, we proceed. Soon I smell campfire smoke. All is silent, though. We go another twenty paces. Storm stops. Just stops dead, and when I try to nudge her, she digs in and gives me a look, as if begging me not to make her go on.

I hesitate. Dalton takes the leash and sets it on the ground. Then he prods me to keep going. I do, with reluctance, but after a few steps, Storm follows. She may not want to continue, but she wants to be left alone even less. Dalton gathers up the leash, and we move slowly through the trees.

The first thing I see is a hide tent. Small and low, shelter for one person.

Dalton's arm springs up to hold me back. I survey the campsite, and after a sweep, I spot what he did — someone sitting by the embers of a fire. The figure is perched on a log and leaning back against a tree. A guard for the night. When I peer, I see the light brown beard of the younger man. I can't tell if he's resting or fallen asleep.

Storm growls, the sound vibrating through her. I bend to reassure her that all is well, and yes, praise her for the growl, proof that these are the settlers who unnerved her earlier.

I take the leash and tell Storm to sit while Dalton moves closer. As he does, I survey the camp again. One tent. A couple of leather pouches hang from trees, along with the brace of rabbits. That tent is much too small for three people, and I'm wondering where they all are when I make out the shape of sleeping blankets, just barely illuminated by the dying fire.

I follow one set of blankets up to the graying hair of the older man. He's sound asleep. I think I spot more blankets beyond him, but they're too far from the fire to be more than dark blobs.

If this is a trap, it's an odd one. I see both male settlers. They could be faking sleep, but it would make more sense to be lying in wait while leaving the woman and girl in sight.

The younger man is across the campsite. Dalton motions that he's going to circle around. Then he stops. Considers. Hefts his gun, held in his left hand, his arm far from healed. He shifts the gun to his right and lifts it. Considers some more.

"Let me," I whisper. I motion at my dark clothing and hair, better able to blend into the shadows.

He nods.

I give him back Storm's leash and whisper, "Stay."

Dalton says, "I will," and then gives me a smile, tight and anxious. I squeeze his arm and set out.

While it's only a quarter moon, the sparser forest here means I can see where I'm putting down my feet. It's mostly bare dirt, and the windswept puddles of conifer needles are damp from spring showers; even when I do touch down, they make no sound.

I head behind the young settler. As I pass the camp, I squint at a second set of sleeping blankets. I think I see a smaller figure. There's no sign of the older woman's white hair, so this would be the girl, Harper.

That means the woman is inside the tent. Where I can't see her and confirm she's fine.

She *should* be fine. The others wouldn't have slept through those screams. Either this is a trap, then, or they woke hearing the screams, recognized them for an animal, and went back to sleep.

I can see my target now. The tree is just inside the clearing. I have my gun out. And then . . .

Well, I'm not quite sure what I should do next. For the sake of a good night's sleep, I'd like to reassure myself that the woman and girl are both fine. I can't do that without marching into camp. I would also like to reassure myself that this isn't a trap. But how do I do that without the risk of waking the settlers, who'll think *we're* raiding *them*?

I circle behind the tree where the young man rests. Then I keep going so I don't emerge behind him, which is never the way to say "I come in peace."

I draw alongside him, close enough to see that he seems to be sleeping, his head bowed. Then I whistle. It's not piercing, but it's enough that even if he's asleep, he should jump up.

He doesn't budge.

Damn it.

Either my whistle is softer than I think, or this *is* a trap, and he's wide awake and waiting.

I whistle again, louder.

No reaction.

I get a better grip on my gun and then retreat behind the tree. From there, I creep forward, no longer worried about startling him. This is a trap. That or . . .

I know what the "or" is. I have from the start.

I slip up behind the tree. I can see the young man's arm, hanging at his side. I take a deep breath and count my steps. Three. Two. One.

The last brings me to his shoulder. I sidestep. Moonlight shines into the clearing, glistening off his half-closed eyes. Glistening off the blood soaking his dark shirt.

THIRTY-NINE

A slash bisects the young settler's throat. It's ragged at one side, cutting upward on an awkward angle. Rushed. But a single slice, deep enough that I see his spinal column. No hesitation cuts, no sign that the killer paused or reconsidered or had to steel himself to do the job.

The killer crept up while the young settler watched the fire. One deliberate slash to end his life before he had time to react. Blood covers the young man's hands as if in his last moments he'd reached up, unable to breathe, grabbing his throat. Too late to even rise from his spot.

I turn to call Dalton, but he's already making his way into the clearing. He sees me bent beside the young settler and knows he is not asleep.

Dalton ties Storm to a tree. She whimpers, but at a firm "Quiet" she lies down. She doesn't want to come closer. She knows what's here. She has always known what's here.

I crouch beside the older man. His eyes are open just enough for me to know he isn't sleeping. The top blanket has been drawn up to his throat, as if the killer tucked him back in. Not an act of contrition — the killer was hiding his work. I tug down that blanket to see the old man's throat has been slashed. There are other cuts, too, on his bare arms, and a clump of gray hair by my foot.

The killer tried to murder the older man in his bed, but something gave him away, an ill-placed footstep or the death gurgle of the younger man. The old man bolted up, maybe getting tangled in his blankets. Rising fast enough to fight, not fast enough to win.

There's a knife by his head. No blood on the blade. As if he'd grabbed it from under his blankets, but it was already too late. The killer had grabbed the old man's hair, yanked back his head and slit his throat. Then he laid him down and tucked the blanket up under his chin.

Dalton is at the tent, sweeping open the front flap. Even from here, I can see it's empty, the old woman gone. Then I remember the second set of blankets by the fire.

The small form within. I stumble over to it and yank back the blanket to see . . .

A pack. There's a large deerskin pack under the blanket. The girl is gone, but someone has made it look as if she's asleep. What's the point of that?

Dalton stands in the clearing. He's peering around, gun in hand, but this doesn't seem like a deliberate trap. The first body wasn't staged in that position. The second was covered, but only — I presume — in case the woman or girl saw a body and panicked.

Kill the two men. Take the woman and girl.

Dalton's circling the camp, scanning it. He walks to the tree where the food has been hung. There are rabbits missing from the brace. Two food packs are missing, too, the cut ropes dangling. Two others remain, and scrapes in the trunk bark suggest someone tried to climb and reach them but couldn't.

"Hostiles?" I say.

Dalton shrugs. He knows I'm just avoiding the obvious conclusion. I don't want to give Brady that power, make him our bogeyman — everything terrible that happens must be him.

Dalton circles the camp. I realize what

he's looking for: items the settlers wouldn't need to secure in trees. I spot cups, some cooking tools, and blankets. No weapons, though, other than the knife the old man grabbed.

On a second circuit, Dalton finds two bows propped by a tree. I check the pack hidden in the girl's bed and find a small knife, a sling with stones, a waterskin, and a pouch of dried meat.

I look again at the girl's sleeping place. There's no sign that the killer went through the pack before putting it there.

Why wouldn't he search the pack for supplies?

Why make it look as if the girl was asleep at all?

I walk to the two bows. Neither has the wolf etching.

"She snuck off," I say.

"Hmm?" Dalton is examining tracks and looks over.

"Harper snuck out." I motion to the bed. "A classic kid's trick. Make it look like you're asleep in case the grown-ups wake and look for you. She took her bow."

I back onto my haunches and survey the scene. "Intruder kills the lookout first. Then the old man. He leaves the girl because either he doesn't see her blankets or she's too small to be a threat. He decides not to bother with the tent — maybe the woman didn't wake up so he ignored her. He takes what supplies he can. But the older woman *does* hear him. She comes out . . ."

I move to the tent and shine my light on the flaps and then inside. "No sign of blood. Does she scare him off? Go after him?"

Dalton points at the forest's edge. I see signs of wild flight, trampled undergrowth and broken branches.

The woman woke and ran.

She did not run far.

We find her body ten meters from the campsite. I would have passed close to it when I'd been circling around, my attention fixed on the campsite, oblivious to the rest.

She is on her stomach. One hand stretches out, fingers dug into soil. Dragging herself away from her killer. A trail of blood smears the ground and undergrowth.

When I see that outstretched hand, I run to her. But she's gone. Long gone, body cooling fast, her eyes as glazed as the two men's. Eyes wide open. Fixed in horror and determination, as if she only needs to get a little farther, and she will be fine.

Stab wounds in her back. Her killer finishing the job as she crawled away.

Dalton turns the woman over.

More wounds there. She was attacked from the front and ran. Realized she could not escape. Turned to fight. Weaponless. Powerless.

A dozen stab wounds perforate her chest.

I'm lifting my head to say something when I see a blur of motion. Dalton does, too, spinning, his gun rising. The running figure gives a roar of rage . . . and then skids to a halt.

It's Harper.

"You," she says, and there is disappointment in her voice. Her brandished knife wavers for a moment. Then it falls.

"They're dead, aren't they?" Harper says. "They're all dead." She looks down at the woman and her voice cracks. "Nonna."

"She was your grandmother?" I ask gently. She nods.

I motion for her to turn away, but her jaw sets.

"I have seen death before," she says. "I am not a child."

I would like to say this is different — and it is — but she can already see the body, and she's not going to listen to me.

"You weren't in your sleeping blankets," I say.

"I wanted to see your dog again." She kneels beside her grandmother's body. "I was heading to where Albie told you to camp. I was almost there when Nonna screamed. I ran back. I . . . I saw him. The man who . . ."

She looks at her grandmother again. Rage flashes in her eyes.

"You saw their killer?" I say.

"I didn't know that. It was just a man on the trail. He had blood on his face, and I . . . I should have done something — I know I should have stopped him but all I could think about was that scream. I raced back here. Then I saw someone in the camp, and I thought the man had circled back. So I hid." She bites her lip and then straightens. "But not like that. Not hiding *from* him. I was preparing for my attack. Waiting until I could see who it was. Only it was just you."

Dalton murmurs to me that he's going to get Storm, whimpering back at the campsite. When he's gone, I say to the girl, "You saw the man who did this?"

"Yes."

"Where was he? How far from camp?"

"A quarter mile southwest," she says, with the assurance of a girl who may not know her times tables but must be able to relate distances and directions accurately, a matter of basic survival in the forest.

"How far away were you?"

"From here to the campsite. I was in the forest, and he was on the path. He was walking away with some of our stuff."

"What stuff?"

"I saw a rabbit and a food pack."

"Can you describe the man you saw?"

"I wasn't that close, like I said. But he was on the path, and there was moonlight. I could see light-colored hair. Straight, I think. Longer than . . ." She gestures toward Dalton, in the clearing. "But not long like yours. No beard. He had pale skin. That's how I saw the blood on his cheek. I couldn't tell his height, but he looked normal-sized. And he was wearing clothing like you people."

She's describing Brady. Oliver Brady killed these settlers. Slit a guard's throat. Slaughtered an old man in his bed. Chased down and brutally murdered a fleeing old woman. There is no way I can say these were acts of desperation.

Also, there was no sign of Jacob with him. Brady was seen a half kilometer from the scene alone.

Brady is not an innocent man.

Brady does not have Jacob.

That is everything I need to hear. Everything I want to hear, too.

FORTY

We hide the bodies under evergreen boughs, which should help mask the smell from scavengers. Then we escort Harper to the First Settlement. She walks while we ride slowly. I offered her a spot behind Dalton, but pride won't let her attempt to ride as a passenger. And, I suspect, it wouldn't have let her ride Blaze alone and risk looking foolish.

Harper walks holding Storm's lead. Now that I'm certain we are dealing with a monster, I cannot risk Storm taking off after her target. I explain that to Harper, who has never heard of using a dog to follow a smell, and she peppers me with questions, distracting herself from the memory of what happened tonight.

We don't talk about what happened. That is how, as a homicide detective, I handled dealing with a victim's loved ones so soon after the deaths. Let them set the tone. If they want to talk about it, I will, while giving away nothing about the investigation. More often, when it's this soon afterward, they either haven't fully processed the death or they are desperate to discuss anything else. For Harper, that distraction is talking about how dogs track scents. Every now and then she'll trail off and look back the way we came, only to shake herself and keep talking about Storm.

It's 4 A.M. when we near the settlement. We don't take Harper inside. We don't even take her to the edge. Three settlers are dead. Edwin — the leader of the First Settlement — will figure out that the killer came from Rockton. That puts us in danger.

The First Settlement is like many splinter groups that break away over issues with its parent organization. They don't hate us. They don't wish us ill. But there is no warmth there either.

I once asked why Dalton doesn't trade with the settlement. We don't need their game, but we can always use it, and what they'd want in trade is paltry to us — some coffee, a new shirt, a gun or ammunition. More important, though, is the bond it would forge. The goodwill it buys. Trade links provide us with valuable partners in this wild life. While Ty Cypher might not tell us that ducks are particularly plentiful on a certain lake, he will mention if he's spotted strangers or a worrisome predator.

To the First Settlement, though, such a partnership would smack of weakness. If we initiate trade, that suggests they have things we need, and that we may be weaker than they think. Weak means ripe for raiding. I will admit I didn't fully believe that until I saw the way the settlers looked at me when I suggested they watch out for Brady. I may have been right — tragically right — but to them, Brady was just a lone outsider. No match for them.

We leave Harper about a kilometer from town. Dalton tells her to explain everything to Edwin and let him know that we had to hightail it back to Rockton, in case the killer heads there. He promises that we'll come by later to discuss the situation. By "later" he means "after we catch Brady."

We don't return for our tent and sleeping blankets. We'll get them another time. Right now we *do* need to hurry back to town. Jacob doesn't seem to be with Brady, and we'll willfully interpret that to mean Jacob is safe. We must return to Rockton, regroup, and organize a full manhunt for Oliver Brady . . . before he *does* circle back to Rockton, once he realizes that escape isn't a simple matter of a half-day hike to the next town.

As we near Rockton, I hear a sound that must be an audio hallucination. I've been working through the case as we ride, and I was analyzing the beginning to figure out what we could have done better. Then I hear the very sound that started this whole mess. Therefore, I am imagining things. Or so I tell myself until Dalton says "What the fuck?" and I glance back to see him squinting up at the midmorning sky . . . as a prop plane flies into view.

Once again, we reach the landing strip just as the plane touches down. Cricket hears the racket and declares she's not going a step closer, and if I insist, then she'll send me there by equine ejection seat. Even Blaze flattens his ears and peers at the steel monster with grave suspicion.

We leave our horses and walk down the airstrip just as the passenger door opens. Out steps the kind of guy who'd seem more at home on a private jet. He's tall and trim, in his late fifties, with silvering dark hair. He has a magazine-cover smile that's dazzling even from fifty meters away. Dressed in pressed khakis and a golf shirt, he looks around with the grin of a big-game hunter, ready for his first Yukon adventure. When he spots us, the smile only grows, and he strides over, hand outstretched.

The pilot climbs from the cockpit. He looks like the passenger's personal assistant, a guy maybe my age, dark-haired and chisel-jawed, wearing stylish glasses that I suspect don't contain prescription lenses. *He* is not smiling. Instead, he bears down on us like we're about to contaminate his boss with our dirt-crusted hands.

"Sheriff Dalton," the younger man says. "Detective."

I know that voice. I can't quite place it, but it's one I've heard . . .

It clicks. Yes, I have heard this voice many times, and I've imagined the man it belongs to so often that I'm sure I'm misidentifying him now. In my head, the voice belongs to an older man, maybe fifty, another middle manager, like Val. A fussy little man with a potbelly and a comb-over.

The younger man passes the older one and puts himself slightly in front, as if shielding him from necessary interaction. Then he extends a hand — to me.

"Phil," he says. "It's good to meet you, Detective."

Phil. The council's spokesperson.

He takes my hand in a firm but perfunctory shake. And for Dalton? A curt nod.

Then he turns to the older man.

"This is —"

"Gregory." The silver-haired man steps past Phil. "Gregory Wallace. I've come to see my stepson."

FORTY-ONE

I glance at Dalton.

Gregory catches the look and says wryly, "Yes, I suspect I'm not your favorite person right now, which is why I'm here. I insisted Phil bring me to see what can be done to make Oliver's stay less taxing."

"Yeah?" Dalton says. "You know what would make it less taxing? If it never happened."

Phil makes a noise in his throat, one manicured hand rising in the gesture you'd give a child, telling him to calm down before he embarrasses you in front of company.

Dalton continues, "I don't know what the hell your understanding of the situation up here was, Mr. Wallace, but we were not equipped to deal with a prisoner of any variety. This town is for *victims*. It is safety. It is sanctuary. It is not a fucking maximum-security prison."

"What Sheriff Dalton is saying —" Phil begins.

"Oh, I believe he's saying it just fine," Wallace says, and while he's smiling, the steel in his voice warns Phil to silence. "Please continue, Sheriff."

"We were not equipped for this," Dalton says. "We were not warned in time to become equipped. Your stepson was dropped off with a fucking bag of coffee. *Here's a serial killer. Please take care of him for us. Oh, and enjoy the coffee.*"

"I don't think this is productive," Phil says.

Dalton turns on him. "You want to talk about productive? How about giving me a damn method to communicate with you when everything goes to hell up here?"

Phil straightens, bringing himself to Dalton's height and looking him square in the eye. "You have a method, Sheriff. Valerie is —"

"Dead."

A moment's pause. Then Phil says, "What?"

"Val is dead." Dalton waves at Wallace. "His stepson took her hostage. Killed her. Dumped her in a river. Casey almost died trying to retrieve her body 'cause a proper burial seems the least we can do. Oliver Brady also murdered Brent, one of our key scouts and local contacts. Shot him and left him to die. Then he massacred three settlers, including an old woman trying to escape. Her granddaughter managed to avoid the carnage, though not without witnessing her grandmother's bloody corpse. We escorted the kid home, but we didn't dare take her inside the settlement and explain what happened, or we might not have walked out alive, considering the killer was one of ours." Dalton pauses. "That's our day so far. And yours?"

Phil's face hardens. "Your insubordination —"

"*Fuck* my insubordination. Go tell the council I was rude to you, Phil. See which of us they declare the more valuable asset."

I turn to Wallace. "I'm sorry we don't have your stepson. Despite the fact we weren't prepared, we do accept responsibility for his escape. I'm also sorry if you were misled about the appropriateness of this solution to your problem."

Wallace rubs his chin. He looks sick, and it takes him a moment to regroup.

"The blame, I'm afraid, is as much mine as anyone's, Detective," Wallace says. "I failed to properly warn you about exactly the sort of monster you were dealing with. I erred on the side of caution, fearing the truth would limit my options drastically. And in doing so —" He inhales sharply and then shakes his head. "Let's get someplace quiet, where we can come up with a solution."

We ride the horses to town, letting Phil and Wallace walk the short distance. When we're out of earshot, Dalton mutters, "Fuck," and I agree, and that's all we say, all that can be said. This wrinkle is the absolute last thing we need to deal with.

When we enter Rockton, Anders and Isabel are striding toward us.

"Did we hear another plane?" Anders says. He notices the two men behind us. "What the hell?"

I jump off Cricket and call Storm over. Dalton wordlessly reaches for my reins, and I hand them over.

"The younger guy is Phil," I say when Dalton leaves for the stable.

"Our Phil?" Anders says.

"Yep."

"Huh. Not what I expected."

"But a not unpleasant surprise," Isabel murmurs as she gives Phil the kind of look I haven't seen her give any guy since Mick died.

"The other one might be more your style,"

Anders says.

She gives him a look. "More my *age* you mean?"

"Nah. I know you like them young."

He gets a glower for that. Wallace is looking about Rockton, his gaze here and there, taking everything in. I can almost see his thought processes — looking for electricity lines, noting the piles of lumber, checking the construction of the buildings and the layout of town, and nodding throughout, as if intrigued and impressed. Phil glances about in mild horror, and I can read his thoughts even better. *Dear God, I had no idea it was this bad.*

"And the older gentleman?" Isabel says, her voice lowered as the men approach. "Judging by his attire, clearly a man of means. An investor, I presume."

"You could say that. He's Gregory Wallace. Oliver Brady's stepfather."

"Oh, hell," Anders mutters.

"Yep."

The men draw close enough for me to say, "Phil? Mr. Wallace? This is our deputy, Will Anders, and one of our local entrepreneurs, Isabel Radcliffe."

Isabel's eyebrows lift at the introduction. I mouth, *Brothel owner?,* asking if she'd prefer *that* introduction, and she rolls her

379

eyes and extends her hand. Phil accepts it with a perfunctory shake, having seen and dismissed her in a heartbeat. Wallace's gaze lingers, and he smiles, as if she is much more than he expected out here.

"Gregory, please," he says, taking her hand and then Anders's. "Detective? If I might speak to you alone, I believe Phil would like to talk to the sheriff."

Phil gives him a clear *What the hell?* look, but Wallace only smiles and says, "I believe you and the sheriff have a few things to discuss. Or *he* has a few things to discuss with you. Detective . . ."

"Casey," I say.

He nods. "Casey and I will be at the police station."

I leave Storm with Anders. As Wallace and I enter the station, he says, "You are correct that I didn't know where I was sending Oliver. I understood the basics, of course. A remote, northern community. Hidden. Untraceable. Designed to conceal and contain those who need concealment and containment. That seemed enough. I made the mistake of presuming this was for people like my stepson."

"It's not."

"I see that now. I should have asked more

questions. An associate told me this was the perfect solution, and I suppose, given what I was willing to pay, Phil's employers had every incentive to agree with me."

"Like Eric said, we just weren't equipped for it." I stoke the fire to start a kettle. "Our police force is just myself, Eric, and Will. We're all experienced law enforcement but none of us has done correctional work. We have a volunteer militia. We have one cell." I cross the room and open the door to show him, and then shut it before Roy can speak. "We couldn't leave Oliver in that for six months, so we were quickly building him a fortified unit. He escaped just before it was completed."

"Can you take me through — ?" The door opens and Dalton comes in, Phil following. Wallace says, "That was quick. Casey was just about to tell me what happened. I'm sure you'll want to hear this, Phil. Please, continue, Detective."

I tell the story.

"The poisoning was real," I say. "Oliver had inside help. He was, as you might expect, protesting his innocence. That's very easy to do when no one here can look up his alleged crimes on the internet. He claimed to have been accused of a shooting spree in San Jose."

Phil's head jerks up, as if he's remembering I'd asked about the shooting.

I continue, "It was far too easy to plant doubt under the circumstances. Yet the alternative was to keep him permanently gagged, which raised suspicions among the residents — they wondered if he had something he wanted to say. We tried to walk a middle line — no gag but limited access. That failed. He found an ally, who got him the poisoned food. We had to take him to the clinic to pump his stomach. We had him restrained while recuperating, but his accomplice provided him with a knife."

"And set the fire," Wallace says. "As a distraction."

"Helluva good one in a town made of wood," Dalton says.

Wallace nods. "As his accomplice knew. I am so sorry this happened. The loss of your town leader . . ." He shakes his head. " 'Sorry' doesn't begin to cover this."

"What was Val doing with the prisoner?" Phil asks.

"She hoped Oliver would see her as a potential ally, possibly even someone he could charm. She was trying to take a more active role in the community."

"Which was her first mistake," Phil says. "The leader of this town cannot become involved in such a way. It blurs lines."

Wallace looks at him. "Are you implying that by trying to *help* her town, she made a fatal error?"

Phil has the grace to color. "Of course not, sir. I misspoke. Val made a questionable choice but what happened was not her fault."

"It was Oliver's," Wallace says. "He is responsible for his actions, something he was never able to grasp, and that is our . . ." He shakes it off. "No blame. Not now. For now, we need to find him before anyone else dies. And then . . ." A pause as he glances away, his voice lowering. "And then we will have to make sure this never happens again, that he never poses a risk to anyone else again."

Wallace squares his shoulders. "That's for later, and whatever needs to be done, it will not involve anyone in this town. I am truly sorry that this happened. I will make it up to you. I know the town was counting on the added income."

"Income?" Dalton snorts. "That's *their* concern." He jerks his thumb at Phil. "We don't give a shit. Not like we were going to see more than a fraction of it anyway."

Phil bristles. "Of course you were. Beyond basic administrative costs —"

"Don't," Wallace says. "I have worked with enough foreign governments to understand the concept of 'basic administrative costs.' Roughly ninety percent, in my experience." He looks at Dalton. "When we get Oliver, you'll tell me what you need for this town. Supplies, infrastructure improvements, and any wish-list items that will make life here easier. I'll pay your *administrators* a reasonable fee for their work, and I will personally take care of everything on your list. Plus I'll pay you and your detective and deputy a bonus."

"Fuck, no," Dalton says.

"He means the bonus isn't necessary," I say. "We'll take the rest, but we don't need added incentive to find your stepson. What he's done is enough."

Wallace dips his chin. "I apologize if I implied otherwise." He looks at Phil. "You can run along now. Fly back to the city, and leave me here with these people to find my stepson."

Phil's jaw sets. "I will be staying and helping."

"Yeah," Dalton says. "Because if you leave, you have to tell the council how badly you all fucked up. Then they'd just order your ass back here anyway."

"If you're staying, stay," Wallace says. "But

you damn well better make yourself useful. Now, let's talk about how to get Oliver back."

FORTY-TWO

Our plans? We're going to look really, really hard for Brady. What else is there to do? We could call in the Mounties with a full search team, blow Rockton's cover to hell for the sake of stopping one killer, and it wouldn't ultimately achieve anything more than we can do on our own, which is, in short, frustratingly little.

I remember hearing once that Alaska is the serial killer capital of America — not for the number of active ones, but the number who have disappeared there. That is, obviously, an urban legend. It's not as if serial killers leave behind a "gone to Alaska" note. Instead, the so-called fact is an acknowledgment that there are likely many people hiding there, who have done something terrible and then fled where they cannot be found.

The same goes for the Yukon. In White-horse, I've heard people joke that the most common question asked of newcomers is

"So, what are you running from?" The answer for most is "Nothing." People run *to* places like Whitehorse. They come on a job placement or a vacation and fall in love, like I have. Whitehorse is a city of transplants. Willing transplants. But yes, everyone knows there are people in the wilderness who are hiding. Asking questions is frowned upon, both for safety and as a courtesy.

We don't know what — or who — might be in these woods. And we don't really care to find out, because the point is moot. Modern tracking equipment can't reliably locate hikers who wander off the Appalachian Trail. It sure as hell won't locate fugitives up here.

We must find lodgings for our unexpected guests.

"I will take Casey's old house," Phil says. "I know it's vacant."

"Yeah, no," Dalton says. "The guy paying the bills gets the house. Casey just needs to move something out first."

"No need," Wallace says. "I won't disturb any of her belongings."

"Thanks," I say. "But there's one item you'll definitely want relocated."

We take Phil and Wallace to my house with their luggage. I open the door and slip inside with a quick, "Give me a sec."

A few minutes later, I emerge with a duffel bag and a sleepy cub.

Phil sees the wolf-dog and turns on Dalton. "We allowed special dispensation for a single canine. Casey's dog, which is a working —"

"This isn't a pet," I say. "It's the remaining cub from the wolf-dog we had to put down."

"And so you brought it here? This isn't a wildlife refuge, Detective."

"This cub bit Eric. We feared it was rabid, and I needed to monitor it."

Phil steps back so fast I have the very childish urge to dump the cub into his arms. I do hold it out toward him. I can't resist that.

"It's fine, see?" I say.

"Then why is it still here?"

"As opposed to dumping it in the forest? Or killing it?"

As he opens his mouth, I spot a familiar figure passing and shout, "Yo! Mathias!"

Mathias makes his way over and arches a brow. "Did you actually hail me with 'yo'?" He speaks in French as his gaze touches on our guests, testing their comprehension. Wallace gives no sign of understanding. Phil squints, as if he recognizes French from long-ago classes.

"We have guests," I say in English. "I'm sure you've already heard that."

"Our illustrious council liaison, and the poor man who married into the family of a serial killer."

Wallace blinks, but then chuckles. "That's one way of putting it." He shakes Mathias's hand as I introduce them properly.

Then I say, "Your timing is perfect. I was just about to tell Phil that you've volunteered to take and train this cub as a guard and hunting dog. But I'm afraid he's going to tell you no."

"No?" Mathias says, as if he doesn't recognize the word. He turns to Phil and fixes him with a smile that has sent many a resident skittering from the butcher shop. "You wish to tell me I cannot have this cub, Philip? That is unfortunate. I was very much looking forward to it."

"I never said —"

"Excellent. Then we are agreed. I will quarantine and then train it properly, as a working beast." He hefts the cub from my arms. "The next serial killer must escape the jaws of a wolf if he wishes to flee." He pauses. "Or she. I would not wish to be sexist."

"Let's just hope we don't have to guard

more serial killers, okay? Now Mr. Wallace is taking my old house while he's here, so you'll need to care for the cub."

Mathias says in French, "You realize you cannot take it back now. You have committed to the course. All for the sake of tweaking poor Philip."

"I couldn't resist."

"A cruel streak. This is why I like you." He takes the bag of supplies from my hand and switches to English. "Do you know where Philip will stay? I do not believe we have empty apartments."

"We can move Kenny out and place him under guard," I say. "Then let Phil take the house we built for Oliver."

"The windowless *box* you built for Oliver?" Phil says. "I am certainly not —"

"Yes," Mathias says. "That would be wrong. You must stay with me. Ah, no — I mean us." He hefts the canine. "Please. I insist."

Phil's jaw works, as if he knows he's being played here. Then he says, his voice tight, "Oliver's intended residence will be adequate."

We leave the men to settle into their lodgings, and we resume our search for Oliver Brady. We're out until dark, and I'm putting my extra gear in the locker when Isabel comes in and says, "We need a fourth for poker."

I laugh. Hard.

"I'm serious," she says.

I close the equipment locker. "I'm exhausted, Isabel. I'm going home with Eric, to a hot meal, a warm bed, and as much sleep as I can get."

"Eric won't be joining you for a while. There's a problem with the lumber-shed reconstruction."

"Of course there is."

"So, poker?" she says.

I shake my head. "If Eric's busy, I'm going to have that hot meal waiting when he's done."

"That's very domestic of you."

"No, it's considerate."

"I'm not sure that's the word I'd use, having heard Will and Eric discuss your cooking." She follows me from the equipment shed. "One of the cooks at the Lion owes me a favor. I'll have her prepare something to put aside for both of you."

"Then I'll rest —"

"That word is not in your vocabulary, Casey." She keeps pace alongside me. "If you want a rest, you'll find it in our poker game. It's an all-estrogen event. You, me, Petra, and Diana."

"Since when do you play poker — or socialize with Diana?"

"Since I requested her presence at this particular game. I know you and I both would have preferred Nicole, but she's busy with the search. Diana is joining us in a wake for the loss of one of our own."

I slow. "Val."

"Yes, and while you might not want the reminder, I think we owe it to Val."

I nod and follow her.

FORTY-THREE

We're in the Roc. Isabel has closed it for the night, both the bar and the brothel. There would normally be two women on "duty" in the evening. There are about six on staff. I say "about" because the number fluctuates, as women come and go from the ranks, most just deciding they're going to give it a try for a few months, for fun.

Isabel argues there is sexual liberation in that, and it isn't so much monetizing their bodies as experimenting with a traditionally more masculine form of sexuality, taking partners where and when they want, without emotional risk. Sounds great. The reality, though, is that if one of them refuses an offer, she has to deal with the prospective client outside these walls, and having a woman refuse *paid* sex is apparently more of an ego blow than just refusing sex. I dealt with an incident recently where the rejected john found a way to retaliate.

When we arrive at the Roc, there's a hopeful client walking inside just ahead of us, and Isabel pulls open the door just in time to see him sidling up to Petra and Diana, with a "So, are you ladies looking for —"

Then Petra turns and he sees who it is and stops short with an "Oh."

"Yes, oh," Isabel calls. "Have I spoken to you about this before, Artie? You do not ever presume that a woman drinking here is looking for *anything* but a drink."

"No harm in asking, Iz," he whines.

"Yes, actually there is. If a woman here wants your company, she will approach you. That is the new rule, as you have been told. If you're looking for company, you'll find it in the search parties. That's where tonight's staff is, and that's where you should be."

"Can I get a drink?"

"Yes, absolutely. I'll get you your drink, and you'll sit on your ass and enjoy yourself while everyone else searches for the man who murdered Val. I'll make sure all my girls know that's what you were doing tonight. They'll be terribly impressed."

Artie leaves. Quickly. I sit with Petra and Diana, and Isabel brings over tumblers and Irish whiskey.

"I don't think Val was Irish," I say.

"Do you have any idea what her heritage

was?"

I shake my head.

"Then in the interests of a proper wake, tonight she was Irish. And we are playing poker."

"Never been to an actual wake, have you," Petra says.

"I'm improvising. Otherwise, we'll sit here and try to come up with things to say about the dearly departed, and it will get very awkward, very fast." Isabel pours the whiskey. "Have any of you ever attended one of those funerals? Where it's very clear that no one actually has anything interesting to say about the deceased?"

"Or anything nice," Diana says as she takes her drink.

"The lack of anything nice would be far worse than the lack of anything interesting. That's what I want for my funeral. I don't give a damn if anyone tells a single story that reflects well on me. Just tell stories."

"Val liked tea," I say.

Diana snickers and then sobers with, "Sorry."

"The point being," Isabel says, "that we have not a single interesting thing to say about Val."

"We didn't know her," I say.

"Not for lack of trying."

"Shortly after she arrived, she got lost in the forest and was attacked."

Isabel nods. "I know."

"She came to you?"

"Val ask for help? Never. But I have counseled enough survivors to know she did not wander out of that forest unscathed. I tried to broach the subject once, to offer support, and she shut me down. Nothing happened, and I should go practice my 'mediocre skills' on real victims." She raises her glass to me. "Kudos on being the one to break through."

"I didn't. When I confronted her, she said that to have 'allowed' herself to be attacked would have been a sign of weakness. Strong women don't do that."

"Ouch," Petra says.

"An unfortunate — and unfortunately common — belief," Isabel says. "Also monumentally wrong and stupid, but that goes without saying."

We take a drink.

"Val, however, was not a stupid woman," Isabel says. "She'd been a mathematician."

"I didn't know that," I say. "I'd seen her doing math puzzles. Not the kind you get in a paperback book, but real puzzles. Theoretical ones."

"Even if she didn't open up to you about

the attack, Casey, you *were* the one to break through. To get her out of that house and into the community."

"Yep." I take a slug of my whiskey. "And look where it got her."

Three mouths open in simultaneous denials. I beat them to it with, "This morning, Phil said Val made a mistake trying to join life in Rockton. That her place was separate and apart from us. He may have had a point."

"Phil is an idiot. Gorgeous, but an idiot. And I don't just say that because he looked at me like I was a bag lady blocking the steps to his brownstone."

"It wasn't that bad," I say.

"Oh, yes it was, but since he wasn't checking you out either, I won't take it personally."

"You both might be the wrong gender," Petra says.

"He didn't give Will more than a passing glance."

"The sneer wasn't a physical assessment," I say. "It was disdain. For everyone and everything here. But I still wonder if he was right about Val. We couldn't afford to lose our leader, and involving herself in our affairs endangered her."

"Well, if that's your reasoning, you'd better tell Eric he has to stay in the station from now on. He's the one we can't afford to lose. Val was . . ." Isabel swirls her drink and shakes her head. "This isn't the proper way to conduct a wake, is it?"

"Does anyone have anything nice to say?" Diana says.

"She liked tea," Petra quips. Then she adds, "The truth is that none of us knew her well enough to eulogize her. But a year ago, no one would have been holding a wake for her either. She was coming out of her shell. She was starting to care. We were starting to care back."

Isabel raises her glass. "Then let's drink to that. A woman we didn't always understand. A woman we didn't always like. But a woman we were looking forward to getting to know better. A missed and mourned opportunity."

We clink glasses.

"Now, poker?" Petra says. "For credits, I hope, because I will clean you all out."

The door opens, and Isabel calls, "Closed!"

Dalton walks in. "Got a situation, Casey. I need you."

I'm getting to my feet when Diana says, "Can't you handle it alone, Sheriff? Casey deserves a rest."

"So does he," I say. "And he hasn't been sitting here drinking whiskey."

She opens her mouth, but a murmur from Isabel stops her. A quiet reminder, I'm sure, that harping on Dalton does nothing to bring Diana back into my good graces.

When we get outside, I say, "We were attempting to eulogize Val. It wasn't going well."

He slows. "Shit, I'm sorry. If you want to go back —"

"The eulogy part was over. It was booze and cards henceforth. Somehow I don't think Val would have approved."

He takes my hand as we walk. I might joke, but he knows that wake wasn't easy. Any reminder of Val is a reminder of how she died. But Isabel is right — Val deserved a few quiet moments of our time.

"So what's up?" I say.

"Kenny's missing."

"What?"

"He was out searching with a party. I wanted him at the lumber shed to deal with the reconstruction issues. When it was definitely dark" — he points at the night sky — "I went to see why he wasn't back yet."

"And?"

"His group returned fifteen minutes earlier. He had to use the bathroom. Someone stood outside waiting, not wanting to rush him."

"Let me guess — he's not in the bathroom."

"Yep."

FORTY-FOUR

There are three levels of occupancy here in Rockton. At the top is having your own house. At the bottom is apartment living — bachelor-style apartments. In the middle, you get the full level of a house, which still only nets you about six hundred square feet. Yes, we aren't exactly living in mansions here. We can't afford the energy costs or the footprint.

Kenny has a ground floor. Which means it was very easy to sneak out the window while his guard was watching at the front.

And his guard? Jen.

"Which is why you should have put a guy in charge of him," she says. "Someone who can stand in the bathroom while he takes a shit."

"Yeah, not even the guys are going to do that," Dalton says. "But next time someone's in there that long? Knock. Ask if he needs medical care."

"He took a book. I knew it was going to be a while."

"A book from the library?" I say.

"Everyone does it."

"Which is why I don't read books from the library," Dalton says. He stands in the bathroom and looks at the window. "Fuck."

"Eloquent as always, Sheriff," Jen says.

"Yeah, well, I'm saving time on a lengthy response." He strides for the door. "Time better spent catching his ass before he rendezvouses with Oliver Brady and gets his fool throat cut."

I join the search for a while, with Storm. The problem? Kenny knows what Storm can and cannot do. Which means he runs straight to the nearest stream.

We lead Storm up one side of it for about a kilometer, as far as we figure he could walk in the icy water. Then we take her down the other side and another kilometer in the opposite direction. Either Kenny managed to steal waterproof boots and three pairs of wool socks or Storm misses his exit spot.

Dalton takes her on a wider circle in the area while I return to town. There are a few things I want to check, and with both Dalton and Storm hunting, I really am a third wheel.

I want to look for a note. Even with what seems like an obvious betrayal, I still can't write Kenny off just yet. I find it much easier to believe he was duped by Brady's protests of innocence rather than jumping at a huge bribe to help a serial killer. If so . . .

If so, I have an alternate theory for his disappearance. One that paints Kenny in a better light. One that fits better with the man I know.

I find the note in the station. Paul said Kenny came in here earlier, to return a flashlight that he claimed belonged to me.

I find the note in the drawer, along with a spare flashlight.

The note is addressed to me. And when I read it, I discover I was wrong. Very, very wrong.

Dalton comes home at three in the morning. From the kitchen, I hear the door open, the solid *boom-boom* of his boots stepping inside and then the skitter and scrape of Storm's nails as she zips past him. After that double boom, his footsteps go silent. He's looking for me in the living room. When he doesn't see me, there's a sigh, and his boots come off, thumping to the floor.

Steps move into the living room. Not the solid boom of his initial ones. Not even his usual purposeful stride. These are dragging and whispery, socks skimming the hardwood. Then the thud of him collapsing onto the sofa.

He doesn't hear me come out of the kitchen, and I catch that first unguarded glimpse of him, forearms on his thighs, shoulders bowed, gaze empty as he stares at nothing. The floorboard creaks with my next step, and he looks over and his face lights in a smile.

I know he thought I'd gone to bed, and while he'd never complain about that, yes, he was disappointed. Now he sees me and smiles. Then he gets a whiff of the dinner I'm carrying, and his gaze goes to it.

"Don't worry, I didn't cook it," I say. "Isabel wouldn't let me."

He shakes his head.

I take the plates of rewarmed dinner onto the back deck, and we eat in silence.

I wait until he finishes before I say, "Kenny left a note."

Dalton's head jerks up at that. Then he snorts and says, "What? Telling us we were fucking idiots for not keeping a closer eye on him?"

Which isn't what he expects at all. He's

just bracing for the worst. This was a person Dalton trusted. He feels betrayed, and so he wants to believe Kenny was not the man he thought. It makes this easier than any of the alternatives.

Tell me he betrayed us. That he deserves whatever happens to him in that forest.

I hand him the note. As he reads it, I watch him, his cheek twitching, gaze skimming the first time through and then slowing to reread. When he finishes, he crushes the paper and whips it across the back lawn.

"God-fucking-damn-it, no," he snarls, pushing to his feet. "Is he an idiot? Yes, obviously he fucking is. The biggest goddamn idiot . . ."

Dalton can't even seem to continue, and he starts pacing instead. Storm scratches at the back door. I've left her inside, and I know she's hurt and confused, certain we've accidentally forgotten her, patiently waiting for us to realize our mistake. Now she hears Dalton curse and she scratches, a tentative whine seeping through the wooden door.

Dalton wheels on me. "This is what I need. Exactly what we both need. Because clearly we're not doing fuck-all here. *Hey, why don't I just take off into the goddamn forest and give you guys something to do.* Or maybe no, we won't chase him because we don't give a shit. That's why he had to take off. Catch this murdering asshole himself. Because we aren't trying. So he'll do it for us and prove he wasn't Brady's accomplice, because otherwise, we'll just punish him and not bother with a fucking investigation."

I let Dalton rant. Let him express my own frustration and my fear and my rage. I still recall every word of that note.

Casey,
   I'm going to fix this. I'm going to find Brady and bring him back for you. It's my fault he escaped and killed Val and your friend and those settlers. I didn't help him. I swear I didn't. But I'm going to bring him back. I'll catch him, and he can tell you who was his real accomplice.
   I'm sorry for all the trouble I've caused.

                                    Kenny

"Trouble he's caused," Dalton says. "He's sorry for the fucking trouble he caused, so the best way to fix that is to cause more. Poor Kenny feels guilty. Blames himself. Fucking awesome. Let's share that blame. Let Jen have some when Kenny dies, for letting *him* escape. Let you have some for suspecting he was the accomplice. Let me have some for trusting him enough to let him out of that cell. Let's all take another helping of the fucking blame pie, because it's clear we haven't eaten enough of it already."

He spins on me. "What am I supposed to do here, Casey? I feel like we're spending this whole damn case searching for people. Brady, Val, Jacob, now Kenny. I tell them not to go into the forest. I regulate every damn step out there until I feel like a paranoid parent. But they keep doing it. They walk out of this town, and they die. Do I need to build a fucking wall? A barbed-wire fence? Post armed guards? Shoot anyone who tries to leave? These are supposed to be responsible adults, but they come here and they act like fucking children, which means we have to be the fucking parents. No, not children. Teenagers. And we're just obstacles standing between them and whatever shit they want to pull. Well, if that's the way they want it, then fuck yeah, that's what they're getting. Prison guards."

My gaze flicks from Dalton as I notice something to the side. A figure stands just around the rear corner of our house. Watching Dalton rage. Listening to him rant. Observing and judging.

I get to my feet. "Can I help you, Phil?"

Dalton spins with a "What the fuck?"

"I wished to speak to you both," Phil says as he walks into the yard.

"It's almost four A.M.," I say. "We're on our own time, and our own property. This is a private conversation."

"At that volume, no, I don't think it is."

There's more judgment in his voice, and I want to snap at him, but I only say, "Then I'll repeat that we are on our own time. We'll speak to you in the morning."

Phil walks over as if I haven't spoken. "I take it you didn't find Kenny?"

"No," I say, as evenly as I can. "We will resume the search tomorrow."

"I don't think that's necessary."

"Excuse me?" Dalton says.

"I understand you suspected him of being Oliver Brady's accomplice."

"We did," I say. "The evidence fit, but it was all circumstantial. That's why we let Kenny out of the cell on work duty. If you wish to debate that decision, I'll suggest it's unnecessary. We already realize that might not have been wise."

"I don't care what choice you made regarding Kenny's incarceration. My point is that the only reason to pursue him is in hopes he'll lead you to Oliver. That is unlikely. Oliver has staff, not partners. He

408

conned this man into helping him, and now he will have abandoned him as unnecessary. Otherwise, Kenny would have fled with him. Correct?"

He doesn't even wait for a response before continuing. "Kenny left because he realized his guilt had been uncovered, and it was only a matter of time —"

"No," Dalton says.

Phil sighs. It's a familiar sigh, one I've heard countless times underscored by the feedback from a radio receiver. "I know you —"

"He left a note." Dalton points at the wadded paper on the lawn. "He blames himself for Brady escaping and wants to bring him back. Kenny accepts responsibility because he left his post. Not because he was in cahoots with Brady."

Another sigh, the sort a supercilious teacher gives a student he considers not terribly bright. "Just because Kenny *claims* that doesn't mean it's true, Sheriff. Of course he'll defend himself. My point is that he isn't your concern. He has made his choice. He might hope to find Oliver. Perhaps even kill him, to cover his own crimes. But he's unlikely to succeed. His flight proves his guilt and therefore, whatever justice the forest metes out . . ." Phil shrugs.

"It saves the council from doing it?" Dalton says.

There's a warning note in Dalton's voice, but Phil only says, "Yes, it does. Casey no longer needs to waste time proving his guilt, and you can both focus on Oliver instead. Take this as a reprieve; do not turn it into a cause for extra effort."

"A *reprieve*?" Dalton says. "Extra *effort*? Kenny was a valued member of my militia, and whatever you might think of what he's done, he deserves my —"

"He deserves nothing. If you feel guilty, take this as an order. You may not search for this man. If you happen to find him, all right. Do what you must."

"Do what I must?" Dalton says, his voice lowering. "Kill him, you mean?"

"Of course not. Bring him back."

"If I must. Because, you know, the alternative is to just let him die out there. Which is worse than killing him. And it's not like, if I bring him back, he's going to live much longer anyway. Maybe I *should* just kill him."

I see where Dalton's heading, and I try to get his attention and cut him off, but before

I can, Phil says, "What are you talking about?"

"Sure, yeah, let's pretend you don't know."

"Eric . . ." I say.

Dalton advances on the other man. "Tell me, Phil, what happens if I bring Kenny back and put him on your plane. What happened to Beth after I dropped her off?"

"Beth Lowry is fine, and to suggest otherwise only proves you are exhausted and need —"

"What if I want her back? We need a doctor. Let's bring Beth back for a while. Can we do that, Phil?"

"Certainly not. After what she did —"

"Forget about bringing her back. We have medical questions. How about the council hires her for satellite consultations?"

"We cannot —"

"Do you know where she is, Phil?"

"I don't care, and neither should you. But she is alive. We are not executioners —"

"No? Then tell me about the deal you tried to make with Tyrone Cypher."

Phil's face screws up. "Who?"

"The sheriff before Gene Dalton."

"That is long before my time, as you well know."

"The council tracked him down in the forest. Tried to cut him a deal. Ty says he

411

knows what it was, because he has one real talent. His former occupation. A hit man."

Phil bursts into a laugh. "Is that what he told you? I'm sure whatever this Cypher man did in his past life, he was not a hired killer. The council would never put such a man in Rockton."

"No? Then tell me about Harry Powys."

"Eric," I say sharply.

"No, please, Casey," Phil says. "It seems the sheriff has a few things to get off his chest. If you are suggesting Harry Powys was a hired killer —"

"Worse," Dalton says. "He was a doctor who drugged illegal immigrants and removed their organs. Sometimes they lived; sometimes they didn't. Being in the country illegally, though, it wasn't like they could complain."

Phil stares at him.

"What Eric means —" I begin.

"Please, Casey. There is no alternative interpretation you can come up with to explain that away, however embarrassing I'm sure you find it."

I bristle. "I don't find it —"

"The sheriff's exposure to our culture is limited largely to his books and videos. Dime-store novels and fantasy television shows."

"That's not —"

"And from those, he clearly has a distorted view on the world, one that someone has exploited by feeding him ridiculous stories. Black-market organ sales are the stuff of pulp fiction and urban legend, Sheriff. Whoever told you Harry Powys did such a thing was pulling a prank."

"Look it up," Dalton says.

"What?"

"Harrison Powers. That's his real name. Google it. You'll find news articles — *legitimate* news articles — about a doctor suspected of exactly what I said. A warrant was issued for his arrest. He disappeared. Check the dates. Check the photograph. Compare it to Harry Powys."

Silence. Three long pulses of it. Then Phil says, "Whoever told you they found this online —"

"I found it. I'm not illiterate, you pompous jackass. I can use the fucking internet and read the goddamn evidence, which I verify against alternate sources."

Dalton steps closer to Phil. "You let a man like that into my town. For profit. And he murdered Abbygail. They chopped up her body and scattered it for scavengers. That's who you let in here. Because it was profitable."

"I'm sorry, Sheriff. I don't know how you came across this information, but it is wrong. Completely and utterly —"

Dalton hits him. A right hook to the jaw. Phil flies off his feet. Dalton steps away. Then he follows me into the house, leaving Phil on the ground outside.

FORTY-FIVE

We're upstairs in our bedroom. Phil is gone
— I checked out the balcony window. I've
let Storm upstairs, only because it would be
more upsetting to keep her out and listen to
her cry. Dalton is in the chair by our bed,
and she's at his feet, her muzzle on his
boots, which he's forgotten to take off. I
bend to untie them, and he removes them
silently. Then he says, "I fucked up."

"Yes."

He looks at me.

"This is the one time I'm not going to
argue," I say. "You opened a hornet's nest
that we should have left alone."

I take his boots and set them outside the
door. "It was going to happen sooner or
later. Probably best that it happened when
it's just Phil, without the council listening
in. That will make it easier for us to control
the damage."

"Our word against his?" He makes a face,

and I know he hates that. It's underhanded and dishonest.

"No, I have another idea. But first I have to ask if you *want* this damage controlled. Or is this scorched-earth time?"

He exhales and leans forward, both hands running through his hair. Then he shakes his head. "There's part of me that says 'fuck, yeah.' Just throw it all out there and end this. Pack our things and go. But that's me being pissy."

"Which you'd regret about twelve hours later."

"Yeah. As much as I'd like to confront the council, what good does it do? They'll pull a Phil — pretend they don't know what I'm talking about, treat me like a delusional idiot. Then they'll shut me up. Exile me. Exile you. Or worse. So, no, this isn't scorched-earth time. This is 'Casey fixes Eric's fuck-up' time. And you have an idea about how to do that?"

"I do."

After Dalton is asleep, I slip over to Anders's place to ask him to take the first search shift this morning. I know he's only been to bed for a couple of hours — and me waking him doesn't help — but when I explain what happened, he offers before I can ask. Then it's back home to make sure the blackout blinds are closed, reset the alarm, and ease into bed.

When the alarm sounds at nine and I admit my subterfuge, Dalton grumbles . . . until I point out that I would much rather *not* trick him and just be able to ask him to stay in bed until he's rested enough to search properly. He agrees. Even apologizes. Whether he'll voluntarily sleep in when I ask is another matter. I can't say I'm any better, though.

Phil is at the station when we arrive. He's waiting by my desk, his arms crossed, as if we're tardy children. Dalton sees him and slows to an amble, perversely acting as if he's just strolled in whenever he feels like it. He walks right past Phil and puts on the kettle for coffee.

"I believe we have an issue to discuss," Phil says.

"Yeah," Dalton says as he stokes the fire. "I'd like to explain."

Phil's voice chills even more. "I don't think that's possible."

Dalton straightens, still holding the poker. "You were right about Powys."

"I should certainly hope —"

"It's entirely possible the council didn't know what he was. I know that, which is why I've never said anything until I lost my temper last night." Dalton puts the poker back. "As for whether he did that shit, the answer is yes. Like I said, it's online. I suspected Powys was involved with making the rydex, especially with his background. According to his entry papers, he was a pharmacist."

"Correct."

"So I went looking online . . . and dug up more than I bargained for."

"Perhaps, but that hardly proves we let him buy his way in."

"Agreed. If you don't know anything about it, then obviously he faked his admission file."

Phil's eyes narrow, as if he's waiting for the punch line.

"I don't like the council," Dalton says calmly. "Never made any secret of that. But, yeah, accusing them of that went too far. So I apologize. Good?"

"No, Eric, it is not good. When I said I wanted an apology, I meant for this." He gestures to the bruise on his jaw.

"Fuck no," Dalton says. "You deserved that."

Phil's sputtering as the door swings open.

"Good, you're still here," Wallace says as he walks in. "I was afraid I'd been left behind. So, when do we start searching for Oliver?"

Dalton does not want to take Wallace into the forest. He argues. Vehemently. Profanely. Loudly. He is overruled by Phil. Both Wallace and Phil are coming along, and there's nothing we can do about that.

We fill thermoses with coffee and grab breakfast to go at the bakery. I think Dalton's hoping that our speedy departure will change Wallace's mind. It doesn't. Within the hour, we're deep in the forest, with the two men and Storm.

Dalton takes the lead with the dog. I hang back with Phil and Wallace. That's deliberate, allowing our trackers to work. I chat with Wallace. Phil tries several times to pull Wallace's attention his way, with topics I can't possibly address — American election issues, a stock-market roller coaster — but Wallace only answers politely and then steers conversation back to include me.

Phil surrenders with a sniff and once-over of me, as if suggesting Wallace is only paying attention to me because I'm female. I get no such vibe from the older man, though. Wallace is just politely keeping conversation on things I can discuss, like the forest itself. When Phil falls back, I warn him to please stay close, but he dawdles just enough that I need to keep shoulder-checking to be sure he's with us.

When Wallace realizes both Dalton and Phil are almost out of earshot, he lowers his voice and says, "I would like to speak to you about something." He pauses. "Or perhaps not so much a discussion as a confession."

"Hmm?"

"About Oliver. I know how this looks from your viewpoint. You are a detective. You're supposed to catch people like my stepson and put them in prison. That is what should have happened to Oliver. And yet it did not. Why? Because we're rich. We can afford alternatives, and the alternative I chose resulted in the death of five more people."

"Yes."

He gives a strained chuckle. "Not going to sugarcoat that for me, are you?"

"I grew up with money. Not your tax bracket, but my parents had very successful careers, and we enjoyed all the privileges that come with that. So I won't rage about the inherent evil of the upper class. But nor do I agree with anyone using their money and their privilege to keep a serial killer out of prison."

We walk in silence for a few minutes. Then

he says, "I told myself I was doing the right thing. The responsible thing. I'm embarrassed to say that now, but it's true. I thought that by incarcerating Oliver, I was saving my country that expense. Doing my civic duty by removing him from the population while not charging the taxpayer for our mistakes."

"It doesn't work like that."

"Oh, I know. The truth is . . ." He exhales. "I love my wife. I wanted to protect her — not only from a trial, but from ever knowing what Oliver did. As soon as the police started questioning, I hired an investigator. I found evidence and confronted Oliver. When I threatened to turn my evidence over to the police, he confessed. So I whisked him away and told my wife that he was innocent, but we couldn't trust the justice system. I said they'd convict him on the grounds of being a spoiled, rich white boy. But my wife wasn't the only reason I did that. I wanted to avoid the business ramifications of having a serial killer for a stepson. It was a sound business investment. Whatever this costs, it is not nearly the blow my finances would suffer if Oliver was arrested."

Storm barks, and I tense. It's just a quick bark, though, with a response from Dalton.

I can see them through the trees around the next curve, and while I can't make out what Dalton's saying, there's no alarm in his voice.

Wallace has gone quiet, and I think he's waiting for me to respond. This is, as he said, a confession. A safe one, too — it's not as if I can tell the newspapers what he's said.

If he wants absolution, he has to look elsewhere. I do, however, credit him for the confession, which is why I just stay quiet.

"I wanted to be clear that I understand my position here," Wallace continues. "I am the interloper who brought this on your town. I realize now what I've done, and I'm sorry it took five deaths for me to understand that." Another few steps in silence. "I really did believe this solution was a valid one. But the hard truth is that anyone who comes into contact with Oliver is at risk. The only truly viable solution is one that doesn't put him into contact with anyone. Ever."

Execution. That's what he means, and I stiffen, fearing he's hinting that we should resolve this with lethal action. But his gaze is straight ahead, distant.

Jail is no longer an option. We both know that. It ceased to be an option as soon as

Brady came here. Put him into custody, and he'll cut a deal any way he can, including talking about Rockton.

I don't know where to go with this, what to say, so after I glance back for Phil, I change the subject with, "You say it'd be a blow to your personal finances, but Oliver claims your family money comes from his father — from a business he started."

Wallace nods. "Yes, that's his version of history, and it's our fault. His mother's and mine. We wanted to keep his father alive for him. Honor him with a legacy of success."

"And the truth?"

"I worked for Oliver's father. At one time, we were partners, but when we formed the business, the money came from his family, so his name went on it. That seemed fair. The problem was that while David was an incredible inventor, he didn't have a lick of business sense. I lacked the clout to over-rule him, and at the time of his death, the company was floundering."

"You brought it back."

A sharp laugh. "There was no place to bring it back *from*. We had investors — David's ideas were incredible — but we'd been scrambling to stay afloat from the start."

"With Oliver's father gone, though, you turned it around."

"Oliver's mother and I did. Together. Yet David's name remains on the company, and we have allowed Oliver the fiction of his brilliant inventor father who launched a billion-dollar corporation. Which led, unfortunately, to Oliver beginning to demand more than a trust fund. When his mother had enough, she showed him the financial records from the year of his father's death. He accused us of forging them. By that point . . ."

He shrugs. "By that point, I knew there was no arguing with him. He was never happy, never satisfied. Everyone was conspiring to keep him from his due."

I check for Phil again and —

The path behind us is empty. Then I spot him, stopped off the path with his back to us. It's obvious from his stance what he's doing.

I turn to give him privacy and call, "Eric? Hold up." I have to shout — he's too far ahead to see on the winding path. Then I say, "Phil, please let us know if you are stopping. The absolute last thing we need —"

At a rustle behind me, I turn. But it's not Phil. It's a man holding an old rifle, trained on me. Two men armed with knives step out in front of Wallace. Behind them, Phil stands frozen, staring at the men. Their

424

backs are to him, and I tear my gaze away before they spot him.

One glance tells me these men are settlers, not hostiles, and I relax at that. I'm cautious, though, gauging the distance to my gun, ready to pull it if that rifle barrel swings out of my way.

I open my mouth to speak. Then I hear:

"Let them go."

As I turn, Dalton appears at knifepoint, his hands on the back of his head. Two men and a woman follow at his rear. The woman holds Storm's lead. My gaze drops to the dog.

"Take Storm and our friend there back to Rockton, Casey," Dalton says. "I've got this under control."

If my heart wasn't thudding so hard, I'd laugh. He said the same thing when Jacob had a knife on him. His brother was drugged and ranting and threatening . . . and Dalton's biggest concern was reassuring me that he could handle it. They'd talk it out. Yeah, just talk it out. No big deal.

"We are not letting your girl go," one of the men says.

"She's my wife," Dalton says, "and if Edwin has one drop of respect for me, he will let her walk away with our guest and the dog, and I will come willingly and answer any questions you have."

Edwin. Questions.

The First Settlement. The massacre.

Oh, shit.

"The girl comes," the man says. "That is what Edwin says. He wishes to speak to the girl."

I swear Wallace snorts softly. He's already realized that, given the choice, *everyone* prefers to speak to me instead of Dalton.

"All right," I say. "Let Eric take our guest and dog home to Rockton. I'll talk to Edwin."

Dalton mouths *Fuck no,* his jaw setting in a way I know well. But before he can speak, the man says, "Edwin will talk to the girl, but he says to bring Steve's boy. That was the order. Do not let him leave. If he tries" — he looks at Dalton — "shoot him."

FORTY-SIX

We walk to the First Settlement. They were willing to let Wallace go, but he refused.

"I don't know my way back," he said.

"Just follow —" I begin.

"Somehow, it seems safer to stay with you two. I've heard quite enough about this forest."

As for Phil, he's gone. Fled without ever being spotted.

I try to talk to the settlers. Defuse this situation. But they have been warned not to speak to us, and they are already wary. So I fall to silence, walking beside Dalton, armed settlers in front and behind.

We're nearing the First Settlement when the men in front of us turn and point their guns.

"Hands behind your back," one says, taking out a length of rope.

"Fuck no," Dalton says.

The woman steps forward. "Get your hands behind your back, boy, or we'll put a bullet through your damn skull."

Dalton wheels on her. "Excuse me?"

"Enough." One of the men turns to Dalton. "We are not letting you walk into our village after what happened. You will be disarmed. You will have your hands bound. People are angry. If we bring you in like guests, there will be trouble."

Dalton grumbles, but puts his hands behind his back, and then lets them disarm us. Wallace silently follows our lead.

The woman glowers at Dalton's grumblings. "You're lucky we don't shoot you and drag your bodies through the settlement."

"What the hell?" Dalton says.

She steps up to him. "Albie. Nancy. Douglas."

"The people who died," I say. "Yes, we take full responsibility for letting their killer escape."

"Escape?"

"What do you expect?" one of the guys says. "They're going to blame this on someone else."

"No," I say carefully. "We acknowledge the killer was one of ours."

"So now you're blaming some innocent

428

person from Rockton?" the woman says. "Was that your plan? Bring us a body and say 'There's your killer'?"

"Or is it him?" The man turns to Wallace. "Are you forcing this old man to take the fall?"

"What the hell are you talking about?" Dalton says.

The woman steps right in front of him and spits up in his face.

I move between them fast. "We don't know what's happening here —"

"Harper told us who killed our people," the woman said. "Your husband. She saw it, and she barely escaped with her life."

FORTY-SEVEN

We cannot even begin to speculate on
what's happened here, which doesn't keep
Dalton from demanding answers. But our
captors are not talking.

We enter the village at gunpoint. The First
Settlement is composed of about ten cabins,
spread over a couple of acres. As people
emerge from homes, the palpable weight of
their rage pulses through the air.

If I had any idea what they thought we'd
done, I'd have fought our captors. Allowing
a dangerous Rockton resident to escape was
one thing. We could have handled that,
though. Made promises. Made apologies.
Made concessions. Now . . . ?

I glance at Dalton. His face is taut, gaze
straight ahead, jaw set as if he's outraged,
but the vein throbbing in his neck tells me
he is afraid.

"In here." One of our captors prods
Dalton toward a dilapidated building.

When I see Harper, I try to catch her eye, not accusing but confused, concerned. I gesture that I would like to speak to her, but she's pretending not to see me. She circles to a man behind us and says something. He shakes his head. She gestures my way and I think it's at me, but then I realize she's pointing at Storm. The man shakes his head and reaches to squeeze her thin shoulder, but she throws him off and stomps away.

Dalton's captor prods him again.

"Yeah, no," he says. "I'll wait here for Edwin."

"You aren't talking to Edwin." The man nods at me. "She is."

"Fine, then I'll sit my ass down right here and wait."

The man points at the building. "You will wait there. She will wait at Edwin's."

Dalton opens his mouth, but I shake my head. He hesitates, and I know this makes him nervous — it makes me nervous, too — but we cannot give them any excuse for using those weapons to *force* us to obey.

Dalton stalks off toward the building, muttering the whole way. Our captors prod Wallace to follow Dalton. I let them take me to Edwin's place. They open the door, and I walk in, as calmly as I can, as if this is an obvious misunderstanding that I know will be cleared up.

Edwin isn't there.

I turn to ask where he is, but they've shut the door behind me.

I take a deep breath and sit on the floor. Storm lowers herself beside me, leaning in hard, panting with nervous tension. I pat her and tell her it will be okay, it will all be okay.

I hope it will be okay.

I've been there about ten minutes when I hear a noise in the next room. The door swings opens, and Harper stands there, an open window behind her, a knife in her hand.

"Put that down," I say.

"I just came here to talk."

"Good. Then you don't need a knife."

She shakes her head. I ask her one more time. Then I take it. She doesn't see that coming. She tries to slash, but I already have her by the forearm. I squeeze just tight enough to hold her steady. Then I pluck the knife from her hand. When I release her, she swings at me. I grab her arm, pin it behind her back, march her to the open window and drop the knife through it.

When I let her go, she backs off, rubbing her wrist.

"That hurt," she says, and there's genuine shock in her voice.

"You attacked. I defended."

She eyes me as if this calm response isn't what she expects. "It was my knife. I was defending *myself.*"

"One shout will bring the guard to your aid. I only put your knife outside. I didn't keep it."

She's still eyeing me. She says, again, "That hurt," and there's a tremor of outrage, as if I should be ashamed of myself hurting a kid. But like she said the other day, she is not a child, not out here.

"What's going on?" I say.

I'm waiting for the look of worry, of guilt. The one that says they've made her blame us. Someone has forced her to make a false statement. Someone she respects. Someone she fears.

I'm waiting for her to apologize. To say she had no choice.

When she says, "I told the truth," my heart sinks. But I am not surprised.

"The *truth?*" I say.

"Eric killed them. I was there."

I could blame post-traumatic stress. Confusion. Even fear.

Instead, I say, "Why?"

"Why what?"

Now I'm the one eyeing her. Sizing her up. There's no point in Harper coming here to talk.

"What do you want?" I say.

I follow her gaze to Storm. "No."

"Yes."

"She's town property."

"She's yours," Harper says. "I heard Eric say that he got her for you."

"Are you sure?"

Her face scrunches up. "That he got her for you?"

"No, that you overheard it. When? As you were running for your life? After Eric killed three of your people?"

"I want her."

She says it as if this is a simple matter. As if she is indeed a child, one too young to have realized that a wish is not a command or an obligation.

But I'm not sure it *is* childlike to her. Out here, it's a very normal thing, at least for some of the settlers and probably all of the hostiles. *I want this thing. You have it. So I will take it from you.*

I remember the young man — Albie — checking out our horses. Suggesting where we might camp, and Dalton being sure *not* to camp there.

You have this thing that I want, and I will

434

take it from you, and that's nothing personal. It's just the way it is.

Harper steps toward Storm, who leans against me, whining.

The girl looks at me. "Tell Eric that you're giving me the dog, and I'll tell Edwin I made a mistake."

"Little late for that, isn't it?" I say.

"What?"

"How exactly do you tell him you made a mistake? Say that you hallucinated Eric murdering your people? Or that the event was so traumatic you forgot what happened and made something up? How will that make you seem?"

I see her mental gears whirring madly as she looks for the trap here. There must be a trap. Why else would I ever advise her *not* to rescind her story?

"You want a new husband," she says.

"What?"

She nods, satisfied. "You have met someone new in your town, and you want him. Or you never wanted Eric, but he is the leader, and you cannot say no to the leader."

"Yes," I say. "He is the leader. My boss. But if he's gone . . ."

"You want his job."

As she says that, I get a glimpse into the woman behind the girl's mask. When she speculates I simply want a new lover, she is dismissive. Now, as I claim it is ambition, respect flashes in her eyes.

"Can you help me?" I say.

"For the dog?"

I nod. "For the dog."

"What do I need to do?"

"Just stick to your story. *Exactly* to it. Can you do that?"

She nods.

"Tell me everything you told Edwin."

FORTY-EIGHT

You can learn so much about a person by how they react to others. In the forest, my view of Harper was formed almost entirely by how she responded to Storm. I love my dog, and Harper found her fascinating, and that made me happy. It made me open up to her, engage her, see her as more than just some settler kid. I never suspected there was darkness in her.

I don't believe she actually realizes what she's done. She is incapable of realizing it. She wants Storm. I have Storm. Therefore she must get her from me, and if Dalton is endangered by her actions, well, he's a stranger, a meaningless bit player in her life drama. And so was I . . . until I "admitted" that I'd like my lover out of the picture so I can take his job. With that, I became someone interesting to her. In her strengths, she also shows me her weaknesses.

After Harper leaves, I wait for Edwin to

finally show up. He'll bring Harper with him, and I'm prepared for that.

The door opens, and my guard walks in.

"Edwin is ready for you," he says.

"Good. I'm here."

The man shakes his head. "*He* is waiting out here."

I tell myself this will still work. Then I step outside, and Storm starts whining, and I look over to see Dalton being led — bound and gagged — across the village.

Wallace follows, bound but not gagged, and he's glancing about, taking everything in, and I don't think he really understands what's at stake here. How can he? He doesn't come from a world where strangers can grab you in the forest, accuse you of murder, and string you up from the nearest tree. To him, this is just an interesting cultural study, a blustering show of force, all sound and fury, signifying nothing, because there's no way these people would actually *hurt* us.

Dalton is being Dalton. Chin up, shoulders squared. He's not worried. Nope, not worried at all. When he sees me, the facade cracks, but only for me — am I okay? He can see I am, and he nods.

Don't worry, Casey, I may be gagged and bound, but I have everything under control.

I could shake my head at that, but he's really just saying that he trusts me to have a plan. Trusts that I will get us out of this.

No pressure.

We are all led to the village square. Where the village waits. I skim-count thirty heads, all adults.

Edwin stands at the front. Someone has brought him a chair, but he's ignoring it. He's a small man, not much bigger than me, wizened by age.

The guard starts leading Storm away, and she digs in her nails, growling.

"She knows Harper," I say. "Let Harper hold her."

The girl takes Storm's lead.

I turn to Edwin. "What do you want?"

"Due process. This is a trial. A murder trial."

"And you're the judge. No lawyers, I'm guessing."

"I was one," he says.

"And one lawyer is quite enough."

He doesn't quite smile, but the glimmer in his eyes awards me a point for that.

I continue, "I'm presuming, though, that if you've gagged Eric, I'm acting as *his* lawyer. Witness and counsel."

"Correct."

"As a former lawyer, *sir,* you'll recognize

the predicament I'm in here," I say. "All I know is that Eric has been accused of killing your people. I don't know what Harper told you. I don't know what you might have found at the scene. There's been no discovery. No formal laying of charges. So I'll skip straight to the biggest missing piece. Motivation. Why did Eric do this?"

Harper tenses, but I nod for her to trust me.

Edwin waves the question off. "As you well know, Detective, motivation isn't important. Fact is what matters."

"Yes, motivation gets in the way of an investigation. It clouds fact. But this is a trial. Unless Eric has confessed, we need motive."

"We have an eyewitness."

I give him a look. Just a look. He grants me another point. Juries love eyewitnesses, but a lawyer knows how unreliable they are.

"Fine," I say. "Set motive aside for now. What is the evidence *beyond* your witness? You returned to the scene to collect your dead, I presume."

"Our people did."

"And you saw how they died? Albie killed at his guard post. The older man in his sleeping blankets. Harper's grandmother running for her life."

A grumble runs through the crowd. This reminder does not please them.

"What evidence do you have that Eric did this?" I ask.

"He fled the scene, which means we can hardly search his belongings for bloody clothes or a weapon."

"What you need then is a second eyewitness."

I glance at Harper. Her face is glowing now. She sees victory — I will be that witness for her.

"I believe I have your motivation," I say, and then I switch to Mandarin with, "Keep your eyes on me, please, sir."

His brows lift, but he does as I ask. I nod discreetly to Harper, who is fairly quivering with anticipation. I do not dare implicate my lover when he stands right there, so I am using another language to do it, a language I share with her leader.

"Motivation," I say to Edwin. I speak slowly, carefully — my Mandarin is rusty and probably the equivalent of a four-year-old's. "You know Eric doesn't have one. You can't even think of one."

His mouth opens. I continue, while sneaking looks at Dalton. Worried looks. Maybe guilty looks. For Harper's benefit. Dalton doesn't even frown. He trusts me.

441

"But I have a motivation for you," I say. "A motivation for Harper to lie. That is right in front of your eyes. I have something that she wants."

"The dog? That's . . ." He doesn't finish.

"I have something she wants," I say.

He shakes his head. "Then she would know you're telling me the truth now. She would be arguing."

"Not if I've convinced her I want Eric's job. And that she can have the dog if she sticks to her story."

"What happened out there?"

I tell him. When I finish, I say, "Which story makes logical sense?"

Edwin says, in English, "So you were tasked with imprisoning a killer. You failed to do that, and we suffered. Is that your story, Detective?"

Oh, shit. I haven't fixed anything. Edwin never believed Dalton did it. This was all for show. We haven't dodged a bullet . . . we just stepped back into the path of the one that's been coming at us since we fled the massacre.

"Yes," I say. "We accept responsibility —"

"You did not. You walked away. You failed to show the basic respect due my people."

"Yeah," says a muffled voice.

I look to see Dalton has managed to get

the gag down just enough to talk over it. He twists, and it drops further, and he shakes it off, saying, "Yeah, I did. That was my choice. Because I knew there was no way in hell we'd come in here, confess to our mistake and you'd let us walk away. And there was no way in hell I was putting up with your bullshit while I've got a killer out there."

"My *bullshit*?" Edwin's voice lowers, heavy with warning.

"Yes, and don't give me that tone. You're in charge here. I'm in charge in Rockton. We're equals. Which means you should have shown me the *basic respect* of marching me in here for a private audience. Not tying me up. Gagging me and talking to my detective instead. You *know* why I didn't come here right away. I wish I could have. Would have saved us all a shitload of grief. But I couldn't, and this is all fucking theatrics, so cut the bullshit and let me get on with my job."

"I think perhaps we should put that gag back on."

"Sure." Dalton meets his gaze. "Go ahead and try."

"He killed —" Harper begins.

Edwin spins on her, snapping as he finds a target for his frustration. "I don't know what you thought you saw out there, girl, but no one from Rockton is going to murder our people for a few bows and supplies. You lost your head in those woods, and you won't be going back out there anytime soon. Turn in your bow and hunting knife. You'll help Mabel with the cooking now."

Rage fills Harper's eyes. Impotent rage. She tried to step out of her assigned role, and she is being smacked right back into it. I want to sympathize, but she accused an innocent man of mass murder because she wanted a dog. Sympathy is a little hard to come by after that.

"Give Casey her dog," Edwin says with an abrupt wave.

Harper grips the leash. "She's mine. In forfeit, for what they did."

"You think we'll share our food so you can have a pet?"

"It's not a pet. It can track and hunt and —"

"The only animals in this town are the ones we cook on a fire. Give Casey her dog. Now."

Harper looks at me, her eyes blazing. Then she drops the leash and knees Storm. The dog falls back in shock, and I race over, and whatever Harper sees in my face, she decides not to stick around.

I crouch beside Storm and pet her, soothing her as she keeps looking at Harper's receding back in confusion.

"We demand justice, Eric," Edwin says behind me. "We demand this killer."

"When we catch —"

"You will not bring him to me. I know you won't. Casey would promise to convey our demand to the council, but you know they'll refuse. So you will tell me only that you'll catch him, and justice will be served. That's not what I want. I am keeping Casey until you bring me this man."

"What?" I rise.

"Hell, no," Dalton says. "Do not even —"

"Casey stays. With the dog if that helps. She will be our guest until you return."

"Guest? We call that a fucking hostage."

"She is *my* guest."

"Yeah?" Dalton strides toward him. "If you keep her, this psycho is never going to *be* caught. She's the goddamn detective. You want a hostage? Take me."

"That is far more trouble than —"

"I remember how my mother was treated here." Dalton stops in front of the old man and lowers his voice. "A child does not forget that. He does not forgive that. The answer is *Fuck, no.*"

"I realize Casey is now your wife and —"

445

"I would not let *any* woman from Rockton stay here. Casey is a fucking *detective,* which means she needs to be out there hunting for this guy."

"So do you." I turn to Edwin. "I understand what you're trying to do, but you need to come up with a solution that won't hinder the actual hunt for this man."

"Take me," says a voice behind us.

I look to see Wallace, who has been so silent I've forgotten he was there. Now he steps forward.

"This is my fault, not theirs," Wallace says. "I hired Rockton to imprison the man who killed your people. They weren't equipped to do so, which the council failed to tell me. Eric and Casey had nothing to do with that. I made the mistake here."

"And who are you?" Edwin says.

"The father of the man who did this to your people."

FORTY-NINE

If I could have stopped Wallace before he said that, I would have. But once the words are out, there is no taking them back. And there is no way of walking out of this village with him.

We must leave Wallace behind. Leave him, and trust that no harm will come to him. He is a smart man. He didn't interfere as we dealt with Edwin, so I feel confident he's not going to do anything that will endanger him in our absence. It just won't be the most comfortable way to spend his Yukon trip.

They don't let us speak to Wallace in private. All we can do is talk to him, within earshot of the others, reassuring him.

A group of settlers escort us into the forest. Then they put our weapons on the ground and tell us to stand with our backs to them while they retreat. We do. Only when they give us the signal do we pick up our guns. Then we walk in the other direction.

"Can we go back to the scene of the massacre?" I say when we're out of earshot.

Dalton nods. He leads me there. The bodies are gone. Even the blood has seeped into the ground and disappeared, and when we arrive, the only thing that tells me this is definitely the right place is a red fox. It's in the clearing, so busy sniffing around that it doesn't see or smell us. It's snuffling madly, smelling death and seeing no sign of it.

When Storm spots the fox, she lets out a bark of greeting. The fox's head jerks up. It sees her. And it bolts into the undergrowth, leaping logs and ripping through dead leaves while Dalton digs in his heels and clenches the leash in both hands.

Once the fox is gone, I pat Storm and head into the clearing. Then I search. After a few minutes, Dalton says, "Tell me what you're looking for, and I can help."

I shake my head, as if I don't know, too distracted to answer. That's not entirely a lie. I don't know specifically what I'm looking for. But I'm here with a purpose, a question niggling the back of my mind, not ready to be voiced. Maybe never ready to be voiced. Not unless I find evidence to support it. So I just look. Then I hunker in the middle of the clearing and observe.

When I finally start to rise, Dalton says, "You gonna tell me what happened?"

"Hmm?"

"With that girl. She lied, didn't she. Outright lied."

"Yes."

Silence.

I take another look around before answering his unspoken question. "She wanted Storm."

More silence. I glance over, and he's just standing there, brow furrowed.

"The dog?" he says finally.

I drop to all fours and peer about near ground level, still searching. Then I say, "An error in judgment on my part. When she was interested in Storm, I jumped on that as a topic of conversation. Of connection."

I rise and brush off my knees. "I told her how we've taught Storm to track. I showed her how well trained she was. I said how gentle she was. How much bigger she'd get. Apparently, that was like showing off your new vehicle's special features to a car thief."

"You're serious?"

I nod.

"That's fucked-up."

"It is."

I stand in the clearing. Think. Think some

more. I'm so enrapt in my thoughts that I don't realize Dalton is right there until I turn and bash into him.

When I lean against him, his arm goes around me.

"You okay?" he says.

"I wasn't the one accused of murdering three people."

I feel him shrug as he says, "It was all for show. Just pissed me off."

I chuckle and shake my head. His arm tightens around me. "Something's bugging you."

"Everything's bugging me," I say as I step back. "We've left Gregory Wallace with people who know his stepson murdered their friends. To get him back, we need to turn over Brady. Which means finding Brady. Which we've been trying to do since this whole damn thing started and —"

Another squeeze as Dalton kisses the top of my head. "We'll get Wallace back. In the meantime, they won't hurt him. No point in it. If we'd left Storm, that'd be a whole different matter, apparently. But no one's going to want Wallace."

I give a strained laugh.

Dalton continues, "This just raises the stakes. Motivates us. Because, you know, we were just sitting on our asses before, trying to decide if we wanted to bother looking for this Brady guy."

I shake my head.

"Let's get to Rockton," Dalton says. "See if Phil made it back okay."

"Phil . . . Oh, *shit.*"

"Yeah, I know. Come on. We'll —"

"One last thing. Sorry. I just want to check . . ."

I trail off as my brain finally homes in on the source of that niggling thought.

As Dalton follows, he says, "Something's up."

"Just . . . I just want to check this."

A grunt says he isn't happy with my answer. He doesn't ask again, though, just lets his dissatisfaction be known.

"This is where we found Harper's grandmother, right?" I say.

"Yeah." He points, and I see that some scavenger has rooted through the dirt, looking for the source of the blood.

"Harper came from . . ." I turn. "This direction."

Dalton nods.

I walk that way and find a spot where vegetation has been crushed. "She watched us from here. Which means . . ." I look around.

"She came that way," Dalton says, pointing. "That's what you're looking for, right?"

"It is. Thanks."

"The path where she saw Brady is over there. We can follow it, but if I thought that would do any good, we'd have tracked him from there right away."

"I know."

A soft growl of frustration. "So what the hell are you looking for, Casey?"

"I don't know exactly."

Three beats of silence as I backtrack on Harper's trail. Then he follows. He wants to demand answers, but he knows that's not how I work. My ego needs proof before I'll voice any outlandish theories.

Harper's trail doesn't lead directly to the path. She meandered, and when Dalton sees that, he says, "She was trying to decide what to do. Follow Brady or go back to the camp."

I'm nodding when I spot something on the ground. I walk over and bend. It looks like the shredded remains of an animal. I prod it with a stick, expecting to see a head or leg or tail. I don't. It's just hide.

"A food pouch," Dalton says.

A hide pouch that must have held food, now ripped apart, with no trace of what it once contained.

He lifts and turns it over in his hand,

examining the craftsmanship.

"First Settlement." He peers into the forest, both toward the camp and out in the direction of the path. "So Harper saw Brady on the path and then followed his trail back to the camp. That's why it meanders. He was making his way in the direction of the path but didn't quite know where it was. He dropped this." He shakes the pouch. "So . . ."

He peers up and down the path. Then he goes still. His head jerks up. Storm's muzzle does the same, her nose wriggling madly.

"Back up," Dalton says.

"Wha— ?"

His hand wraps around my wrist as he starts propelling us backward. I take each step with care, rolling it, but Storm's paws crunch down on dead leaves. Dalton whispers a curse just as she starts to whine. *Loudly* whine, while straining at the lead.

Dalton stops. His gaze swings across the landscape. Storm dances and whines.

"What did you see?" I whisper.

"Movement. Something big."

Something big that Storm desperately wants to get to. Dalton has the leash wrapped around his hand, but he's distracted, looking about. When I see Storm hunker down, I know what's coming.

"Eric!" I say, and I lunge to grab the lead.

Storm leaps. A powerful leap that catches Dalton off guard, and he stumbles, the leash whipping free, my fingers grazing it, wrapping around it, only to feel the leather burn through my hand as the dog takes off.

"Storm!"

I run after her. I am aware, even before Dalton shouts, that I'm making the exact same mistake I made when she went after the cougar. But that doesn't mean I stop. I can't.

I hear Dalton coming after me, and I double down, terrified he's going to stop me. The messed-up muscles in my bad leg scream for mercy but —

Dalton shoots past.

"Gun," he snarls. "Get your damn gun out."

I do. Ahead, I can still see Storm, her black rump bobbing. Then I spot a figure with its hands out to ward her off. Dalton shouts. The figure says "Whoa —" and Storm takes him down. Then laughter rings out. Sputtering laughter.

Dalton slows, shaking his head. As I jog over, Jacob struggles to get to his feet while pushing Storm off.

"No one can sneak up on you guys, can they?" Jacob says.

"Yeah, because sneaking up on people who have these" — Dalton waves his gun — "is such a good idea."

"Cranky." Jacob grins my way. "That's the word you use for him, right?"

"Yes," Dalton says. "I'm cranky because my damn fool brother just tried to get himself killed by sneaking up on me when I'm in this fucking forest looking for —"

"The guy who killed all those people?"

Dalton eases back. "Yeah. He escaped and —"

"Found him."

"What?"

Jacob's grin widens. "Does that make you less cranky, brother?"

"Depends on how much longer you stand here instead of taking me to him."

FIFTY

We'd speculated that Jacob might have abandoned his camp because he got wind of irresistible prey.

And he had. His prey was Oliver Brady.

Jacob was camping after taking down the bull caribou when he spotted the man he'd met with us a week ago, and he knew Brady ought not to be out wandering the forest alone.

Jacob had his bow and knife and a waterskin, and that was all he needed. He followed Brady for two days, waiting for an opportunity to take him down. He didn't get one. The first night — when Brady massacred the settlers — Jacob lost him late in the day. He managed to find him again yesterday afternoon and planned to capture him that night but . . .

"He met up with a guy," Jacob says.

I glance at Dalton. He says nothing but shoves his hands deeper into his pockets.

"Can you describe the person?" I ask.

"I didn't get too close, but I could tell he was smaller than your guy." Jacob moves a limb from the path. "No, not smaller. Shorter."

Jacob goes on to say the guy had short, dark hair, maybe graying, but he wore a hat so it was hard to tell. Clean-shaven. Dressed in jeans, boots, and a bulky jacket. Carried a gun.

I reach for Dalton's hand, our fingers interlocking. Jacob notices and says, "He's one of yours?"

I nod. "Our lead militia. He took off last night. He was due to go home the day Brady arrived. We suspected he helped Brady escape, but we hoped Brady had just conned him into it, convinced our guy he was innocent."

"That could still be the case, though, right? Brady tells your guy he's innocent, and gets his help escaping, and then they meet to get through the forest. Paid escort."

"Yeah," Dalton says, "but if we keep telling ourselves there's a logical explanation, we're going to end up on the business end of a gun, finding out there isn't."

"I guess so."

We keep walking. I ask Jacob where Brady has been, what he's been doing. Jacob first encountered him over by the mountain, where we found Val's body. From there, Brady wandered. Or so it seemed to us, but as Dalton points out, without wilderness navigation experience, he probably thought he was getting someplace.

It's even possible that he climbed the mountain to get a better vantage point and in the distance spotted the First Settlement. Because that's the direction he seemed to head. From the mountain, he must have met up with the hunting party and killed them. When Jacob found Brady's trail again the next day, he saw him *watching* the First Settlement.

"He scaled a tree on the far side. He kept his distance, but he stayed up there until early evening before he came down and took off."

Had he seen the village from the mountain, thought it was a town, and made his way there, only to realize those people lived even more primitively than we did? That they had no ATVs or motor vehicles or horses he could steal?

But the First Settlement was only two hours' walk from where Brady massacred settlers for their belongings. Why do that if he thought he was close to the end of his journey?

So many questions. All of them unanswerable until we have Brady.

Jacob had spent today tracking his quarry. Plan A had been to capture him at night and march him back at knifepoint. Plan B had been to wound him from afar and do the same. But Kenny's arrival kiboshed that.

Then, as Jacob tracked them, he heard the First Settlement men who'd escorted us into the forest. He overheard enough to realize we were in the area. So he'd made note of Brady's current location and hurried to find us.

We reach Brady's camp. He's not there. That's only mildly disappointing — we figured he'd only pulled over to rest. But he's been here, very recently, so we'll find him.

There are two wrappers in the clearing where Jacob had seen Brady and Kenny sitting on logs. Protein bar wrappers. The kind we keep stashed in the militia equipment shed.

I pick one up and examine it.

"Yeah, that's ours," Dalton says.

"I know." Something about the wrapper nudges at me, though, telling me to look closer. I see these bars almost daily — Dalton insists we inventory any pack before taking it out.

This flavor is my personal favorite — chocolate peanut butter. Or it used to be my favorite. The company revamped the recipe lately and changed the packaging, sticking on a *New & Improved Taste!* band, which I'd grumbled should read *New & Cheaper Ingredients!* because it definitely did not taste better.

"This is old stock," I say, confirming as I check the expiration date.

Dalton shrugs. Jacob has already headed out to find the trail, and Dalton's struggling against telling me to put the damn wrapper away and come on before the trail gets cold.

"We ran out of these months ago," I say.

"Yeah, okay." He peers into the forest, head tilting as if he's listening for his brother. Storm tugs at the leash, seconding his impatience.

"Did we have old stock anywhere?" I ask.

"I don't know," he says. "Is that important?"

It isn't. Not right now. But it's bugging me, like so many things.

I fold the wrapper and put it in my pocket as I follow him from the clearing.

Jacob finds the trail easily. Brady is no outdoorsman. Once he got far enough from Rockton, he stopped using even amateur methods of hiding his trail. He's walking along what he probably thinks is a path, but it's really just a deer route. That means it's narrow, and we find freshly broken twigs and crushed vegetation, and even footprints when the ground gets marshy.

Jacob is in the lead, maybe twenty paces ahead. It's impossible to walk silently with an eighty-pound Newfoundland panting and lumbering alongside us, so we're hanging back. When Jacob finds the footprints, he gives a birdcall and, through the trees, I see him gesture at the ground. Then he keeps going.

We reach the spot, and I see what he was indicating and crouch to examine footprint impressions in the soft ground. Some of the prints are partials, just a toe or heel squelching down, the rest of the foot on harder ground. But I count five nearly complete and distinct shoe impressions. Three come from sneakers. Brady had been wearing sneakers the last time I saw him.

When I motion for Dalton, he puts his foot beside one print and I can confirm it's the same size, a nine. Average-size feet from an average-size man. Yet they give me that now-familiar niggle. I didn't expect Brady would still be wearing sneakers. Why not, though? That's what he fled wearing, and it's not as if he'd have been able to find

461

other footwear in the forest.

"Those are his," Dalton says. "Since you seem to be wondering."

"I am."

"They match the prints he left when he first ran. I remember thinking they're shitty shoes. The kind of fancy sneakers that wear out after a month out here."

I nod. He's right. But something . . .

I turn to the other prints. These are boots. Rockton boots. We don't exactly have a shopping mall of selection in town. Dalton finds a couple of styles that fit his criteria — good for outdoors, readily available, durable, and reasonably priced — and that's what you get. These are the type I wore until I went down to Whitehorse with Dalton and bought a pair better suited to my small feet.

I flash back to last month, in the station, waterproofing my new boots. Anders came in with Kenny and picked up the boot I'd already done.

He whistled. *"Nice."*

"Yep, I'm spoiled. Perks of sleeping with the boss."

"You mean compensation for sleeping with the boss."

Kenny chuckled at that and took the boot from Anders. "These *are* nice. Good arches. That's the problem with mine. Not enough support for high arches. Hurts like a bitch after a daylong hunt."

"How long have you been here?" Anders said. "And you're just telling us now?"

Kenny shrugged. "I didn't want to complain."

It'd been too late to get him special boots, and when Dalton said we had a stash of other ones — different designs for those who couldn't wear the usuals — Kenny had brushed it off. That's how he was. Never wanted to make waves. Never wanted to ask for anything special. Like the bullied kid who found his way into the cool clique and just wanted to ride that out, behave himself in case the others decided he was a pain in the ass and kicked him out.

Which is why helping Brady doesn't —

I rub my neck. Stop making excuses. My flashback does prove something: that I know Kenny left Rockton wearing boots like these.

Dalton moves his foot beside one print without prompting. It's smaller than his. Smaller enough to be noticeable, and yet significantly larger than my ladies' size five. A men's seven maybe.

I remember Anders joking that Kenny should try on mine — that they might fit. Which suggested Kenny's feet were small.

"Casey?"

I nod and straighten. This is the worst part of community policing — investigating a crime when the person responsible is someone I know, someone I like. I need to remind myself that beyond the few people I associate closely with, I don't *really* know anyone in Rockton. I cannot know their pasts. Even people without that past can come here and commit horrible crimes.

I grieve for the loss of the Kenny I thought I knew. I'm deep in my thoughts, following Dalton, and —

"Stop right there," a voice rings out. "Hands on your head, you son of a bitch, or I swear I'll — I'll fucking shoot you and drag your . . . fucking ass back to Rockton."

I know that voice. I even know the diction — a poor imitation of Dalton by a guy who wants to be him.

"Kenny?" I whisper. I was just thinking of Kenny, and therefore I must be mishearing or —

Dalton is running. Doubled over, running full out. I'm taking off after him, my gun out as he pulls his. We pass a tree, and ahead I see Kenny holding a gun at Jacob's back.

FIFTY-ONE

"Turn around," Kenny barks.

Jacob says something I can't hear, his voice low, words calming. He turns, and Kenny gives a start.

"Eric?" Kenny says to Jacob.

Jacob lowers his hood.

"Who the hell are — ?" Kenny begins.

"Kenny!" Dalton thunders.

Kenny wheels, gun lowering, the perfect opportunity for Jacob to grab it, but he just stays with his hands on his head. Kenny realizes he's lowered his weapon and corrects his stance, but Dalton sees that gun go up, trained on his brother, and he lets out a roar. When he snarls "Drop that fucking —" he doesn't even need to finish. Kenny literally throws the gun aside.

The gun hits the ground hard enough that I half expect it to fire, but it only bounces into the undergrowth as Dalton knocks Kenny flying.

Kenny babbles something from the ground. I reach them, but I still can't make out what he's saying.

Then Dalton has his gun trained on Kenny, saying, "Get your ass in the air," and when Kenny doesn't obey within 1.5 seconds, "Get your fucking ass in the air!"

Jacob says, "Eric . . ."

"You think I'm being an asshole?" Dalton snarls. Then he turns to Jacob. "*This* is the head of my fucking militia. The man who let Brady get away and then came out here to join him."

"Wh-what?" Kenny says. "No. I mean, yes, I let him get away. I didn't do my job right. I screwed up. But I didn't come out here to —"

"Get in position," Dalton says. "Now."

Getting in position means assuming the position that's like a downward dog, feet and hands on the ground, butt in the air. The first time I saw Dalton make a guy do it, I thought Dalton was trying to shame the guy, make him look ridiculous. And while it does, that's just a bonus. The beauty of the position is that the average person cannot leap out of it and attack. If he tries to rise, a foot on the ass will put him down again.

It is also, as I later discovered, a trick Dalton learned from Cypher.

466

Kenny gets into position, saying, "Just listen to me, Eric. I left a note. Didn't you get —"

"Yeah, Casey found it. Covering your ass, in case we found you alone. You weren't alone a couple of hours ago, were you."

"What?"

"You were seen with Oliver Brady."

Kenny starts sputtering denials, which only pisses Dalton off, and Jacob is trying to interject until finally I step in, arms waving for silence. Dalton gets the last word, of course, but then backs down, a jerk of his chin telling me to handle this.

"Kenny?" I say. "Just be quiet and listen, okay?" I turn to Jacob. "Is this the guy you saw with Brady?"

"I didn't get a look at the guy's face," Jacob says. "This *could* be him. That's all I can say."

"It wasn't —" Kenny begins.

"Wait," I say.

"He's the right size," Jacob continues. "Jeans. Boots. Jacket. All the same or close enough to what I remember."

"Which is town-issue clothing," I say, and Kenny nods, relieved.

"Eric? Can you give me one of Kenny's boots?"

I train my gun on Kenny while Dalton

467

removes a boot and hands it to me. It's the one I expect. Town-issue. Same tread as the prints I saw with Brady's.

"Have you been tracking Brady?" I say.

"I've been trying," Kenny says. "But I'm not Eric. I made a lot of noise, and I figured maybe Brady would see me and think I looked like easy pickings, and then I'd get the jump on him. It was a stupid plan. I haven't even heard anyone until this morning, and that was you guys." He glances at Jacob. "You're . . . one of Eric's contacts?"

The inflection tells me he knows full well Jacob is more. The resemblance is undeniable. But I only say, "Yes, Jacob is a local scout."

"I thought he was Brady. He's about the right size. And he's got light hair. His hood was up or I'd have noticed his hair's too long. Plus, uh, the beard." Kenny exhales. "I'm sorry. I heard someone, and then I saw a guy the right size, and I jumped the gun."

I compared Kenny's boot to Dalton's. Kenny's is a couple of sizes smaller.

"Have you been on this path?" I say.

"I was on a bigger one over there." He points left. "I might have been on this one earlier, but I don't think so. I've been heading for that mountain." He points to our right.

I look at Jacob. "The person you saw with Brady . . . He was definitely *with* him. Talking to him? Sitting with him?"

"I heard voices. They seemed to be talking. They sat together, and I saw the guy pass Brady food."

"Eric? Can you empty Kenny's pockets and backpack?"

He does. There's a waterskin and basic tools. For food, he's brought dried meat and a handful of protein bars.

"You took these from the supply cabinet?" I say, waving the bars.

Kenny nods. "I'll repay them."

"Not my biggest concern right now." I go through the handful of bars. "You already ate the chocolate peanut butter ones?"

"I didn't take any. I know those are your favorite, so I leave them for you. The cookie ones are good, though."

"She's not asking because she's hungry," Dalton says.

"Right. Sorry. I didn't take any of the chocolate peanut butter."

"What about old stock?"

"Old stock?"

"There was a box of chocolate peanut butter that went missing a while ago. Do you know anything about that?"

Dalton's gaze cuts my way, but he says

nothing. I'm bullshitting about the missing box. The truth is that we don't monitor the bars that tightly, figuring if the militia want to sneak a few extras, that's a perk for their help.

When I say that, though, Kenny looks uncomfortable.

"Kenny . . ." I prod.

"Someone took a bunch of old stock," he says. "I don't know what flavors. I just know that when I did inventory a while back, we had out-of-date bars and I put them aside to ask Will what to do with them, and they went missing. I decided not to say anything. They *were* old stock."

"You have no idea who took them?"

That uncomfortable look again. "I . . . No. I don't."

He's lying. I don't know why, but I need this answer. I study Kenny — the set of his jaw, the look in his eye — and I see it's not time to press the matter.

"Eric?" I lift Kenny's boot, and he nods.

When I pass Storm's lead to Jacob, Dalton's ready to argue, but I say, "I'll be quick," and I get a reluctant nod.

I take off at a jog back to the footprints. They're just around the corner, and when I reach them, I look back to see Dalton. He's moved about ten steps from Kenny, his gun

470

still on the suspect but staying within sight range of me.

I crouch with the boot in hand. First, I confirm, beyond a doubt, that the tread is correct. Eyeballing it, I'd also say the size is, but when I lower the boot below the prints, I see that the ones in the soft earth appear to be a size smaller.

I prod the edge of the print. While the ground is damp, it doesn't seem wet enough for the print to have contracted a size. That's possible, though. Soft ground shifts. If the boot is the right type and almost the right size . . .

Wait.

It's not the same boot. Closer examination shows that the wear pattern doesn't match. Kenny's are worn, with an uneven tread, maybe the result of unsupportive boots and high arches. The prints look like new boots, the tread very distinct.

I check the tag inside Kenny's. Then I look at the prints again.

New boots. Rockton-issue. Size-seven men's. Small for a man's shoe.

Not small for a woman's. Not unreasonably large either. That works out to maybe a nine. While we have women's boot sizes, many choose to wear the guys', finding them sturdier.

I work through Jacob's description of the person he spotted with Brady. Clean-shaven. Shorter than Brady. A bulky jacket, which would hide breasts.

There is a person with Brady. This person showed up at some point between day one and last night. This person is from Rockton, as evidenced by the clothing and the bars.

Someone has betrayed us. That person does not seem to be Kenny.

One name keeps coming to mind.

My other suspect for the poisoning, for Brady's accomplice.

Jen.

I'm working through how much of it fits when Dalton calls, "Casey?"

I've been bent over and out of his sight too long, and it's a testament to his self-control that he didn't shout "Butler!" the second I disappeared.

I rise and see him farther down the path, anxiously straining to spot me, resisting the urge to run and check. When I wave, I swear I hear him exhale from thirty feet away.

I glance down at the prints one last time, but they aren't telling me anything new. I'm turning from them when I see a flicker in the bush. I drop Kenny's boot and raise my gun.

Dalton gives an alarmed "Casey?" and his

boots thump as he runs toward me. In the bushes, I can see a form big enough to be dangerous, and I back against a tree, my gun raised.

A woman steps out. She's filthy with snarled hair and ragged clothes, and I think of Nicole. A woman, lost in these woods or taken captive, escaping and hearing voices and making her way toward us.

Then I see the knife. A rusted one with a broken blade and a makeshift handle. When I see that, I realize I'm looking at a hostile.

I have not seen one since I arrived in Rockton. I have heard some stories from Dalton and read others in the archives, but I am still not prepared. This woman could have just crawled from a pit after a decade of captivity. Matted hair. Dirt-crusted skin and clothing. When she draws back her lips, I see chipped and yellowed teeth. But she has not crawled from a pit. She has not been held captive. She has chosen to do this to herself.

And yet . . .

And yet I am not certain she has chosen. Deep in my brain, tucked away into the morass of "things I will pursue later," I have a theory. A wild theory that I used to joke sounded like I'd been spending too much time with Brent. I will never make that joke again, but the truth of it remains — that I have a theory about the hostiles that I am ashamed to admit to anyone but Dalton because it smacks of paranoia.

A theory for which I have zero proof, and that only makes it worse, makes me fear it is truly madness arising from hate and prejudice, a place no detective can afford to draw from.

My theory is that the hostiles are not Rockton residents who left and "went native" in the most extreme way. That such a thing is not possible, not on such a scale, because that is not what happens to humans when they voluntarily leave civilization. Jacob is not like this. The residents of the First Settlement are not like this. To become this, I believe you need additional circumstances. Mental illness. Drug addiction. Medical interference.

My theory is that the council is responsible for what I see here. I don't know why they'd do that. I have hypotheses, but I won't let them do more than flit through my brain or I may begin to believe I truly am losing my mind in this wild place.

I see this woman. I see what she has done to herself. And it's not just dirt and lack of care. Those only disguise what Dalton's stories have told me to look for. The dirt

474

isn't from lack of bathing. It has been plastered on like war paint. Under it, I see ritualized scar patterns. And the teeth that appear chipped have actually been filed.

I see a woman who should not exist outside of some futuristic novel, a world decimated by war, ravaged by loss, people "reverting" to primitive forms in a desperate attempt to survive, to frighten their enemies.

Which would make perfect sense . . . if people up here *had* enemies. If there was not enough open land and fresh water and wild game that the only force we need fight is the fickle and all-powerful god of this world: Mother Nature.

I stare at this woman . . . and she stares back.

I point my gun; she brandishes her knife.

Dalton is running toward us. Running and paying no attention to anything except me and this woman. Movement flashes in the trees, the bushes rippling.

"Eric!" I shout. "Stop!"

He sees something at the last second. He spins, gun rising, but his back is unprotected and there is another movement behind him. Then something white flying toward him. I yell "Eric!" and he dodges, and what looks like a sliver of white flies past his head.

It's a dart. A bone dart.

He's turning, and then there's a figure, in flight, leaping from a tree.

Dalton lashes out with his gun. A *thwack*, and the man goes down, howling. Another figure lunges from the forest. Jacob races around the bend, and Storm barrels past. And I fire. I lift my gun over my head and fire.

Fifty-Two

When I fire overhead, everyone stops. Even Storm.

The man who was charging at Dalton sees the dog, and he raises something in his hand, and Jacob drops on Storm, covering her.

"Stop!" I say.

I don't know if it will do any good. I believe they are capable of understanding the word; I do not believe they are capable of caring about it. I'm not even sure the guns matter, if the shot didn't just startle them.

Then I hear a voice, and the words are so garbled, it doesn't sound like English.

"Get on the ground," one of the men says again, slower, clearer, as the man Dalton knocked down rises.

Two others step up beside Dalton. Two men armed with clubs. One raises his and barks what I am certain is not a word, but

477

the meaning is clear.

"Do as he says, Eric," Jacob says. "Please just do as he says." He glances over his shoulder and says, "You, too," and that must be for Kenny, sneaking up.

Dalton holsters his gun, and I wait for someone to tell him to hand it over instead, but no one does.

Dalton kneels and puts his hands on his head. His expression is blank, but I see the rage in his eyes. This is the second time today we have been ambushed, and that feels like failure, as if we are characters in a bumbling-cop movie. But the truth is that this is the Yukon wilderness, and we are always one step away from ambush, by human or beast. The forest swathes her threats in bush and shadow, and we can walk all day and see no more than hares . . . or we can be forced to lower our weapons twice.

In all this, the woman before me has not moved. When I fired, she flinched, but now she stands exactly where she was, watching me, studying. No one else pays me any mind. I'm standing with my gun out, but they don't seem to care. They have assessed our party and dismissed me. One man watches Jacob — still atop Storm — but makes no move to go closer.

Four men surround Dalton, and something tells them that this is all that matters.

Which is not wrong. Not wrong at all.

The man who spoke before prods Dalton with his club. "Jacket."

Dalton glowers, but even before Jacob can speak up, Dalton takes off his pack and tosses it aside. The jacket follows.

"Gun."

He lays that down.

"Shirt."

"What the hell — ?"

"Eric?" Jacob says, and there's a quaver in his voice.

Jacob has spent his life avoiding the hostiles. There was an encounter years ago, when he'd been a young teen, after his parents died. I don't know details, but he's said enough for me to suspect it was not unlike the ordeal Nicole faced . . . in every way.

"We'll be fine," I say. "We'll be fine."

Dalton grunts and strips off his T-shirt. "There. If you want the rest, you're gonna need to —"

"We will take the rest."

The leader grabs Dalton's gun and swings it up.

I shout "Eric!" and lunge.

Dalton drops to the ground. The gun fires. And I fire.

I shoot the leader. I do not think about what I'm doing. I saw that gun rise on Dalton, and I knew what was happening. They made Dalton remove his jacket and shirt so they didn't ruin the garments when they put a bullet through him.

The leader falls. Dalton's gun drops from his hand, and Dalton scrambles for it. It takes only a split second, and then we're back-to-back, our guns raised.

The leader lies on the ground, blood pumping, his hands over the hole through his chest. His mouth works, his eyes wide. And not one of his own people even looks his way.

He is defeated. He is useless. He is forgotten.

"Jacob! Kenny!" Dalton shouts. "Go!"

There is a pause, and I know Jacob and Kenny are both assessing. Waiting for one of the remaining hostiles to turn on them, to raise a weapon, let loose a dart. But they do not. All they care about is us.

"Jacob," Dalton says again.

Then there's a rustle in the undergrowth, and while neither of us dares look that way, I know Jacob and Kenny are retreating. That's the smart move. This is bad enough already, with Dalton and me back-to-back, guns drawn, three armed men surrounding us, a woman with a knife just a few feet away.

"Back the fuck up!" Dalton says to the men.

The one with the club steps toward us.

"That is *not* backing the fuck up," Dalton says. "I know you understand English, so do not pull this bullshit caveman routine on me. I know where you are from. The same place I am, and you will not pretend you don't fucking understand me."

One of the other two men raises a knife.

"Drop that!" Dalton barks. "If you take a step toward us with that —"

The man draws back as if to throw the knife. I shoot his hand. He lets out a howl, blood spraying, knife dropping. Then he charges.

I kick. I don't aim for his groin, but that's where my foot connects. He falls back yowling, and the two other men run at us, weapons raised.

Dalton fires. I kick again and then swing my gun, hitting my attacker in the face. I hear Dalton snarl for the men to stop, just fucking stop before we put fucking bullets through their fucking heads. We do not want to do that. To them, though, that does not make us merciful. It makes us weak.

It makes us vulnerable.

481

I kick. I pistol-whip. Dalton shoots, aiming to wound, not kill. My foot makes contact. So do my gun and Dalton's bullet, and the three men are bleeding. Bleeding and enraged, club flying, knife slashing. I hear an *oomph* as the club strikes Dalton in the chest. I wheel to fend off his attacker, and a knife slashes my jacket.

I remember a story Brent told once, about a wolverine. He'd watched it defend its kill from a grizzly. Defend it to the death, the wolverine knowing it had no chance of winning against the bigger predator but unable to surrender. That's what this is. Only we cannot walk away. Cannot just say, "You win — take our stuff and go." That is not an option; it never was an option.

The hostiles can't win this fight against our guns. It doesn't matter. Our reluctance to use those guns is like blood in the water. The smell of weakness drives them into a frenzy, even if they *must* realize we won't let them beat and stab us to death while we hold loaded guns. They will force our hand.

The club blow winded Dalton. He lowers his gun, and his attacker is pulling back to strike him again. Dalton raises his gun, but he hesitates, and I know he will not pull that trigger. Something in his brain says he doesn't need to just yet.

He will not use lethal force until he is moments from death himself.

I can fix this.

Don't worry. I can fix this.

Dalton diverts his aim to the man's arm. His finger moves to the trigger, and I fire. I must fire. I will not gamble on his life. I have already killed one man today, and if I have to kill three more to walk away from this, then that is what I must do. They leave us no choice.

I fire.

My aim isn't perfect. This is not a slow dance. Only a few heartbeats pass between Dalton being clubbed and me realizing I must shoot before he is hit again. I pull the trigger, and my bullet hits Dalton's attacker in the shoulder. It is enough. He goes down, and I spin on the other two men.

Dalton shoots one in the leg. The other is coming at me, and I raise my gun and Dalton has his up, yelling, "Stop, you stupid son of a bitch! Just stop!"

A shot fires. The man flies sideways, and Kenny stands there, gun gripped in both hands, his eyes wide. The hostile slumps to the ground, shot through the chest. Kenny stands frozen, breathing hard.

"Eric?"

I hear the voice, and I think it must be

Jacob. It isn't Kenny, and it comes from off to the side. It's pitched high, but I am still sure it is Jacob — he's frightened. Then there's a movement on my right as Jacob and Storm cautiously approach from the left.

I turn toward the voice.

The woman stands on the path.

I have forgotten the woman. She's gripping her knife, and there are four of her people on the ground, two dead and two injured, moaning and bleeding, and she doesn't seem to see them. She's staring at Dalton.

"Eric?"

FIFTY-THREE

Even before Dalton says "Maryanne?" I know who this is. A woman who left Rockton years ago. A biologist who'd mentored Dalton, taught him, shared his insatiable curiosity about the world around them.

When Maryanne left with others, his father made the militia pursue. Rockton did not allow residents to become settlers. Dalton had been the one to find their camp, with evidence they'd been attacked by hostiles. A year later, he saw Maryanne again, and she *was* a hostile — did not recognize him, tried to kill him, almost forced him to kill her. Maryanne is one of those pieces that makes me think my theory is not so far-fetched after all.

I look at this woman, and I try to imagine a biologist, rapt in conversation with a teenage boy. A brilliant woman with a doctorate who decided to go live in her beloved natural world, and who made that choice willingly. Chose that and ended up as this.

She looks at me, and she's squinting, studying me as she did before, when we faced off and she did not attack. She squints as if trying to place me, too. Or maybe it's more than that. Maybe she's looking at me and seeing a mirror, reflecting something that sparks forgotten memories.

I used to look like that. Used to dress like that. Talk like that.

"Maryanne," I say carefully, too aware of that knife in her hand. "I'm Casey. This is Eric Dalton. You remember him, right? From Rockton."

Dalton gives a start, as if snapping out of the shock of seeing her. "Right. It's Eric." He pauses for a second. "Eric Dalton. Gene was my father. We talked about biology. You specialized in black bears. I found papers you wrote, on vocalizations and body language. I read them a few years ago. You were a professor at a university in Nova Scotia."

Her brow furrows, as if she's trying to understand the language he speaks. Intently trying to understand. She might even be struggling to hear — I see the blackened ear he mentioned, lost to frostbite. But there's more to her expression than incomprehension. It is as if she's peering deeper into that dark mirror, catching wisps of shadows that

486

look like people she once knew.

"Bears," she says.

Dalton nods. "Right."

"Eric?" Kenny says.

Dalton lifts a hand to tell Kenny to stay where he is. He never takes his eyes from Maryanne. "I found your camp after you left Rockton. I know something happened to you."

"Eric," she says. "The boy with the raven."

"Uh, right." He shoots an almost sheepish glance at me and then looks back at Maryanne. "I was trying to train a raven. I wanted to see if it could be taught to use tools. You told me there'd been studies on that, and you thought it might be possible."

Dalton has never told me this. That look says he finds it a little embarrassing now. But I remember when he first caught me training "my" raven. He rolled his eyes then, but I'd gotten a sense that my experiment pleased him.

"Eric with the raven," she says. Then she pauses. "Eric with the gun."

"Yes. You wanted to learn to shoot. I showed you, but you couldn't actually do it. You couldn't shoot anything."

He's giving as much as he can, trying to prod those memories, like speaking to someone with amnesia, but I can tell it's not quite getting through. It's like talking to a small child, one who is listening mostly to the sound of your voice and picking up familiar words. She is making connections, though. She is remembering.

And she is not attacking. That is the most important thing, because in her restraint I see hope. The others attacked. The others now lie, bloody, on the ground. And yet it isn't fear that holds her back. She could have attacked. She could have fled. But she sees Dalton, and something has changed from the last time. The rage is gone.

"Do you remember Rockton?" he asks. "Where we lived? Where you met me?"

"Eric. The boy with the raven."

He nods. "I'm going back to Rockton. I would like you to come with me. You'll be safe there. We have . . ." He pauses, as if struggling to remember something. "We don't have ice cream. That's what you said you missed most from down south. Ice cream. But we've shaved frozen milk before. You can have that. It's *like* ice cream."

There's no sign that she understands what he's saying, but when he says, "You'll come with me?," she tilts her head, listening. I put out my hand, and she stares at it.

"Come with us?" I say.

She looks at Dalton. He moves my way, a

sidestep, motioning for her.

"It's okay," he says. "It's your choice. You can come with us or . . ."

He doesn't say "or not." He glances at me, and we exchange a look that says that isn't an option. We want her to come willingly, but what is the alternative? To leave her out here, with her people dead?

There is opportunity here. So many opportunities. For her, to return to what she had been. For Dalton, to exorcise this particular ghost from his past. And yes, for me, to answer my questions about the hostiles. Both Mathias and Cypher have said we need live subjects, and while the very concept has horrified me, Maryanne is the perfect subject — not a lab rat but a woman we can help.

We walk a few steps. Then we motion for her to come with us. She looks about. She sees the men on the ground. Sees the two bodies. Sees the two wounded. Then she nods, and I can't tell whether it's acceptance or satisfaction. Whether she sees her comrades fallen through their own mistakes . . . or her captors finally getting their comeuppance. Either way, she nods. And then she follows. One step. Another.

There's a noise behind us. Kenny or Storm must step in undergrowth, and it crackles beneath their feet. Maryanne wheels. Dalton says "It's okay. We're —" and I don't hear the rest. I see her face. I see her reaction, as pure and unthinking as my own.

There is a noise in the forest. There is a threat.

She catches sight of Jacob and Storm on the path and lets out a howl, barely human. She charges. I'm right behind her as she runs, knife raised. Jacob only yanks the dog back behind him, no panic, knowing he's fine. He realizes she's just startled, and he can stop her, or I will, or his brother will, and she is no threat.

Dalton shouts, "Maryanne! It's okay!"

That's when she sees Jacob. Sees his face. Sees the resemblance to Dalton and begins skidding to a stop, a few feet from him and —

A shot fires.

For exactly one second, I think it's Dalton. Then I know it is not. Maryanne may have been running toward his brother with a knife, but Dalton has both a brain and a conscience. He will not shoot until he is absolutely sure his brother is at risk.

"Case —" Dalton begins, and then stops, having the exact same reaction as me. One moment of thinking I am shooting at Maryanne before realizing I am not.

Another shot. A half shout. Then Maryanne spins sideways. I run, and Jacob runs, and I hear Dalton's strangled cry and the thud of his footsteps.

Yet another shot. This one whips right past me, and I stop. I see Maryanne. There's blood. She's standing against a tree, and there's blood.

"Mary —" I begin.

She runs. She races into the forest, and I go after her, and there's a fourth shot. I feel pain. Then I'm falling.

"Casey!" Jacob yells.

Dalton hits me, and I drop as he's shouting his brother's name and I have no idea what the hell is going on, and the next thing I know I am on the ground under Dalton and Jacob is on top of Storm.

I twist, ready to leap up. That's when Dalton's eyes round, his mouth forming my name as he grabs my chin. I feel a hot burn, and my fingers rise to my cheek. There's a bullet graze across my cheek.

"I'm fine," I say quickly. "It just . . ."

Just grazed me.

Just about killed me.

"Who — ?" I begin.

Another shot. This one hits the tree near our heads.

"Kenny?" I say as I try to twist.

That's all I can think. It isn't me shooting. It's not Dalton. Jacob doesn't have a gun. So it must be Kenny.

Dalton's gaze flies to Jacob and Storm. His brother is crouched and pulling Storm along with him, his free hand motioning to us. Behind them is Kenny, hunkered down, gun lowered at his side.

I look up and scan the treetops and . . .

There's a figure in a tree. A dark figure.

Sniper.

"Off the path!" Dalton shouts. "Get off the path. Into the forest."

We creep into the undergrowth. Dalton has one hand wrapped in my jacket, not unlike Jacob with Storm. I only need to see Dalton's face to know not to argue. He tugs me to a clump of bushes, and we crouch behind it, both of us breathing too hard for the minor exertion, both of us fighting panic.

The forest has gone quiet except for the moans of the dying hostiles. The sniper has his — or her — position and is holding it.

I look up into the trees. It's dense enough over here that I won't spot someone on a limb. It's *not* dense enough, though, that we can just run, certain of cover.

I glance to my right. Jacob has Storm

behind a cluster of tall undergrowth. He's gesturing. Dalton is looking that way now, and they both motion, pantomiming a retreat plan.

I know what I want to do. Tell them to stay where they are while I make my way *toward* the shooter. Attack the problem.

Stay here, Eric. Stay there, Kenny. Jacob, hold Storm. Be safe. Please, I need you to be safe. Let me handle this.

Let me finish this.

If I even mention that to Dalton, he won't hold me here by force — he'll realize this is indeed the correct plan . . . and go to take down the sniper himself.

So when he taps my shoulder and nods to our next point of cover, I force myself to creep to that spot.

We reach it, and we make sure Kenny, Jacob, and Storm reach theirs.

Then we set out for the next point of cover. And the next. Each takes us deeper into the forest. Farther from the path. Farther from the sniper and the groans of the dying.

There is no sound except those moans. One turns to soft sobs. I hear a woman's name choked in those sobs, and I think of the men we are trying so hard *not* to think about. The dying hostiles. Just hostiles.

That's what I want to think. Not people. Not men who may have been no different from Maryanne once upon a time, no less deserving of mercy and salvation.

The dying man keeps saying the name, over and over. A wife? Lover? Child? Sister? Someone he remembers in his final moments. Someone he calls for. And then there is a shot, and the crying stops.

The crying stops, and the other man lets out a string of unintelligible babble. The crunch of undergrowth. A thump, as if he's rising, and that babble keeps coming. He's begging for his life. Begging someone who is not in a distant tree but standing right over him and —

Another shot. Silence.

I hear a click beside me and turn to see Dalton topping up his gun. I do the same with mine after he's finished, and I can see that makes him nervous — he doesn't want my weapon unusable even for a second. When I finish, he nods, and I lean against him for a moment of comfort. Then I look out again.

I can see nothing. No one. Instead I listen, and I catch the telltale crinkle of dead foliage under a careful foot. It is off to our left, the sniper attempting to circle wide and surprise us that way.

Dalton taps my shoulder. He points as his brother does the same, both of them indicating rocks to our right. The foothills. Dalton nods. Then Jacob motions that we are to go, and he will stay. In explanation, he gestures at his side, where I know Storm lies.

He cannot run with her. We can't tell her to be quiet or careful, and if she runs with him, they will be spotted.

Dalton swallows hard. I squeeze my eyes shut and make a choice. A choice I know I have to make even if every fiber in me screams against it. Even if this might be the one thing I do that I will never forgive myself for. If I am a good person, if I love Dalton, if I care for his brother, then I must make a monstrous suggestion.

"He should let her go," I whisper in his ear.

Dalton's gaze swings to mine.

I force the words out. "Tell him to drop the leash and run, and she'll follow but . . ."

But she won't be right at his side. She will be ahead or behind and that makes her a target, and I can hope to God the sniper decides not to bother with a dog, but this . . . This is what I must suggest, isn't it? I cannot risk Jacob's life to save my dog.

Dalton shakes his head. I shake mine harder, giving him a look that tells him I will not back down. His jaw sets. Then he motions for Jacob to drop the leash. Even from here, I see Jacob's face screw up, like he must be misunderstanding.

Dalton motions more forcibly, and Jacob looks at me.

I nod, and mouth, *Please.*

He slowly and carefully lays down the lead, watching us for any sign that he has misunderstood. Once the leash is on the ground, Dalton gestures for Jacob to run into the rocky foothills. One final moment of hesitation, and a glance at Storm. Then Jacob runs.

Kenny takes off behind Jacob, and Dalton gives me a shove, making me go before I can even see what Storm does. When I also hesitate, he pushes harder, and I take a deep breath, and then I run.

I run as fast as I can, veering away from Jacob and Kenny so we separate, giving multiple targets, multiple sources of noise and movement. And I do not look at Storm. I do not try to see where she is and what she's doing.

I have never prayed in my life, but at that moment, I send one up. Wherever the sniper is, let him realize what he sees is a fleeing dog, and there is no point in wasting precious ammo on it.

I run, and I know Dalton follows, but his footsteps fade fast as he heads in another direction. He must, same as I did with Jacob and Kenny.

Dalton has run to my left, which I don't like. It takes him closer to the sniper's likely location. But there's nothing I can do except curse him —

A whistle. A bark.

No. Fuck, no. Eric. Tell me you are not . . .

Of course he is. Of course he will, and I'm a fool if I thought otherwise.

Another whistle. Calling Storm to him as he runs. I glance over to see him bend in midstride and grab her leash and then run with her at his side, with all the noise an eighty-pound Newfoundland makes running through the forest.

You fool. You goddamn fool.

That's what we are, isn't it? We are those vampires who cannot continue until we have picked up every grain of rice. The shepherds who cannot ignore a sheep in danger. The law keepers who cannot shoot to kill if there is room for mercy. The humans who cannot put their dog at risk, cannot let their lover suffer the loss of her pet.

No matter what the cost to ourselves, we keep making these damn mistakes, and we know they are errors in judgment, but we truly are no more able to stop ourselves than those vampires of lore. Compelled to help, to protect, to save.

It is weakness. I know it is weakness. I hate that weakness. But I know we won't overcome it, no matter how many times we are shown that it's a mistake.

We keep running, and I try not to think about Storm being with Dalton, Storm endangering Dalton. Try, try, try . . .

A shot hits the tree above my head.

"Cover," Dalton yells. I'm already diving. I hit the ground just as another shot passes over me. I roll fast. Keep moving, keep moving. That is the trick here. Do not try to hide and hope for the best. Present a moving target.

I roll and then leap up and weave through trees. Jacob and Kenny are safe — they've reached the rocks and gone behind one, disappeared from sight. Dalton sticks to thicker forest with the dog, opting for safety over speed. I can see a rock ahead. I just need to —

A shot passes so close that I swear I feel it. I'm not going to make it. I'm too exposed, and the sniper has gauged my speed and is refining his shots.

I can't go faster. I don't dare go slower.

Just a little closer, a little closer . . .

"Hey!" There's a shout behind me. "Hey, you! Over here!"

I think it is Dalton — it's exactly the kind of fool thing he'd do. But I can see him, and I know where Jacob and Kenny went, and there's no way either of them has circled behind me.

Another shot, and it goes nowhere near me. The sniper accepting the newcomer's invitation.

"Here!" someone calls ahead, and Jacob peeks out.

He's gesturing at a rock. It's farther than the one I chose, but bigger, and while the newcomer distracts the sniper, I cross the last few paces and dive. Then I twist to see who is helping us.

I am almost afraid to see who it is. Afraid it is Anders or Sam or Paul come to find us. Afraid it is Cypher or some other settler who has come to our rescue and may pay the ultimate price for it. I even think it may be Wallace, that he has escaped captivity.

It is not any of those.

It is the absolute last person I expect.

Oliver Brady.

FIFTY-FOUR

It is a trap. It must be. But at this moment, all I care about is getting Dalton out of a sniper's sights, and if this is a trap, we'll deal with it later.

I wave for Dalton. He's running my way, aiming for another rock. A shot fires. A tree behind him splinters, and I leap from my hiding spot and wave my arms, shouting, "Hey!"

Dalton motions for me to get the hell back under cover. Then he's diving, and I withdraw. I make sure Dalton and Storm are safe, Dalton crouched behind the rock, his arms around her.

I spin toward Brady. He's coming straight at me. Running at me. Motioning for me to stay where I am, remain hidden.

I aim my gun.

Behind me, Dalton snarls, "Stay the fuck away from her or I swear I'll shoot your ass
—"

Brady goes into a slide. The moment he does anything the least bit threatening, I will shoot him. If he gets within a foot of me, Dalton will shoot him.

But he does neither. He slides behind a smaller rock, one that barely hides him. Then he pokes his head out and says, "We're sitting ducks here. There's a spot farther down."

Dalton says, "If you think, for one fucking minute —"

"I just saved you, Sheriff. You and your girlfriend. I risked my *life* to save you two. What the hell else do I need to do to prove myself? Take the bullet?"

"Depends on where it hits," Dalton says. "And whether you survive."

Brady's eyes narrow, but Dalton is right. We know Brady has an accomplice. Of course that accomplice wouldn't kill him. Which means he could easily pretend to draw fire while leading us to our deaths.

Jacob whistles. He's gesturing toward a spot we can't see, presumably big enough for the three of us and the dog. He's ignoring Brady, his gaze going between me and Dalton, making sure we see where he's pointing. Then he disappears.

"Go," Dalton murmurs.

I do. Behind me I hear, "You stay where

501

you are, Oliver, or I'll blow your fucking head off."

"Head or ass. Make up your mind, Sheriff."

"Whichever presents the bigger target. Right now, I'm figuring it's about fifty-fifty."

I run from rock to rock, and wherever the sniper is, he doesn't see me. Or he doesn't care, now that I'm with his partner.

I find Jacob disappearing into a crevice. By the time I reach it, he's turned and pokes his head out. Then he waves and retreats. I look in to see Kenny inside, safe.

I gesture for Dalton to drop the leash. He does, and I whistle for Storm. She comes running. When she reaches me, I pass her leash to Jacob and turn back to wave for Dalton. He's already on the move, and I curse him for that, because for a few seconds there, I didn't have my gun trained on Oliver Brady.

I remedy that, and when Dalton arrives, I make him go into the cave, which means giving him a shove. He gets halfway in before realizing that leaves *me* outside. He balks. I may kick his ass, possibly literally. Because here's the thing: we can't all crawl into this cavern and sit there, with Brady knowing exactly where we've gone. So I get Dalton inside, and then I look up to see

Brady hightailing it our way.

I meet him with my gun drawn. I've plunked myself in front of that opening, ignoring Dalton's pokes from within. I'm crouched there, gun trained on Brady when he arrives.

The first words out of his mouth are "Oh, come on . . ." like we're kids on the playground, and I'm being terribly unreasonable.

He even rolls his eyes, and I swear he's lucky I don't put a bullet between them for that alone.

"I saved —" he begins.

"You lured us in. Diverted fire to convince us you're innocent. After you massacred a hunting party of settlers."

"What? Wait. What?"

"Casey?" That's Dalton. I'm about to ignore him, but he yanks on my jeans leg and says, "Back door."

He means there's a second way out. We won't be trapped in this cavern.

When I hesitate, Dalton sticks his head through and says, "You do realize you're arguing with this asshole while there's a sniper out there."

Point taken.

I twist and get my legs into the opening. Then I'm wriggling backward while trying to keep my gun trained on an exasperated Brady.

After a moment, Dalton just drags me inside. It is indeed a cavern. Not a big one, but there's a passage big enough for Storm to get through, evidently, because I don't see her . . . or Jacob and Kenny.

Dalton wants me to go through first this time, and I grant him that, but not before I say, "That stunt with Storm —"

He cuts me off with a kiss, and that startles me enough to stop talking, which may be the point. It's not just a quick smack of the lips, either, but a deep one, dark with residual fear and confusion, a kiss that says he was scared shitless out there — for all of us — and may still be.

When it breaks, I rest my head on his shoulder and I breathe. Just breathe. Then I inhale and say, "Onward?"

"Yeah," he says.

I'm turning to go, and I see Brady, his head and shoulders pushed through the opening, paused there, watching us.

Dalton turns on him. "Get the fuck —"

"You're going to kick me out there to get shot?"

Dalton meets his gaze. "Yes."

"Fuck you, Sheriff." Brady pulls through into the cavern and crouches in front of us.

"I had nothing to do with what happened to those people. Yeah, I saw it — the tail end of it, when I heard voices and came to investigate. But if you're saying I massacred —"

"Not them," I say. "The others."

"What others?"

"A hunting party two nights ago."

"I have no idea —"

"Of course you don't. So where's your partner?"

"What partner?"

Dalton squeezes my shoulder. "Go with Storm. I'll handle this."

"Handle this?" Brady says. "By what, shooting me?"

"If I have to. I'd prefer if you just came along quietly. Saves me having to drag a corpse back to Rockton."

"And they call *me* a psychopath? You —"

I grab Brady's shirtfront, my hand wrapping in it, yanking him forward, and the surprise of that nearly topples him onto me. He tries to jerk back, but he's crouched in this cavern and can't get the balance to do more than weakly pull against my hold. I lift my gun and point it at his temple, and that gets him struggling hard, but I have a good grip.

"The person you need to worry about

505

shooting you?" I say. "It's not Eric. I watched a good friend die in agony because of you. Saw a woman I cared about dead in a river because of you."

"No, not Val. I did not hurt Val."

"You took her hostage, you son of a bitch."

My finger moves to the trigger, and the only reason I don't pull it? Because another gun barrel flies up. Dalton lifts his gun, and his finger is on the trigger, and I know that if I shoot, so will he. That has nothing to do with agreeing that Brady deserves to die. He cannot stop me from killing Brady, so he will join me. Do something he would never do on his own, and do it to keep me from being the one who kills Oliver Brady, as I killed Blaine Saratori twelve years ago.

I see that gun rise, and I see the resolve on Dalton's face, and I release my trigger.

"Oliver Brady," I say. "You're under arrest. Get your ass through that hole" — I point at the opening where Kenny, Jacob, and Storm have gone — "and if you scream or fight or do *anything* that calls the attention of that sniper out there, I will shoot you. I swear I will."

We lock gazes. Hold them. When he tears his away, I see his outrage, the look that says he won't forget this, that no one treats him this way.

He goes through the hole after me. Dalton follows. There isn't any sign of Kenny, Jacob, and Storm until we go through another passage. I watch Brady come in, so I witness his first glimpse of Kenny. He sees him . . . and reacts no more than he does to Jacob.

They're crouched in a cubbyhole not big enough for all of us, and Storm is whimpering. She has no idea what's going on or what to make of this cave-crawling business. Dalton takes the lead and her leash, and Jacob falls in behind.

The exit is a tight squeeze, and my poor dog cries as she's being tugged by Dalton and pushed by his brother. But she trusts us and she doesn't fight, just lets herself be propelled through.

We come out a couple of hundred feet from where we went in. We move as quickly and quietly as we can, through the forest, getting at least a kilometer away. Then Dalton wheels and grabs Brady so fast that Jacob and Kenny dive for cover. But Dalton just puts Brady up against a tree and says, "If you fucking ever tell us you haven't killed anyone again —"

"I did accidentally shoot your friend. The old man. I'm sorry. I know you don't believe that, but I am."

Brady looks my way, still pinned to the tree.

"I told you before, Detective, whatever I do comes from desperation. My stepfather wants me dead. He has the money and the power to make that happen. I've run out of options. I will do pretty much anything to stay alive. That includes intimidating an old man. But I did not mean to shoot him. We fought for the gun, and he got shot, and I ran. Panicked and ran."

"You ground your fist —"

"I *panicked.* I needed to know where to find the sheriff's brother, and I did a horrible thing in my desperation to get that information. When he still refused, I didn't try again. I ran."

"And Val?" I say.

"If Val is dead, then I am sorry for that, too, but I didn't kill her. I took her to that spot. That wolf was there. Only it was rabid." He gives a ragged laugh. "Of course it was. It's not enough to just have wolves out here. They need to be rabid, too."

"So you saw the wolf . . ." I say.

"I saw it. Shot it. And it kept coming, like something out of a damn horror movie. So I ran. At first, Val was behind me, but then she apparently realized I wasn't holding her at gunpoint anymore. So she took off. I have no idea what happened to her after that."

"Then you did what?" Dalton says. "Wandered around hoping for fucking signs to the nearest town?"

"Yes, Sheriff, I kinda did, okay? Not an actual signpost — I'm not that naive — but I figured if I just kept walking, I'd reach a road, and I could hitchhike to town."

"Yeah, good luck with that. You hear any cars out here?"

"I've realized my mistake, okay? Which is why, when I heard voices, I just said 'screw it' and headed toward you. I've been out here for days, and I feel like I'm walking in circles — hell, I probably am. I'm exhausted. I have no supplies. No weapons. I saw a grizzly bear yesterday. A fucking grizzly bear. I may have pissed myself, but by now, I stink so bad, it's not like you're even going to notice. I give up, okay? I throw myself on your mercy. The only thing I'm going to ask is that if my stepfather orders you to kill me, you walk up behind me and just do it, before I know what's happening. I can't win here. Can't escape. I get that now."

I slow clap. He turns on me, but Dalton still has him pinned, and all Brady can do is glower.

"Just applauding the performance," I say.

"It's really good. Unfortunately, while you can explain away Brent and Val and just play dumb about the settler massacre, we have an eyewitness who has seen you out here. Eating bars from Rockton." I take the wrapper from my pocket. "And you weren't alone."

"What? No. Just . . . Look, I have no idea who this eyewitness is, but if someone told you that, then my stepfather got to him — or her. Bribed him. Blackmailed him. *Something.*"

Brady turns to Kenny. "It was you, wasn't it?"

"No, it was me," Jacob says.

"What?" He turns to Jacob. "You're the scout. The one I met on the walk with the wolf and the sniper. The sheriff's brother, right?"

"Yeah," Dalton says. "And he lives out here. Which means he's not working for your daddy."

I wave at the forest. "This isn't the big city. Your stepdaddy can't post on Craigslist for a spy."

"I realize that," Brady says coolly. "I presumed that whoever he paid off was a resident of your town." He glances at Kenny. "You or one of my other prison guards."

"It wasn't me," Kenny says.

"I saw you eating that bar with someone," Jacob says to Brady. "I saw you walking with someone. Heard you talking with someone."

"I don't even know what to say to that, except that I wasn't. Flat-out wasn't."

"So you're calling my brother a liar?" Dalton says.

"No, I'm actually not. I grew up with the biggest liar you could hope to meet — my stepfather. I know when someone's bullshitting, and I can tell your brother isn't, which leaves me . . ." A helpless shrug. "I don't even know. I just don't. Obviously he saw someone out here who looks like me. Same size or whatever."

"It was you," Jacob says. "Those jeans. Those shoes. That shirt."

"Then I . . ." Brady trails off and looks over at me. "I do not know what to tell you, Detective. I just don't know."

"Any identical twins we should know about?" I ask.

His lips tighten. Then he says, "I realize you're being sarcastic, but at this point, I'm starting to wonder myself. The only thing I can even think of is that my stepfather sent someone out here who resembles me, dressed like me. Which makes me sound like a raving lunatic. So I've got nothing, Detec-

511

tive. Absolutely nothing but my solemn word, with a promise that if you find out I'm lying, you don't need to shoot me. Walk me to one of these mountain gorges, and I'll swan-dive. Save you the bullet."

FIFTY-FIVE

Jacob leads the way. Brady is right behind him, with Dalton and Kenny following. I'm lagging back with Storm. I've given her food from my pack, and we've found water, but she's exhausted. Like a small child who senses this is not the time to complain, though, she troops silently beside me.

We're heading toward the First Settlement. That's what Dalton told me, murmuring, "I'll work it out," and, "Only thing we *can* do." Which is correct. We cannot risk Edwin finding out that we have Brady and didn't bring him. He would execute Wallace for that — he must, to keep the respect of his people.

So I'm lagging behind, and I'm thinking. I'm not thinking of how to get out of this without handing our prisoner over to people who'll execute *him.* I need to work through something else first.

We've been walking in silence for about

thirty minutes when Dalton falls back with me.

"You know one of the best things about having you?" he says quietly, and I have to replay his words, so out of context here.

"Having *someone,*" he continues. Then he pauses. "Yeah, that didn't come out right. Sounds like I'm one of the guys from town, desperate for a woman, any woman."

I manage a chuckle. "You've never had that problem."

"Yeah. But you know what else I've never had? A partner. Not just for sex. Not just for work. Not just for friendship. Someone who is all that and more. Lover. Colleague. Friend. Even using those words to describe other people? Seems like they should have different definitions altogether."

"I know."

And I do. I'm just not sure where this is coming from, if he's unsettled by what's happened and looking for distraction.

He continues, "Even 'partner' is a shitty word. Sounds like a business arrangement. The other day, when you said you were my wife, that . . ." He shoves his hands in his pockets. "It sounds lame, but that means something to me. We don't get that in Rockton. My parents — the Daltons — they were a couple, but I've never heard them use the vocabulary much. To me, husband or wife means . . ."

He takes his hands out of his pockets and flounders, as if looking for a place to put them, finally settling for taking Storm's lead in one and my hand in the other.

"My dad always used it," he says. "My, uh . . ."

"Birth father."

"Right. In the First Settlement, he used it a lot, and my mom would call him her husband. That was because they were reminding people — warning the men to leave her alone — but I didn't realize that at the time, so husband and wife, that seemed like their special words. And they were . . ." He shakes his head. "Fuck, they were in love. The kind of stupid, crazy love that makes you run into the forest when someone tries to separate you. Dumb kids. But they made it work, and they were partners — real partners — in everything. I told you Jacob says they died together, in a dispute with hostiles, but I wonder if maybe just one was killed and the other didn't . . ." His hand clenches mine, reflexively tightening. "Just didn't try very hard to get out alive after that."

We walk a couple of steps, and I say softly, "I don't know much about your parents, but from what Jacob has said, I don't think they'd have left him alone if they had a choice."

A moment of silence. Then he nods. "Yeah, you're right. If one could have made it back, they would have. For him. For their . . ." He swallows. "Fuck."

His hand grips mine so tight it hurts. Here is the discrepancy he cannot resolve: that the parents who didn't rescue him from Rockton were not parents who would ever shrug and say, *Well, that's one fewer mouth to feed.*

"The point," he continues, "is that this is important to me. What we are. You and me. One of the best parts is that I don't have to do this on my own anymore. Yeah, I know, I've always had help. But it's just been that: help. People who listen to me and do what I tell them because they trust my judgment. But fuck, you know what? Half the time I'm not sure *I'd* listen to me. Now I have you. Someone I can talk to, share with, confide in, ask for advice and, yeah, someone who'll tell me if I'm full of shit."

"Uh-huh."

"So my question is, Casey" — his gaze slides my way — "is that just me?"

"I don't understand."

"I want to be that for you, too."

"You are."

"Am I? Or am I the junior partner here?"

I look over sharply. "What?"

"The trainee. A promising one, but still new at this detective shit, and not ready to work at your level."

"What — ?"

"I don't think that's it. But I like the alternative even less — the feeling that if you're holding back, it's not because I haven't proved myself, but because you want to protect me. I'm a little bit naive. A little bit idealistic. You like that. You want to preserve that. Which might seem fine to you, but I feel patronized. Like I'm years younger than you, not just a couple of months."

"I —"

"When we got Nicole back, I know Mathias left that asshole in a hole somewhere. Poetic execution. You know it, too, and I'm sure you confronted him. But you kept that from me."

"No, I did not, Eric. Yes, I confronted Mathias and didn't tell you — because he wouldn't admit to anything. He knew if he did, I would tell you. I have to. Not just because you're my boss, but because keeping it from you *would* be treating you like a child."

He relaxes at that. But he has a point, one

I'm not going to admit right now. I *would* have told him if Mathias confessed, and I'm glad he didn't, because that would have meant Dalton needed to launch a hunt for a man who deserved his horrible fate.

I didn't push Mathias because I wanted to protect Dalton. And that is wrong. Not wrong to protect him, but wrong if, in protecting him, I'm trying to preserve his innocence, to shield him.

It is patronizing. It's what you do to your children and, at one time, it was how you treated your wife, presuming she didn't have the fortitude to face life's ugly truths. It is *not* what you do to someone you consider an equal, however good your intentions.

"I'm sorry," I say. "If I've done that, I apologize."

"So we can stop protecting Eric's delicate sensibilities?" he says.

I manage a smile. "We can."

"Good. Then tell me what you were thinking."

"Thinking . . . ?"

"Right before I came back here and gave you a hard time. What you've been thinking all day . . . whenever we haven't been trying to stay alive, which has been, admittedly, the bulk of our morning and afternoon."

"It's only afternoon?"

He shows me his watch. It isn't even 3 P.M. I curse, and he chuckles.

"I'm working on a theory," I say.

"Kinda guessed that."

"It's not one I like."

"Yep."

"If I've been keeping it from you, it isn't to protect your sensibilities. It's to protect your opinion of my mental health. And maybe your opinion of *me.*"

"Because if you tell me what you're thinking, I'll wonder what kind of fucked-up person even imagines something like that."

"Yes."

"Then let me help. Are you wondering whether Harper killed the settlers?"

I blink over at him.

He continues, "She claimed to have seen Brady there but gave little more than what might be extrapolated from our description of him. She was the one found with blood-soaked clothing, explained away by trying to save her grandmother. Then there's the shredded food pack. If Brady killed the hunting party for their supplies, he'd have taken much better care of that. Instead, it was abandoned and ripped apart by animals. You just don't want to admit you're considering her because you're afraid it reflects badly on you, thinking a kid could do something that horrific."

He looks over. "So, am I close?"

"Uh, dead-on, actually."

"Good. Proves I'm making progress with this detective thing. And that maybe my view of people is a little more jaded than you'd like to think."

"Or just that I'm rubbing off on you."

He puts his arm around my shoulders. "Sorry, Detective. I'm pretty sure it's not possible to have lived my life up here and be completely unaware of what people are capable of doing to each other. I just don't like to jump to that for the default. Innocent until proven guilty. Good until proven evil. And there's a huge spectrum between those two poles. What matters is where you *want* to sit on that spectrum, and where you *try* to sit if you have a choice. Like when you need to shoot a hostile who's about to kill me."

I say nothing.

He glances at me. "You think I don't know that's bugging you, too? I'm the one who screwed up back there. I tried to avoid killing that man, and all I did was sentence him to a slow death. They had no chance of crawling back to their camp. No chance of being rescued. No chance of surviving. The sniper who shot that hostile did him more of a favor than I did in trying to just wound him."

"You —"

"I'm not looking for redemption, Casey. Just stating facts. I learned my lesson. Doesn't mean I won't leave someone alive if they *can* get to help, but I won't make that mistake again. Either way, I killed a man today, too."

"Have you ever . . . ?"

"No," he says, and shoves his hands in his pockets. "No, I haven't."

We are back in the clearing where the three settlers were massacred. I have watched Brady's expression the whole way, waiting for the flicker of recognition, of concern, of worry. Why are we returning him here? Is there something we might find that will prove he's guilty?

He must be guilty, right?

No. That is the hard truth I've come to accept. The likelihood that Harper killed these settlers. That Brady's claim of innocence is correct. At least in this.

As we approach, he gives no sign that he recognizes the location. We enter the clearing, and he's looking around. Then he's checking his watch, as if wondering whether we're stopping for the night.

"Turn around," I say.

He does. He's been quiet. Past the point of denials. Past the point of anger. Just exhausted and resigned to whatever his fate might be.

Earlier, I patted him down for weapons and found only Kenny's knife, which I have returned. Brady claims he had a stick, too — he'd sharpened it with the knife, as a spear, and he'd been proud of his ingenuity in that. He'd been unable to find anything to eat out here, but at least he had a sharp stick. Or he did until we crawled into that cave and he had to abandon it outside.

Now I more thoroughly pat him down, and he has nothing but crumbs in his pocket. Apparently Devon had delivered cookies to Val while she sat with Brady, and before Brady escaped, he shoved them into his pocket. A survival plan as pathetic as that sharp stick.

Those crumbs clearly came from sugar cookies rather than our protein bars, and Brady seems as weak as one might expect after three days. That does not mean I accept that Jacob made a mistake about seeing him with another man, eating our old bars. I'm just not sure how to reconcile that, so I've put it aside.

The lack of food isn't ironclad proof that

he didn't kill the hunting party. Yet there is also the most damning evidence for a homicide detective. His clothing.

Brady is wearing what he left Rockton with. Right down to his socks and boxers. As filthy as his clothes are, I see no more than a smear of blood on his shoulder, as if he'd wiped a bloodied nose after fighting Brent.

Whoever killed the settlers had slit one man's throat. Stabbed another. Brutally murdered a woman. That much blood won't come out by rinsing your shirt in a mountain stream.

I would not take this evidence before a court of law — not unless I was a defense attorney, desperate to get my client exonerated. Brady might have taken off his shirt for the attacks. He might have hidden whatever food and supplies he stole from the settlers.

But I cannot continue to say he even makes a good suspect.

Which leads to a very uncomfortable admission. That he might actually be telling the truth . . . about all of it.

Brent's death was manslaughter, rather than murder. As for Val, I don't know how she died. I wasn't able to recover her body to autopsy it. I wasn't even able to get *to* her body for a closer look. I can only say that she was dead in that river, with no obvious signs of trauma.

Yet there are other things that don't fit.

Who did Jacob see in the forest, if not Brady? I trust Jacob implicitly, and I can't imagine he was mistaken, so what is the alternative? If it was Brady, wouldn't he come up with an excuse? *Why, yes, I did meet someone on the trail — a stranger who took pity on me and shared his stash of protein bars.*

Who the hell shot at us? Executed the two wounded hostiles? Tried to kill the rest of us?

It makes sense that it was the same person who shot at Brady a few days ago. Was Brady really the target, though? He was nowhere in sight when the sniper executed the hostiles and opened fire on us.

There are too many loose ends that "Brady is innocent" does not explain.

Yet none stamp him as guilty either.

We're missing a piece of the puzzle here. A huge one. And I'm starting to think I know what it is — or at the very least, I know where to begin this trail.

A few words from Brady, dismissed as the rantings of a killer, determined to lay blame anywhere he could.

Words that could have come straight from
the serial killer handbook.

I'm being set up.

Why?

Because I know a secret.

FIFTY-SIX

"We're taking you to Edwin," Dalton says to Brady as we leave the scene of the settler massacre.

"Who?" Brady says.

"We need to get Gregory back," I say.

"Greg — ? My *stepfather*? He's here?" Genuine fear spikes Brady's voice.

"He's being held hostage," I say. "In exchange for you."

"What?"

"You massacred three people from a settlement out here. They wanted a guarantee that we'd hand you over. Your stepfather volunteered."

"Volun . . . ?" He stares at us. Then he laughs. "Oh, that's funny. I know you don't mean it to be. You're trying to scare me into thinking you're handing me over to these crazy mountain men. I don't know why you'd bring Greg into this, but telling me he voluntarily turned hostage in exchange for me?" He shakes his head. "That bastard wouldn't *voluntarily* piss on me if I were on fire. He doesn't do anything for anyone except himself."

"Well, he did. Unless you're suggesting the guy we left as a hostage is an imposter."

I describe Gregory Wallace, and Brady's ashen complexion answers for him.

"No," he says. "That's not — He has an agenda. Goddamn it, no. He's up to something and . . ."

"And what?"

"And I have no idea what it is, but I can promise you — Wait. Hell, yes." He wheels on us so fast he startles Storm. "What are you about to do?"

I glance at Dalton.

"Didn't you just say you're taking me to trade for Greg?" Brady says.

"No, we're taking you to work this out," I say. "We aren't going to turn you over for execution. That's not —"

"But it's what Gregory expects. That in order to get him back, you'll need to hand me over. Which means he doesn't need to kill me. You guys handed me over. Some crazy mountain men killed me. Not his fault."

"So he wants you dead."

Brady stares at me, eyes bugging. He

blinks. Stares some more. "Have you listened to a word I've said since I got here? Yes, Greg wants me dead. Why the hell did he send a sniper to shoot me? Why did he show up himself when that failed? To make sure — one way or another — that the job gets done."

"For the money." I turn to Dalton. "Seems a little overcomplicated, doesn't it?"

"Just a little," he drawls.

"I've never even been down south," Jacob says. "And that sounds crazy to *me.* Accuse you of killing a bunch of people, ship you off into the wilderness, and *then* execute you?"

"Gotta be easier ways of killing an inconvenient heir," Dalton says.

"At the risk of sounding like a rich prick lecturing the local rednecks, it's not that easy to get rid of me. My mother loves me more than she *trusts* Greg. If I died down there, she'd suspect him. In a few months, he'll tell her the so-called truth. By then, he'll have fabricated all the evidence he needs to convince Mom that her darling boy was a psychotic serial killer. Then he'll show her all the steps he took to keep me safe . . . only to have me die in these woods, through no fault of his own."

"There must be more to it," I say.

Brady growls under his breath. "I don't want to call you stupid, Detective . . ."

"Then don't. And please remember that I *am* a detective. Your story stinks. Back at the start, even *you* said there was more to it. A secret you knew, about your step-father."

"It doesn't matter. What matters is —"

"Eric, can you cuff him? We really need to get him back to Edwin. We may need to find a gag, too."

Brady wheels . . . to find my gun pointed at his face, Dalton's at the side of his head.

"Hands behind your back," I say.

"You think you want my secret, Detective? Actually, you don't. Because if there's any doubt in your mind that I'm a lying son of a bitch, this will erase it. The only person who gets to hear it is my stepfather. One final card I can play to beat him at his game. It's my ace in the hole, and I'm not letting you take it away from me."

"Then I guess you're going to get the chance to play that ace very soon. Put your hands behind your back."

We are marching Brady to the First Settlement, and I'm trying to figure out what the hell to do about that. He's called my bluff, and right now, the only solution I can think of involves showing him it's not a bluff. Handing him over to Edwin and seeing what Brady plans to do about that. Which is a shitty, shitty plan.

It shouldn't come to that. Brady's smart enough to realize that no secret is going to fix this solution. His leverage is with Wallace, who has no power here.

So how does Brady think he's going to get out of this?

He doesn't. He really is calling my bluff, and he expects me to cave.

Okay, fine. Forget the hostage exchange. Let me take you back to town, and we'll work this out.

I already know his secret. I've figured that one out. But if I confront him with it, I lose ground.

I need him to tell his secret. Break down and confess. Hand me that ace in his pocket. Give me what he thinks is his power.

I need it before we reach the First Settlement.

I look at Dalton, walking behind me, but he's deep in thought, also trying to see a way out of this predicament.

I pause to let him catch up. We need to talk. I'm not sure how but . . .

Dalton stops. He's looking to the side. I go still and listen. I don't need to focus very hard to hear the distinct clomp of boots on hard ground. Kenny's looking over, too. Brady opens his mouth, but at a sharp wave, he shuts it. Dalton motions for Jacob and Kenny to take Brady and Storm, and for me to follow him.

The boot steps continue along the path. There's no attempt to be stealthy or to avoid the path. That makes me hopeful — hopeful that as we sneak up through the trees, I'll see Anders. Or any familiar face from Rockton.

Instead, I catch the guttural tones of a settler.

Dalton lifts a hand, sees I've already stopped, and grants me a nod of apology. We both go still as we listen.

"We'll split up here," a man says. "You go left. I'll take right."

"Edwin said to stay together."

"We're tracking a southerner. An unarmed southerner."

"Didn't stop him from almost killing Martha."

"But he failed. He couldn't even take down a woman. He's soft. Old, too."

"He didn't seem that old. And he still got away. He's smart —"

"Not as smart as us."

Gregory Wallace has escaped the First

Settlement. There's no other way to interpret this, but I still mouth the words to Dalton. He nods — he's come to the same conclusion.

I creep back to Brady, who's looking the other way, gazing into the forest. I slip up to him, put my gun to his chest, and whisper, "One word, and I pull this trigger."

His glare is icy rage. He hates me. I don't know if he would have hated me no matter what the circumstances. I don't know if my actions thus far have led to this. But whether he's a killer or not, I suspect that if Oliver Brady got hold of a gun, his first bullet would go between my eyes.

We wait until the settlers are out of earshot. Then we wait a little more, before Dalton nods, telling me they are gone.

"There is no exchange," I say to Brady, and he smirks.

Called your bluff, Detective.

"There's no exchange because your stepfather has escaped."

His lips form a curse, quickly swallowed.

"He'll return to our town," I say. "Which is where we're going. We're done with this bullshit. We've lost two friends, and I don't care if you murdered them or not, they would still be alive if you hadn't shown up. This ends now. We are taking you back to

532

your stepdaddy, and we're putting both your asses on the plane. Eric will fly you within a day's walk of the nearest town. He'll point you in the right direction. He'll give Gregory a gun. What your stepfather chooses to do with the gun is up to him."

Brady's eyes widen, his mouth opening.

"You say you have a secret for his ears only?" I whisper. "You'll have plenty of time to confront him with it, after Eric kicks you both off that plane. Until then? You're gagged."

"No," he says, and there isn't any defiance in it. Only fear. "You can't —"

"Can. Will. You may say you aren't a killer, but people die a little too often around you, Oliver. So we're terminating the contract that brought you here. This is family business. Yours, not ours."

"I didn't kill —"

"Like I said, we don't care. We did, once upon a time. But then you went and escaped, which led to the whole 'two dead friends' issue."

His face hardens. "You had no intention of listening to me —"

"You never gave us a chance to dig deeper. So off you go. Tell Gregory your secret. Maybe you two can work this out." I pause. "Unless it's a secret you plan to threaten him with . . . when the two of you are alone in the forest, and only one of you has a gun. That would be inconvenient."

I lift my gaze to his. "Yes, flare your nostrils at me, Oliver. Give me that look that says you're considering all the ways you could kill me. Relishing the options. In fact, why don't you just tell me what you'd like to do? Get it off your chest."

"I have done nothing." He can't even unclench his jaw to speak clearly. "I made mistakes out here, and your friends died. But that was desperation. I did not kill those people in Georgia. If you can prove otherwise, you would. You can't. So go ahead and put me and Greg on a plane. Let us go in the forest. But I want a gun, too. I deserve a fighting chance."

"Like those people you shot in . . ." I frown and look at Dalton. "Wait, did he just say Georgia?"

"Yeah," Dalton says. "Weird. I coulda sworn he said he was being blamed for a shooting in San Jose. You slip up there, Oliver?"

Another nostril flare. "No. I'm cutting through the bullshit. You know he's not accusing me of the San Jose shooting. He's saying I murdered five people in Georgia. Fucked-up, psychopath serial killings."

"Which you did not commit."

"No, I did not."

"Yet you know who did. Who would do . . . ? Wait. Don't answer. Let me guess. Could it be . . . your stepfather?"

Brady jerks forward. Dalton's gun barrel slams into his temple. Brady reels. Dalton catches him by the arm and presses his gun against the young man's forehead.

"You gonna call Casey a lousy detective now?" Dalton says.

"So you figured out Greg is the real killer," Brady says. "Fine. Now you see —"

"I see you're a desperate man," I say. "Desperate enough to accuse your own stepfather of the crimes you committed."

A string of obscenities follows, his face contorting with rage. "This is exactly what I knew would happen. See? See?"

As his voice rises, I say, "Do you want that gag? Or do you want the chance to keep talking?"

"Why bother? This is how it is. How it will always be. You want me to play nice, Detective?" He leans toward me. "I don't know how. Never learned the skill. Or maybe I lack the genes. You look at me, and you see a spoiled white boy. Self-centered. Entitled. An unpleasant son of a bitch. And you know what? You aren't wrong."

He eases back. "I'm an asshole. But that doesn't make me a killer. I'm probably not a good person. But that doesn't make me evil. I don't think that's such a difficult concept for you to understand, Detective. You're a stone-cold bitch. Doesn't mean you aren't good at your job. Doesn't mean you don't care about your people. The sheriff here doesn't bat an eye when you threaten me, and it doesn't stop him from looking at you like the sun shines out of your ass."

He locks gazes with me. "I *am* responsible for your mountain-man friend's death. Court of law would lock me up for man-slaughter. I accept that. I am also responsible for Val's death. I promised you'd get her back, and you didn't. But those murders back home? Those were committed by a guy who makes me look like a saint."

"Gregory Wallace."

"You liked him, didn't you? Of course you did. Everyone does. Let me guess how it went. He showed up, apologized for all the trouble he put you through, promised to compensate you for it, while being clear he knows money won't fix this. Am I close?"

Brady doesn't wait for an answer. "I know I am. I know him. He was charming and gracious and humble. Probably confided in

536

you, too, Detective. He wouldn't bother with the sheriff. He decided you were the brains of the operation. The moral compass, too, he'd presume, because he's a sexist ass-hole, and you know the problem with being a sociopath? You're so busy acting your role that you can't see through the performances of others. He bought the sheriff's redneck routine and your quiet-but-thoughtful one. Am I right? Did he confess to you? Admit he made mistakes? Of course he did."

I say nothing.

Brady continues, "I bet he volunteered to help search for me. Insisted on it. He feels *so* bad about the situation that he wants to help find me. Take the risks alongside you two. The truth? He doesn't trust you. He wanted to be there when you caught me, to make sure you brought me in and maybe use the opportunity to stage a tragic ac-cident."

"Yeah," Dalton says. "That explains why he *offered* to stay behind as hostage. In Casey's place."

"Because that guaranteed you'd turn me over to those savages."

"Except he escaped," I say.

Brady finally goes silent. At least a minute passes.

"Can't explain that away?" Dalton says.

"No, Sheriff, I can't. I could speculate that he overheard something that made him think he might not survive the exchange. But that's speculation. I only know something happened in that camp, and he decided he'd overstayed his welcome. I bet he took out a few of the locals on his way, too."

"Actually, no," I say. "He hurt a woman, but he left her alive and made his escape."

"Okay, that makes sense. It's hard to keep pretending you're a good guy if —"

"Down!" Dalton shouts.

He falls onto me and, for a moment, I think he's been hit. Then I realize he's pinning me down. There's a shot. Then Storm lets out a yelp of pain.

FIFTY-SEVEN

My dog has been shot. There's a sniper in the trees, and Storm has been shot. I try to scramble up, but Dalton holds me fast, whispering, "I'm sorry. I'm sorry, Casey."

I fight the urge to snarl at him. To get free of him. To get to her.

I dig my fingers into the ground to hold myself still, and I listen, as hard as I can. After a moment, I hear a labored pant, each breath ending in a whimper.

She's been shot.

Definitely shot.

As I twist toward her, I catch a blur of motion. It's Kenny rolling into the undergrowth, his arms around Storm.

"I've got —" Kenny starts.

Another shot. Kenny's whole body jerks.

Dalton starts to leap up. I tackle and yank him into the undergrowth.

"Careful," I say. "We have to be careful."

He nods, and we creep on our bellies.

We're on the same side of the path as Kenny and Storm, and I can see their shapes ahead.

As we move, I hear Jacob whispering, "You're okay, you're okay, just stay still. Play dead."

"Kenny?" I whisper, as loudly as I dare.

"I've got him," Jacob whispers back. "I have Kenny and Storm. Stay down. Casey. Keep Eric *down*. Stay where you are. Do not move."

He's right. Any movement we make is going to draw fire. I reach out for Dalton's hand and clasp it, and we lie there, listening to Kenny's ragged breathing.

That's when I see Brady crawling away.

Dalton squeezes my hand hard, getting my attention, and then he shakes his head.

Let him go.

Don't take the risk of going after him.

But I have to, don't I? As long as Oliver Brady is out there, people will keep dying.

I look in the direction of the shots. I see nothing. It isn't like the city, where I could scan the buildings and know which is most likely to hold the gunman. This is a forest filled with towering trees, all perfect for a sniper.

And as long as this gunman is out there, we are sitting ducks. Eventually we need to come out, and all the sniper has to do is

540

track us and wait for us to stop moving.

So we can't stop moving.

We can't wait for the shooter to figure out where we are. We have a wounded man and dog, and we need to get them someplace safe.

I watch Brady sneak off, and I wait for Dalton to relax, convinced I'm giving up on my prey. Then I leap up to a crouch, call, "Get them someplace safe!," and break into a run.

Dalton grabs for me. His fingers brush my leg. But I'm gone.

I zigzag. One shot fires into a tree several feet away. Another does the same. I'm careful, though, moving up, down, left, right, zipping behind every tree and bush in my path.

Behind me, Dalton whispers urgently to Jacob. I can't slow enough to focus on words, but I know Dalton's trusting that I'm okay while he gets the others to safety.

Brady hears me coming. He straightens to run faster. A shot hits a tree, clearly intended for me, but when he hears that hit, and he sprawls into a home-plate slide. I sprint and leap on his back. He bucks. I grab his still-bound wrists and wrench them so hard he howls.

"Shut the hell up," I say, slamming his

541

head into the dirt. "I'm doing you a favor. Exactly how long do you think you'd survive out here with your hands tied behind your back?"

He glowers over his shoulder.

"Yeah, yeah," I whisper. "I'm a stone-cold bitch. I've heard it already. You would do well to note that you're still alive, when it would be a hell of a lot more convenient for me to change that. I *will* kill you, Oliver, but I need a reason. So don't give me one."

I wait until I'm sure the shots have stopped, the sniper trying to find targets again. I'm checking whether we're hidden enough to move when something thumps in the trees to my right. A family of ptarmigan explodes from the bushes, startled by whatever Dalton must have thrown at them.

The sniper fires toward the birds.

I prod Brady forward with "Move!" and "Stay down."

He does both. I steer him through the clearest patch of forest floor, where we don't make enough noise to draw the sniper's attention. The forest has gone silent again. Then there's a shot, one too loud to be the sniper. A tremendous crash. Brady dives. I grab him by the collar and propel him forward.

"That's Eric providing cover," I say.

This time, he's fired his gun at a dying sapling or dead branch, something that will break and fall, the noise again drawing the sniper's attention.

I get Brady behind rocks. We're back in the foothills. There's no conveniently located cave this time, but we wind through the rocks and tree cover until I see Dalton ahead, flagging me. I arrive to see he's found a sheltered spot where he's moved the others.

I spot Storm first. Dalton whispers, "She's fine. Bullet grazed a hind leg. She can't run, but she's fine."

I crawl to her and rub her neck, and she whines but stays lying down, muzzle on her paws, her gaze on . . .

Her gaze on Kenny.

I see him, and I stifle a gasp. He's lying on his stomach, his head to the side, eyes closed. Eyes closed, not moving.

As I scramble over, Jacob says, "He's unconscious, but he's . . ."

Jacob looks at Dalton.

"Where did he . . . ?" I trail off as I see the answer.

Kenny has been shot in the back. The lower back, the bullet passing through near his spine.

I forget that there's a sniper out there and

a possible killer beside us. That doesn't matter. Kenny has been shot, and this is not a graze or a bullet passing through soft tissue. This is . . .

I drop beside him. I check his vital signs first. They're strong enough to suggest he's only fainted. He isn't in shock, not from internal bleeding or neurogenic shock — the injury is too low on his back for that.

I peel up his jacket and shirt, as carefully as I can. It's soaked with blood, front and back, but the bleeding is slow.

I tend to the injury as best I can while Dalton stands guard. It's quiet out there. Our sniper seems to have a remarkably short attention span. He — or she — is not the trained professional we first thought. With the exception of Kenny, everyone has suffered only minor injuries. Given Kenny, though, the intent does *seem* lethal. The sniper just doesn't have the skills to pull it off without a perfect target. The wild shots support that theory, as does the fact that it's been easy to draw his fire.

This is still someone who knows distance shooting — knows how to find a good perch and hit a clear target. That's more than I could manage with a rifle, but it's no better than Dalton or Jacob could do, with their hunting experience.

As for the sniper's intentions, I have no idea. Initially, Brady seemed to be the target. But he hasn't actually hit Brady. Nor has he fired only at those standing nearby. By this point, I'm almost wondering if the sniper is a completely separate situation — that we have a settler with a rifle who's decided to kill himself some Rockton residents. Because that's just what we need.

We must get help for Kenny. The best plan seems to be to leave Jacob and Storm with the remainder of our supplies and a sidearm. Both Dalton and I must take Brady back to Rockton, to guard each other from the sniper. That's not even considering the fact that we have settlers hunting for Wallace, who'd be quite happy to vent their outrage on us.

And then there's Wallace himself. Could he be the real serial killer? At this point, I'm beyond guessing. If someone lined Brady and Wallace up and told me I had to pick which one to shoot, I might as well make them play rock-paper-scissors to decide who gets the bullet.

With no knowledge of the crimes, no evidence to consider, no way of *getting* any evidence swiftly, it comes down to "Which man do I believe?" And the answer right now is neither.

Dalton and I scale the mountain partway to get a better look at our situation. We've climbed about a hundred meters up when a voice drifts over from the forest. A voice that has me thinking I'm clearly hallucinating, because it makes no sense in this context.

"Is that . . . ?" Dalton looks over at me. "Diana?"

She stops talking, and a man answers. I hear him speak, and I grin.

"Will," I say. "They're out searching —"

Oh, shit. Anders and Diana are out searching for us. In the forest. With a sniper and Wallace nearby. And some really pissed-off settlers. If we can hear Diana and Will, then others will, too.

FIFTY-EIGHT

"I'm going to go to them," I say. "Can you cover me?"

Dalton nods.

I slide down the mountainside as Dalton positions himself, gun ready. I reach the bottom and scamper from one point of cover to the next. I hear Anders again, but his voice is muffled now that I'm on ground level, and I can tell he's farther away than I thought.

I turn and see Dalton shielding his eyes, watching me. I pantomime that they're at least a kilometer away, and he motions that he'll stand guard for as long as he can see me. I'm zipping past the others, quietly calling to Jacob that I hear Anders . . . when Brady lurches out.

"I am not staying out here," Brady says. "If you're on the move, so am I."

I want to put my damn gun to his head. I might, too, if I could spare the time to slow down . . . and the time to chew him out . . . and the risk of being overheard by our sniper. I see Dalton watching from above. He gives a dismissive gesture, one I'd love to interpret as "Just shoot the son of a bitch," but I know better.

"Keep up," I say. "You want to try escaping again? That sniper isn't the only one in this forest with a gun."

"You don't need to keep reminding me," he grumbles as he jogs over.

When I glance back to Dalton, he puts a finger gun to his head and shakes his head, and I have to smile at that. By this point, we don't really give a shit if Brady is innocent. Killing him on principle seems like a fine idea.

He catches up and stays behind me. I'd rather he was in front, where I can watch him, but that won't help me find Anders and Diana quickly. I can no longer hear them. I'm moving at a slow jog, and Brady has the sense to do the same, making minimal noise.

Shortly after I start, I think I hear something, but it quickly goes quiet. I'm long out of Dalton's line of sight, unable to see more than the mountaintop over the trees. I'm mentally trying to pinpoint where the sound might have come from when I hear

Diana, her voice harsh as she argues with Anders.

I'm not sure whether to breathe a sigh of relief that I hear her . . . or hiss in exasperation at her loudly bickering with him. Diana and Anders had a one-night stand after she arrived, and then I showed up and to her, it seemed that he suddenly turned his attentions my way. Not entirely true. Their affair had been a drunken one-nighter, which he regretted, realizing he might have taken advantage of her at a vulnerable time. But to have him hanging out with me a day after sharing her bed? Humiliating, and she hasn't forgiven him. I don't quite blame her. It's an awkward situation all around.

Now I'm just wishing they hadn't had the harebrained idea to team up and come find me. Why Diana? Even at our closest, I'd never have chosen her as a search-team partner.

"I am not —" she begins.

Anders answers, his voice pitched higher than normal, clearly feeling the strain of this pairing. I can't make out what he's saying, but it must be some variation on *Hell, yeah, you will, Di,* because she comes back with, "Absolutely not, you crazy —"

A hiss of pain cuts her short, and I stumble to a halt.

Will?

The question lasts only a split second. I know Will Anders, and it doesn't matter if he isn't *really* Will Anders, if he's a soldier named Calvin James, who shot his CO in cold blood. Anders would be the first person to call himself a killer, a monster. But even when I once suspected him of brutally murdering four residents, I'd struggled with my own conclusion. As naive as it sounded, I could not believe he'd done it. And he hadn't.

I know Will Anders. I also know Calvin James. I know exactly what happened, even if he doesn't understand it himself. Once I stood in front of a man I hated, pointed a gun at him, and pulled the trigger. I snapped. Anders did the same, spurred on by tragedy and rage and misprescribed medication.

When I hear Diana's words and that hiss of pain, I know that the other speaker is not Anders.

"Casey!" Diana calls, and her companion doesn't stop her. "Casey? If you're out there, and you can hear me . . ." She pauses, as if expecting to be interrupted. "Run. Run like hell —"

A smack cuts her short. Whoever has her hostage told her to call to me. This just isn't the message he wanted imparted.

"Casey?" she shouts. "It's Brady's father. He's knocked out Will —"

Another *thwack*, hand against flesh. Then I hear Wallace talking to Diana, his voice clearer now as he tells her to stop it, he hasn't hurt Anders, hasn't hurt her, stop being so melodramatic.

"And you think I'm fucked-up?" Brady mutters behind me. "He's holding your friend hostage, smacking her around, and telling her she's overreacting."

"So he *is* dangerous?" I say.

Brady stares at me. "Have you been listening to anything I said? He's killed at least five people. Tortured them. Watched them *die.* Oh, but he seems like such a nice guy." He jabs a finger in the direction the voices came from. "Does *that* seem like a nice guy? Of course he's fucking dangerous. He's going to kill your friend and —"

"Just checking," I say as I kick out his knee.

Brady drops, and I grab his arms with one hand, wrenching them up again as I put my gun at his head and plant my foot on his back.

"Wallace!" I shout. "It's Casey."

"What the fuck are you — ?" Brady begins.

551

"You just confirmed he's dangerous. Which means he'll kill Diana and Will if he doesn't get what he wants. I'm going to guess what he wants is you."

Brady goes wild, struggling and snarling. I keep wrenching his arm and warning him to stop. There's a crack as his wrist breaks. He howls in pain.

"You bitch. You —"

"Shhh," I say. "I can't hear your daddy."

I push Brady's face into the dirt and shout, "Wallace?"

"Yes . . ." The reply comes slow, tentative.

"You've got something I want," I say. "I'm going to guess I have something you want, too."

"If it's that sadistic bastard my wife whelped, you would be correct, Detective."

"Then bring Diana and follow the sound of my voice."

I keep Brady pinned, muffling his rage as I scan the treetops, all too aware of the chance we're taking with this confrontation. The chance that our voices will tell our sniper friend exactly where to find us.

Wallace eventually appears, Diana in the lead, a knife at her back.

"He ambushed us," she says. "Knocked out Will."

I mouth to ask if there are others. Anders

and Diana can't be the only searchers. But her gaze sweeps over the forest in a desperate look that tells me, yes, there are others, but they aren't close enough to come running.

"I just want what I came for," Wallace says. "I haven't killed anyone. I've only done what I had to. I need you to give me Oliver."

"But that was the deal, wasn't it?" I say. "So why the sudden need to force my hand, Gregory? To start hurting my people?"

"I know you have doubts, Casey. I've seen it in your face. In Sheriff Dalton's. You've spoken to Oliver, and whatever he has said, it's made you wonder if you've been misled. I don't blame you, which is why I'm doing my best *not* to hurt your people. But I can't take the chance that you won't use lethal force to stop Oliver if he escapes. The very fact he's still alive tells me I'm right. You'll let him run, and others will die."

"You son of a —" Brady begins.

I push the gun against the back of Brady's neck.

"Oliver here is telling a new story," I say. "One that says *you're* the monster. The serial killer."

"What?" Wallace's eyes round. "My God, Ollie, you *are* desperate. You're actually accusing me —"

"I caught you," Brady snarls. "With that boy. I followed you to where you were keeping him, and I saw what you'd done. What you were doing. You murdered him right in front of me. Slit his throat while he begged me to save him."

"You know, Ollie, I recognize that story. It sounds very familiar. Maybe because it did happen . . . only I was the one following you. I was the one who saw that poor kid." Wallace's voice rises. "And I was the one begging. Begging you to let him go as he sobbed, gagged and bound, covered in blood and filth. A boy. A teenage *boy.* You tortured him. Murdered him. I don't even want to know what else you'd done to him."

Brady struggles to get up from under me. "You bastard. You sick, sick bastard. Do you think I've forgotten what you did to me when I was his age? I kept my mouth shut because you said you'd kill my mother if I told her. Maybe I should have *let* you, if it meant stopping you before anyone else died."

Wallace looks at me. "He will say anything to get out of this, Casey."

"So will you," Brady spat.

Wallace keeps his gaze on me. "I know you're angry at me for threatening your friends. But I have done the minimum damage possible. Same as with that woman in the village. I just want to get Oliver out of here before he kills more people. However angry you are right now, Casey, the difference in our behavior should speak for itself. Oliver has murdered multiple people up here. I've knocked out two. I've threatened this woman and, yes, I've struck her in anger. Ask her if I've done more. Check to see if she's suffered even a bruise."

Diana gives a reluctant shake of her head.

"We have no actual proof Oliver killed anyone except Brent," I say, "and even Brent says the bullet was fired accidentally, during a fight."

Brady stops struggling.

"I won't know about Val until I retrieve her body," I say. "I saw no signs of trauma that couldn't have been inflicted by a fall. As for the settler massacre, I believe someone else was responsible."

"Some *other* random killer roaming the woods?" Wallace says. "I'm sorry, Detective. I realize Oliver is an attractive young man, and he can be charming —"

"Stop right there," I say.

Brady gives a harsh laugh. "Yeah, no, Greg. Don't even try that. She hates my fucking guts, whether I'm guilty or not. The only reason she isn't shooting me is that she's actually a damn fine cop, one who gives a shit about —"

"You, too," I say. "Enough. I don't want patronizing bullshit from him or bootlicking flattery from you."

"She's right," Diana says. "I've known Casey half my life. Don't insult her. Don't flatter her. She'll see through that crap and stomp you both like bugs."

"Just give me my stepson," Wallace says. "That's all you need to do. Hand him to me, and I will lead you to your deputy, and we'll all walk back to town. It's not as if I can hijack the plane and fly out on my own."

"He can do exactly that," Brady says. "He has a *fleet* of small planes, and he insists on flying them himself, like he insists on doing everything himself. Including murder."

Wallace sighs. "And here is the problem, Casey. Lies. His endless lies. I don't know how to fly. I don't own any planes. If I did, why would Phil have brought me? Oliver is spouting nonsense. He'll say whatever it takes to make you doubt me."

And so they go, accusing one another and protesting their innocence, leaving me feeling like the therapist for the most dysfunctional family ever.

Except I'm not their therapist. I am their

judge, jury, and, yes, executioner.

I can end this now. Decide who is lying and shoot him. I have Brady pinned under me, and Wallace is barely even bothering to hold the knife on Diana, too caught up in defending himself against his stepson's accusations.

All I have to do is decide who is telling the truth. Who is the real killer. Which is impossible, when I have nothing to go on but their say-so.

Maybe after all my years as a detective, my gut should tell me which one is guilty. But right now, it wants me to shoot both of them. It says they're both full of shit, and I don't think it's wrong. Neither is being completely honest. But one is a serial killer, and the other is just a garden-variety dangerous son of a bitch. One deserves death. One does not. And I have no idea which is which.

I catch Diana's eye. She's looking straight at me, tuning out father and son as she waits for me to resolve this, like I always do.

Casey to the rescue. Just trust Casey.

See how well that worked out for Val and Kenny.

I failed them. I will not fail Diana.

I could signal to her that she can jump

aside and get free of Wallace, but that's a risk.

No more risks. No more being a homicide cop. I need to channel Dalton here. I am the guardian of those under my protection, and they are all that matters.

"He's yours," I say to Wallace.

Brady screeches, "What?"

"You'll escort him back to town," I say, "and I don't really give a damn what happens then."

Which is a lie. I have every intention of getting to the bottom of this. I just can't do it out here, with them raging at each other, drawing the attention of everyone around. And not while Anders lies unconscious and Kenny is in desperate need of medical attention. Just let me get them to town, and I'll figure out my next move there.

I haul Brady to his feet. When he resists, I squeeze his broken wrist. He howls . . . and a bullet hits the tree right beside Wallace's head.

Wallace spins. But he doesn't dive for cover. He grabs Diana, yanking her in front of him. When she tries to pull away, the knife flashes and blood sprays, and I forget Brady.

I run for Diana. Wallace holds her like a human shield. I knock her in the side, shoving her away. Wallace grabs my upper arm and yanks me into Diana's place. When I see the look on his face, I know what he is.

I finally know.

I swing my gun up. The idiot has forgotten I have it. He slashes with the knife, the blade aiming for my face. I wrench from his grasp.

"On the ground!" I say, gun barrel pressing up under his chin. "Get on the goddamn ground or —"

"You'll shoot?" Wallace says. "You haven't yet, Casey."

"Because I hadn't figured out which of you bastards is guilty. Now I have." I push the gun barrel in harder. "Do you notice which one I let escape? And which is at the end of my gun?"

"You're wrong. You —"

His whole body convulses so fast I'm sure it's a trick. I'm about to pull the trigger when I see Diana beside him, holding the knife, blood dripping from the blade. Wallace's mouth works. Then he topples.

I kick Wallace as he falls, and then I'm on him. He lies facedown on the ground, my gun to his head. Blood gushes from his side.

"I stabbed him," Diana says, and she's clutching the weapon in both hands. "I took the knife, and I stabbed him. He —"

"Get *down*," I say.

I look around, but there have been no more shots.

Brady is gone, and the sniper has stopped shooting.

That is no coincidence.

"It's your shooter, isn't it?" I say to Wallace. "You put someone out here to kill him. You paid the council to let you bring in an assassin."

Wallace gives a ragged chuckle. "You have seen too many movies, my dear. And Oliver was wrong. You're a lousy detective. You picked the wrong —"

"No, I did not. The minute that gun fired, you grabbed Diana to shield you. You stabbed —"

I look over sharply to see she's got her jacket off and is wrapping it around her arm.

"He sliced me good," she says. "You're going to need to give me a few stitches. I'm fine, though. Not that he gave a damn."

She's right. I saw Wallace's face when he pulled her to shield him. When he stabbed her. When he tried to stab me.

Backed into a corner, we cannot conceal our true selves. I saw his, and I still don't know exactly what we're dealing with here, but Gregory Wallace is not an innocent man.

I bind and gag him. Then I leave him

where he lies, while Diana takes me to
Anders.

FIFTY-NINE

When we arrive, Anders is conscious and struggling to get free from an old hemp rope tying him to a tree. His wrists are bloodied, and as much as I want to carefully tend to his injuries and Diana's, Kenny's situation is a much graver concern.

Our path takes us past Wallace. Diana offers to stay with him. I don't actually give a damn if *anyone* stays — he's not escaping those ties and if the cougar finds him and thinks he's a fine dinner, I'm okay with that. But I leave Diana behind, armed with a knife and a whistle.

When we set out again, Anders says, "Rough day?"

I'm not sure whether to laugh or cry. I think I do a little of both, and he puts his arm around my shoulders as we walk.

"Kenny was alive and stable when you left him," he says after I explain. "I'm not going to lie and say he'll be fine, but he was alive and he was stable. Also . . ." He glances over. "What happened to him wasn't your fault."

"He only came out here to clear his name."

"No, he comes out here all the time as a member of the militia. Odds are just as good that he could have been shot by this psycho sniper while just doing his job. You don't really feel guilty about him being out here. You feel guilty for thinking he was Brady's accomplice."

I nod.

"Lesson one in Rockton?" he says. "Trust no one. Except Eric. Well, trust him to not be a killer or a killer's accomplice. I know he has secrets, but I'm sure you already know those."

I glance over.

He shrugs. "I can tell. And I'm never going to push. That's his business. But I know his secret isn't *our* secret — that we've killed people. If you and I have that in our background, though, anyone could. Even Kenny. He was the most likely suspect for Brady's accomplice. So stop beating yourself up. I'll do whatever I can for him. Hopefully he'll be fine."

We walk a few more steps, and then he says, "There's more, isn't there? Something else happened out there."

"The sniper shot someone Eric knew, a hostile we . . ." I swallow. "A hostile might have helped. It was a misunderstanding. She ran into the forest. And there were others. Hostiles. Eric had to shoot them, and he tried to just wound them and . . . things got worse."

"Shit." He looks over. "And you?"

I shrug.

"Casey . . ."

"I shot one. Had to. Me or him. You know how —" I stop myself. There's a lightness in my voice. Forced casual, sardonic. *You know how it is. You were a soldier.* Which is not anything he needs to be reminded of.

"I do know," he says, brushing his shoulder against mine.

"I'm sorry. I didn't mean —"

He cuts me off with a quick embrace as we walk. "I do know. And it sucks every last goddamn time."

"I'm worried about Eric."

"I know you are."

"I'm also worried I may have . . ." I inhale. "He may have seen a side of me I'd rather he didn't."

"You mean the side that just told Wallace he's a piece of shit who deserves to be carved up and fed to the ravens?"

"Uh . . . possibly."

Anders laughs. "If you think Eric would be the least bit surprised by that, you are underestimating the man. You might try to hide that part, but you do a lousy job of it. Sorry. Wallace is alive, and you're doing everything you can to keep him that way until he can face his crimes. That's enough."

I look at him. "Is it too much? If only I'd killed Brady back in Rockton —"

"Yeah, don't even go there. You aren't that person. If we'd killed him then, yes, people would still be alive, but we had no way of knowing that, and we were right to suspect the council's story, considering Brady turned out to be innocent."

"Did he?"

Anders frowns at me. "You still have questions?"

Yes. Yes, I do.

We're halfway to the spot where I left Kenny with Dalton and Jacob when we hear the pound of feet on a nearby path.

"Brady," I say. "That's . . ."

When I trail off, Anders reaches into his pack and hands me his whistle. "Go on."

"No, I should —"

"You've done what you can for Kenny. I'm reasonably sure even I can't do any more until we get him back to Rockton. That's my real role here — the muscle to help make that happen. If I need a nurse, Eric does a fine job. You go get Brady."

"It might not be him."

"It is. Go."

I take off. As I jog along the path, I think.

So many questions.

And maybe, just maybe, an answer.

But for now, I will only say that I have questions. It seemed logical that the sniper works for Wallace. It might also seem logical that the sniper would stop shooting when Brady — his target — fled.

But that does not explain the fact that the first bullet was aimed at Wallace. That Wallace instinctively grabbed for a human shield. Would you do that if you'd hired the man firing the gun? Of course not.

And if you did hire that man, and he saw you being taken captive, would he not turn his rifle on those attacking you? You can't collect payment if your client is dead.

When Diana and I went to free Anders, we left Wallace bound and gagged. And the sniper never returned to check on him, never returned to free him.

The sniper is not Wallace's man.

Yet Wallace is guilty.

I saw that mask slide from Gregory Wallace's face. I could say it was just the mask of civility falling away, like the hostiles in this forest, stripped of what passes for humanity when they are forced to fight for their lives.

That is bullshit.

Strip away my mask of civility, and you get someone who would shoot a man who left her to be beaten to death . . . and then blamed her for it. Someone who would have shot Wallace or Brady — not caring which was innocent — if it saved a friend.

What I saw in Wallace was more than my brand of darkness. It was evil.

When faced with danger, he pulled an innocent bystander into the path of the bullet.

Does that mean Wallace has done what Brady claims?

He could have. For now, I'll only say that. He is entirely capable of it.

As for Brady . . .

A theory. That's what I have. Now I need the man himself.

SIXTY

It's easy enough to sneak up on Brady. He hasn't transformed into a master woodsman. The problem has always been simply getting close enough to find him in this endless wilderness. Once I am, I can hear him, stopped to catch his breath. Those gasps cover my approach. Then I grab his broken wrist, still bound by my handcuff tie. He lets out a shriek, half pain, half surprise.

When he sees me, he deflates.

"Oh, come on, Detective," he says. "I'm starting to feel like that guy in *Les Miz,* chased by the cop who just won't give up, even when he knows the poor guy is innocent."

"Javert didn't know anything of the sort," I say. "And neither do I."

"Seriously?" He slumps, shaking his head, like I'm a patrol officer who pulled him over for speeding. Just a pain-in-the-ass cop, wasting the taxpayers' money trying to pin some silly little misdemeanor on him.

"I'm going to ask you again," I say. "How far do you think you'll get with your hands tied behind your back?"

"Does it matter?"

"Sure it does." I walk in front of him, my gun lowered. "A few years ago, I went to a party where they played a game called Would You Rather. It's supposed to be two equally shitty choices. Except the host didn't quite get the point and kept giving choices where there really was no choice at all. Like 'Would you rather take a bullet to the head or die of slow starvation in the forest?' Whatever fate you'd suffer out here is much worse than what your stepfather would do to you."

"Uh, did you miss the part where he's a fucking psychopath? He didn't shoot those people in the head. He tortured them."

"Yes, I'm sure being tied up and beaten wasn't —"

"Tied up and beaten? Is that your idea of torture? He cut them. He burned them. He pulled out their fingernails. Their teeth. He did the kind of things you see in movies, when they're trying to get spies to talk. Only he didn't want these people to talk. He wanted them to scream. To cry. To beg. To break."

"You got a good look then, at that boy you caught him with."

A heartbeat's pause before he plows on with, "Yes, yes, I did, Detective."

"And he molested you as a child."

A glimmer of relief as I move on, and he nods, "Yes."

"Tell me about that."

"What the hell is this? A therapy couch?"

"No, it's an interrogation room. You have accused your stepfather of molesting you. I've dealt with victims of that. I've had to interview them, lead them through it, and it was a horrible part of my job, but it was necessary to properly prosecute the offenders. So I know the stories. I know all the reactions a victim gives. Go on, Oliver. Convince me."

He starts to rage that he won't give me the satisfaction. That he won't play this bullshit game. Rage. Deflect. Rant.

I'm lying, of course. I have dealt with those victims. I have interviewed them. But there is no way in hell that I can tell a real accusation from a false one just by speaking to the accuser. Every response is different. I just want Brady to believe I can do it. He does, and so he says not one word about the abuse. He just rages at me until he finishes with, "You want me to talk about that? Put me in front of a real professional."

"With a lie detector?"

"Fuck you. My stepfather is a sadistic bastard, and whatever he did to me pales in comparison to what he did to his other victims."

I ease back. "I don't know. One could argue otherwise. I'm sure a defense attorney would. Gregory may not have molested you, but turning you into a killer? That's some seriously bad parenting."

"What? No. He's the killer. He's the one —"

"Yes, I suspect he is. You both are. Partners in crime, who turned on each other. How did it happen, Oliver? Not how he lured you into it. You're right — that's a story for a therapist, and I don't really care. I'm curious about the schism. The break. How did it come to this? Former partners, each desperately trying to pin the crimes on the other."

It takes three long seconds for him to say, "What the hell are you talking about?," and with that I know I've hit on the truth. The reason I couldn't pick a side. The solution that makes so much more sense than all the ones they've spouted.

Not a man trying to steal his stepson's inheritance. Not one trying to shield his wife from her son's horrible crimes. Not a young man who stumbled over his stepfather's horrible crimes.

Shared crimes. Shared blame. Equally shared? I don't give a damn.

"I've taken Wallace into custody," I say. "I'm doing the same with you. Eric will fly you both back down south and tie you up in a hotel room and place an anonymous call to the police."

"Sure, do that," Brady says. "And we'll tell them all about you and your town. Do you think you haven't given us enough information to pass on to the authorities? I know your name, Detective Casey Butler. I know his, Sheriff Eric Dalton. I know the names of a half dozen people in your town. I know I'm in Alaska — I've been here before, and I recognize the terrain. They will track you down and . . ."

He trails off, and I smile.

"Can't even finish that threat, can you?" I say. "They'll do what? We've given them two serial killers. You tell them that you were turned in by some secret prison camp in Alaska? Why would they care? And why would you presume they don't already know about us?"

He blinks at me.

"Turn around," I say. "And start walking —"

"Not so fast, Casey," a voice says behind me.

It's a familiar voice, but on hearing it, my heart skips.

Not possible. That is not . . .

I turn, and I see Dalton. But it wasn't his voice I heard. It was a woman's. Then I see Dalton's hands on his head, as he's prodded down the path by a woman.

"Hello, Casey," Val says. "You look surprised to see me."

"I — I saw your . . ." I don't finish. I will sound like a fool if I do, and I already feel the sting of my mistake.

But *how* was it a mistake?

I saw the bloat of her corpse. I know she was not alive.

Sharon, Dalton mouths, and with that, I understand.

Sharon. One of our winter dead. The woman who'd died of a heart attack last week. Whom we'd been burying when Brady arrived.

Sharon was not a perfect doppelgänger for Val. She was older. With longer hair. Heavier. Shorter. But none of that mattered for a water-bloated corpse floating facedown in the water. Cut the gray-streaked hair to

573

Val's length. Dress her in Val's clothing. Put her corpse in the water and send it downstream, and even if we had managed to pull it out, between the rot and the bloat, it would have been hard to say it wasn't Val.

Peter Sanders had pulled that same trick with Nicole — found a dead hostile or settler and put her in Nicole's clothing and damaged the body enough that Dalton naturally concluded he'd found Nicole. Val knew we didn't have the equipment to test DNA, and that told her the trick might work again.

"Eric stopped to help me," Val says. "He couldn't resist, even when he considers me deadweight on your precious town. All I had to do was lie in his path, and he holstered his gun and raced over to help."

"And that's weakness to you, isn't it?" I say. "That he came to your aid, no questions asked, despite all the shit you've put him through."

"Put *him* through? I'm the one who's gone through hell in that god-forsaken town. Condemned to coexist with people who lack the IQ to carry on a proper conversation with me. Yet they all tried. Even you, Casey. Especially you. You had to try to help a poor fellow female, trapped in her home, cowering like a mouse. I wasn't cowering, you idiot. I was waiting. You said once that the council constructed a prison for me — made me too afraid to leave my house. No. I constructed it. It was my refuge, and you couldn't leave me well enough alone."

"Yeah," Dalton says. "We're all assholes for giving a shit."

My look warns him not to antagonize her. I'm all too aware of that gun at his back.

"You *should* have left me alone, Casey," she says. "But you couldn't. You had to dig and poke and prod. Destroy what little sanctuary I had. Rob me of what few allies I had."

"Allies?" I say. "You mean the council? Because I proved they set you up to be *raped*?"

"I was not raped." Her voice shakes along with the gun, and I give myself the same warning I gave Dalton. *Stop. Just stop.*

She continues, "I *escaped.* If you don't believe that's possible, it's because you didn't escape your attackers, Casey. You let them beat you. Let them almost kill you. Almost certainly let them rape you. You could not get away, so you cannot conceive of the possibility that another, stronger, smarter woman might have."

"Okay," I say, and it's a calm, even response, but she keeps shaking, wanting to

575

fight, to defend herself, and I change the subject fast. "So you helped Oliver here. You ingratiated yourself with him, while pretending you were spying for us."

"And you bought it." She smiles. "You couldn't help yourself. Your pet project was showing signs of improvement. Joining the community. Making herself useful. I manipulated you into giving me access to him and you jumped at the chance."

"You brought supplies," I say. "Food. Weapons. That's why Oliver didn't bother retrieving my gun after he shot Brent. And you sent him *to* Brent. You knew Brent could lead you both to Jacob."

She says nothing. It doesn't matter. Not now.

Focus on the facts. On how this fills in the holes.

Brady attacked Brent because Val said Brent could get them a better hostage: Jacob. Who could also guide them out of the wilderness. And the companion Jacob saw with Brady? Val. From a distance, Jacob mistook her for a man. She brought those protein bars they shared, old stock she had access to. Brady had been so confident, he'd outright lied about it. Didn't even bother making up a story.

I have no idea what you're talking about,

Detective.

Dalton jerks his chin toward Val, and it takes a moment to see what he's gesturing at — the rifle barrel poking over Val's collarbone, a gun slung at her back.

"You're the sniper," I say.

"Yes, I know my way around a gun, too, Casey," she says. "Did you presume I was too weak and timid? I told you I used to stay on my grandparents' farm. They had guns. I insisted on learning. I'm good at it — my aptitude for mathematics comes in handy with distance shooting. Of course, my grandparents didn't think it was a proper sport for a girl, so while they humored me as a child, I had to shoot in secret when I got older. Which was useful, as it turns out. Do you recall those boys who taunted me? Chased me? Tried to assault me? One died the month before he graduated from high school. Shot by a stray bullet in the forest. A careless hunter, it seems."

"And you shot Kenny," I say. "Who was no threat to you. Was never anything but respectful —"

"Respectful? He was a toad. Always trying to talk to me. Ask what he could do for me. I *know* what he wanted to do for me."

"So you shot him?"

"He was in the path of my actual target."

"Casey," Dalton says, when I don't respond. "You wanted to kill Casey. You felt threatened —"

"Threatened? By this *child*?" Val laughs. "No, Sheriff. I only wanted her out of the way. She stood between me and the one thing that really can get us out of this godforsaken wilderness."

"Him," I say. "Eric. Shooting him on our walk was accidental — you just wanted it to look as if someone was trying to assassinate Oliver. When Oliver couldn't get Brent to take him to Jacob, you decided Eric would do. He can guide you out. Keep you alive. You'd kill me and force him to help you escape."

"Now I don't need to kill you, so I won't. Proving I'm not threatened by you, Casey, I'll just borrow your lover for a week. If he gets us where we want to go, I'll set him free."

"And I'm supposed to trust you?"

"He's no threat to us once we escape, so why would we kill him?"

"Because you can. Because Oliver here is a sadistic —"

"It was Greg," Brady snarls. "He made me do it. He forced me to help him, and he said if I ever told anyone, he'd kill me."

"Which would be hard for him to do from

a prison cell. He might have groomed you, Oliver, but that's only because he saw you for what you are — as much a narcissistic, sociopathic sadist as he is. And you, Val?"

I turn to her. "You felt like a prisoner in Rockton because you were. You weren't there by choice. Which means that farm boy isn't the only person you've killed. That's the thing about pulling a trigger. Either you're horrified and suffer a lifetime of guilt . . . or you realize it wasn't so bad after all. You tried to kill Kenny because he literally stood in your way. You tried to do the same to me because I figuratively blocked your path. You're no different than this psycho. Which means I can't trust you to let Eric go once he guides you out."

"I don't think you have a choice here, Casey. Drop to your knees with your head down or I'll put a bullet —"

I shoot her between the eyes.

I don't think about it. I cannot second-guess. I have my gun in my hand, and I have exactly one chance here, while she's talking, while she convinced she's won.

I swing my gun up, and I fire. I see her eyes. There is a moment there, a terrible moment, between her seeing the gun fire and death. A moment when she knows what has happened. A moment of horror that I

579

will not forget.

Val drops to the ground.

"Holy shit," Brady says. "Holy —"

I point the gun at him, and he stops. I'm waiting for Dalton to tell me no, don't shoot Brady. But he says nothing. Does nothing. I glance back, and his face is ashen. He isn't in shock, though. He says nothing because he knows he doesn't need to. I had to shoot Val . . . and I don't have to shoot Brady.

"Start walking," I say to Brady.

"Hell, no. I am not —"

He stops talking. I think that means he's realized there's no point arguing. Then I see the blood blossoming on his chest.

His mouth works. He falls to his knees. And he topples face-first to the ground.

I spin, gun raised. That shot did not come from me. It did not come from Dalton. I didn't hear a gun fire, meaning it came from one with a suppressor. We don't have suppressors in Rockton.

Both of us turn, our guns raised, scanning the empty forest. Then I see a flash of motion. A killer in flight.

I tear off. Dalton passes me, but the gap is too wide, the killer dressed in camouflage, little more than a blur through the trees.

I let myself slow, gait smoothing as I squint at the shooter.

A slight figure. Narrow shoulders. Hips just as wide. It's a woman. She's fast and she's agile, and she knows how to move in the forest, racing down the path, leaping over obstacles, outrunning Dalton.

He shoots. The sound of that shot surprises me. It's wild, though. Intentionally wild — no matter what has happened, he's not aiming to bring down someone who shot a serial killer. He's just trying to get her attention. He does, and she glances over her shoulder, and I catch a flash of pale skin and light hair and a face I recognize.

Even from this distance, I recognize it.

She doesn't slow, though. And in trying to surprise her, Dalton got a shock himself, one that has him stumbling. Then she's around the corner, too far ahead to ever catch.

After a pause he heads back to me as I cover him. I *will* fire — if she turns and I see her gun trained on Dalton, I will shoot her.

She doesn't turn.

Dalton breaks into a jog and says, "Did you see . . . ?"

"I did."

"That was —"

"Petra."

■ ■ ■ ■

We leave Val's and Brady's bodies behind. We cover them and mark the spot. Then we set out to Rockton.

"I killed Val," I say.

"You did what I couldn't. Last winter. With Peter."

He's looking straight ahead as we walk.

"I froze up," he says. "All I could see was Peter holding a knife on you, and I panicked. I should have shot him."

"No, you couldn't. If you had killed him, we'd have lost Nicole."

A few steps before he says, his voice low, "I didn't care. Not at that moment. I just froze."

"And I just reacted. I panicked. With another result."

He shakes his head. "You thought it through. Made a choice. I still regret not shooting Peter. I go over it and over it in my head. What if I lost you because I froze up? And now you'll second-guess making the opposite choice."

More quiet walking. Then he says, "We're both going to suffer. Wonder if we made the wrong decision. But I guess that's better than the alternative."

"Which is?"

"Not giving a shit." He looks back in the direction of the bodies. "Being like them."

SIXTY-ONE

We're nearing town when we meet Anders, pacing the path. He looks behind us and says, "You didn't find Brady."

"We did," I say. "Someone didn't want us bringing him back alive."

Anders swears. "The sniper."

I make a noise he can interpret as assent for now.

"How's Kenny?" I say, dreading the answer.

"Stable. That's all I can tell you. We got him back, and now we're getting the swelling down so Mathias and I can see the bullet. Unfortunately, that's not our biggest problem right now. Phil is ready to put Wallace on a plane and fly him out of here. I was giving you guys another sixty seconds before I stopped him at gunpoint."

We break into a jog, and I say, "Is Phil in on it? Or is this the council?"

"No idea. I told Phil what Wallace did.

Told him you think he's the killer, not Brady. It seemed like he believed me. Then he starts packing. I say hell, no, not until you guys get back. He reminds me that, in Val's absence, he's in charge. I argued, but he ignored me. Acted like the walls were talking and then went to check the plane."

"Where is he now?"

"He ordered me to bring Wallace to the hangar. I told him to go fuck himself and came to see if you guys were nearby."

We head straight for the hangar. Anders tells us Jacob and Storm are fine. He managed to persuade Jacob to sneak into my old place through the back door, and he's recovering there.

We're nearing the hangar when we hear the plane start.

"Shit!" Anders says.

We're about twenty meters away when Phil appears, doing a last visual check of the runway.

"I'm taking the prisoner, Sheriff," he calls when he sees us.

"The hell you are," Dalton says.

"Actually, yes, I am, and while I know you need to bluster in front of Will and Casey, let's skip that part. Your protest is duly noted. But it doesn't change the fact that you are not in charge here. I can assure you,

Mr. Wallace will be properly dealt with."

"We have a patient in urgent need —" I begin.

"And you have Dr. Atelier. Plus the sheriff's plane, should the council decide to extract Kenny."

"I want to talk to Wallace," I say. "I have questions that require answers."

"No, Casey, you have questions you would like answered, and you wish to stall me while you figure out how to stop me."

"I want to figure out how you can take him safely," I say. "He's a dangerous psychopath —"

"Yes, yes, I know," Phil says, as if I'm telling him Wallace might prove an annoying seatmate.

Dalton's gaze swings toward the hangar. Then he starts to run.

Phil holds his ground, saying, "If you physically try to stop me, Eric —"

Dalton swerves around the hangar instead, heading for the rear door. I follow, and Phil calls, "Whatever you two have in mind, it is a waste of time. If you attempt to stop me, there will be consequences. I would suggest, Casey, that you . . ."

I don't catch the rest, drowned out by the sound of the plane.

The back door to the hangar stands open.

Dalton circles into the trees to sneak up on the other side. Anders has joined us, and he gets into the trees, angled where he can cover me.

I swing through the doorway. There's a figure at the open passenger side. A small one wearing a hooded jacket. When I see her, there's a moment of confusion as complete as when I first spotted Val. Then it's like dominoes falling, connections made in an instant.

"Harper," I say. "Step away from the plane."

She turns and sees the gun. Hers starts to rise, but Anders barrels through, saying, "Drop the weapon!"

She looks toward the open main doors. Dalton appears there with his gun trained on her.

"Weapon down!" Anders barks. "Now!"

"Do as he says, hon." Wallace's muffled voice emerges from inside the plane. "They *will* shoot you."

She lowers her gun to the ground.

"Shit, it's just a kid," Anders says as he gets his first good look at her.

"A kid who murdered three of her fellow settlers. Including her own grandmother."

Harper just levels her gaze on me, and I've seen that look before, in teens I've arrested.

587

Some cry. Some rage. Some just give me this look, a cold *So what?*

It's chilling enough when it's a kid I've arrested for breaking into a house. For this? "Chilling" does not begin to describe it.

I want to ask, "Why?" But I know better. I'll just see another look like I did when I arrested those kids, when I felt compelled to ask why, and they rolled their eyes like I was just another stupid grown-up, asking stupid questions.

The "why?" isn't about motive. It's more of a "how?" *How could you do such a thing?* That is a question Harper cannot answer. No one can.

"You said Albie wanted to go back and steal the horses," I say. "But your grandmother and the other man stopped him. You still wanted to do it, though. You told Albie that, after the others went to sleep, didn't you?"

"He acted like I was a little kid. He ignored me. I had a plan for getting the horses. He wouldn't listen. When I said I'd go myself, he threatened to whip me. *Whip* me. Then he said even if I stayed in camp, he was going to tell my grandmother. She'd have to tell Edwin, and I'd never get to go on another hunting trip again."

"So you waited until he went back to his

588

guard post, snuck up, and slit his throat.
Except the old man heard, so you had to
kill him. And then your grandmother. She
tried to get away. You couldn't let her. You
chased her down and stabbed her."

"It was Albie's fault. He was going to
tattle on me because I offered to *help* him
get those horses."

"It wasn't the horses you wanted. It was
the dog."

Her lip curls. "I don't care now. I don't
need a dog. I'm going down south."

"And Mr. Wallace here is going to buy all
the puppies you want, right? You really are a
child, aren't you, Harper?"

She yanks a knife from her pocket. I just
hold my gun on her.

She sneers. "You won't shoot me."

She reaches into the cockpit to cut the
strap on Wallace's hand. I lunge to grab her,
but a voice says, "I can't let you do that,
Casey."

Phil's pointing a gun at me.

"She's a child," he says. "I know you're
upset, but we can resolve this without violence."

Anders lets out a ragged laugh. "Please
tell me you're part of this escape attempt.
Because otherwise you're the biggest idiot
alive."

He's not part of it. If Phil planned to spirit Wallace off to safety, Wallace wouldn't be letting Harper free him. She's cut the strap on his hands, and now she's pointing the knife at me as Wallace climbs into the pilot's seat.

"Guess you have your pilot's license after all," I say.

"Of course," Wallace says. "Harper?"

She backs into the passenger seat.

Phil comes around the side of the plane. "This is pointless, Gregory. You will be a hunted man. Don't take a child into that."

"Oh, for God's sake," I mutter. "You really are an idiot." I raise my gun. "Wallace? Get out of the plane."

Harper's hand swings up, and I'm thinking it's just the knife. It's not.

I backpedal. Phil grabs me as if I'm . . . I don't know. Fleeing? Out of the corner of my eye, I see Dalton lunge. Then Harper presses the button, and the pepper spray hits me full in the face. I double over, blinded. Phil howls in agony. Even Dalton curses, as stray particles hit him.

Anders shouts "Stop!" but he's the farthest away, unable to fire from his angle. I hear the door slamming, the plane rolling, Anders yells. A shot fires. Another, hitting metal. Then the engine roars as the plane takes off.

Sixty-Two

Wallace and Harper escape. Dalton goes to get our plane out, but Harper has cut wires in the engine. By the time he could fix it, they'd be gone.

The council claims they'll go after Wallace. I don't know if that's true. I don't think Phil does either. I don't bother asking him. I can barely get him to tell me what they've said. He walks out of that radio meeting and says, "I have to stay."

"Until they figure this out?" I ask.

A slow shake of his head, his gaze blank. "I don't know. I don't . . . They said this is my fault. So I stay."

At that moment, seeing the look on his face, if I could muster any sympathy for him, I would. But I can't. All I can think is *Not again.* Once more, we are saddled with a leader who does not want to be here. The council has learned nothing from Val.

I must talk to Petra. That is obvious, but

my gut screams at the idea. It tells me I'm mistaken — that both Dalton and I were obviously mistaken. Petra? No. Never Petra. She's my friend.

Which doesn't mean shit, does it? Diana was my friend. Beth became my friend. Even Val had been inching toward something akin to friendship.

I can tell myself no, not Petra, but then I remember her on the back deck of the station, going after Jen. I remember the look in her eyes.

I tell Dalton that I want to do this alone.

I find Petra at home, working on a sketch, and she welcomes me in, as she always does, with a big smile, and again I tell myself I'm wrong. I must be wrong.

She starts to lead me inside, but I stay in her front entryway.

"I saw you in the forest."

"Ah."

That's what she says. It's all she says, and I feel anger surge, outrage, and yes, hurt.

"I saw you shoot Oliver Brady," I say.

"Are you sure?"

Are you sure?

Not a moment of surprise, just a cool semi-denial, a lackluster defense that cuts deeper than any feigned confusion.

The anger flares, white-hot, and I advance

on her. She doesn't step back. She doesn't flinch. She just meets my gaze with a level stare.

"I saw you," I say, "Eric saw you. We were not mistaken."

She says nothing.

"I just told you that Oliver Brady is dead, and you didn't bat an eye. No one else in town knows. That alone proves you were there, Petra."

"I'm not denying I was there. I'm asking if you're sure I'm the one who shot him."

"You —"

"Am I your friend, Casey?"

It takes everything I have not to throw her against the wall, like she did to Jen.

"Don't you dare —" I begin.

"I'm not asking you to drop this because I'm a friend. I'm asking you to trust me because I'm a friend."

"Trust that you didn't kill —"

"Just trust me." She meets my gaze. "I am your friend. Yours. Eric's. Rockton's. Whatever happened out there wasn't a tragedy. It was cleanup."

"Who gave you the right — ?"

"I'm not saying I shot Oliver Brady, Casey. I'm saying that it doesn't matter who did. Not really. He's dead, and that's what had to be done, and if you'd like to come in and discuss it . . ."

I turn and walk out.

This isn't over. This isn't like it was with Mathias, a resident who saw our predicament and solved it for us. Petra might play it that way, but it isn't the same. Even with Mathias, he is no "random resident," no ordinary citizen driven to act outside his nature.

This was an execution. An *ordered* execution. Otherwise, we have a resident who somehow found a gun and a silencer lying around and wandered into the forest in hopes of finding us, then saw and shot Brady to protect us. Despite the fact that, at that moment, he posed no threat.

Someone told Petra to kill Brady. And she did. Which means there is so much more to this — and to her.

Dalton doesn't know what to say about Petra. For now, there's no time to discuss it, much less pursue the matter. We have Kenny to worry about.

A bullet that close to the spine is a dangerous thing. Even moving him may have made the situation worse. To take him up in a plane and fly him to Whitehorse? We could do no more than pray we don't make things worse. We almost certainly will.

Dalton and I sit on the back porch of the clinic, after seeing Kenny and assessing the situation.

"Fuck," Dalton says. "I don't even know what to do."

"Is there any chance the council will fly in a surgeon?"

He shakes his head. "They can't even get us a doctor. Where the hell will they find a neurosurgeon?"

I take a deep breath. "April."

He looks over. "Your sister? Right, she's a neuroscientist, isn't she?"

"Yes, but she was a medical doctor first. She specialized in neurosurgery. She didn't care for it, so she got her doctorate and went into research instead. Did I mention I come from a family of overachievers?"

I give a wry smile. Dalton lays his hand on mine, and I realize I'm tugging a thread on my shirt, anxiously winding it around my finger.

"Are you sure you want to do that?" he says. "I know you and April . . ."

"I can try," I say. "For Kenny, I can try."

"Then let's go talk to the council."

ABOUT THE AUTHOR

Kelley Armstrong graduated with a degree in psychology and then studied computer programming. Now, she is a full-time writer and parent, and she lives with her husband and three children in rural Ontario, Canada.

The employees of Thorndike Press hope you have enjoyed this Large Print book. All our Thorndike, Wheeler, and Kennebec Large Print titles are designed for easy reading, and all our books are made to last. Other Thorndike Press Large Print books are available at your library, through selected bookstores, or directly from us.

For information about titles, please call:
 (800) 223-1244

or visit our website at:
 gale.com/thorndike

To share your comments, please write:
 Publisher
 Thorndike Press
 10 Water St., Suite 310
 Waterville, ME 04901